7

THE
BLOOD
OF
FLOWERS

THE
BLOOD
OF
FLOWERS

A NOVEL

ANITA AMIRREZVANI

LITTLE, BROWN AND COMPANY

New York   Boston   London

Little, Brown and Company
Hachette Book Group USA
237 Park Avenue, New York, NY 10169
Visit our Web site at www.HachetteBookGroupUSA.com

First Edition: June 2007

Designed by Paula Russell Szafranski

Library of Congress Cataloging-in-Publication Data
Amirrezvani, Anita.
   The blood of flowers : a novel / Anita Amirrezvani. — 1st ed.
      p.   cm.
   HC ISBN 978-0-316-06576-4
   Int'l ed. ISBN 978-0-316-02100-5
   1. Young women—Fiction.   2. Women weavers—Fiction.   3. Rugs—Fiction.
   4. Iran—History—Safavid dynasty, 1501–1736—Fiction.   I. Title.
   PS3601.M57B56 2007
   813'.6—dc22   2006023034

10   9   8   7   6   5   4   3   2   1

Q-FF

Printed in the United States of America

For my family —
Iranian, Lithuanian, and American

THE
BLOOD
OF
FLOWERS

Prologue

First there wasn't and then there was. Before God, no one was.

Once there was a village woman who longed for a child. She tried every-thing—praying, taking herbs, consuming raw tortoise eggs, and sprinkling water on newborn kittens—but nothing helped. Finally, she voyaged to a distant cemetery to visit an ancient stone lion, and there she rubbed her belly against its flank. When the lion trembled, the woman returned home filled with hope that her greatest wish would be fulfilled. By the next moon, she had conceived her only child.

From the day she was born, the girl was the light of her parents' eyes. Her father took her on mountain walks every week, treating her as if she were the son he always wanted. Her mother taught her to make dyes from orange saf-flowers, cochineal bugs, pomegranate rinds, and walnut shells, and to knot the dyed wool into rugs. Before long, the girl knew all her mother's designs and was deemed the best young knotter in her village.

When the girl turned fourteen, her parents decided it was time for her to marry. To earn money for the dowry, her father worked hard in the fields, hoping for a large harvest, and her mother spun wool until her fingers grew rough, but neither brought in enough silver. The girl knew she could help by making a carpet for her dowry that would dazzle the eyes. Rather than using ordinary village reds and browns, it should glow turquoise like a summer sky.

The girl begged Ibrahim the dye maker to reveal the secret of turquoise, and he told her to climb a hillock in search of a plant with jagged leaves, and then to search for something inside herself. She didn't know what he meant by that, but she gathered the leaves and boiled them into a dye, which was a dirty purple color. When her mother saw the liquid, she asked what the girl was doing. The girl replied in a halting voice, watching her mother's eyebrows form a dark, angry line across her forehead.

"You went to Ibrahim's dye house alone?"

"Bibi, please forgive me," the girl replied. "I left my reason with the goats this morning."

When her father came home, her mother told him what the girl had done. "If people start talking, her chances of finding a husband are finished!" she complained. "Why must she be so rash?"

"Always has been!" roared her father, and he chastised her for her error. The girl kept her head bent to her mending for the rest of that evening, not daring to meet her parents' eyes.

For several days, her Bibi and her Baba watched her closely as she tried to unlock the riddle of the dye. One afternoon, when the girl was in the mountains with her goats, she hid behind a boulder to relieve herself and a surprising thought struck her. Could Ibrahim possibly have meant . . . that? For it was something inside herself.

She returned home and made another pot of the purple dye. That afternoon, when she went to the latrines, she saved some of the liquid in an old pot, mixed it with the dull purple dye and the wool, and left it overnight. When she lifted the lid on the dye pot the next morning, she cried out in triumph, for the dye had paled into a turquoise like the pools of paradise. She took a strand of turquoise wool to Ibrahim's dye house and tied it around the knocker on his door, even though her father had forbidden her to go there alone.

The girl sold her turquoise carpet to a traveling silk merchant named Hassan who desired it so much that he paid silver while it was still unfinished on *the loom. Her mother told the other village women about her daughter's success, and they praised the skill of her hands. Now that she had a dowry, the girl could be married, and her wedding celebration lasted three days and three nights. Her husband fed her vinegared cucumbers when she was pregnant, and they had seven sons in as many years. The book of her life had been written in the brightest of inks, and Insh'Allah, would continue that way until —*

"That's not how the story goes," I interrupted, adjusting the rough blanket around my shoulders as the wind howled outside. My mother, Maheen, and I were sitting knee to knee, but I spoke quietly because the others were sleeping only a few paces distant.

"You're right, but I like to tell it that way," she said, tucking a lock of her gray hair into her worn scarf. "That's what we were expecting for you."

"It's a good ending," I agreed, "but tell it the way it really happened."

"Even with all the sad parts?"

"Yes."

"They still make me weep."

"Me, too."

"Voy!" she said, her face etched with distress. We were quiet together for a moment, remembering. A drop of freezing rain struck the front of my cotton robe, and I moved closer to my mother to avoid the leak in the roof. The small oil lamp between us gave off no heat. Only a few months before I had worn a thick velvet robe patterned with red roses, with silk trousers underneath. I had painted my eyes with kohl, perfumed my clothes with incense, and awaited my lover, who had torn the clothes from my body in a room kept as warm as summer. Now I shivered in my thin blue robe, which was so threadbare it looked gray.

My mother coughed from deep in her lungs; the sound ripped at my heart, and I prayed that she would heal. "Daughter of mine, I can't get all the way to the end," she said in a thick voice. "It's not over yet."

I took a deep breath. "Thanks be to God!" I replied, and then I had an idea, although I wasn't certain I should ask. My mother had always been the one with a voice like mountain honey. She had been famous in our village for spinning tales about Zal the white-haired who was raised by a bird, Jamsheed who invented the art of weaving, and the comical Mullah Nusraddin, who always made us think.

"What if — what if I told the story this time?"

My mother considered me for a moment as if seeing me anew, and then relaxed her body more deeply against the old cushions that lined the walls of the room.

"Yes, you are grown now," she replied. "In the last few months, I believe you have grown by years. Perhaps you would never have changed so much if you hadn't done what you did."

My face flushed and then burned, although I was chilled to the bone. I was no longer the child I had once been. I would never have imagined that I could lie and, worse yet, not tell the whole truth; that I could betray someone I loved, and abandon someone who cared for me, although not enough; that I could strike out against my own kin; and that I would nearly kill the person who loved me the most.

My mother's gaze was gentle and expectant. "Go ahead, you tell it," she said.

I swallowed a mouthful of strong tea, sat up straight, and began speaking.

CHAPTER ONE

In the spring of the year that I was supposed to be married, a comet launched itself over the skies of my village. It was brighter than any comet we had ever seen, and more evil. Night after night, as it crawled across our skies spraying its cold white seeds of sorrow, we tried to decipher the fearsome messages of the stars. Hajj Ali, the most learned man in our village, traveled to Isfahan to fetch a copy of the chief astronomer's almanac so we would know what calamities to expect.

The evening he returned, the people of my village began assembling outside to listen to the predictions for the months ahead. My parents and I stood near the old cypress, the only tree in our village, which was decorated with strips of cloth marking people's vows. Everyone was looking upward at the stars, their chins pointing toward the sky, their faces grave. I was small enough to see under Hajj Ali's big white beard, which looked like a tuft of desert scrub. My mother, Maheen, pointed at the Sunderer of Heads, which burned red in the night sky. "Look how Mars is inflamed!" she said. "That will add to the comet's malice."

Many of the villagers had already noticed mysterious signs or heard of misfortunes caused by the comet. A plague had struck the north of Iran, killing thousands of people. An earthquake in Doogabad had trapped a bride in her home, suffocating her and her women guests moments before she was to join her groom. In my village, red insects that had never been seen before had swarmed over our crops.

Goli, my closest friend, arrived with her husband, Ghasem, who was much older than we were. She greeted me with a kiss on each cheek.

"How are you feeling?" I asked. Her hand flew to her belly.

"Heavy," she replied, and I knew she must be worried about the fate of the new life inside her.

Before long, everyone in my village had gathered, except for the old and the infirm. Most of the women were wearing bright bell-shaped tunics over slim trousers, with fringed head scarves over their hair, while the men were attired in long white tunics, trousers, and turbans. But Hajj Ali wore a black turban, indicating his descent from the Prophet Mohammad, and carried an astrolabe wherever he went.

"Good villagers," he began, in a voice that sounded like a wheel dragging over stones, "let us begin by heaping praise on the first followers of the Prophet, especially upon his son-in-law Ali, king of all believers."

"May peace be upon him," we replied.

"This year's predictions begin with poor news for our enemies. In the northeast, the Ozbaks will suffer an infestation of insects so fierce it will destroy their wheat. In the northwest, troop desertions will plague the Ottomans, and even farther west, in the Christian kingdoms, inexplicable diseases will disarrange the lips of kings."

My father, Isma'il, leaned toward me and whispered, "It's always good to know that the countries we're fighting are going to have miserable luck." We laughed together, since that's how it always was.

As Hajj Ali continued reading from the almanac, my heart skipped as if I were climbing a mountain. I was wondering what he would say about marriages made during the year, which was what I cared about the most. I began fiddling with the fringe on my head scarf, a habit my mother always urged me to break, as Hajj Ali explained that no harm would come to paper, books, or the art of writing; that earthquakes would occur in the south but would be mild; and that there would be battles great enough to tinge the Caspian Sea red with blood.

Hajj Ali waved the almanac at the crowd, which is what he did when the prediction he was about to read was alarming. His assistant, who was holding an oil lamp, jumped to move out of his way.

"Perhaps the worst thing of all is that there will be large and inexplicable lapses in moral behavior this year," he read, "lapses that can only be explained by the influence of the comet."

A low murmur came from the crowd as people began discussing the lapses they had already witnessed in the first days of the New Year. "She took more than her share of water from the well," I heard Zaynab say. She was Gholam's wife, and never had a good word to say about anyone.

Hajj Ali finally arrived at the subject that concerned my future. "On the topic of marriages, the year ahead is mixed," he said. "The almanac says nothing about those that take place in the next few months, but those contracted later this year will be full of passion and strife."

I looked anxiously at my mother, since I expected to be married at that time, now that I was already fourteen. Her eyes were troubled, and I could see she did not like what she had heard.

Hajj Ali turned to the last page in the almanac, looked up, and paused, the better to capture the crowd's attention. "This final prophecy is about the behavior of women, and it is the most disquieting of all," he said. "Throughout the year, the women of Iran will fail to be acquiescent."

"When are they ever?" I heard Gholam say, and laughter bubbled around him.

My father smiled at my mother, and she brightened from within, for he loved her just the way she was. People always used to say that he treated her as tenderly as if she were a second wife.

"Women will suffer from their own perverse behavior," Hajj Ali warned. "Many will bear the curse of sterility, and those who succeed in giving birth will wail in unusual pain."

My eyes met Goli's, and I saw my own fear reflected in hers. Goli was worried about childbirth, while I was troubled by the thought of a disorderly union. I prayed that the comet would shoot across the firmament and leave us undisturbed.

Seeing me shiver, my father wrapped a lamb's wool blanket over my shoulders, and my mother took one of my hands between hers and rubbed it to warm me. From where I stood in the center of my village, I was surrounded by the familiar sights of home. Not far away was our small mosque, its dome sparkling with tile; the hammam where I bathed every week, steamy inside and dappled with light; and the scarred wooden stalls for the tiny market that sprang up on Thursdays, where villagers traded fruit, vegetables, medicines, carpets, and tools. A path led away from the public buildings and passed between a cluster of mud-brick homes that sheltered all two hundred souls in my village, and it ended at the foot of the mountain and the rutted paths where my goats roamed for food. All these sights filled me with comfort, so that when my mother squeezed my hand to see how I was feeling, I squeezed back. But then I pulled my hand away because I didn't want to seem like a child.

"Baba," I whispered to my father in a small voice. "What if Hajj Ali's predictions about marriage come true?"

My father couldn't hide the concern in his eyes, but his voice was firm. "Your husband will pave your path with rose petals," he replied. "If at any time, he fails to treat you with honor . . ."

He paused for a moment, and his dark eyes looked fierce, as if what he might do were too terrible to imagine. He started to say something, but then stopped himself.

". . . you can always come back to us," he finished.

Shame and blame would follow a wife who returned to her parents, but my father didn't seem to care. His kind eyes crinkled at the corners as he smiled at me.

Hajj Ali concluded the meeting with a brief prayer. Some of the villagers broke off into family groups to discuss the predictions, while others started walking back to their homes. Goli looked as if she wanted to talk, but her husband told her it was time to go home. She whispered that her feet ached from the weight in her belly and said good night.

My parents and I walked home on the single mud lane that pierced the village. All the dwellings were huddled together on either side for warmth and protection. I knew the path so well I could have walked it blind and turned at just the right moment to reach our house, the last one before our village gave way to sand and scrub. My father pushed open our carved wooden door with his shoulders, and we entered our one-room home. Its walls were made of packed mud and straw brightened with white plaster, which my mother kept sparkling clean. A small door led to an enclosed courtyard where we enjoyed the sun without being seen by other eyes.

My mother and I removed our head scarves and placed them on hooks near the door, slipping off our shoes at the same time. I shook out my hair, which reached my waist. For good luck, I touched the curved ibex horns that glowed on a low stand near the door. My father had felled the ibex on one of our Friday afternoon walks. Ever since that day, the horns had held a position of pride in our household, and my father's friends often praised him for being as nimble as an ibex.

11

My father and I sat together on the red-and-brown carpet I had knotted when I was ten. His eyes closed for a moment, and I thought he looked especially tired.

"Are we walking tomorrow?" I asked.

His eyes flew open. "Of course, my little one," he replied.

He had to work in the fields in the morning, but he insisted he wouldn't miss our walk together for anything other than God's command. "For you shall soon be a busy bride," he said, and his voice broke.

I looked away, for I couldn't imagine leaving him.

My mother threw dried dung in the stove to boil water for tea. "Here's a surprise," she said, bringing us a plate of fresh chickpea cookies. They were fragrant with the essence of roses.

"May your hands never ache!" my father said.

They were my favorite sweets, and I ate far too many of them. Before long, I became tired and spread out my bedroll near the door, as I always did. I fell asleep to the sound of my parents talking, which reminded me of the cooing of doves, and I think I even saw my father take my mother in his arms and kiss her.

THE NEXT AFTERNOON, I stood in our doorway and watched for my Baba as the other men streamed back from the fields. I always liked to pour his tea for him before he walked in the door. My mother was crouched over the stove, baking bread for our evening meal.

When he didn't arrive, I went back into the house, cracked some walnuts and put them in a small bowl, and placed the irises I had gathered in a vessel with water. Then I went out to look again, for I was eager to begin our walk. Where was he? Many of the other men had returned from the fields and were probably washing off the day's dust in their courtyards.

"We need some water," my mother said, so I grabbed a clay jug and walked toward the well. On my way, I ran into Ibrahim the dye maker, who gave me a peculiar look.

"Go home," he said to me. "Your mother needs you."

I was surprised. "But she just told me to fetch water," I said.

"No matter," he replied. "Tell her I told you to go back."

I walked home as quickly as I could, the vessel banging against my knees. As I approached our house, I spotted four men bearing a limp bundle between them. Perhaps there had been an accident in the fields. From time to time, my father brought back stories about how a man got injured by a threshing tool, suffered a kick from a mule, or returned bloodied from a fight. I knew he'd tell us what had happened over tea.

The men moved awkwardly because of their burden. The man's face was hidden, cradled on one of their shoulders. I said a prayer for his quick recovery, for it was hard on a family when a man was too ill to work. As the group approached, I noticed that the victim's turban was wrapped much like my father's. But that didn't mean anything, I told myself quickly. Many men wrapped their turbans in a similar way.

The front bearers got out of step for a moment, and they almost lost hold of the man. His head lolled as though it were barely attached to his body, and his limbs had no life in them. I dropped the clay vessel, which shattered around my feet.

"Bibi," I whimpered. "Help!"

My mother came outside, brushing flour from her clothes. When she saw my father, she uttered a piercing wail. Women who lived nearby streamed out of their houses and surrounded her like a net while she tore the air with her sorrow. As she writhed and jumped, they caught her gently, holding her and stroking the hair away from her face.

The men brought my father inside and laid him on a bedroll. His skin was a sickly yellow color, and a line of saliva slid out of the corner of his mouth. My mother put her fingers near his nostrils.

13

"Praise be to God, he's still breathing!" she said.

Naghee, who worked with my father in the fields, didn't know where to look as he told us what had happened. "He seemed tired, but he was fine until this afternoon," he said. "Suddenly he grabbed his head and fell to the ground, gasping for air. After that, he didn't stir."

"May God spare your husband!" said a man I didn't recognize. When they had done all they could to make him comfortable, they left, murmuring prayers for good health.

My mother's brow was furrowed as she removed my father's cotton shoes, straightened his tunic, and arranged the pillow under his head. She felt his hands and forehead and declared his temperature normal, but told me to fetch a blanket and cover him to keep him warm.

The news about my father spread quickly, and our friends began arriving to help. Kolsoom brought the water she had collected from a spring near a saint's shrine that was known for its healing powers. Ibrahim took up a position in the courtyard and began reciting the Qur'an. Goli came by, her boy asleep in her arms, with hot bread and stewed lentils. I brewed tea to keep the warmth in everyone's body. I knelt near my father and watched his face, praying for a flutter of his eyelids, even a grimace — anything that would assure me life remained in his body.

Rabi'i, the village physician, arrived after night had fallen with cloth bags full of herbs slung on each shoulder. He laid them near the door and knelt to examine my father by the light of the oil lamp, which flickered brokenly. His eyes narrowed as he peered closely at my father's face. "I need more light," he said.

I borrowed two oil lamps from neighbors and placed them near the bedroll. The physician lifted my father's head and carefully unwound his white turban. His head looked heavy and swollen. In the light, his face was the color of ash, and his thick hair, which was flecked with gray, looked stiff and ashen, too.

Rabi'i touched my father's wrists and neck, and when he did not find what he was looking for, he laid his ear against my father's chest. At that moment, Kolsoom asked my mother in a whisper if she would like more tea. The physician lifted his head and asked everyone to be silent, and after listening again, he arose with a grave face and announced, "His heart beats, but only faintly."

"Ali, prince among men, give strength to my husband!" my mother cried.

Rabi'i collected his bags and removed bunches of herbs, explaining to Kolsoom how to brew them into a heart-enlivening medicine. He also promised to return the next morning to check on my father. "May God rain His blessings on you!" he said as he took his leave. Kolsoom began stripping the herbs off their stalks and throwing them into a pot, adding the water my mother had boiled.

As Rabi'i left, he stopped to talk with Ibrahim, who was still in the courtyard. "Don't halt your praying," he warned, and then I heard him whisper the words "God may gather him tonight."

I tasted something like rust on my tongue. Seeking my mother, I rushed into her arms and we held each other for a moment, our eyes mirrors of sorrow.

My father began to make wheezing sounds. His mouth was still slack, his lips slightly parted, and his breath rasped like dead leaves tossed by the wind. My mother rushed away from the stove, her fingers green from the herbs. She leaned over my father and cried, "Voy, my beloved! Voy!"

Kolsoom hurried over to peer at my father and then led my mother back to the stove, for there was nothing to be done. "Let us finish this medicine to help him," said Kolsoom, whose ever-bright eyes and pomegranate cheeks testified to her powers as an herbalist.

When the herbs had been boiled and cooled, Kolsoom poured the liquid into a shallow bowl and brought it to my father's side. While my mother raised his head, Kolsoom gently spooned the medicine into his mouth. Most of it spilled over his lips, soiling the bedroll. On the next try, she got the medicine into his mouth, but my father sputtered, choked, and for a moment appeared to stop breathing.

Kolsoom, who was usually so calm, put down the bowl with shaking hands and met my mother's eyes. "We must wait until his eyes open before we try again," she advised.

My mother's head scarf was askew, but she didn't notice. "He needs his medicine," she said weakly, but Kolsoom told her that he needed his breath more.

Ibrahim's voice was starting to sound hoarse, and Kolsoom asked me to attend to him. I poured some hot tea and served it to him with dates in the courtyard. He thanked me with his eyes but never stopped his reciting, as if the power of his words could keep my father alive.

On the way back into the room, I bumped against my father's walking stick, which was hanging on a hook near the door to the courtyard. I remembered how on our last walk, he had taken me to see a carving of an ancient goddess that was hidden behind a waterfall. We had inched our way along a ledge until we found the carving under the flow of water. The goddess wore a tall crown that seemed to be filled with clouds. Her shapely bosom was covered by a thin drapery, and she wore a necklace of large stones. You could not see her feet; her clothing seemed to swirl into waves and streams. She stretched out her powerful arms, as big as any man's, which looked as if they were conjuring the waterfall at will.

My father had been tired that day, but he had marched up the steep trails to the waterfall, panting, to show me that wondrous sight. His breath sounded even more labored now; it crackled as it left his body. His hands were beginning to move, too, like small, restless mice. They crawled up his chest and scratched at his tunic. His long fingers were brown from working in the fields, and there was a line of dirt under the nails that he would have removed before entering the house, had he been well.

"I promise to devote myself to tending to him, if only You will leave him with us," I whispered to God. "I'll say my prayers every day, and I will never complain about how hungry I am during the fasting month of Ramazan, even silently."

My father began clutching at the air, as if he were fighting his illness with the only part of his body that still had vigor. Kolsoom joined us by the bedroll and led us in prayers, while we watched my father's hands and listened to his anguished breath. I told my mother how tired he had seemed during our walk in the mountains, and asked if it had weakened him. She put her hands on either side of my face and replied, "Light of my eyes, it probably gave him strength."

In the blackest hour of the night, my father's breathing quieted and his hands stopped doing battle. As my mother arranged the blanket over him, her face looked calmer.

"He will get some rest now," she said with satisfaction.

I went into the courtyard, which adjoined our neighbor's house, to bring more tea to Ibrahim. He had moved to a cushion near my turquoise carpet, which was unfinished on my loom. My mother had recently sold the carpet to a traveling silk merchant named Hassan, who was planning to return later to claim it. But the source of the turquoise dye that had pleased Hassan's eyes was still a tender subject between me and my father, and my face flushed with shame when I remembered how my visit alone to Ibrahim's dye house had troubled him.

I returned to the vigil at my father's side. Perhaps this terrible night was nearly over, and daylight would bring a joyful surprise, like the sight of my father's eyes opening, or of him being able to swallow his medicine. And then, one day when he was better, we would take another walk in the mountains and sing together. Nothing would be sweeter to me than hearing him sing out of tune.

Toward morning, with no other sound than Ibrahim's river of prayers, I felt my eyelids grow heavy. I don't know how much time passed before I awoke, observed that my father's face was still calm, then fell asleep again. At dawn, I was comforted by the sound of sparrows breaking the silence with their noisy calls. They sounded like the birds we had heard on our walk, and I began dreaming about how we had stopped to watch them gather twigs for their nests.

A wheeled cart creaked outside, and I awoke with a start. People were beginning to emerge from their homes to begin their chores at the well, in the mountains, or in the fields. Ibrahim was still saying prayers, but his voice was dry and hoarse. My mother was lighting an oil lamp, which she placed near the bedroll. My father had not moved since he had fallen asleep. She peered at his face and placed her fingers under his nostrils to feel his breath. They lingered there, trembling, before they drifted down to his slack mouth. Still searching, they returned to his nose and hovered. I watched my mother's face, awaiting the contented expression that would tell me she had found his breath. My mother did not look at me. In the silence, she threw back her head and uttered a terrible wail. Ibrahim's prayers ceased; he rushed to my father's side and checked his breath in the same way before dropping to a squat and cradling his head in his hands.

My mother began wailing more loudly and tearing out her hair in clumps. Her scarf fell off and lay abandoned near my father. It was still tied and kept the shape of her head.

I grabbed my father's hand and squeezed it, but it was cold and still. When I lifted his heavy arm, his hand dangled brokenly at the wrist. The lines in his face looked deeply carved, and his expression seemed aggrieved, as if he had been forced to fight an evil jinn.

I uttered one short, sharp cry and collapsed onto my father.

Kolsoom and my mother let me remain there for a few moments, but then Kolsoom gently pulled me away.

My father and I had both known that our time together must soon come to an end, but I had always thought I would be the one to leave, festooned with bridal silver, with his blessings alive in my ear.

THE DAYS AFTER my father died were black, but they became blacker still.

With no man to harvest the fields that summer, we received little grain from my father's share of the planting, although his friends tried to be generous with theirs. And with little grain, we had little to barter for fuel, for shoes, or for dyes for wool. We had to trade our goats for grain, which meant no more cheese. Every time we gave up a goat, my mother cried.

Toward the end of the long, warm days, our supplies started to diminish. In the mornings, we ate the bread my mother made with cheese or yogurt brought by kind neighbors, but it was not long before our evening meals became less and less plentiful. Soon there was no question of eating even a morsel of meat. My mother began trading my father's belongings for food. First went his clothes, then his shoes, then his turbans, and finally his precious walking stick.

Other people would have turned to their family for help, but my mother and I were unfortunate in having no elders. All of my grandparents had died before I was old enough to remember them. My mother's two brothers had been killed in a war with the Ottomans. My father's only relative, a distant half brother named Gostaham, was the child of my father's father and his first wife. Gostaham had moved to Isfahan when he was a young man, and we hadn't heard from him in years.

By the time it started to become fiercely cold, we were living on a thin sheet of bread and pickled carrots left over from the previous year. I felt hungry every day, but knowing that there was nothing my mother could do, I tried not to speak about the pains in my belly. I always felt tired, and the tasks that used to seem so easy to me, like fetching water from the well, now seemed beyond my ability.

Our last valuable possession was my turquoise rug. Not long after I finished knotting its fringes, Hassan the silk merchant returned to pick it up and pay us what he owed. He was startled by our black tunics and black head scarves, and when he learned why we were in mourning, he asked my mother if he could help us. Fearing that we would not survive the winter, she asked him if he would find our only relative, Gostaham, when he returned to Isfahan, and tell him about our plight.

About a month later, a letter arrived for us from the capital, carried by a donkey merchant on his way to Shiraz. My mother asked Hajj Ali to read it aloud, since neither of us had learned our letters. It was from Gostaham, who wrote that he felt great sorrow over the losses we had endured and was inviting us to stay with him in the capital until our luck improved.

And that's how, one cold winter morning, I learned that I would be leaving my childhood home for the first time in my life and traveling far away. If my mother had told me we'd been sent off to the Christian lands, where barbarian women exposed their bosoms to all eyes, ate the singed flesh of pigs, and bathed only once a year, our destination could hardly have seemed more remote.

Word of our upcoming departure spread rapidly through the village. In the afternoon, women began arriving at our home with their smallest children. Pulling off their head scarves, they fluffed their hair and greeted the others in the room before arranging themselves in clusters on our carpet. Children who were old enough to play gathered in their own corner.

"May this be your final sorrow!" said Kolsoom as she came in, kissing my mother on each cheek in greeting.

Tears sprang to my mother's eyes.

"It was the comet," Kolsoom added sympathetically. "Mere humans couldn't defeat a power that great."

"Husband of mine," my mother said, as if my father were still alive. "Why did you announce that life was going so well? Why invite the comet's wrath?"

Zaynab made a face. "Maheen, remember the Muslim who traveled from Isfahan all the way to Tabriz to try to outrun the angel of death? When he arrived, Azraeel thanked him for meeting him there on time. Your husband did nothing wrong; he just answered God's command."

My mother's back bent a little, as it always did when she felt grief. "I never thought I would have to leave my only home," she replied.

"God willing, your luck will change in Isfahan," said Kolsoom, offering us the wild rue she had brought to protect us from the Evil Eye. She lit the herb with a coal from the oven, and soon its acrid smell purified the air.

My mother and I served tea to our guests and offered the dates that Kolsoom had brought, for we had nothing of our own to serve. I brought a cup of tea to Safa, the eldest villager, who was sitting in a corner of the room with a water pipe. It bubbled as she drew in smoke.

"What do you know of your new family?" she asked as she exhaled.

It was such an embarrassing question that it quieted the room for a moment. Everyone knew that my grandfather had married my father's mother many years ago while he had been visiting friends in our village. My grandfather was already married to his first wife, and lived with her and Gostaham in Shiraz. After my grandmother bore my father, he visited occasionally and sent money, but the families were understandably not close.

"I know very little," replied my mother. "I haven't seen Gostaham for more than twenty-five years. I met him only once, when he stopped by our village on his way to visit his parents in Shiraz, the city of poets. Even then, he was becoming one of the exalted carpet designers in the capital."

"And his wife?" asked Safa, her voice tight from the smoke in her lungs.

"I know nothing of her, except that she bore him two daughters."

Safa exhaled with satisfaction. "If her husband is successful, she will be running a grand household," she said. "I only hope she is generous and fair in her division of work."

Her words made me understand that we would no longer be mistresses of our lives. If we liked our bread baked dark and crisp but she didn't, we would have to eat it her way. And no matter how we felt, we'd have to praise her name. I think Safa noticed my distress, because she stopped smoking for a moment to offer a consolation.

"Your father's half brother must have a good heart, or he would not have sent for you," she said. "Just be sure to please his wife, and they will provide for you."

"Insh'Allah," said my mother, in a tone that sounded unconvinced.

I looked around at all the kind faces I knew; at my friends and my mother's friends, women who had been like aunts and grandmothers to me while I was growing up. I could not imagine what it would be like not to see them: Safa, with her face crinkled like an old apple; Kolsoom, thin and swift, renowned for her wisdom about herbs; and finally Goli, my truest friend.

She was sitting next to me, her newborn daughter in her arms. When the baby started to cry, she loosened her tunic and put the child to her breast. Goli's cheeks glowed pink like the baby's; the two of them looked healthy and contented. I wished with all my heart that my life were like hers.

When the baby had finished nursing, Goli placed her in my arms. I breathed in her newborn smell, as fresh as sprouting wheat, and whispered, "Don't forget me." I stroked her tiny cheek, thinking about how I would miss her first words and her first halting steps.

Goli wrapped her arms around me. "Think of how big Isfahan is!" she said. "You'll promenade through the biggest city square ever built, and your mother will be able to choose your husband from thousands upon thousands!"

I brightened for a moment, as if my old hopes were still possible, before remembering my problem.

"But now I have no dowry," I reminded her. "What man will take me with nothing?"

The whole room became quiet again. My mother fanned the rue, the lines in her forehead deepening. The other women began speaking all at once. "Don't worry, Maheen-*joon!* Your new family will help you!"

"They won't let such a fine young girl get pickled!"

"There's a healthy stud for every mare, and a lusty soldier for every moon!"

"Shah Abbas will probably desire your daughter for his harem," said Kolsoom to my mother. "He'll fatten her up with cheese and sugar, and then she'll have bigger breasts and a rounder belly than all of us!"

At a recent visit to the hammam, I had caught my reflection in a metal mirror. I had none of the ripeness of nursing mothers like Goli, who were so admired at the hammam. The muscles in my forearms stood out, and my face looked pinched. I was sure I could not be moonlike to anyone, but I smiled to think of my thin, bony body in such a womanly form. When Zaynab noticed my expression, her face twisted with mirth. She laughed so hard she began pitching forward over her stomach, and her lips wrapped back over her teeth until she looked like a horse fighting its bit. I flushed to the roots of my hair when I understood that Kolsoom had only been trying to be kind.

IT DIDN'T TAKE us long to pack our things, since we had so very few. I put one change of black mourning clothes into a hand-knotted saddlebag along with some heavy blankets to sleep in, and filled as many jugs as I could find with water. The morning of our departure, neighbors brought us gifts of bread, cheese, and dried fruit for the long journey. Kolsoom threw a handful of peas to divine whether it was an auspicious day for travel. After determining that it was excellent, she raised a precious copy of the Qur'an and circled our heads with it three times. Praying for a safe journey, we touched our lips to it. Just as we were setting off, Goli took a piece of dried fruit out of my bag and slipped it into her sleeve. She was "stealing" something of mine to make sure that one day, I would return.

"I hope so," I whispered to her as we said good-bye. It pained me to leave her most of all.

My mother and I were traveling with a musk merchant named Abdul-Rahman and his wife, who escorted travelers from one city to another for a fee. They often journeyed all the way to the northeastern borders of our land, looking for musk bladders from Tibet to sell in big cities. Their saddlebags, blankets, and tents smelled of the fragrance, which commanded princely prices.

The camel that my mother and I shared had soft black eyes that had been lined with protective kohl, and thick, bushy hair the color of sand. Abdul-Rahman had decorated his pretty nose with a strip of woven red cloth with blue tassels, a kind of bridle. We sat on his back atop a mountain of folded rugs and sacks of food, and held on to his hump. The camel lifted his feet delicately when he walked but was ill-tempered and smelled as rotten as one of the village latrines.

I had never seen the countryside north of my village. As soon as we stepped away from the mountains' life-giving streams, the land became barren. Pale green shrubs struggled to maintain a hold on life, just as we did. Our water jugs became more precious than the musk bladders. Along the way, we spotted broken water vessels and sometimes even the bones of those who had misjudged the length of their trip.

Abdul-Rahman pushed us onward in the early-morning hours, singing to the camels so they would pace themselves to the cadence of his voice. The sun glinted off the land, and the bright white light hurt my eyes. The ground was frozen; the few plants we saw were outlined with frost. By the end of the day, my feet were so cold I could no longer feel them. My mother went to sleep in our tent as soon as it was dark. She couldn't bear to look at the stars, she said.

After ten days of travel, we saw the Zagros Mountains, which signaled our approach to Isfahan. Abdul-Rahman told us that from somewhere high in the mountains flowed the very source of Isfahan's being, the *Zayendeh Rood,* or Eternal River. At first, it was just a pale blue shimmer, with a cooling breath that reached us from many *far-sakhs* away. As we got closer, the river seemed impossibly long to me, since the most water I had ever seen before had been in mountain streams.

After arriving at its banks, we dismounted from our camels, for they were not permitted in the city, and gathered to admire the water. "May God be praised for His abundance!" cried my mother as the river surged past us, a branch flowing by too quickly to catch.

"Praise is due," replied Abdul-Rahman, "for this river gives life to Isfahan's sweet melons, cools her streets, and fills her wells. Without it, Isfahan would cease to be."

We left our camels in the care of one of Abdul-Rahman's friends and continued our journey on foot on the Thirty-three Arches Bridge. About halfway across, we entered one of its archways to enjoy the view. I grabbed my mother's hand and said, "Look! Look!" The river rushed by as if excited, and in the distance we could see another bridge, and another gleaming beyond that one. One was covered in blue tiles, another had teahouses, and still another had arches that seemed like infinite doorways into the city, inviting travelers to unlock its secrets. Ahead of us, Isfahan stretched out in all directions, and the sight of its thousands of houses, gardens, mosques, bazaars, schools, caravanserais, kebabis, and teahouses filled us with awe. At the end of the bridge lay a long tree-lined avenue that traversed the whole city, ending in the square that Shah Abbas had built, which was so renowned that every child knew it as the Image of the World. My eye was caught by the square's Friday mosque, whose vast blue dome glowed peacefully in the morning light. Looking around, I saw another azure dome, and yet another, and then dozens more brightening the saffron-colored terrain, and it seemed to me that Isfahan beckoned like a field of turquoise set in gold.

"How many people live here?" my mother asked, raising her voice so it could be heard above the din of passersby.

"Hundreds of thousands," replied Abdul-Rahman. "More than in London or Paris; only Constantinople is bigger."

My mother and I said "Voy!" at the same time; we could not imagine so many souls in one place.

After crossing the bridge, we entered a covered bazaar and passed through a spice market. Burlap bags overflowed with mint, dill, coriander, dried lemon, turmeric, saffron, and many spices I didn't recognize. I distinguished the flowery yet bitter odor of fenugreek, which set my mouth watering for a lamb stew, for we had not tasted meat in many months.

Before long, we reached a caravanserai run by Abdul-Rahman's brother. It had a courtyard where donkeys, mules, and horses could rest, surrounded by a rectangular arcade of private rooms. We thanked Abdul-Rahman and his wife for escorting us, wished them well, and paid for our lodgings.

Our room was small, with thick windowless walls and a strong lock. There was clean straw on the floor, but nothing else for bedding.

"I'm hungry," I said to my mother, remembering the lamb kebab I had seen grilling near the bridge.

She untied the corners of a dirty piece of cloth and looked sadly at the few coins remaining there. "We must bathe before seeking out our family," she replied. "Let's eat the last of our bread."

It was dry and brittle, so we endured the emptiness in our bellies and lay down to sleep. The ground was hard compared with the sand of the desert, and I felt unbalanced, for I had become used to the gentle tipping motion of my camel. Still, I was weary enough from our long journey to fall asleep not long after putting my head down on the straw. In the middle of the night, I began dreaming that my Baba was tugging on my foot to wake me for one of our Friday walks. I jumped to my feet to follow him, but he had already passed through the door. I tried to catch up; all I could see was his back as he advanced up a mountain path. The faster I ran, the faster he climbed. When I screamed his name, he didn't stop or turn around. I awoke in a sweat, confused, the straw prickling my back.

"Bibi?"

"I'm here, daughter of mine," my mother replied in the darkness. "You were calling out for your Baba."

"He left without me," I mumbled, still caught in the web of my dreams.

My mother pulled me to her and began stroking my forehead. I lay next to her with my eyes closed, but I couldn't sleep. Sighing, I turned first this way, then the other. A donkey began braying in the courtyard, and it sounded as if he were weeping over his fate. Then my mother began speaking, and her voice seemed to brighten the gloom:

First there wasn't and then there was. Before God, no one was.

My mother had comforted me with tales ever since I was small. Sometimes they helped me peel a problem like an onion, or gave me ideas about what to do; other times, they calmed me so much that I would fall into a soothing sleep. My father used to say that her tales were better than the best medicine. Sighing, I burrowed into my mother's body like a child, knowing that the sound of her voice would be a balm on my heart.

Once there was a peddler's daughter named Golnar who spent her days toiling in her family's garden. Her cucumbers were praised for being crisp and sweet; her squashes for growing into large, pleasing shapes dense with flesh; and her radishes for their fragrant burn. Because the girl had a passionate love of flowers, she begged her father to allow her to plant a single rosebush in a corner of the garden. Even though her family was poor and needed every morsel of food she grew, her father rewarded her by granting her wish.

Golnar traded some vegetables for a cutting from a rich neighbor's bush and planted it, uprooting a few cucumber plants to make room. In time, the bush pushed forth extravagantly large blossoms. They were bigger than a man's fist and as white as the moon. When a warm wind blew, the rosebush swayed, dancing as if in response to the nightingales' song, her white buds opening like a twirling skirt.

Golnar's father was a liver-kebab seller. One afternoon, he returned home and announced that he had sold the last of his kebabs to a saddle maker and his son. He had bragged about what a good worker his daughter was — not a girl who would fall ill at the rancid fumes of tanning leather. It wasn't long before the boy and his family paid a visit to the liver seller and his daughter. Golnar was not pleased: The boy's shoulders and arms were thin, and his small, beady eyes made him look like a goat.

After some tea and an exchange of compliments, the girl's parents urged her to show the boy her garden. Reluctantly, she led him outside. The boy praised her healthy vegetables, fruits, and herbs and admired the rosebush's beauty. Softening, she begged him to accept a few blossoms for his family and cut several long stems with her shears. As the two reentered the house, their arms filled with white blossoms, their parents smiled and imagined them on their wedding day.

That night, after the boy and his family had left, Golnar was so tired that she fell into a deep sleep rather than visiting her roses. The next morning, she arose with a feeling of alarm and rushed outside. The rosebush drooped in the early-morning sun, its flowers a dirty shade of white. The garden was silent, for all the nightingales had flown away. Golnar pruned the heaviest flowers tenderly, but when she removed her hands from the thorny bush, they were streaked with blood.

Penitently, the girl vowed to take better care of the bush. She poured a bloody bucket of water she had used to clean her father's kebab knives onto the soil around the bush, topping it with a special fertilizer made of tiny pearls of liver.

That afternoon, a messenger arrived with a marriage proposal from the boy's family. Her father told her that a better boy could not be found, and her mother whispered to her coyly about the children they would make together. But Golnar wept and rebuffed the offer. Her parents were angry and puzzled, and although they promised to send a letter of refusal, they secretly sent a message to the boy's family asking for time for reflection.

Early the next morning, Golnar arose to the sweet music of nightingales and discovered that once again her roses stood large and proud. A wealth of blossoms had opened, nourished by the organ meat; they shone in the still-dark sky like stars. She clipped a few flowers from the bush, tentatively at first, and the plant caressed the tips of her fingers with its silky petals, exuding a musky perfume as if it desired her touch.

On the morning of the family's annual picnic to celebrate the New Year, the girl had so much to do that she failed to water her rosebush. She helped her mother prepare and pack a large picnic, and then the family walked to a favorite spot near a river. While they were eating, they happened to see the boy and his parents, who were picnicking, too. The father invited them to drink tea and share a meal of sweetmeats. The boy passed the finest pastries to Golnar, a kindness that surprised her now that she had rebuffed him (or so she believed). At their parents' urging, the two took a walk together near the river. When they were out of sight, the boy kissed the tip of her index finger, but Golnar turned and ran away.

When she and her family returned home, it was already dark. Golnar ventured into the garden to give the thirsty rosebush a drink. As she bent forward with a bucket of well water, a sudden wind whipped up and tangled her hair in the bush's stems; the bush embraced her and held her tight in its long, thin arms. The more she struggled, the tighter its thorns gripped her, slashing her face. Screaming, she tore herself out, blinded by blood, and crawled back to the house.

At the sight of her in the doorway, her parents howled as if she were an evil jinn. At first the girl refused to let them touch her. Her father grabbed her flailing arms and held them down so her mother could treat her wounds. To their horror, they discovered a fat black thorn lodged in her index finger as firmly as a nail. When her mother pulled it out, it left a hole that bled like a fountain.

With a great roar of rage, her father rushed out of the house. Within moments came the sound of an ax as it struck the bush, cracking it at its core. With each blow, Golnar shuddered and tore at her own hair in the fury of her grief. Her mother put her to bed, where she stayed for several days, burning with fever and crying out in delirium.

At her parents' insistence, she was married two weeks later to the boy who looked like a goat. The two lived together in a room in his parents' house, and the boy came home every afternoon stinking of the blood and rot of the tannery. When he reached for Golnar, she turned her face away from him, shuddering at his touch. Before long, she became pregnant and bore him a son, followed by two daughters. Every day, she arose in darkness, dressed herself in old garments, and clothed her children in hand-me-downs even more ragged than her own. She never had time to grow her own flowers again. But sometimes, when she passed the walled garden where she used to tend her rosebush, she would close her eyes and remember the smell of its blossoms, sweeter than hope.

When my mother stopped speaking, I rolled this way and that to free my legs and back from the prickling straw, but I couldn't get comfortable. I felt as distressed as if a buzzing bee had gotten stuck in my ear.

My mother took my face in her hands. "What is it, daughter of mine?" she asked. "Are you ill? Are you suffering?"

An unhappy sound escaped my lips, and I pretended I was trying to sleep.

My mother said, as though thinking aloud, "I'm not sure why I told you that story. It poured out of me before I remembered what it was about."

I knew the tale, for my mother had told it once or twice in our village. Back then, it hadn't troubled me. I had been anticipating a life with a husband who paved my path with rose petals, not with a boy who smelled of rotting cowhides. I had never thought that my fate might be like Golnar's, but now, in the darkness of a strange room in a strange city, the story sounded like a prophecy. My father could no longer protect us, and no one else was duty-bound to do so. My mother was too old for anyone to want her, and now that we had no money for a dowry, no one would want me. With the first pass of the comet, all my prospects had been ruined.

My eyes flew open; in the wan streaks of light creeping into our chamber, I saw my mother studying me. She looked frightened, which made me feel sadder for her than for myself. I took a sharp breath and forced calm into my face.

"I felt ill for a moment, but now I'm better," I said.

The relief in my mother's eyes was so great that I thanked God for giving me the strength to say what I did.

31

CHAPTER TWO

We arose the next morning to the sound of travelers loading up their mules for the day's journey. My black trousers and tunic were stiff with dust and sweat, as I had been wearing them for more than a week. With the last of our money, my mother paid for us to enter a nearby hammam, where we scrubbed the grime off our bodies and washed our hair until it squeaked. When we were clean, we performed the Grand Ablution, submerging our bodies in a tank large enough for twenty women. The bath attendant rubbed my back and legs until I felt all the tightness from our long journey dissolve. As she worked, I cast my eyes over my bony ribs, my concave stomach, my callused fingers, and my stringy arms and legs. In my daydreams, I had imagined myself as a pampered woman, my hips and breasts round like melons. But it was no use: Nothing had changed except for the color of my face and hands, which to my dismay had darkened after all the days of travel.

When we were clean, we dressed in fresh black clothes and black head scarves and went in search of Gostaham at the Image of the World, which Shah Abbas had built after naming Isfahan his new capital. We entered the square through a narrow gateway that gave no hint of its vastness, but once inside we halted in our tracks, astonished.

"Our whole village . . . !" I began to say. My mother finished the sentence, for she was thinking the same thing.

". . . could fit in this square two times over. No wonder people say Isfahan is half the world!"

The square was so large that the people at either end looked like figures in a miniature painting. The minarets of the Friday mosque were so long, thin, and tall that when I looked up at them, I felt dizzy, for they seemed to vanish into the sky. The mosque's huge turquoise dome appeared to be suspended in space; surely the hand of man must have been aided by God to make clay seem so light! The tall gateway to the bazaar was surmounted by a mural — the first I had ever seen — of a battle, which looked as real as if the men were fighting before our eyes. Everything about the square seemed to defy the ordinary laws of possibility.

"*Khanoom,* please move forward," cried a man behind us, using the respectful term for a married woman. We apologized and stepped away from the entrance. Looking back as he passed, he added with a smile, "First time? I still enjoy seeing the wonder on visitors' faces."

Wonder was right. On the shorter sides of the square, Shah Abbas's blue-and-gold palace faced his private yellow-domed mosque, which glowed like a tiny sun. On the longer sides, the gateway to the Great Bazaar faced the entrance to the vast Friday mosque — a reminder to God-fearing merchants to be honest.

"Power, money, and God, all in one place," remarked my mother, looking at the buildings around us.

"And *chogan,*" I replied, noticing the goalposts for polo at the far ends of the square, which was long enough to host a competition.

From the top of one of the Friday mosque's minarets, the muezzin began the call to prayer, piercing the air with his sweet nasal voice. "Allah-hu-Akbar — God is great!" he cried, his voice drifting above us.

As we walked into the square, I noticed that most of the buildings were tiled in the purest colors of sun and sky. The dome of the Friday mosque looked all turquoise from afar, but up closer I could see it was enlivened with swirling vines in yellow and white. Garlands of white and turquoise blossomed on the dome of the Shah's lemon-colored mosque. The arched gateways to the mosques sprouted a profusion of tiled white flowers that looked like stars sparkling in the blue of twilight. Every surface of every building glittered with ornament. It was as if a master goldsmith had selected the most flawless turquoise, the rarest of blue sapphires, the brightest yellow topaz, and the purest of diamonds, and arranged them into an infinity of shimmering patterns that radiated color and light.

"I have never seen anything so wonderful," I said to my mother, forgetting for a moment the sadness that had brought us here.

My mother hadn't forgotten. "It's all too big," she replied, gesturing at the wide square, and I understood that she missed our tiny village, where she knew everyone she saw.

The square was full of people. Young boys zoomed around us, balancing cups of hot, dark liquid, yelling, "Coffee!" "Coffee!" which I had never tasted but which smelled as rich as a meal. Two jugglers performed a swift exchange of balls, begging the audience to be generous with their coins. Hawkers stopped us a dozen times, asking us to examine cloth, kohl, and even the tusk of an elephant, an enormous animal from India with legendary powers of memory.

After a few minutes of walking, we reached the Shah's palace. Compared with the Friday mosque, it seemed modest. It was only a few stories high, and it was protected by a pair of thick, carved wooden doors, eight brass cannon, and a row of guards armed with swords. My mother approached one of the guards and asked how we could find Gostaham the carpet maker.

"What is your business with him?" asked the guard with a frown.

"He told us to seek him out," said my mother. The guard smiled scornfully at the sound of her long village vowels.

"He invited *you?*"

"He is part of my husband's family."

The guard looked as if he doubted her word. "Gostaham is a master in the Shah's carpet-making workshop, which is behind the palace," he said. "I will tell him you are here."

"We are the dust beneath your feet," said my mother, and we went back into the square to wait. Nearby, there was a bazaar of metal beaters, and we watched the smiths pound the shapes of birds and animals into teapots, cups, and spoons.

Before long, the guard found us and led us to meet Gostaham, who was waiting near the palace door. I was surprised by how little he and my father resembled each other. It was true that they were only half brothers, but while my father had been tall with features cut as cleanly as if with a knife, Gostaham was short and as round as a potato, with drooping eyes, a nose curved like a falcon's beak, and a large gray beard. He greeted us kindly and welcomed us to Isfahan. Beaming at me, he grabbed my two hands between his. "Well, then!" he exclaimed. "So you're Isma'il's child. You've got his walnut color and his straight black hair, and I would know those tiny, perfect hands anywhere!"

He made a show of examining my hands, which made me laugh, and compared them with his own. They were very small for a man and, like mine, narrow with long fingers.

"The family resemblance is obvious," he said. "Do you make rugs?"

"Of course," said my mother. "She's the best knotter in our village." And she told him the story of how we had sold my turquoise rug while it was still on my loom.

"May the hand of Ali always be with you!" said Gostaham, looking impressed.

He asked my mother for news of home. As we followed him out of the square, she began telling him about my father. The words poured out of her as if they had been bottled up for too long, and she told the story of his death with so much feeling, it brought tears to his eyes.

We left the Image of the World through a narrow gateway and walked for a few minutes through a district called Four Gardens to get to Gostaham's home. The district was divided into pleasure parks, which were barren now that it was winter. A cedar tree marked the beginning of Gostaham's street. From the outside, all the houses looked like fortresses. They were situated behind tall, thick walls that protected the inhabitants from prying eyes.

Gostaham led us through thick wooden gates, and we stood for a moment looking at the outside of his home. It was so large we didn't know where to go at first. Gostaham entered a narrow corridor, walked up a few steps, and led us into the *birooni,* or outside rooms, where he entertained male guests. His Great Room had long glass windows depicting two green swans drinking blue water from either side of a fountain. Carved white plaster flowers and vines adorned the ceiling and the walls. Ruby-colored carpets, made with the tightest knots I had ever seen, supported thick cushions in warm crimson tones. Even on this cold winter day, the room seemed to radiate warmth.

Gostaham lifted the windows, which opened all the way to the ground, and we stepped out into the large courtyard. It had a pool of water shaded by two poplars. I thought of the single tree in my village, a large cypress. For one family to have its own shade and greenery seemed to me the greatest of luxuries.

We met Gordiyeh, Gostaham's wife, in the courtyard. She was an ample woman, with large round hips and heavy breasts, who advanced slowly to kiss us on both cheeks. One of her servants had just boiled water, and I watched him make tea out of previously used leaves. It was strange that a household this grand would use its leaves twice. The tea was as tasteless as water, but we thanked Gordiyeh and said, "May your hands never ache."

"How old are you?" she asked me.

"Fifteen."

"Ah! Then you'll have to meet Naheed. She's fifteen, too, and is the daughter of a woman who lives nearby."

She turned to my mother. "Naheed comes from a very good family. I have always hoped that they might commission a carpet from us, but they haven't yet."

I wondered why she hoped to sell more carpets, since to my eyes she already had everything a family could want. But before I could ask any questions, Gordiyeh suggested that we must be tired, and led us through the courtyard to a tiny room squeezed between the kitchen storerooms and the latrine. There was nothing in it but two bedrolls, blankets, and cushions.

"My apologies that the room is so unworthy of your presence," Gordiyeh said, "but all the others are occupied."

My mother struggled to keep the dismay from her face. The walls were dingy, and the floor was streaked with dust. Gostaham's house was a palace compared to our little village home, but the tiny room we were to share was more humble.

"Not at all," replied my mother politely, "your generosity far exceeds what we deserve."

Gordiyeh left us for the afternoon rest. I straightened my bedroll, raising dust, which brought on a fit of coughing. After a few moments, I heard one of the house servants enter a room next to ours, while another opened the door to the latrines, releasing a thick, earthy smell even more pungent than the odor of our camel.

"Are we servants now?" I asked my mother in alarm. She was stretched out on a bedroll, her eyes wide open.

"Not yet," she replied, but I could see that she was worried about that very question.

AFTER SLEEPING, we arose and joined Gordiyeh and Gostaham in the birooni for the evening meal. What a feast was laid on cloths before us! I had not seen such food even at weddings, yet for Gordiyeh and Gostaham it seemed to be everyday fare. There was a chilled yogurt soup with dill, mint, green raisins, walnuts, and rose petals, cold and refreshing on the tongue; stewed chicken with tart sweetened barberries; tender eggplant cooked with garlic and whey; saffron rice with a crunchy brown crust; tangy sheep's cheese; hot bread; and a plate of radishes, fresh mint, and bitter greens for good digestion. I ate too much the first evening, as if to make up for the times in my village when we hadn't had enough.

When we were all sated, my mother began to speak. "Exalted hosts," she said, "we are honored that you have taken us into your household and fed us as if it were only yesterday that we last parted. And yet, I haven't seen you, honorable Gostaham, for more than twenty-five years. In that time, you have risen faster than the highest star. How did you come to be here, in this grand house, with all the good fortune that a man could desire?"

Gostaham smiled and put his hands on his large stomach. "Indeed, sometimes when I arise in the morning and look around, I can't believe it myself. And then when I see Gordiyeh beside me, I know my dreams have become real, and I thank God for my many blessings."

"May they be forever plentiful," replied my mother.

"It wasn't always like this, though. Long before you were born," Gostaham said to me, "my father realized that if he was to remain in his village, he would always be poor. Knowing there would be little

39

to inherit, he moved to Shiraz to test his fortune. We were so poor that I had to help by making rugs. When I was twelve, I discovered that I could knot faster than almost anyone."

"Just like my daughter," my mother said proudly.

"Our home was so small that there was no space for a loom. When the weather was fine, I set up my loom outside, just as you must have done," Gostaham said to me. "One day I was knotting a rug with such speed that a small crowd gathered to watch. It was my good fortune that one of the passersby owned the largest rug workshop in Shiraz. He never looked for apprentices outside the workshop — why should he, when he could just train his workers' sons? But when he saw me, he offered to hire me, for my speed would increase his profits.

"The next few years were the harshest of my life. The workshop owner made his demands according to ability, not age. Because I was fast, I was required to finish rugs more quickly than anyone else. Once, when the owner caught me away from the loom, he told one of his bullies to throw me onto my back and beat the soles of my feet until I screamed. No one but a fool would destroy a knotter's hands, but what did he care if I couldn't walk?"

His story made me shiver. I had heard of children younger than me, mostly orphans, who had been forced to spend long hours at the loom. Sometimes, at the end of their day, they couldn't unbend their legs to stand up, and their caretakers had to bear them home on their backs. After they spent years laboring with folded legs, their bones grew twisted and their heads seemed too large for their bodies. When they tried to walk, they tottered like old people. I was glad I had grown up in a village where no one would allow a loom to break a child's body. Even so, when I was working at my loom on a warm spring day, I used to envy the birds and even the scrawny dogs, who were free to roam as they liked. To be young and have to sit quietly and work, when your blood is racing and you long to be chattering and laughing — that will make a child grow old quickly.

"The truth is, the owner of the workshop was right," Gostaham continued. "I tried to shirk my duties because I didn't want to remain a knotter. Whenever I could, I spent time with his master designer and master colorist. The designer allowed me to copy some of his patterns, and the colorist took me with him to the bazaar to show me how he selected shades of wool. Secretly, I learned all I could."

It had never occurred to me that it was possible to be more than just a knotter. Although I was sleepy from the large meal, I listened to Gostaham's tale with care.

"My husband didn't need much teaching," Gordiyeh burst in. "His eye for color is better than any man's."

Gostaham leaned back into the cushions with a smile, enjoying his wife's praise. "I was so ambitious that I told the master designer I wanted to make a carpet of my own. He offered me a design on paper that he wasn't using anymore and allowed me to copy it. Taking all my earnings, I went to the bazaar and bought the best wool I could afford. I spent hours choosing the colors, taking so long at it that the merchants yelled at me to buy something or leave their shops. But I had to be certain beyond certainty that I was choosing the right hues.

"By then I was seventeen, and it took me nearly a year to knot that carpet outside of working hours. It was the best I had ever made. My mother was pleased with me, for it would bring money into our household. But then I took the biggest risk of my life, which is the reason you see me here today in this fine home, with a wife who outshines the brightest stars of the age."

I sat up straighter, eager to learn how he had made such a fortune.

"I heard that Shah Abbas the Great was coming to Shiraz and would be holding audiences for his subjects every afternoon. I finished the rug, rolled it up, and carried it to his palace on my back. Presenting it to one of his guards, I explained that it was a gift. The guard unrolled it, making sure there were no assassins, animals, poisons, or the like hidden within — and promised to place it before his eyes."

"How bold to part with your only treasure!" exclaimed my mother.

"The rug was presented to the Shah after he heard testimony from a servant accused of stealing and ordered him to be punished with a beating," Gostaham continued. "I think he was ready to enjoy some sweeter news. When my carpet was unrolled before him, he flipped over a corner to check the tightness of the knots. I worried that he was simply going to tell his servants to carry it away, but then he asked that its maker make himself known.

"Looking at me with eyes that seemed to understand my poverty and my ambition, the Shah said, 'Every day, kings offer me gifts of gold, but not one compares with the sacrifice you have just made.' It was my great fortune that he had just started the royal rug workshop in Isfahan to make the finest rugs for his palaces and to sell to rich men. He liked my carpet enough to invite me to join the workshop for a year's trial. My mother almost beat me when she heard I had given away the carpet. When I told her how my fortunes had changed, she praised the Shah's name."

"That is a story beyond stories!" said my mother.

"There was a long road yet ahead," said Gostaham. "When I started at the royal rug workshop, I was the lowliest of the low. I was lucky because all of us were paid an annual salary, and even though mine was the smallest, it was enough for me to live on and send money to my family. Conditions were much better at the Shah's workshop than in Shiraz. We worked from dawn until midday, but then we were at liberty to work for ourselves. In the afternoons, I freely learned from the masters with the approval of the Shah."

"So you have come to know him?" I asked with wonder, for the Shah was second only to God.

"Just as his humble servant," said Gostaham. "He takes great interest in carpets and knows how to knot them himself. From time to time he stops by the workshop, which is, after all, adjacent to his palace, to see how the carpets are progressing, and sometimes we exchange a few words. But to return to my story, one of his chief colorists took an interest in me and trained me to master the way hues are combined in a carpet. That has been my job for nearly twenty years, and after my dear mentor went to meet God, I became one of the assistant masters for color."

"They are second only to the master," said Gordiyeh proudly. "And perhaps he will one day become master of the whole workshop."

"There is no certainty in that," Gostaham said. "I have a strong competitor in Afsheen, the assistant master designer, and I believe the Shah is more impressed by designers than colorists. Still, I wouldn't change anything about the course of my life. Because it was that very colorist — the one who made me his apprentice — who taught me everything I know, and who also gave me his daughter as his wife." And here he smiled at Gordiyeh with so much affection and desire that it reminded me of the way my father used to look at my mother. My mother noticed, too, and for a moment her eyes filled.

"What kind of rugs do you make in the royal workshop?" I asked quickly, hoping Gostaham would stop smiling at his wife.

"The finest carpets in the land," he said. "Carpets that require an army of specialists. Carpets that the Shah keeps rolled up and stored in dark rooms so they will never be ruined by light. Carpets ordered by foreign kings with their coat of arms depicted in silver-wrapped thread. Carpets that will be treasured long after we're all dust."

"May God rain His blessings on Shah Abbas!" exclaimed Gordiyeh.

"If not for him, I would still be a knotter in Shiraz," agreed Gostaham. "He is responsible not only for the rise in my own fortunes, but for exalting the craft of rug making above others."

It was getting late. My mother and I said good night and went to sleep in our little room. As I pulled the blankets around me, I thought about how for some families, good fortune rains down with no end. Perhaps now that we were in Isfahan with a fortunate family, our luck would finally change, despite what the comet had foretold.

THE NEXT DAY, Gordiyeh sent a messenger to Naheed's mother to tell her that I was her daughter's age and was visiting from the south. Her mother sent back an invitation for us to visit them that afternoon. When Gordiyeh told me it was time to go, I smoothed my hair behind my scarf and announced that I was ready.

"You can't leave the house like that!" she said, sounding exasperated.

I looked down at my clothes. I had dressed in my long-sleeved robe, a long tunic, and loose trousers, all black because I was still in mourning. I patted the hair at my temples, pushing back the locks that had strayed out of my scarf. My clothing had always been thought modest enough for my village.

"Why not?"

"It's different in the city," she replied. "Women from good families keep fully covered!"

I was speechless. Gordiyeh took my hand and led me into her quarters. She opened a trunk stuffed with cloth and rummaged through it until she found what she needed. Pulling me in front of her ample body, she removed my scarf and smoothed my hair on both sides of my head. It was unruly, I could tell. Then she wrapped a lightweight white cloth around my head and fastened it under my chin.

"There!" she said. "Now you'll look like Naheed and other girls when you're at home or visiting."

She held up a metal mirror so I could see. The cloth shielded my hair and neck, but I didn't like how exposed and fleshy my face looked. The days in the desert sun had made my face darker, especially against the whiteness of the scarf.

I looked away from the mirror, thanking her and turning to go.

"Wait, wait!" protested Gordiyeh. "Let me finish."

She shook out a hood and placed it expertly over the top of my head. Even though the hood was white, it was dark and airless inside.

"I can't see!" I complained.

Gordiyeh adjusted the hood so that a portion of lace covered my eyes. The world was visible again, but only as if looking through a net.

"That's your *picheh*," said Gordiyeh. "You should wear it when you're outside." It was hard to breathe, but once again I thanked her, relieved that we were done.

"Oh, but you are a funny little one!" said Gordiyeh. "Small, quick as a hare, and just as nervous. What's your hurry? Wait while I find you everything you need!"

She moved slowly, sorting through the cloths until she found a large white length of fabric. She draped it over my head and showed me how to hold it closed by clutching the fabric in my fist right under my chin.

"Now you look as you should, all snug inside your chador," she said.

I led the way out of her room, feeling as if I were carrying around a nomad's tent. Although I could see well enough if I looked straight out through the lace, I had no side vision. I was not used to holding a chador around me except at the mosque, and I tripped on it until I learned to position it above my ankles.

As I walked unsteadily down the hallway, Gordiyeh said, "For now, everyone will be able to tell that you are not from the city. But very soon, you will learn how to move as quietly and gently as a shadow."

When we returned to the birooni, Gostaham congratulated me on my new attire, and even my mother said she wouldn't recognize me in a crowd. Gordiyeh and I walked together to Naheed's house, which was a few minutes away through the Four Gardens district. It was a refreshing walk, for Shah Abbas had built a grand avenue through the district, lined by gardens and narrow canals of water. The road was wide enough for twenty people to stroll side by side, and it was filled with plane trees, whose hand-shaped leaves would form a shady green canopy in spring and summer. The road led to the Eternal River and the Thirty-three Arches Bridge, and had a view of the Zagros Mountains, whose jagged tips were covered with snow. The homes we passed had gardens as large as parks and seemed like palaces compared with the tiny, clustered dwellings in my village.

Hidden by my picheh I felt free to stare at those around me, since no one could see where I was looking. An old man who was missing part of his leg begged for alms under the cedar tree near Gostaham's house. A girl dallied aimlessly, her eyes darting around as if she were seeking something too embarrassing to name. On my left, the turquoise dome of the Friday mosque hovered over the city like a blessing, seemingly lighter than air.

Shortly after Thirty-three Arches Bridge came into view, we turned down a wide street toward Naheed's house. As soon as we stepped inside the door, we removed our chadors and pichehs and gave them to a servant. I felt lighter after relinquishing them.

Naheed reminded me of the princesses in the tales my mother liked to tell. She wore a long robe of lavender silk with an orange undergarment that peeked out at the neck, the sleeves, and the ankles. She was tall and thin, like a cypress tree, and her clothing swayed loosely when she moved. She had green eyes—the gift of her Russian mother, Ludmila—and her long hair, partially covered by an embroidered white head cloth, was wavy. Two loose tresses lay on her bosom. In back, her hair was in wefts that reached almost to her knees. The wefts were held by orange silk ties. I wanted to talk to her, but both of us had to sit quietly while our elders exchanged greetings. Naheed's mother noticed our eagerness and said to her, "Go ahead, *joonam*—soul of mine—and show your new friend your work."

"I'll be glad to," said Naheed. As she led me into her small, pretty workroom, whose carpet was made in soothing shades of gray and blue, she whispered, "At last we can talk without the old folks!" Her irreverence delighted me.

Naheed opened a trunk full of paper with black marks on it and pulled out a sheet to show me. I stared at it for a moment before I realized what she could do.

"God be praised!" I said. "You can write!" Not only was she beautiful, but a scholar, too. Almost no one in my village could read or write; I had never even met a girl who knew how to use a pen.

"Do you want me to show you how I do it?"

"Yes!"

Naheed dipped a reed pen into a vessel of black ink and brushed off the excess. Taking a fresh piece of paper, she wrote a word in large letters with the ease of long practice.

"There!" she said, showing me the page. "Do you know what that says?"

I clicked my tongue against my teeth.

"It's my name," said Naheed.

I stared at the graceful letters, which had a delicate dot on top and a dash below. It was the first time I had ever seen anyone's name recorded in ink.

"Take it—it's for you," she said.

I pressed the paper to my chest, not realizing it would leave a wet mark on my mourning clothes. "How did you learn?"

"My father taught me. He gives me a lesson every day." She smiled at the mention of him, and I could see that she was very close to her Baba. I felt a pang in my heart and I looked away.

"What's the matter?" Naheed asked. I told her why we had come to Isfahan from so far away.

"I'm sorry your luck has been so dark," she said. "But now that you're here, I'm sure things will change for you."

"God willing."

"You must miss your friends back home," she said, searching my face.

"Just Goli," I replied. "We have been friends since we were small. I would do anything at all for her!"

Naheed had a question in her eyes. "If Goli told you a secret, would you keep it quiet?" she asked.

"To the grave," I replied.

Naheed looked satisfied, as if an important concern about my loyalty had been addressed.

"I hope we can be good friends," she said.

I smiled, surprised by her swift offer of friendship. "Me, too," I replied. "Can I see more of your writing?"

"Of course," she said. "Here—take the pen yourself."

Naheed showed me how to make a few basic letters. I was clumsy and spilled pools of ink on the paper, but she told me everybody did that at first. After I had practiced for a while, Naheed stoppered the vessel of ink and put it away. "Enough writing!" she said imperiously. "Let's talk about other things."

She smiled so invitingly, I guessed what she wanted to talk about. "Tell me: Are you engaged?"

"No," I said sadly. "My parents were going to find a husband for me, but then my Baba—"

I couldn't finish the thought. "How about you?" I asked.

"Not yet," said Naheed, "but I plan to be soon."

"Who is the man your parents have chosen?"

Naheed's smile was victorious. "I've found someone myself."

"How can you do that?" I asked, astonished.

"I don't want some old goat that my parents know, not when I've already seen the most handsome man in Isfahan."

"And where did you find him?" I asked.

"Promise you won't tell?"

"I promise."

"You must swear that you will never breathe a word, or I'll put a curse on you."

"I swear by the Holy Qur'an," I said, frightened by the idea of a curse. I didn't need any more bad luck.

Naheed sighed with pleasure. "He's one of the best riders in the polo games at the Image of the World. You should see him on a horse!" She arose and imitated him taming a bucking stallion, which made me laugh.

"But Naheed," I said with concern, "what if your mother finds out?"

Naheed sat down again, slightly breathless. "She must never find out," she said, "for she would refuse a man of my own choice."

"Then how will you ensnare him?"

"I'll have to be very clever," she said. "But I'm not worried. I always find ways to make my parents do what I want. And most of the time, they think it's their own idea."

"May Ali, prince among men, fulfill all your hopes!" I replied, surprised by her boldness.

Few girls were as confident about their future as Naheed. I admired her for her certainty, just as I was dazzled by her smooth white skin, her green eyes, her lavender silk tunic, and her skill with the pen. I couldn't understand why she wanted to be my friend, as I was just a poor village girl and she was a learned child of the city, but it seemed that Naheed was one of those girls who could make or break rules as she liked.

ON THE NEXT DAY, Friday, my mother and I arose before the sun and went to the kitchen, looking for breakfast. A pretty maid named Shamsi gave us hot bread and my first vessel of coffee. The rich taste of it brought tears of pleasure to my eyes. No wonder everyone talked about the wonder of the bean! If tea enlivened the appetite, coffee was rich enough to quench it. It was sweet, but I stirred in another spoonful of sugar when no one was looking. I began chattering with my mother about nothing in particular. Her cheeks were flushed, and I noticed that she, too, was chirping like a bird.

While we were eating, Gordiyeh stopped by and told us that her daughters would be visiting with their children, as they did on every holy day, and that everyone would be needed to help make the festive midday meal. It would be a large task, as the household was even grander than it looked at first. There were six servants: Cook; Ali-Asghar, who was responsible for men's jobs like slaughtering animals; two maids, Shamsi and Zohreh, who scrubbed, polished, and cleaned; a boy named Samad whose only job was to make and serve coffee and tea; and an errand boy, Taghee. All these people would have to be fed, plus my mother and I, Gordiyeh and Gostaham, their daughters and their children, and anyone else who happened to visit.

Ali-Asghar, a small, wiry man with hands as big as his head, had already killed a lamb in the courtyard that morning and suspended it to let the blood flow out of its body. While we peeled eggplant with sharp knives, he stripped off its skin and chopped the body into parts. Cook, a thin woman who never stopped moving, threw the meat into a cauldron over a hot fire, adding salt and onions. My mother and I cut the eggplant into pieces and salted them to make the sour black juice erupt.

50

Gordiyeh appeared from time to time to check on the preparations. Looking at the eggplant, which had only just begun to sweat, she told my mother, "More salt!"

I could feel words behind my mother's lips, but she didn't speak them. She sprinkled more salt and then paused.

"More!" Gordiyeh said.

This time, my mother poured until the eggplant was nearly buried and Gordiyeh told her to stop.

After the sourness had drained out, we rinsed the chopped eggplant in cool water, and my mother fried it in a pot bubbling with hot oil. When each piece was cooked, I patted it with a cloth to remove the grease, and put it aside. The eggplant would be laid on top of the lamb just before serving to allow it to marry the meat juices.

Since the meal was still hours away, Gordiyeh told us to make a large vessel of vegetable *torshi*, a spicy relish that added flavor to rice. Cook's recipe called for eggplant, carrots, celery, turnips, parsley, mint, and garlic by the basketload, all of which we had to wash, peel, and chop. Then Cook measured out the vinegar she had made and mixed everything together. By the time we had finished, my hands were tired and raw.

Gordiyeh's daughters, Mehrbanoo and Jahanara, arrived and dropped in to the kitchen to see what we were cooking. Mehrbanoo, the eldest at twenty-two, had two daughters, who were dressed and groomed like little dolls, in yellow and orange tunics with gold earrings and gold bracelets. Jahanara was a year younger and had one son, Mohammad, a three-year-old child who seemed small for his age and who had a runny nose. Both of the women lived with their husbands' families but came to visit their parents at least once a week. I was introduced to them as their father's half brother's daughter—"a distant relative," Gordiyeh said.

"How many of *those* do we have?" Mehrbanoo asked her mother, with a big laugh that revealed several rotten teeth. "Hundreds?"

"Too many to count," said Gordiyeh.

I was taken aback by this airy dismissal. As if in explanation, Gordiyeh said to my mother, "Our family is so large that my girls can't keep up."

Shamsi entered the kitchen just then and said to Gordiyeh, "Your revered husband has arrived."

"Come, girls, your father is always hungry after Friday prayers," Gordiyeh said, ushering them out of the room.

The whole kitchen began to bustle. "Hurry!" Cook hissed, handing me a few cotton spreads. "Lay these over the carpets in the Great Room. Don't delay!"

I followed Gordiyeh and her daughters, who had arranged themselves on the cushions and were chatting without paying me the least attention. I was eager to sit and eat with them, but Cook called me back to the kitchen and handed me a tray of hot bread and a dish of goat cheese and mint; she followed with the plate of honor, heaped with eggplant and herbs, while Zohreh tottered under the weight of the rice. My mother emerged with a large vessel containing a cool drink she had made of rose water and mint.

Back in the kitchen, Cook said, "We may as well begin the washing," although we hadn't eaten yet. She handed me a rag and a greasy pot encrusted with eggplant. I stared at them, wondering when we'd be called in to dine. My mother pushed a strand of hair back into her scarf and began cleaning the rice pot. Surely we'd be asked to join the family soon! I tried to catch my mother's eye, but her head was bowed over her task and she didn't seem to be expecting anything.

After we had completed most of the cleanup, Cook sent me back to the Great Room with a vessel of hot water so the family could wash their hands. Everyone had finished eating and was reclining comfortably against the cushions, their bellies large with food. My stomach growled, but no one seemed to notice. Zohreh and Shamsi collected the platters, and then Cook divided the remaining food among the six members of the household staff and the two of us. Ali-Asghar, Taghee, and Samad ate together outside in the courtyard, while we women ate in the kitchen.

Although the meal had been served, Cook couldn't seem to quit her labors. She'd take a bite, then rise to clean a serving spoon or return a stopper to a vessel. The flavors in her food achieved an exceptional marriage, but her nervousness dulled the pleasure of it. The moment we finished, Cook told each one of us what to do to finish the cleanup. When the kitchen was spotless again, she dismissed us for our afternoon rest.

I threw myself onto my bedroll, my limbs aching. Our room was so small that my mother and I were nose to nose and foot to foot.

"I have nothing left," I said, with a large yawn.

"Me, neither," my mother replied. "Did you like the food, light of my eyes?"

"It was fit for a shah," I said, adding quickly, "but not as good as yours."

"It was better," she replied. "Who'd have thought they would eat meat every week! A person could live on the rice alone."

"God be praised," I replied. "Hasn't it been a year since we've eaten lamb?"

"At least."

It had felt good to eat as much as I wanted for two days in a row.

"Bibi," I said, "what about the eggplant? It was too salty!"

"I doubt that Gordiyeh has had to cook in many years," my mother replied.

"Why didn't you tell her it was too much?"

She closed her eyes. "Daughter of mine, remember that we have nowhere else to go."

I sighed. Safa had been right; we were not our own mistresses now. "I thought Gordiyeh would have invited us to share the meal with them again," I said.

My mother looked at me with pity. "Oh daughter, whom I love above all others," she said, "a family like this one keeps to itself."

"But we *are* their family."

"Yes, and if we had arrived with your father, bearing gifts and good fortune, it would have been different," she said. "But as the poor relatives of your grandfather's second wife, we are not good news."

Feeling more tired than I could remember, I closed my eyes and slept as if dead. It seemed only moments before Cook knocked on our door and asked for help. The family would be up and about soon, she said, and they'd be anxious for their coffee, fresh fruit, and sweetmeats.

"What a honeyed existence!" I muttered under my breath, but my mother did not reply. She was asleep, her eyebrows knitted together in a furrow of worry. I couldn't bear to wake her, so I told Cook I'd work for two.

TWICE A YEAR, Isfahan's Great Bazaar was closed to men so that the ladies of the royal harem could shop in freedom. All the shop-keepers' wives and daughters were sent in to run the stores for three days, and all the women, whether buyers or sellers, were allowed to walk around the bazaar without their heavy chadors.

Gostaham kept an alcove in the bazaar with a few rugs on display, not so much for sale but to remind people such as the royal courtesans that he was available for commissions. Since these could be the most lucrative of jobs, and since they improved his contacts within the harem, he always put his most fashionable wares on display for the women.

Gostaham normally sent his daughter Mehrbanoo to run his shop during the harem's visit, but she became ill the night before. Gordiyeh was sent to sell the carpets instead, and I begged Gostaham to let me accompany her. I had heard stories about the

Shah's women, who were gathered like flowers from every region of our land to adorn him. I wanted to see how beautiful they were and admire their silken clothes. I had to promise I would be as quiet as a mouse if Gordiyeh was making a sale.

On the first day of the harem's visit, we walked to the Image of the World just before dawn. The vast square, normally so busy with nut sellers, hawkers, musicians, and acrobats, was now the province of girls and pigeons. All men had been ordered away under penalty of death, lest they catch a glimpse of the unveiled women. The empty square looked even larger than before. I wondered how the Shah made his way between the palace and his private mosque on the other side of the square. It seemed a long way for royalty to walk in public.

"How does the Shah go to pray?" I asked Gordiyeh.

"Can you guess?" she asked, pointing to the ground beneath us. It looked like ordinary dirt to me, and I had to think for a moment.

"An underground passageway?" I asked, incredulous, and she dipped her chin in assent. Such was the ingenuity of the Shah's engineers that they had thought of his every convenience.

When the sun rose, the burly bazaar guards opened its gates and permitted us to enter. We waited near the doors until the women of the harem began to stream in, mounted on a procession of richly decorated horses. They held their chadors closed with one hand and the reins in the other. Not until all the horses and horsemen had disappeared did they shed their wraps and pichehs, throwing them off with merriment and frivolity. They lived in palaces only a few minutes' walk away, but such ladies were not allowed to travel on foot.

There were thousands of shops in the bazaar to answer every desire, whether for carpets, gold jewelry, silk and cotton cloth, embroidery, shoes, perfume, trappings for horses, leather goods, books, or paper, and on normal days, all kinds of foodstuffs. The two hundred slipper makers alone would occupy the women for some time. Although we could hear their chattering and their laughter, it wasn't until the end of the day that we spoke to any of them.

I had imagined that all the women of the harem would be beauties, but I was wrong. The Shah's four wives were in the fifth or sixth decade of life. Many of the courtesans had been in his harem for years and were no longer beautiful. And most of them weren't even ample. One pretty girl caught my eye because I had never seen hair like hers, the color of a flaming sunset. She looked lost among her sisters, though, and I realized that she didn't speak our language. I felt sorry for her, for she had probably been captured in battle.

"Look!" said Gordiyeh in a tone of awe. "There's Jamileh!"

She was the Shah's favorite. She had black curls surrounding her tiny white face and lips like a rosebud. She wore a lacy undershirt slit from the throat to the navel, which showed the curve of her breasts. Over it, she had chosen a long-sleeved silk sheath dyed a brilliant saffron. Flowing loosely on top was a red silk robe, which opened at her throat to reveal a golden paisley pattern on the reverse side. She had tied a thick saffron sash around her hips, which swayed as she walked. On her forehead pearls and rubies hung from a circlet of gold, which shimmied when she turned her head.

"She's the very image of a girl the Shah loved when he was a young man," Gordiyeh said. "They say she spends her days in the harem quizzing the older women about her dead predecessor."

"Why?"

"To curry favor with the Shah. She pinches her own cheeks all the time now, because the other girl's always bloomed with pink roses."

By the time Jamileh and her entourage reached our alcove, Gordiyeh was as nervous as a cat. She bowed practically to the ground, inviting the ladies to have something to drink. I fetched hot coffee, hurrying so that I wouldn't miss anything. When I returned, the white-cheeked Jamileh was flipping up a corner of each rug with her index finger and examining the knots.

After I served her coffee, she sat down, explaining that she was refurnishing the Great Room in her part of the harem. She would need twelve new cushions for reclining against the wall, each of which was to be about as long as my arm and knotted with wool and silk.

"To make him comfortable, you know," she said significantly.

Hiring Gostaham to design cushion covers was like paying a master architect to design a mud hovel, but Jamileh would have only the best. A fluent stream of flattery poured from her lips about his carpets, "the light of the Shah's workshop, by any measure."

Gordiyeh, who should have been immune to such flattery, melted as quickly as a block of ice in the summer sun. When the two began bargaining, I knew she was doomed. Even her first price for the work was too low. I calculated that it would take one person three months of knotting to make the cushion covers, not including the work on the design. But whenever Jamileh arched her pretty eyebrows or pinched her small white cheeks, Gordiyeh slashed a few more *toman* off the price or made another concession.

Yes, she would make some of the knots out of silver-wrapped thread. No, the cushions would look nothing like her predecessor's. Yes, they would be ready in three months. By the time the bargaining was over, a sly expression had stolen into Jamileh's eyes, and she looked for a moment like the village girl she had once been. No doubt she would make the ladies of the harem laugh out loud over the tale of what a good deal she had made on this day.

One of the Shah's eunuchs wrote up two copies of the agreement and stamped them with the Shah's elaborate wax seal. The deal was done.

When dusk fell, we returned home and Gordiyeh went straight to bed, complaining of a headache. The house was unusually quiet as though awaiting a catastrophe. Indeed, when Gostaham came home and read the receipt, he went straight to Gordiyeh's room and yelled at her for breaking his back.

The next day, Gordiyeh retaliated by staying in bed, leaving him to manage the household and all the visitors on his own. In desperation, Gostaham sent my mother to run his shop, and I went with her. He couldn't have made a better choice: My mother knew the value of every knot. This was a surprise to the junior harem women with limited shopping allowances who had heard of Jamileh's triumph. All day, my mother drove hard bargains with these women, who whined over her stiff prices but nonetheless agreed to pay them because they, too, wanted carpets from the same maker used by the Shah's favorite courtesan.

That evening, when Gostaham looked at the receipts, he praised my mother for her skill with money.

"You have earned us a fine profit, despite Jamileh's wiles," he said. "Now what can I offer you as a fitting reward?"

My mother said she'd like a new pair of shoes, for hers were frayed and dirty from our journey through the desert.

"Two pairs of new shoes, then, one for each of you," Gostaham said.

I had been waiting for a chance to ask Gostaham for what I really wanted, and this seemed the most auspicious moment.

"Shoes are very nice," I blurted out, "but instead, will you take me to see the royal rug workshop?"

Gostaham looked surprised. "I didn't think any young girl could resist a pair of shoes, but no matter. I'll take you after the bazaar returns to normal."

My mother and I went to bed that night filled with glee. As we spread out our bedrolls, we began whispering together about the peculiarities of the household we were fated to live in.

"Now I understand why Gordiyeh reuses the tea leaves," my mother said.

"Why?" I asked.

"She's a bad manager," she replied. "She loses her head in one situation, then tries to make it up in another."

"She'll have to reuse a lot of tea to make up for the loss she took on Jamileh's cushions," I said. "What a funny woman."

"Funny is not the word for it," my mother replied. "We'll need to show Gordiyeh that we're working hard instead of draining her household. After all, Gostaham hasn't said how long we can stay."

"But they have so much!"

"They do," said my mother, "but what does it matter if you have seven chickens in a shed when you believe you have only one?"

My parents had always taken the opposite approach. "Trust God to provide," my father used to say. It may have been equally uncertain, but it was a much sweeter way to live.

A FEW WEEKS later, after I had covered myself in my picheh and chador, Gostaham and I left the house and walked to his workshop near the Image of the World. It was a mild day, and signs of spring were alighting on the Four Gardens district. The trees had their first shimmer of green, and purple and white hyacinths were blooming in the gardens. The first day of the New Year was only a week away. We would celebrate it on the vernal equinox at twenty-two minutes past five in the morning, the precise moment when the sun crossed the celestial equator.

Gostaham was looking forward to the New Year because he and his workers would take a two-week holiday. He began telling me about the latest projects. "We're working on a rug right now that has seventy knots per *radj*," he said proudly.

I stopped so suddenly that a mule driver with a cargo of brass pots yelled at me to move out of the way. A radj was about the length of my middle finger. My own rugs might have had as many as thirty knots per radj, but no more. I could hardly imagine wool fine enough to produce so many knots, or fingers nimble enough to do so.

Gostaham laughed at my astonishment. "And some are even finer than that," he added.

The royal rug workshop was located in its own airy building near the Great Bazaar and the Shah's palace. The main workroom was large, with a high ceiling and plenty of light. Two, four, or even eight knotters were busy at each loom, and many of the carpets in process were so long they had to be rolled up at the foot of the loom to allow the workers to keep knotting.

The men looked surprised to see a woman in the shop, but when they saw I was with Gostaham, they averted their eyes. Most were small in stature — everyone knows that the best knotters are small — but they all had larger hands than I did, and still they formed knots that could hardly be seen. I wondered if I could learn to make even smaller ones.

The first carpet we looked at reminded me of Four Gardens, the parklike district near Gostaham's home. The carpet showed four square gardens divided by canals of water, with roses, tulips, lilies, and violets as beautiful as real ones. Floating above them, a single peach tree with white blossoms gave life to seedlings in each garden. It was like watching nature at work, feeding and renewing her own beauty.

At the next loom we stopped to admire, the carpet was so dense with patterns that my eyes couldn't follow them at first. The most visible design was a red sunburst, which gave birth to tiny turquoise and indigo blossoms edged with white. Somehow, unbelievably, the knotters had made a separate layer of curved vines and another simultaneous layer of arabesques, as delicate as breath. Despite the intricacy of these patterns, none interfered with another, and the carpet seemed to pulse with life.

"How do they make it so fine?" I asked.

Gostaham laughed at me, but it was a kind laugh. "Touch one of the skeins," he said.

I stood on my toes to reach a pale blue ball hanging from the top of the loom. Each thread was thinner and softer than the wool I used at home.

"Is it silk?" I asked.

"Yes."

"Where does it come from?"

"Long ago, a couple of Christian monks who wanted to curry favor with our Mongol conquerors smuggled some cocoons into Iran. Now it's our biggest export, and we sell more of it than the Chinese," he finished with a chuckle.

Iraj, the man in charge of the sunburst rug, called his workers to their labors. After they settled on their cushions, he assumed a crouching position behind the loom and began reciting the sequence of colors needed for a blue-and-white flower. Because the carpet was symmetrical, the knotters could work on a similar flower at opposite ends of the loom. Every time Iraj called out a color change, two pairs of hands reached simultaneously for the silk and made the knot. The men held a knife loosely in their right hands, which they used to separate the knot from its connection to the skein.

"Abdullah," said Iraj abruptly, "go back. You missed the change to white."

Abdullah uttered an oath and slashed at a few knots with his blade. The other man stretched while he corrected his mistake. Then the chant started up again, and they were off.

From time to time, I saw Iraj look at a sheet of paper to refresh his memory of what came next.

"Why do they use a design on paper instead of in their heads?" I asked.

"Because it is an exact guide to where every knot and every color should appear," Gostaham replied. "The results are as close to flawless as any human can attain."

In my village, I always knotted my patterns from memory, inventing little details as I went along. I had been used to thinking of myself as an accomplished knotter, even though my rugs weren't perfectly symmetrical, and curved shapes like birds, animals, or flowers often looked more square than round. But now I had seen what master craftsmen could do, I wanted to learn everything they knew.

Before returning home, Gostaham decided to check on sales at his alcove in the bazaar. As we twisted and turned through the bazaar's alleys, we passed hammams, mosques, caravanserais, schools, endowed wells, and markets for everything, it seemed, that man had ever made or used. The smells told me which section we were passing, from the nose-tingling spice market redolent of cinnamon, to the richness of leather used by the slipper makers, to the blood of freshly slaughtered lamb in the meat market, to the crispness of flowers that would soon be distilled into essences. "I've worked here for twenty years," a rug merchant told me, "and there are still many parts of the bazaar I've never set foot in." I didn't doubt his word.

After Gostaham picked up his receipts, we looked at rugs on display in other merchants' shops. Suddenly, I noticed a carpet that made me cry out.

"Look!" I said. "There's the rug I sold to the merchant my mother was telling you about!"

It was hanging at the entrance of a shop. Gostaham approached and checked it with expert fingers. "The knots are nice and tight," he said. "It's a fine piece, though it shows its village roots."

"The design is a little crooked," I admitted. Its flaws were obvious to me now that I had seen better things.

Gostaham stood looking at the design for some time. "What were you thinking when you chose the colors?" he asked.

"I wanted it to be unusual," I said. "Most of the carpets from my village use only camel, red, or white."

"I see," he said. The look on his face made me afraid that I hadn't chosen wisely.

Gostaham asked the merchant to name his price. Upon hearing his answer, I was speechless for a moment.

"What's the matter?"

"It's so expensive, it's as if they're asking for my father's blood," I said angrily. "Perhaps we could have survived in my village if we had been paid such a large amount."

He shook his head sadly. "You deserved much more."

"Thank you," I said, "but now that I've seen your workshop, I know how much more there is to learn."

"You are still very young," he replied.

My blood rushed to my head, for I knew exactly what I wanted and hoped that Gostaham would understand. "Will you teach me?" I asked.

He looked surprised. "What more do you want to know?"

"Everything," I said. "How you make such beautiful designs and color them as if they were images from heaven."

Gostaham considered for a moment. "I never had a son that I could train to carry on my work," he said. "Neither of my daughters ever needed to learn. What a pity you're not a boy! You're the right age to apprentice in the workshop."

I knew there was no possibility of working among all those men. "Perhaps I could help you on your projects at home — if you found I was good enough," I said.

"We'll see," he replied.

His answer wasn't as encouraging as I had hoped. He himself had once begged his master to let him learn, but he seemed to have forgotten what that was like.

"May I watch you design Jamileh's cushions?" I prompted. "I promise you, you won't even know I'm there. I'll fetch you coffee when you're tired and help in any way I can."

Gostaham's face softened into a smile, which made his kindly eyes droop even further. "If you're truly interested, you must ask Gordiyeh if you will have time outside of your household duties," he replied. "And don't feel too badly about your rug. Things are much more expensive in the city. Just remember, it's a sign of appreciation that the price was so high, and the rug displayed so boldly."

His words soothed me and gave me an idea. I could make another rug to sell, and perhaps I would earn all the money that Hassan had pocketed for himself.

THAT AFTERNOON, I found Gordiyeh in her rooms looking through bolts of silk velvet brought by a visiting merchant. He had never seen her, of course; he conveyed the fabric through her servants and waited in the birooni while she made her selections.

Gordiyeh's fingers were lingering on a bolt patterned with leaves in autumn shades of red and yellow.

"Look at this!" she said. "Won't it make a beautiful long robe for cooler weather?"

Staring at my black mourning clothes, I could only imagine how it would feel to wear something so beautiful. After admiring the thick silk, I told Gordiyeh about my visit to the workshop and asked if I might be permitted to observe Gostaham when he worked at home. Having seen how Gordiyeh had melted under Jamileh's flattery, I spiced my request with awe over Gostaham's carpet-making mastery.

"Why do you want to spend your time that way?" Gordiyeh asked, reluctantly putting aside the bolt of silk. "You will never be allowed to learn in a workshop full of men, nor will you be able to do such fine work without an army of specialists."

"Still, I want to learn," I said stubbornly, feeling my top and bottom teeth pressing against each other. My mother said I always looked like a mule when I didn't get my way.

Gordiyeh looked doubtful. Remembering my mother's words from a few nights before, I added quickly, "Perhaps I might one day become good enough to help Gostaham with small tasks for his commissions. That way, I would relieve some of the burden on him and on your household."

That idea seemed to please Gordiyeh, but she wasn't prepared to say yes. "There is always more work in the kitchen than there are hands," she replied.

I was ready with an answer. "I promise to do everything for Cook that I always do. Nothing will change in how much I help."

Gordiyeh turned back to her bolts of silk. "In that case," she said, "since my husband has given his approval, you may learn from him, but only if you don't shirk your other duties."

I was so jubilant that I promised to work harder than usual, though I believed I was already doing as much as any maid could.

All through the next week, I worked long hours alongside my mother, Shamsi, Zohreh, and Cook in preparation for the New Year. We scrubbed the house from top to bottom and aired out all the blankets. We lifted the bedrolls, cleaning and polishing underneath them. We filled the house with vases of flowers and with mountains of nuts, fruit, and pastries. We cleaned what seemed like a field of greens for the traditional New Year's dish of whole white-fish cooked with mint, coriander, and parsley.

On New Year's Day, my mother and I were awakened in the dark by the bustle in the household. At twenty-two minutes past five, we kissed each other's cheeks and celebrated with coffee and rosewater pastries. Gostaham and Gordiyeh gave their children gold coins and presented every member of the household with a small gift of money. I said a prayer of thanks to God for permitting us to survive the year, and for guiding us to a household with so much to teach me.

GOSTAHAM'S WORKROOM at home was located in the birooni. It was a simple place with carpets and cushions on the floors and alcoves for paper, ink, pens, and books. He drew his designs sitting cross-legged on a cushion with a wooden desk propped on his lap. I joined him the day he began the design for Jamileh's cushions and watched him sketch a vase of tulips partially encircled by a garland of other flowers. I marveled at how natural his flowers looked and how quickly they sprang from his pen.

Gostaham decided that the blossoms were to be pink and yellow, with pale green leaves, against a black background. Touches of silver-wrapped silk thread would outline the blossoms, as Gordiyeh had promised. When I commented on how quickly he designed the cushions, he only said, "This is one commission that has already cost me far more than it's worth."

The following day, he laid out a piece of paper that had been ruled by one of his assistants with a grid. With great care, he drew the finished tulip design on top of the grid and painted it with watercolors. The grid underneath remained visible, dividing the design into thousands of tiny colored squares, each of which stood for a knot. With this guide in hand, the designer could call out the colors or the knotter could read it himself, like a map that tells a traveler where to go.

When he was finished, I begged him to give me a task to practice on my own. The first thing he taught me was to draw a grid. I took pen and ink to my little room and practiced on the floor. In the beginning, I had trouble managing the flow of ink. It pooled and smudged, and my lines were crooked and irregular. But before long, I learned how to dip the pen exactly, brush off the excess, and make a clean, straight line, usually while holding my breath. It was tedious work; one sheet of paper took me the better part of an afternoon, and when I stood up, my legs were stiff and cramped.

When I was able to make a proper grid, Gostaham rewarded me with my very own pen. It had been cut from a reed in the marshes near the Caspian Sea. Although it weighed little more than a feather, to me it was better than a gift of gold. From then on, Gostaham entrusted me with preparing the grids he used to make the final designs for private commissions. He also began giving me assignments to improve my drawing skills. He would toss off sketches of flowers, leaves, lotus blossoms, clouds, and animals, and tell me to copy them exactly. I especially liked to copy complicated designs that looked like flowers within flowers within flowers.

Much later, when I had gained more confidence, Gostaham gave me the pattern he had designed for Jamileh's cushions and told me to reverse it, so that the bouquet of tulips leaned to the right instead of the left. Larger carpets often had patterns that went first one way, then the other, so a designer needed to know how to draw both. Every afternoon, during the hours when the household was sleeping, I practiced drawing. I sang folk songs from my village while I worked, happy to be learning something new.

WHENEVER I HAD TIME, I visited Naheed. We were becoming close quickly, now that we shared not just one secret, but two.

After my first experience of seeing her name in ink, I had asked Naheed to teach me to write. She gave me lessons in her workroom whenever I visited. If anybody came to talk with us, I was to pretend I was just drawing. It was not common for a village girl to learn to write.

We started with the letter *alef*. It was simple to draw, a heartbeat and the letter was done.

"It is long and tall like a minaret," said Naheed, who always thought of shapes that would help me remember the letters.

Alef. The first letter in *Allah*. The beginning of everything.

I filled a page with tall, straight strokes, watching Naheed out of the corner of my eye. Sometimes I added a curving top to the letter to give it a long, low sound in the throat. When my efforts had met with Naheed's approval, she taught me the letter *beh*, which was curved like a bowl with a dot underneath. This letter was much trickier. My *beh*'s looked graceless and childish compared with hers. But when she looked over my labors, she was satisfied.

"Now put the two together, *alef* and *beh*, and you make the most blessed thing in our land," said Naheed.

I wrote them together and mouthed the word *ab:* water.

"Writing is just like making rugs," I said.

"What do you mean?" asked Naheed, with a touch of scorn in her voice. She had never made a rug.

I put down my pen to explain. "Words are made letter by letter, in the same way that rugs are formed knot by knot. If you combine different letters, they make different words, and the same is true when you combine colors to make different patterns," I said.

"But writing is from God," objected Naheed.

"He gave us thirty-two letters," I replied, proud that I knew this now, "but how do you explain that He gave us more colors than we can count?"

"I suppose that's true," said Naheed, in a tone that made it clear that she thought letters were superior, like most everyone did.

Naheed took a deep breath and sighed. "I should be working on my writing exercises," she said. Her father had given her a book of calligraphic drills she was supposed to copy before attempting to pen a lion that spelled *Allah-hu-Akbar:* God is great. "But I can't sit anymore," she added, her green eyes jumping around the room. "My mind is too full."

"Could this have something to do with a handsome polo player?" I said.

"I found out his name: Iskandar," Naheed said, pronouncing it with obvious delight.

"And what about his family?"

She looked away. "I don't know."

"And does he know who *you* are?" I asked, feeling jealous.

Naheed smiled her prettiest smile. "I think he's starting to know," she said.

"How?"

"Last week, I went to the Image of the World with a friend to watch the polo game. Iskandar scored so many goals for his team that the spectators roared with excitement. After the game, I

walked to where the players were being congratulated and pretended to carry on a conversation with my friend until I was sure he
noticed us. Then I flipped up my picheh as if I needed to adjust it and
let him see my face."

"You didn't!"

"I did," Naheed said triumphantly. "He stared, and it was as if
his heart had turned into a bird that had found the right spot for its
nest. He couldn't stop looking, even after I had covered my face."

"But now how will he find you?"

"I shall have to keep going to the games until he knows who
I am."

"Be careful," I said.

Naheed looked at me with slightly narrowed eyes, as if she
wasn't sure she could trust me. "You would never tell anyone,
would you?"

"Of course not: I'm your friend!"

Naheed looked unconvinced. Abruptly, she turned away and
called for a servant, who returned soon with refreshments. Naheed
offered me a vessel of coffee and a plate of dates. I refused the fruit a
few times, but since it would have been impolite to insist, I selected
a small date and placed it in my mouth. It took all my spirit to prevent myself from making a childish face of disgust. I swallowed the
date quickly and ejected the pit.

Naheed was watching me closely. "Was it good?"

One of the stock phrases rushed to my lips—"Your hospitality
shames me, your obedient servant"—but I couldn't say it. I shifted
on my cushion and gulped a mouthful of coffee while I tried to think
of what to say.

"It's sour," I said finally.

Naheed laughed so hard that her slender body shook like a cypress in the wind. "You are so much yourself!" she said.

"What else could I say but the truth?" I asked.

"So many things," she replied. "Yesterday, I served the same dates to friends, including the girl I took to the polo game. She ate one and said, 'The dates of paradise must be like these,' and another girl added, 'But these are sweeter.' I tasted a date after they left and discovered the truth."

Naheed sighed. "I'm tired of such *ta'arof*," she said. "I wish people would just be honest."

"People from my village have a reputation for being plain-spoken," I replied, not knowing what else to say.

"That's one of the things I like about you," she replied.

Right before I rose to go, Naheed asked if I would grant her a special favor.

"It's about the polo games," she said. "My friend is too afraid to accompany me any longer, so will you come instead?"

I imagined that the games would be full of young men who assembled in packs and shouted for their favorite teams. Even though I was new to the city, I knew it was not a place for two girls of marriageable age to go alone.

"Aren't you worried about what your parents would think?"

"Don't you understand?—I have to go," she said with a pleading look in her eyes.

"But how will we do it without our families knowing?"

"I'll say that I'm visiting you, and you'll tell your family you're visiting me. We'll be wrapped up in our chadors and our pichehs, so no one will recognize us once we leave the house."

"I don't know," I said doubtfully.

A look of disdain clouded Naheed's eyes, and I thought I must seem spineless. I didn't want her to think of me that way, so I agreed to accompany her and help her ensnare her beloved.

NAHEED HAD SURPRISED me with her boldness in showing a glimpse of herself to a man she admired. Only a few days later, I revealed myself to a man I had never seen before. It was a Thursday afternoon, and I was returning from the hammam with my hair still wet. As soon as I passed through the tall, heavy door that led into Gostaham's home, I tore off my chador, my picheh, and my head scarf and shook my hair free. I failed to notice a stranger waiting to be shown in to see Gostaham; a servant must have just gone to announce him. He wore a multicolored turban shot with golden thread, and a blue silk robe over a pale orange tunic. I caught a faint, fresh whiff of grass and horses. I was so startled I said, "Ya, Ali!"

If the stranger had been polite, he would have looked away. Instead, he kept his eyes fixed on me, enjoying every minute of my surprise and discomfiture.

"Well, don't just stand there looking!" I snapped, walking quickly to the andarooni, the part of the house where women were safe from male eyes. Behind me, he burst out laughing. Who was this insolent fellow? There was no one around to ask. To find out, I flew up to the second floor of the house, which was little more than a passage to the roof. We used it to go outside and hang laundry. Like all the women of the house, I had discovered that there was a tiny nook off the stairwell where I could hide and observe events occurring in the Great Room. The plaster flowers and vines that adorned the walls formed a lattice through which I could see and hear.

Peering into the room, I saw the well-dressed stranger sitting in the place of honor and heard Gostaham saying ". . . deeply honored to be the instrument of your desires."

I had never heard him talk so respectfully to anyone, particularly not to a man half his age. I hoped I hadn't insulted anyone too important. I took a more careful look at the visitor. His slim waist, erect bearing, and sun-darkened skin made me suspect that he was a trained horseman. He had thick, fuzzy eyebrows that met perfectly above his nose, dominating eyes shaped like half-moons. His long nose curved toward his lips, which were plump and very red. He wore a beard cropped close to his skin. He was not handsome, yet he had a powerful beauty like a leopard's. While Gostaham spoke, the visitor sucked on a water pipe, narrowing his eyes with pleasure as he inhaled. Even from my perch I could smell the sweet tobacco cured with fruit, which made the inside of my nose tingle.

Gostaham made sure that his guest felt welcome by inviting him to converse about his recent travels. "The whole town is talking of the army's exploits in the north," he said. "We would be most honored if you would tell us yourself what happened."

The visitor recounted how one hundred thousand Ottomans had bombarded a fortress that guarded the country's northwestern frontier. Hidden in tunnels, they had hurled cannonballs at its gates. "For many days, we thought that God had chosen to give victory to the other side," he said.

From inside the fortress, he led a team of men through Ottoman lines to bring back supplies that helped the army withstand the siege. After two and a half months, the Ottomans began to starve. About forty thousand soldiers were dead by the time their army began its retreat.

"The men inside the fortress were starving as well," said the visitor. "Toward the end, we were eating nothing but bread made out of flour crawling with bugs. After a six-month campaign, I am grateful every time I eat hot bread cooked in my own oven."

"As any man would be," said Gostaham.

The visitor paused, drawing smoke from the water pipe.

"Of course, a man never knows what will happen while he is at battle," he said. "I have a three-year-old daughter, dearer to me than my own eyes. She grew ill with cholera while I was gone and has survived only through the grace of God."

"*Al'hamd'Allah.*"

"As her father, I am bound to give alms in thanks for her survival."

"It is the act of a true Muslim," agreed Gostaham.

"The last time I visited the Seminary of the Four Gardens," said the visitor, "I noticed that some of their floor coverings had become threadbare."

He sucked on the water pipe and exhaled slowly, while we waited and hoped.

"But even as I consider commissioning a carpet to glorify God, I have a special desire," he continued. "This carpet is to be made to give thanks for my daughter's health, and I want it to contain talismans to protect her in the future."

"With God's grace," said Gostaham, "your child shall always be free of illness."

At that moment I heard Gordiyeh calling my name, so I had to go. I hoped she might tell me more. I found her in the courtyard examining several donkeyloads of pistachios from Kerman, which Ali-Asghar was unloading into the storerooms. They needed another hand.

"Who is our visitor?" I asked her.

"Fereydoon, the son of a wealthy horse trader," she said. "We could do nothing better for our future than appeal to his heart."

"Is he . . . *very* wealthy?" I asked, trying to gauge how important he was.

"Yes," she replied. "His father breeds some of the finest Arabian stallions in the land on farms in the north. He used to be just a country farmer, but he has made a lot of money now that everyone wants to own a horse of status."

No one in my village had a horse of status, for even a nag cost more than most people could afford. I supposed she meant the high-class families of Isfahan.

"Fereydoon's family is buying houses all over the country, and each one will need rugs," Gordiyeh continued. "If we can please Fereydoon, we could earn a fortune from his family alone."

Gordiyeh handed me a few pistachios to eat while we were unloading the heavy sacks. I loved pistachios, but I felt discomfited inside. Too often, my tongue leapt out ahead of me. Now that I was in a new city, I must learn to be more careful, for I hardly knew a man of power from a servant.

Later, Gordiyeh told me that Fereydoon had commissioned a rug and had promised to pay a very good price. I was so relieved that I offered to help Gostaham in any way I could. In celebration of the day's good fortune, Gordiyeh freed me from most of my household tasks, and I went to visit Naheed.

AFTER FEREYDOON'S VISIT, Gostaham pushed aside all his other commissions and began working on the new design, and I joined him in his workroom and watched him sketch. I was expecting the design to emerge as easily as it had with Jamileh's cushions, but now it was as if a demon had possessed his pen. He worked at the design for hours before flipping over the sheet of paper and starting over. When he didn't like the new design any better, he balled up the paper and threw it across the room.

Gostaham's hands became black with ink, and soon the workroom was littered with abandoned designs. When Shamsi tried to clean it, he roared, "How can I finish my work if you keep bothering me?" From time to time, he got up and picked through the discarded sheets of paper, searching for an idea.

The only reason he tolerated my presence was that I kept quiet. When he needed more paper, I prepared a new piece of the right size, and when his ink was running low, I refilled his bottle. If he looked tired, I fetched coffee and dates to revive him.

A few days later, when Gordiyeh saw the mess, she tried another tactic, complaining about the cost of the paper. "Woman of mine," Gostaham bellowed, "stay clear! This is not just any carpet for any man!"

While Gostaham was preoccupied with his drawings, I thought about the talismans Fereydoon had requested in his rug. In my village, we used to knot in all manner of symbols, like roosters to en-courage fertility or scissors as protection against evil spirits. But village symbols would have looked peculiar in a city rug, and in any case, a rug designed for a religious school must show no living crea-tures except for trees, plants, and flowers, to avoid the worship of idols.

One afternoon, when Gostaham had cast aside yet another sheet of paper and left the room in a rage, I put my hand to my neck and touched a piece of jewelry that my father had given me as protection against the Evil Eye. It was a silver triangle with a holy carnelian in its center, and I often touched it for blessings. Even though I knew I shouldn't, I picked up Gostaham's pen and paper and began to draw. I was not thinking very hard, just enjoying the feeling of the pen sliding across the page, and I watched it make the shape of a triangle with a circle in its center, just like my necklace. At the bottom of the triangle, I attached delicate hanging shapes resembling beads, coins, and gems.

Gostaham returned to the room, looking tired. "What are you doing?" he asked, as I dipped the pen in his ink.

"Just playing," I said apologetically, returning the reed to the pen rest.

Gostaham's face seemed to grow bigger under his turban, which looked as if it might explode off his head. "Your father is a dog!" he shouted. "No one touches my pen without my permission!"

Gostaham reclaimed the pen and ink with an angry look. I sat as still as a loom, fearing he would yell at me again. He quickly became preoccupied once again by the problem of the design, but I could see from his furrowed brow that he didn't like what came forth. With an exasperated sigh, he got up and walked around the room, passing near me. He snatched the paper I had been working on, mumbling that he might as well use the other side.

Then he stared at the page. "What's this?" he asked.

I flushed as Gostaham returned to his cushion. "It's a talisman," I said, "like Fereydoon wanted."

Gostaham stared at the paper for a long time, while I kept my peace. Before long, he became absorbed in a new drawing, and his pen seemed to fly over his work. I watched him transform the crude, simple drawing I had made into a thing of beauty. He sketched triangular shapes with hanging beads, coins, and gems, connecting them so that they formed a delicate tiered design. The shapes looked pretty and dainty, which is how I imagined Fereydoon's daughter.

When he was finished, Gostaham looked pleased for the first time in weeks. "Good work on the sketches," he said, but I also saw an ember of anger in his eyes. "Let me make it clearer than daylight that you must never, ever touch my pen again."

Looking down at the carpet, I begged forgiveness for being so bold. Later I told my mother that I had contributed to the design, but not exactly how, for she would have thought me rash.

Not long after, Gostaham took the design to Fereydoon for his approval. He had never seen a design like it before and wanted to know where it had come from. Gostaham was secure enough in his own mastery to tell him that a distant relation had contributed to the dangling gems design.

"It's so delicate, just like my girl," Fereydoon had replied.

"Indeed," Gostaham said, "it is based on women's jewelry from the south."

Fereydoon had imitated the southern accent, and Gostaham had laughed and told him that was how his visiting niece talked. Remembering the way I had snapped at Fereydoon in that very accent, I realized that he now knew exactly who I was. I consoled myself that he must not have taken offense at my abrupt words, for he had accepted the design.

After his meeting with Fereydoon, Gostaham praised me and told my mother I had been a loyal helper. As a reward, he promised to take me to see a special rug, which he described as one of the lights of the age.

BECAUSE FEREYDOON'S COMMISSION was so important, Gostaham decided to have the wool for the carpet dyed to his specifications. He favored a dyer named Jahanshah who had a shop on the banks of the Eternal River, and he allowed me to accompany him one morning to see how he commissioned indigo, that most coveted of colors, whose recipe is cloaked in secrecy.

Jahanshah had thick white eyebrows, a white beard, and ruddy cheeks. He greeted us near his metal pots, which were full of water. Since the pots were cool, I thought he had forgotten about our visit.

"Her first time?" Jahanshah asked Gostaham.

"Yes."

"Ah!" he replied, with a broad smile. "Watch closely."

He wet a few skeins of wool and put them gently into a pot. The water inside was a strange greenish color, and when I peered at the wool, it looked unchanged.

We sat on stools overlooking the river. While the men discussed the rising price of lamb's wool, I watched pedestrians cross the old Shahrestan Bridge, with its thick pilings, built four centuries before I was born. Older still were the swordlike Zagros Mountains, which thrust their pointed tips heavenward as if to carve the sky. No one had ever climbed to the top of those mysterious peaks, not even shepherds.

A gust of wind lifted off the water, threatening to pull off my head cloth. I held the ends down and waited impatiently for Jahanshah to add the magical indigo, but he seemed in no hurry. We drank tea while he languidly stirred the wool.

Nearby, another dye maker was hard at work over his boiling pots. He poured in a bag of dried yellow larkspur flowers, which danced their way into the liquid and whirled into a bright streak of yellow. I watched him drop in the skeins of white wool. They licked up the shade, transforming into the color of sunshine.

I wanted to observe more closely, but Jahanshah handed me a pronged tool and said, "Lift out one of my skeins."

I dipped the tool into his pot and fished until I caught a skein, which I raised in the air. It had turned an unappealing shade of green, like the puddles left behind by a sick horse.

I turned to Jahanshah, puzzled. "Aren't you going to add the indigo?" I asked.

He burst out laughing, and Gostaham joined him while I stood holding the dripping skein. I couldn't see any reason for their great mirth.

"Don't take your eyes off the wool," Gostaham said.

For some reason, the skein didn't look as sickly as before. I blinked, feeling like one of those weary travelers who imagine greenery in the desert. But blinking didn't change what I saw: The skein now bore the color of a pale emerald. After a few moments, it changed into an intense green like the first leaves of spring, which deepened into a blue-green, perhaps like the Caspian Sea, and then became deeper still, like the color at the bottom of a lake. I thrust the prong toward Jahanshah and exclaimed, "May God protect us from the tricks of jinn!"

Jahanshah laughed again and said, "Don't worry, it is only one of the tricks of man."

The skein was now such a rich blue that it brought joy to my eyes with its boundlessness and depth. I watched it, amazed, and then I demanded, "Again!"

Jahanshah let me pull out another skein and observe its transformation through a rainbow of green and blue hues until it became a rich lapis lazuli.

"How?" I asked, astonished.

But Jahanshah only smiled. "That has been a family secret for a little more than a thousand years," he said, "ever since the Prophet Mohammad led his followers to Medina, home of my ancestors."

Gostaham wanted the wool to be a slightly darker hue, so Jahanshah immersed it again until Gostaham was satisfied. Then he cut a strand of it for Gostaham and kept the rest for himself, so both men would be able to verify the color of the order.

When we arrived home, I had hardly removed my outdoor coverings before I asked Gostaham what I could do next.

He looked surprised. "Don't you want to rest?"

"Not even for a moment," I said, for seeing the magic of indigo had made me eager.

Gostaham smiled and put me to work on another grid.

From then on, the more I begged Gostaham to allow me to help him, the more he wanted me by his side. There was always something to do: grids to be drawn, colors to be mixed, paper to be sized. Before long, he let me copy the simplest parts of his designs onto the master grid. Sometimes, he even snatched me away from kitchen work. I relished those moments, for I despised the long hours of cleaning and chopping. When he beckoned to me, I relinquished my knife or mortar and pestle gratefully to join him. The other servants mumbled with indignation behind me, especially Cook, who asked sarcastically if the deer and onagers I was learning to draw would fill my belly at the evening meal. Gordiyeh didn't like it, either. "With so many mouths to feed, everyone has to help," she once said, but Gostaham ignored her. With my assistance, he was starting to complete his commissions more quickly, and I think he enjoyed my company during the long hours of design work, for no one could have been more keen.

Things were not as easy in Isfahan for my mother. She remained in the kitchen at Gordiyeh's mercy and had to do the jobs I left behind. Gordiyeh always corrected her work as if scornful of our village ways. I believe she felt my mother's resistance to her and tried to break it whenever she could. She must rinse the rice six times, no more or less, to remove the starch; must cut the radishes lengthwise instead of into roses; must make chickpea cookies with extra pistachio chips on the outside; yet for the heavenly sharbat, must use less fruit and more rose water. My mother, who had been mistress of her own household since she was my age, was being ordered around like a child.

One day, during the afternoon rest, my mother burst into our little room so angry that I could feel the heat burning off her skin.

"Ay, *Khoda*," she said, calling on God for mercy, "I can't bear it anymore!"

"What is it? What happened?"

"She didn't like the pastries I made," replied my mother. "She wanted squares, not ovals! I had to throw all the dough to the dogs and make it again."

That kind of waste would have been unimaginable in my village, but Gordiyeh demanded perfection.

"I'm sorry," I said, feeling guilty. I had spent the day with Gostaham, and my work had been pleasant and light.

"It's not just the pastry," my mother said. "I'm tired of being a servant. If only your father were alive, we could be in our own home again, doing things our own way!"

I tried to console her, for I loved what I was learning. "At least now we eat well and have no fear of starving."

"Unless she throws us out."

"Why would she do that?"

My mother snorted in exasperation. "You have no idea how much Gordiyeh would like to be rid of us," she said.

She was exaggerating, I thought. "But look at how much we do for the household!"

She kicked off her shoes and collapsed on her bedroll. Her feet were bright red from standing so long while making the pastry.

"Oh, how they ache!" she moaned. I arose and put a cushion underneath them.

"In Gordiyeh's mind, we are draining this household, yet we're not hired help that she can dismiss whenever she likes. She told me today that dozens of Isfahani women would give one of their eyes to work in her kitchen. Women who are young and who can work long and hard without complaint. Not women who want to spend valuable kitchen time learning about rugs."

"What can we do?" I asked.

"We can only pray for a husband for you so that you can start a household of your own," she said. "A good man who will consider it his duty to care for your mother."

I had thought the discussions about my marriage had ended now that we had nothing to offer.

"Without a dowry, how am I to find such a husband?"

My mother stretched her feet to release the pain. "What an unkind comet, to have taken him away before you were settled!" she complained. "I have decided to make herbal remedies and sell them to neighbors to help build a dowry for you. We must not wait much longer," she added, in a tone of warning.

It was true that I was getting old. Everyone I knew had been married by the age of sixteen, and most were married well before.

"I will start another carpet for my dowry," I promised.

"Marrying you is the only way we can hope to live on our own again," said my mother. She turned away and fell asleep almost immediately. I wished there were a way to make her life sweeter. I turned toward Mecca and prayed for a speedy end to the evil influences of the comet.

ONE EVENING, WHEN I didn't have anything to do, I picked up a large piece of paper Gostaham had thrown away and took it to the room I shared with my mother. Hunching under an oil lamp, I began drawing a design for a carpet that I hoped would grace a wealthy man's guest room and make his other rugs blush. My design was filled with all the motifs I had been learning—I managed to fit in every one of them. I sketched leaping steeds, peacocks with multi-colored tails, gazelles feeding on grasses, elongated cypress trees, painted vases, pools of water, swimming ducks, and silver fish, all connected by vines, leaves, and flowers. While I was working, I thought about an unforgettable carpet I had seen in the bazaar. It showed a magnificent tree, but rather than sprouting leaves, its branches ended in the heads of gazelles, lions, onagers, and bears. The merchant called it a "vaq-vaq tree," and it illustrated a poem in which the animals discussed humans and their mysterious ways. I thought that such a tree could gossip all night about the mysteries of our new household.

I waited until Gostaham seemed in a cheerful mood before asking if I could show him the design. He seemed surprised by the request, but beckoned me to follow him into his workroom. We sat on cushions, and he unrolled the paper onto the floor in front of us. It was so quiet in the room that I could hear the last call to prayer from the Friday mosque. The evening caller, who sat high in the minaret, had a clear, sweet voice that always filled me with happiness and hope. I thought his call might be a good omen.

Gostaham glanced at the design for only a moment. "What's the meaning of all this?" he asked, looking at me.

"W-well," I stammered, "I wanted to make something very fine, something that . . ."

An unpleasant silence fell on the room. Gostaham pushed aside the paper, which curled up and rolled away. "Listen, joonam," he said, "you probably think that carpets are just things—things to buy, sell, and sit down on. But once you become initiated as a rug maker, you learn that their purpose is much greater, for those who care to see."

"I know that," I said, although I didn't grasp what he meant.

"You *think* you know," said Gostaham. "So tell me — what do all these patterns have in common?"

I tried to think of something, but I couldn't. I had drawn them because they were pretty decorations. "Nothing," I finally admitted.

"Correct," said Gostaham, sighing as if he had never had to work quite this hard before. He tugged at one side of his turban as if trying to pull out a thought.

"When I was about your age," he said, "I learned a story in Shiraz that affected me deeply. It was about Tamerlane, the Mongolian conqueror who limped his way toward Isfahan more than two hundred years ago and ordered our people to surrender or be destroyed. Even so, our city revolted against his iron hand. It was a small rebellion with no military might behind it, but in revenge Tamerlane had his soldiers run their swords through fifty thousand citizens. Only one group was spared: the rug makers, whose value was too great for them to be destroyed. Even after that calamity, do you think the rug makers knotted death, destruction, and chaos into their rugs?"

"No," I said softly.

"Never, not once!" replied Gostaham, his voice rising. "If anything, the designers created images of even more perfect beauty. This is how we, the rug makers, protest all that is evil. Our response to cruelty, suffering, and sorrow is to remind the world of the face of beauty, which can best restore a man's tranquillity, cleanse his heart of evil, and lead him to the path of truth. All rug makers know that beauty is a tonic like no other. But without unity, there can be no beauty. Without integrity, there can be no beauty. Now do you understand?"

I looked at my design again, and it was as if I were seeing it through Gostaham's eyes. It was a design that tried to cover its ignorance through bold patterns, one that would sell only to an unwashed *farangi* who didn't know better. "Will you help me make it right?" I asked in a meek voice.

"I will," said Gostaham, reaching for his pen. His corrections were so severe that there was almost nothing left of my design. Using a fresh sheet of paper, he chose to draw just one of the motifs that I had selected: a teardrop-shaped *boteh* called a mother and daughter because it had its own progeny within it. He drew it neatly and cleanly, intending for there to be three across the carpet and seven down. That was all; and yet it was far more beautiful than the design I had made.

It was a sobering lesson. I felt as if I had more to learn than I had time on earth. I leaned back in the cushions, feeling tired.

Gostaham leaned back, too. "I've never known someone as eager to learn as you," he said.

I thought perhaps he had — himself. Yet I felt ashamed; it was not a womanly quality to be so eager, I knew. "Everything changed after my father . . ."

"Indeed, it was the worst luck for you and Maheen," Gostaham said gravely. "Perhaps it's not such a bad thing for you to distract yourself by learning."

I had more than distraction on my mind. "I was hoping that with your permission, I might make the carpet you just designed for use as my dowry . . . in case I ever need one."

"It's not a bad idea," said Gostaham. "But how will you afford the wool?"

"I would have to borrow the money," I replied.

Gostaham considered for a moment. "Though it would be simple compared with the carpets we make at the royal workshop, it would certainly be worth many times more than the cost of the wool."

"I would work very hard," I said. "I promise I won't disappoint you."

Gostaham was looking at me in a fixed fashion, and for a moment he didn't say anything. All of a sudden, he jumped off his cushion as if he had been startled by a jinn.

"What is it?" I asked, alarmed.

Gostaham uttered a big sigh and settled back into the cushions. "For a moment," he said, "I had the strangest feeling that I was sitting next to my younger self."

I smiled, remembering his story. "The young man who gave his finest possession to a shah?"

"The very one."

"I would have done the same thing."

"I know," said Gostaham. "And therefore, as a tribute to all the good fortune that has come to my door, I will give you my permission to make the rug. When you finish it, you can keep what you earn after paying me back for the wool. But remember: You are still responsible to Gordiyeh for your household duties."

I bent and kissed Gostaham's feet before going to tell my mother the good news.

NAHEED DIDN'T HAVE to trouble herself with making her own dowry, but she had other problems. When she knocked at Gostaham's door and invited me to visit her, I knew what she wanted to do. Sometimes we went to her house and I continued my writing lessons under her supervision. Other times, instead of going where we said we would, we took a shortcut to the Image of the World and went to the perch near the bazaar where Naheed had first shown Iskandar a glimpse of her face. I watched in fascination the people milling around during the game — sunburned soldiers with long swords, dervishes with ragged hair and begging bowls, strolling minstrels, Indians with trained monkeys, Christians who lived across the Julfa Bridge, traveling merchants come to trade their wares, veiled women with their husbands. We tried to lose ourselves in the crowd, as if we were attached to the families around

us. When the game started, Naheed sought out her beloved and followed his form the way other spectators followed the ball, her body
straining toward his.

Iskandar was handsome like Yusuf, who in tales was so renowned for his beauty that he made women lose their reason. I remembered a line that my mother always used: "Blinded by his
beauty, the Egyptian ladies merrily sliced their own fingers, their
shiny red blood dripping onto the purple plums." They would have
done the same for Iskandar, I thought. I was especially drawn to the
beauty of his mouth. His white, even teeth sparkled like stars when
he smiled. I wondered how it would feel to be a girl like Naheed,
who could set her heart on such a man and conquer him. I had no
such hopes of my own.

One afternoon, we arrived at the square just before the game
started. I noticed that people kept looking toward the Shah's palace
with an air of excitement. Suddenly, the royal trumpets blasted and
the Shah emerged onto his balcony high above the square. He wore
a long dark blue velvet robe embroidered with small golden flowers,
a green tunic, and a sash that married layers of green, blue, and
gold. His turban was white, with an emerald aigrette; his mustache
was long and gray; and even at a distance I could see that most of his
teeth were missing.

"Vohhh!" I said in surprise and awe at my first glimpse of royalty. Naheed laughed at me, for she was a child of the city.

The Shah sat upon a low throne placed in the middle of a blue-
and-gold carpet. Once he was comfortable, the men in his retinue
knelt around him in a semicircle and sat back on their heels. The
Shah made a sign with his hand and the game began.

When I had had my fill of staring at him through my picheh, I
left Naheed to examine the carpets for sale in the bazaar. I didn't
enjoy polo that much, with all the dust and dirt kicked up by the
horses, and the people weaving back and forth for a better view and

yelling out for their favorites. I checked on the carpet that I had made and discovered that it was no longer hanging in the shop. The merchant told me it had sold the day before to a foreigner. When I returned to Naheed's side to tell her the news, her response was short and full of reproach. She wore her picheh and chador so she couldn't be recognized, but still, she oughtn't to be there at all, and to be seen alone was even worse. She needed me.

Naheed turned back to the game. She was hoping for a sign from Iskandar, even though the square was thronged with spectators. How could he distinguish her tiny, white-shrouded form among hundreds of other women? She was standing in the same corner where she had shown him her face. That afternoon, we watched him score three goals in a row and drive the spectators into a frenzy of delight. After the game, he was called back to ride to each of the four corners and salute the crowd. When he arrived at ours, he reached into his belt and drew out a leather polo ball, which he threw in the air. It rose high before dropping straight into Naheed's outstretched hand. It was as if a *pari*—a fire-born fairy—had brought it right to her.

We lingered as the players were being congratulated and the crowd thinned. Naheed was still holding the ball in the palm of her hand. After a while, a little boy with crooked teeth appeared in front of us and revealed a slip of paper hidden in his sleeve. Naheed took his hand discreetly and slipped the letter into her own sleeve before paying him with a small coin. After concealing the ball under her clothes, she linked her arm through mine and we began walking home. She unfurled the letter when we were away from the crowd, and I peered over her shoulder, wishing I could read.

"What does it say?" I asked eagerly.

"There's just one line, written in haste," she said. "'*In a crowd of thousands, no one else shines like you, the brightest star of my heart.*' It is signed, '*Your loving servant, Iskandar.*'"

I couldn't see Naheed's face, since she was completely covered in her picheh and chador, but I could hear the excitement in her voice.

"Perhaps your fates are intertwined," I said with amazement.

"I must know if that's possible," said Naheed. "Let's have Kobra tell our fortunes!"

Kobra was an old servant of Naheed's family who was known throughout the neighborhood for the accuracy of her readings. She reminded me of some of the women of my village who could look at the sky or a handful of peas and tell you whether the moment was auspicious for your desires. Her skin was the color of dates, and the fine wrinkles in her forehead and cheeks made her look wise.

Naheed summoned Kobra to her rooms a few moments after we arrived, and she came bearing two vessels of coffee and told us to drink it without disturbing the grounds. We consumed it in one or two gulps so that she could read our future in the remaining froth. First, she peered into Naheed's cup and smiled, showing us her nearly toothless gums. She began describing Naheed's marriage to a handsome young man with lots of money and a body as strong as the hero Rostam's, an event that was to be followed by the birth of more children than she could count. "You'll be spending a lot of time with your feet in the air!" she said.

The prediction was exactly what her mistress wished to hear, which made me wonder about its truth.

When it was my turn, Kobra peered into my cup for a long while. Several times it seemed as if she wished to say something, but then she stared into the cup again as if its message were troubling.

"What does it say?" Naheed prompted.

Looking at the grounds, Kobra mumbled that my future would be exactly like Naheed's. Then she gathered the cups and fled the room, declaring that she had work to do.

"That was strange," I said. "Why didn't she say what she saw?"

"She did!"

"How could my future be the same as yours?"

"Why not?" said Naheed. "You, too, can marry a handsome young man and have plenty of sons."

"But if it was that simple, why did she seem so afraid?"

"Oh, pay no attention to her," said Naheed. "She's old. She probably just needed to visit the latrines."

"I'm afraid the evil comet must still be following me," I said in despair. "It seems as if Kobra thinks my future is fated to be dark!"

"Certainly not," said Naheed. She summoned Kobra again and asked her to tell us more about what she had seen. Kobra clapped both her hands to her chest, one on top of the other.

"There's nothing more I can wring from the grounds," she protested, "but I can tell you the old tale that came to my mind while I was looking at them, although I don't know what it means."

Naheed and I settled back into the cushions and listened to Kobra's story.

First there wasn't and then there was. Before God, no one was.

Once there was a prince whose sleep was troubled almost every night. In his dreams, he saw the image of a woman who was moonlike beyond compare. Her curly hair framed a milk-white face. Beneath her rose silk tunic, the womanly parts of her body swelled like melons. As the prince dreamed more deeply, he could see that she was crying, opening her arms to the sky to show her desperation and helplessness. The prince awoke in a sweat, for he could not bear to see her suffer. He longed to help her, but first he had to find her.

One day, the prince set out to do battle with a fierce warlord who robbed travelers when they tried to cross a bridge through his territory. The prince and his men stamped across the bridge to invite an ambush, then fought the warlord and his tribe for hours in the midday sun. At one point, the warlord ran his sword through one of the prince's best soldiers before heaving his body off the bridge. With a great roar of rage, the prince jumped on the warlord, vowing to avenge his friend's death. The two clashed swords but the prince was stronger, and he forced the weapon out of his opponent's hands, threw him onto the ground, and sat on his armored chest. Then he drew his dagger, planning to savor the end of the man who had tossed his best man over the bridge like a leaf.

"Stop!" cried the warlord. "You know not what you kill."

"All men beg for mercy in their final moments," said the prince, "but you shall soon be begging before God." He raised his dagger.

"At least let me remove my armor so you can see who I am."

The warlord lifted off his helmet, revealing a face as smooth as a woman's and long, dark curly hair.

The prince was astonished. "What a pity that such a fair youth shall soon be dust! You fought so fiercely, I thought you must be a grown man."

"Not even," said the warlord. He removed his chest armor and raised his tunic to reveal a muscled abdomen and tiny breasts, like red rosebuds in the sun.

The prince's dagger wavered, then dropped. The lust to kill had been replaced by a different kind of lust. He bent forward and kissed the young woman's tender lips.

"What caused you to don armor?" he asked.

The woman's face toughened so that she looked like a warrior again. "My father was a warlord who raised me to kill. After he died, I continued to care for his men and protect his property."

During the next few days, the prince came to know and admire the fierce young woman. She could ride as well as he could, goad him into a sweat when they jousted with swords, and best him in a race up a hill. Her muscles were tight and lean, and she was as agile as a deer. She was nothing like the woman he had dreamed about so often, but before long he was smitten, and he married her.

After a year of happiness, the prince started being troubled again by his dreams. The moonlike woman began appearing to him every night on her knees, her head bent, as if her plight were more severe than ever. One morning, after another disturbed night, he kissed his warrior woman good-bye.

"Where are you going?" she protested.

"I have to find someone," he said. "Insh'Allah, we'll see each other again one day."

He mounted his horse and rode away without looking behind him to see the expression on her face.

The prince traveled for months, describing what he had seen in his dreams to anyone who would listen, only to hear the reply, "There's no one like that in this town." Finally, he came to a city where people wouldn't answer his question, and the prince knew he was in the right place. At night, under a full moon, he walked silently to the town's palace and hid himself outside its walls. Before long, he heard a piteous wail. He scaled the palace walls, landing on the other side as softly as a cat, and observed the woman his heart had longed for. She was kneeling on a roof, her arms stretched toward the heavens, her body shuddering with sobs. Her curly black hair gleamed in the moonlight, and the sight of her rounded form filled him with longing. He called to her from the palace grounds.

"Dear distressed woman, don't make the clouds weep. I have come to help you."

The lovely princess raised her head and looked around, astonished.

"Tell me the source of your suffering, and I will destroy it," said the prince, his muscles flexing with pleasure at the thought.

"Who are you?" she asked suspiciously.

The prince revealed himself in the moonlight, recited his lineage and the great deeds of his family, and repeated his desire to help the princess vanquish her sorrow.

She wiped away her tears. "My maidservant has my father's ear," she said. "By day she serves me; by night she wraps herself around his body. She has threatened to tell my father I have been conspiring against him with his top advisor. I have already given her all my jewelry and money. What if my father should believe her lies? I'll be banished or killed."

The prince hauled himself onto the roof and offered to take the lady away. Revealing his love, which had persisted in his dreams for so many years, he promised to treat her honorably by marrying her. Together they fled the town on horseback, and as soon as they reached a sizable settlement, the prince married his lady under the authority of a mullah. The two spent their first night as man and wife in a caravanserai fit for shahs. The princess was just as the prince had imagined, round and ripe like a summer peach. At last, his dream of many years had been fulfilled.

The prince took his new bride to the house of his first wife, the warrior woman, who bared her teeth at his new acquisition. Nonetheless, all three returned together to his father's house. Much had changed since he had left. He was a married man now and a proven warrior, not the dreamer who had set off on a seemingly impossible quest years before.

His father invited the prince to a special dinner in honor of his return. The warrior woman advised him to be careful about any food that he was served. He took her advice and fed his portion to a cat, who immediately had convulsions and died. His father, who had decided he wanted to take the warrior woman as his own wife, ordered his favorites to tear out his son's eyes and set him loose in the desert.

Left alone, the prince wandered for hours with his eyes in his hands, unable even to cry. When he heard the sound of a spring, he patted the earth until he felt wetness. He drank to satiation and sat down to rest. Leaves fell on him from above, and he crushed them in his palms and rubbed his eye sockets, seeking relief. They immediately stopped burning. The prince took each eye and popped it back in its socket. He could see again!

The prince returned toward the city. At its outskirts, he came upon a full-fledged battle. Even from far away, among the armor-clad soldiers he recognized the lithe figure of his warrior woman, whose sword flew mercilessly through the air. With a great war cry, he joined her in battle, and together they vanquished his father's men.

When the battle was over, the prince and the warrior woman returned to the city. He became shah and installed each of his women in her own lodgings, making sure he visited them equally and gave them the same number of gifts. With his first wife he hunted, jousted, and discussed battle plans; with his second, he explored the art of passion and lived contentedly until the end of his days.

When Kobra finished her story, Naheed and I were both silent. Kobra stood up and returned to her work.

"That was a strange tale," I said. "I've never heard that one before."

"Nor I," said Naheed. "What a lucky talisman that prince must have had, to get everything he wanted!"

She yawned and stretched out on her side on a group of flat cushions, putting her hands under her cheek. I had the feeling Naheed imagined herself as lucky as the prince. I remembered sadly how I used to feel the same way about the tale of a princess who rejected all suitors until the right one wooed her.

Opposite Naheed, I stretched out on my cushions so we faced each other, and put my hands under my cheek to match hers.

"Do you think he told his second wife that he already had a woman?" Naheed asked.

"I hope so."

"I would hate that," said Naheed, looking angry.

"Being a second wife?"

"Or a third, or fourth," she said. "My parents will never let that happen. I'll be the first wife or nothing."

"That's the only good thing about coming from a humble family," I said. "Most suitors of mine wouldn't be able to afford a second wife, or even a concubine."

Naheed raised her eyebrows. "Rich men always seem to have a few," she said. "I think if my husband married another woman, I would try to cause her grief." Her smile had a wicked edge.

I thought about what had happened in my own family. "After my grandfather took his second wife, who was my grandmother, the two families remained apart, and my father and my uncle Gostaham almost never saw each other," I said. "But sometimes it's not like that. When the richest merchant in my village married a younger woman, his first wife loathed her. But then she became ill, and the younger one took such good care of her that they became fast friends."

Naheed shuddered. "Insh'Allah, that will never happen to me."

"I don't want to share, either," I said. "But we don't know what happened to the wives in Kobra's story. She didn't tell us that part."

"That's because the story wasn't really about them," said Naheed. "What man wouldn't want a warrior woman to ride with and a fleshy woman to ride in bed?"

We laughed together, knowing that we could be looser with our language when only the two of us were present.

I had stayed with Naheed much longer than I had intended. Because it was nearly dark, she insisted on having a maid accompany me home. When we arrived, the maid handed me a large parcel, saying it was a gift. It was packed with bright cotton robes in shades of saffron, pink, and red, with matching sheaths to wear underneath and loose embroidered trousers that looked as if they had hardly ever been worn. The most dazzling item was a thick purple robe that fell to the knees, with fur at the cuffs, around the hem, and at the breast. I danced with joy at the sight of the bright clothing, and when I showed it to my mother, she gave me permission to stop wearing my mourning clothes, although she herself planned to wear black for the rest of her life. I was overjoyed; I could hardly believe my luck in having Naheed as a friend.

CHAPTER THREE

I awoke one summer morning, after we had been in Isfahan for half a year, thinking of a poem my mother often recited, about a beloved with cheeks like roses, hair as black as coal, and a teasing beauty mark near ruby lips.

> *Look in the face of your beloved,*
> *For in that mirror, you will see yourself.*

My beloved was not Naheed's handsome polo player, nor the powerful old Shah, nor any of the thousands of sweet-faced young men who congregated on Isfahan's bridges, smoked in its coffee-houses, or lingered around Four Gardens. The one I loved was more unknowable, more varied, and more marvelous: the city itself. Every day, I bounded out of my bedroll, longing to explore it. No eyes were hungrier than mine, for they had so memorized the buildings, people, and animals in my village that I was eager to feed myself with new sights.

Isfahan's bridges were the perfect place to begin. From there, I could see the mighty Zagros Mountains, the river rushing below me, and the city's domes twinkling like stars amid its earth-colored buildings. One of my favorite spots was the Thirty-three Arches Bridge, our first point of entry into the city. Standing in one of its famed archways, I would stare at the people streaming in and out of Isfahan. Some were from the Gulf, with skin as black as naphtha, while others, from the northeast, had Mongol ancestors who bequeathed them slanting eyes and straight black hair. Sometimes I even saw nomads with legs like tree trunks, for they walked high into the mountains in search of pasture for their lambs, carrying the newborns on their backs.

The city also fed my love of carpets, because everywhere I looked, I saw patterns. I studied the plants, trees, and flowers in Four Gardens to understand how rug designs were modeled on nature; the district itself seemed to me like a garden carpet writ large. For the same reason, I sought out the dead game and trophy animals for sale in the bazaar: the tough, muscled onager, the airy gazelle, even the magisterial lion, whose mane was tricky to draw. "They say you can draw steeds for a hundred years before the animal springs to life under your pen," Gostaham had said.

I also scrutinized the carpets, which hailed from all parts of Iran, and learned to recognize the knots and patterns from each region. Even the buildings in the Image of the World had something to teach me. One day, I was passing the Shah's private mosque when I observed that the tile panels near the doorway were like prayer rugs. They were indigo, with vivid white and yellow flowers surrounded by a field of clover-green. I promised myself that one day, I would learn to make a design just as intricate.

At home, carpets consumed most of my waking thoughts. I was determined to learn what Gostaham knew, and I worked day and night on the projects he gave me. I quickly finished drawing the boteh design and received his approval to make the rug. One of his workers set up a simple loom in our courtyard, which I strung with cotton. Taking the money Gostaham had lent me to buy wool, I went to the bazaar to shop for colors, just as he had as a young man. I had planned to buy simple hues like those we used in my village — rich camel-brown made from walnut husks, purple from the roots of old madder plants, red made from cochineal bugs, and yellow from safflowers. But in the Great Bazaar, what a richness of shades was at hand! I was enraptured by the sight of thousands of balls of wool hanging like fruit on a tree. Blues ranging from the turquoise radiance of a summer sky all the way to darkest indigo. And that was just blue! I stared at the bolts of wool and imagined different colors side by side in a rug. How about that lime-green with a startling orange? Or wine next to royal blue? I chose twelve hues that delighted my eyes, more colors than I had ever used in a rug. I found myself drawn to the bright colors: baby-chick yellow, grassy green, sunset-orange, pomegranate-red. Taking the brilliant balls of wool home, I attached them to the top of my loom and painted my design with watercolors, so that I would have a guide to knotting the colors I planned to use. I was eager to make the rug, knowing how important it was to prove my worth to the household. While everyone else was sleeping in the afternoons, I knotted for hours, and the rug quickly took shape under my fingers.

While I was consumed by the rug, my mother managed to separate herself from Gordiyeh's supervision by making herbal cures. Medicines were costly, and although my mother had never been adept at brewing them, Gordiyeh agreed to the proposal because she seemed to think that my mother's village origins gave her special powers.

My mother took daylong excursions to the foothills of the Zagros Mountains, where she collected plants, roots, herbs, and insects. She also haunted the apothecaries in the bazaar for information about herbs local to Isfahan. Back in our village, Kolsoom had given her a few recipes for fever medicine when I had been ill, which she still remembered. She also began learning about medicines for headaches and womanly complaints, brewing them over a fire in the courtyard. The resulting concoctions were black and slimy, but Gordiyeh believed in their powers. Once when her head was aching, my mother gave her a liquid that relieved her pain and made her sleep. "Such fine medicines should be made in abundance," Gordiyeh declared. She promised my mother that once she had brewed enough for the household's use, she could sell what remained and keep the money. That gladdened my mother's heart, for now she could preside over her own domain, one that Gordiyeh knew nothing about.

NAHEED VISITED ME one day to see how I looked in her old clothes. I donned her saffron sheath and trousers, which my mother had hemmed, and the dashing purple robe. "You look so pretty!" Naheed said. "Your cheeks are as pink as roses."

"It's nice to wear bright colors after more than a year of black," I replied. "Thank you for your generosity."

"It is yours for the asking," she replied. "And now I hope I may call on yours. Will you come with me to polo?"

I hadn't planned on going to the Image of the World that day, because I had too much work to do. "Naheed-joon, I wish I could, but I have my chores," I replied.

"Please," she begged. "I need your help so much."

"How will I finish all my work?"

"Call in Shamsi," said Naheed, in an authoritative tone. Shamsi arrived wearing a pretty orange head scarf and a cheap beaded necklace from the bazaar. Naheed put a few coins in her hand and whispered to her that there were more coming to her if she took care of my work for the day. Shamsi left jingling the coins, a gleeful smile upon her face.

I still didn't want to go, though. "Aren't you afraid we're going to be caught someday?"

"We never have been before," she said. "Now let's go."

"Only for a short while, then," I said, although I felt apprehensive about leaving. We slipped out when Gordiyeh wasn't looking.

Naheed's purpose this time was to convey a letter to Iskandar revealing her feelings for him. She didn't read it aloud, saying she wanted his eyes to be the first to see it. It professed eternal love and admiration for him in fine sentiments like the poets use, she said. I knew that her elegant calligraphy would make her words go straight to his heart.

The sun beat down without mercy as we walked to the Image of the World. The sky was a blue dome with not a single cloud to shelter us from the sun. Breathing under my picheh was like inhaling fire, and I was sweating through my clothes. When we arrived, the game had already started. The spectators were shouting more than usual, for neither side could win. Dust hung in the air and settled on our garments. I hoped the game would end soon so that I wouldn't be discovered away from my chores. But it went on and on until the players became sluggish and the game was finally called a draw.

Naheed hardly seemed to notice that Iskandar's team had not won. "Did you see how masterfully he played?" she asked. Her voice sounded high-pitched and excited, as it always did after she had watched her beloved. As the crowd began to disperse, she found Iskandar's boy and carefully slipped him her letter and a coin. Then we returned to our homes, parting shortly after we left the square. Because the horses had kicked up a veil of dust that coated my outer clothes, I planned to hide them as soon as I arrived home, but Zohreh was waiting for me at the door under orders to lead me straight to Gordiyeh. That had never happened before. With my heart pounding, I shed the outdoor clothing and balled it up in my arms as I went to her rooms, hoping she wouldn't notice the dust. She was sitting on a cushion and applying henna paste to the tops of her feet. Without a word of greeting, she asked me angrily, "Where have you been?"

"At Naheed's," I said, although the lie stuck to my tongue.

"You were not at Naheed's," said Gordiyeh. "I couldn't find you, and I sent Shamsi to her house to fetch you. You weren't there."

She beckoned me toward her because she didn't want to disturb the henna. "Give me your hand," she said.

I stretched my hand out innocently, and she struck the top of it with the thin wooden paddle she used to apply the henna.

I rocked back on my heels, my hand aflame. I was far too old to be hit like a child.

"Just look at your clothes," she said. "How could they become so dirty if you had stayed inside?"

Afraid of being struck again, I quickly confessed. "We were at the game."

"Naheed doesn't have permission to go to the game," said Gordiyeh. "A girl like her can lose everything if people start to talk — even if she has done nothing."

There was a knock at the door and a servant showed in Naheed's mother. Ludmila entered the room looking as sorrowful as if she had lost her only child. "How could you?" she said to me in a quiet, disappointed tone that was even worse than Gordiyeh's slap. She spoke very slowly in Farsi accented by her native Russian. "What you did was very wrong. You don't understand how much a girl like Naheed can suffer if seen in the wrong places."

"I'm very, very sorry," I said, with my wounded hand behind my back.

Like my mother and me, Ludmila was an outsider to Isfahan. She always reminded me of a delicate bird, flitting around her home as if she didn't belong there, even after twenty years. Because of what she had seen during the wars in her country, she had an aversion to human blood. If a servant cut her finger while chopping meat, she trembled and took to her bed. Sometimes, Naheed told me, she screamed in her sleep about fountains of blood gushing out of men's chests and eyes.

Ludmila's face was white and scared. "Naheed told me how much you love polo and how often you beg her to go to the games. That is very selfish of you. I hope you understand the disruptiveness of your actions."

I must have looked startled, for I couldn't believe Naheed had blamed her misbehavior on me. But I decided to keep silent, knowing she would be in dire trouble if her mother found out what drew her to the games.

"I don't always understand the ways of the city," I said in a meek voice. "I will never do such a thing again."

"As punishment, you are to collect the night soil every morning from all the rooms of the house until the next moon," said Gordiyeh.

It was as if I were the lowliest of servants. To know the state of every person's innards, every day, and to have to pour all the slop into one big basin for the night-soil collectors and then clean all the pans—I could hardly think of the task without feeling as if I might lose what was in my belly.

I was told to go to my room and confess to my mother what had happened. She was not at all sympathetic.

"Bibi, she hit me!" I complained.

"Why did you do such a thoughtless thing?" she asked. "You could have ruined Naheed's reputation in a single day, not to mention your own!"

"You know that I have never liked polo," I said, wanting my mother to take my side. "Naheed was the one who always begged me to go."

"Why?"

I didn't want to reveal Naheed's secret, for that would bring her grave trouble. "It was exciting for her. Her parents keep such a close watch over her otherwise."

"You should have refused," said my mother. "You know better!"

"I'm sorry," I said. "I just wanted to do her a favor."

My mother softened. "I know you were only trying to help," she said. "But since you were wrong, I expect you to take your punishment without complaint."

"I will," I said bitterly.

"Now come here." She rubbed the burning spot on my hand with a poultice made of lamb's fat, which she had concocted from recipes that Kolsoom had once used. The poultice soothed away the sting.

"That's much better," I said.

"I finally found the right herbs," my mother said. She was thoughtful for a moment. "Tell me this: Didn't Naheed blame her escapade on you?"

"Yes," I said.

"What kind of a friend would do that?"

"I'm sure she didn't mean anything by it."

"I certainly hope not," said my mother sharply.

"No doubt she was caught by surprise," I replied, but the thought that she had sacrificed me to save herself plagued me for days.

That was the last time Naheed and I went to the games. For the next two weeks, she was punished by not being allowed to leave home, as I was. I stayed home, did my chores, and collected the night soil. After that, when Naheed wanted to see me, a servant accompanied her to my house and waited for her there until it was time for her to go home.

Despairing over how to contact Iskandar during her confinement, Naheed confided in Kobra and offered silver for her help. The next time there was a game, Kobra went by herself and found the spot where Naheed and I used to stand. She brought the polo ball Naheed had caught, casually holding it in view after the game. Iskandar's boy was sharp enough to realize that she was a messenger from Naheed, who had after all been holding the ball the first time he found her. From then on, Kobra met the child near the bazaar every few days to allow the lovers to exchange letters.

AFTER NAHEED AND I had fulfilled our punishments, we started meeting on Thursday afternoons at the sparkling hammam used by the wealthy residents of our district. As a precaution against further straying, Naheed's family warned her that a maid would be dispatched sometime during the afternoon to make sure we were there.

I had been to that hammam a few times after I arrived in Isfahan, but it was too expensive to attend regularly, so Naheed paid the coin for me. I was grateful to her, because the hammam was one of our greatest pleasures. We spent most of the afternoon soaking, talking, and peeking at other women's bodies. It was there that we learned of births, deaths, and engagements in the neighborhood, or discovered that a woman was pregnant from the slight thickening of her belly, or gleaned that a new bride had mingled with her husband the night before, and therefore had to make the Grand Ablution on a different day than usual.

Homa, the head bath attendant, was a great-grandmother whose skin had stayed almost as moist as a young woman's from all her years in the steam. She washed and massaged me like a mother, and she always had stories to tell about the comings and goings of everyone at the bath. Homa was a skillful questioner, and often I let slip information about myself when I was nearly senseless from soaking in hot water and being massaged. She knew all about my life in the village, my father's death, our poverty, and how it had ruined my marriage plans. I even whispered to her from time to time about the hardships in my household and my desire to marry one day and have a home of my own. "May God grant your fondest wish!" she would always say, but sometimes I thought I saw a doubtful look in her eyes.

Homa had to leave Isfahan for several months to take care of a sick uncle. The first time I saw her after her return, she was walking around the hammam as usual with her white hair loose, her long breasts nearly reaching the thin cloth tied around her waist. After many kisses and greetings of delight, Naheed and I disrobed and gave her our clothes, which she piled into a basket for safekeeping. Then Homa scrubbed Naheed with a *kisseh* to remove the dead skin from her body and washed her hair, while I rested in one of the hammam's warm pools.

When Homa was ready for me, she called out my name. Her round face and white hair were illuminated by a beam of light that entered the hammam from oval windows in the roof. As I walked naked out of the darkness to the tap where she was crouched, Homa's eyes widened with surprise.

"How you have changed!" she said.

"Things are so different here in the city," I mumbled.

"No, that's not what I meant," said Homa. She pulled me into the light. "Look at you!" she said in a loud voice.

Naheed looked up from where she was soaking, and several women who were bathing nearby stared at me, too. My body was exposed in the sunlight streaming down from above. I tried to bend over at the waist to shield myself, but Homa wouldn't let me.

"Last time I saw you, you looked like a little girl," said Homa. "You had almost nothing here," she said, poking the top of my chest, "and nothing there," slapping my hip. "Now see what has happened in only a few months!"

It was true. I was still as short as ever, and my hands and feet had remained the size of a child's. But from neck to hips, my body had rounded in ways that surprised me. My breasts, which had been so small, were now like two ripe apples, and my hips curved like a melon.

"What is the reason, are you secretly engaged?"

"No," I said, blushing. All I knew was that I had been eating more meat, cheese, and bread than ever.

"Well, soon you will be," she said good-naturedly.

Homa turned me this way and that, peering at every curve. I flushed red all over. In the hammam, there was nowhere to hide.

"Your body is as perfect as a young rose," Homa announced with finality. "You will soon be blessed with a husband, God willing, who will cherish every petal."

Homa began singing an old marriage song from the south in a voice as beautiful as a nightingale's:

Oh mountain girl among the flowers,
With hair like violets and tulips on your cheeks.
Listen to the song of the birds no more,
For a fine young shepherd has come to sing your heart away.

A few of the women in the hammam joined in, and before I knew it, a group of them were on their feet, stamping and clapping. Not knowing what else to do, I began singing, too. The women encouraged me as if it were my wedding day. As I sang, I stood tall and forgot my shame.

When the song was over, there was much laughter and teasing. "I hear those fine young shepherds know how to tend to their wives!" said one woman, smirking.

"Why shouldn't they, they watch their flocks at it all day!" cried another.

It was Homa's gift to me to sing out my maturity to all the women in the hammam, who might know of a suitable husband. She was also showing me that I had something worth offering.

"Now you are one of us," Homa said with approval, "except for a few details that you will learn about soon." As the women in the hammam settled back into their bathing routines, she pulled me close and began scrubbing my back with the kisseh. She looked over at Naheed, whose body was still long and thin like a cypress tree. "Whatever you have been eating, Naheed should be eating, too," she said.

Naheed's eyes were closed, and she didn't reply. I couldn't tell if she was asleep or just pretending.

Why is it that we always think our neighbor's chicken must be tastier than our own goose? For the rest of that afternoon, it didn't bother me that Naheed's skin was so white, her hair so curly, and her eyes so emerald-green.

AS MY REWARD for helping him with the dangling gems carpet, Gostaham had promised to show me a rare and wonderful rug, and one day he instructed me to meet him at the royal workshop after the last call to prayer to see a carpet that would be cherished for centuries to come. I could not imagine such a treasure: The rugs in my village were used until they frayed and were ground into dust.

I walked through Four Gardens right after the last call to prayer. People were streaming out of the Image of the World, for that call marked the end of the day. The hawkers in the square had loaded up their wares and were heading home. I passed a man with a cargo of unripened almonds, which I loved. The almond flesh was as soft as cheese, but more delicate.

I found Gostaham in the workshop I had visited previously, the one with all the looms. It was silent and empty of workers.

"*Salaam,*" I said, looking around. "Where has everyone gone?"

"Home," said Gostaham. "Follow me quickly."

He led me through room after room of carpets in various stages of completion. At the end of a long hallway, we reached a door bolted with a thick metal lock shaped like a scorpion. Looking around to make sure no one was near, Gostaham pulled a key out of his tunic and unlocked it. He lit two small oil lamps and handed me one of them. In the soft light, I could make out a large rug on the loom.

We approached it together, holding our lamps before us. "Look closely," he said, holding the light to the surface of the rug. "Eight men have been working on it for a year, and it is only one-quarter completed."

The carpet was already as tall as I was, but it was to be four times my height when finished. It had nearly ninety knots per radj, which made the design as detailed as a miniaturist's drawing. Horsemen dressed in orange and green silk tunics, with white and gold turbans, pursued antelope and gazelle. Striped tigers and wild asses wrestled together like cousins. Musicians played their lutes. Celestial birds preened, displaying their jewel-bedecked tails. The creatures and humans looked alive, they were so true to nature. It was the finest rug I had ever seen.

"Who could ever afford such a costly rug?" I asked.

"It is for the Shah himself, to decorate his personal rooms," said Gostaham. "It embodies all that is finest in our land — the softest silk, the richest dyes, and the best designers and knotters. This carpet will last long after you and I, and the children of our children, are dust."

I peered more closely at the rug, holding my lamp well away from it. A figure seated near a cypress tree caught my eye.

"How do they capture a man so well?" I asked.

"It is not so much his figure, but rather his face, that requires skill of the highest order," said Gostaham. "The other knotters bow to specialists when it is time to make a man's eye. Otherwise, a face might look distracted, vacant, or even malicious."

"What do you think of the colors?" I asked Gostaham.

"They are what is best in a rug that excels above others," he said, with a teasing smile that I didn't understand at first. "Look how the sparkling gold lightens the density of the pattern. Notice in particular how the dull tones — the faded green, the humble beige, the pale blue—emphasize the beauty of the more brilliant colors, just as the female peacock highlights the male's more dazzling plumage."

"The choices are remarkable," I replied. "Whose work is it?"

"My own," replied Gostaham, and we both had a good laugh.

After that, we looked at Fereydoon's rug, which was almost finished. The gems in its design glimmered in the light of our lamps as if they were real stones. Gostaham had set each one of them off with thin lines of color, just as a jeweler separates gems with gold or silver. The carpet looked very delicate and feminine, I thought, compared to the Shah's hunting rug.

"It is even more beautiful than your design," said Gostaham, as if I had done it all myself. His generosity knew no bounds.

As we left the workshop, I felt a twinge of sorrow. Had I been a boy, I might be working as one of the apprentices at Gostaham's side, learning all the techniques he knew so well. I thought back with envy to the young knotters I had seen in the workshop on my last visit. They could devote themselves all day to their learn-ing, while I had to work for long hours in the kitchen before turn-ing my attention to carpet making. Yet I knew I had more privileges than most girls, for Gostaham had taken me under his care and helped me improve at my craft. For that I was grateful every day.

I RETURNED HOME elated. Gostaham had shown me a pearl that few eyes were ever permitted to see; and just a few days before, Homa had praised my new womanliness at the hammam. For the first time since my father had left us, I felt full of hope.

Passing through the courtyard, I stopped to look at my rug and saw my work in a new light. The boteh design was fine: Gostaham had seen to that. But I worried that I had done a poor job choosing the colors. I had once seen Gostaham looking at the rug with an odd expression, as if he had tasted something sour. Although he had not commented on my choices, he had told me several times that he would help me select the colors for my next carpet. Now I was sure I knew why. I had chosen each color for its beauty rather than how well it worked with the others.

Why hadn't I asked for Gostaham's help? I had been so eager to press forward, and so intoxicated by all the colors available, that I had leapt ahead. I hadn't understood that a design of such intricacy demanded a more masterful approach to choosing hues. I could hardly sleep that night. While the stars were still shining, I arose and looked at my carpet again. The colors were not only bad, they were at war. I had an urge to strip the rug off the loom and begin again.

What had been good enough in my village was laughed at here. Ever since we had arrived in Isfahan, I had been reminded of my humble origins. Unlike a wealthy child of the city, I had not learned to read and write, to enrobe myself like a flower, or to behave with courtly courtesy. I wanted to shine as bright as anyone in Isfahan, the only city worth the title "half the world." If my first carpet showed how much I had learned, perhaps I could escape the ill effects of the comet and set myself and my mother on the perfumed path of good fortune.

I had never heard of anyone starting a rug over. I could almost hear my father's voice telling me not to do it, for I had already completed thousands of knots. But then I thought about how I had gone to Ibrahim's dye house to discover the secret of the turquoise dye and made a carpet that had delighted the eyes of strangers, even though my parents had at first disapproved. I thought about how I had borrowed Gostaham's pen and drawn a design that had resolved his quandary, even though he yelled at me for touching his things.

Filled with the same fierce desire as I had felt on those other occasions, I grabbed the sharp knife I used for slashing wool and began cutting the rug off the loom, string by string. Each one went slack as I released it. The thousands and thousands of knots I had made began to lose their shape; the very surface of the carpet warped and wobbled. When Gostaham arises, I thought, I'll admit my error in choosing the colors right away. I'll ask him for help, and then I'll make a rug he'll be proud of.

Before the first light of morning, I had removed the rug and started to restring the loom with cotton thread. Gordiyeh was the first person to see what I had done. She was bringing a large jar of sour cherry jam from the storerooms to the kitchen when she saw the empty loom and the ruined rug. She screamed, dropping the jar, which cracked and spilled its sticky contents around her feet, forming a deep red pool that looked like blood. Within seconds, the servants were all rushing into the courtyard. I stood rooted near the loom, quaking.

"Crazy!" Gordiyeh shouted. "You are crazy like that madman of the desert, Majnoon! What were you thinking?"

There was a big commotion as everyone tried to understand what had happened. Ali-Asghar bent down to ask Taghee, the errand boy, for information. Shamsi rushed to Gordiyeh's side to ask if she needed a whiff of rose water to revive herself. Cook put her hands on either side of her head as if she were at a funeral. Gostaham hurried into the courtyard and stared at the carpet, which sagged on the ground as if broken. He looked from me to the carpet and back again, disbelief in his eyes.

My mother arrived in a panic, patting her scarf into place on her head. "What has happened?" she asked in a pleading voice.

No one even looked at her. "You village idiot!" Gordiyeh yelled at me.

Only then did she turn to my mother, appealing for an explanation, but my mother stood dumbfounded when she realized what I had done.

"Do you have any idea how much wool you've wasted — how much wool and how much work? Are you trying to destroy this household?" asked Gordiyeh, hitting her chest over and over with the palm of her hand.

"We take them in, and they try to ruin us! Why? Why has God put this burden on us? Tell me why!" Gordiyeh demanded of her husband.

Her words chilled my bones.

Gostaham turned to me with anger in his eyes. "Explain yourself," he commanded.

He was the one person I had hoped to please. I could hardly force words out of my throat.

"The colors were bad," I said haltingly. I put my hands to my flushed face, trying to hide myself.

Gostaham didn't contradict me. "Your eyes were dazzled after last night, which is what happens to novices. But now you have destroyed months of work! Why didn't you ask me first?"

"I humbly beg your pardon," I whispered, for I still could not find my voice. "I did it because I thought I could make a better one."

"Of course you could make a better one," he said. "But why didn't you stop to think that you might sell the first one and make the second one superior?"

"What a fool!" exclaimed Gordiyeh.

I cringed at that word. They were right; I should have thought of that, but I had been too excited that morning, possessed by the thought that I could do better. Now I could hardly believe what I had done. I stood abjectly by the loom, suffering even more under the pitiless gaze of the servants, who stared at me with scorn and disbelief.

My mother threw herself on her knees and reached forward to kiss Gordiyeh's feet, her black sash trailing in the jam.

"Get up!" said Gordiyeh, with annoyance in her voice.

My mother arose, her arms outstretched in a plea. "Please pardon my wayward daughter," she said. "I'll pay you for the wool. I'll brew extra medicines and sell them to neighbors. My daughter just wanted to make something pleasing. She has always been that way—sometimes she loses her reason."

I hadn't known that before she said it, but it was true. I stood there, shamed by my own inability to see the difference between a good idea and a calamitous one.

"Loses her reason? What reason?" asked Gordiyeh, hitting her own chest again.

Gostaham grimaced and pressed his hands together, as if he were trying to hold himself back. "Such a reckless action cannot go unpunished," he said angrily. "From this moon until the next, you will not leave the house. You will do whatever my wife says. You will not even draw a breath without her permission."

I knew better than to speak unless asked a question. I kept my eyes averted, my face burning with shame.

"First she goes to the polo games," said Gordiyeh, "and now this. Why do we even give such people shelter?" she continued, as though talking to herself. My mother shivered, her worst fears hanging in the air. Gordiyeh tried to walk away but couldn't move. She looked down in horror. Clumps of jam had pasted her feet to the ground. She kicked off her shoes and continued barefoot to her rooms, muttering, "Imbecile!" as she left.

Gostaham followed, trying to console her. The servants began cleaning the jam and broken crockery, whispering together about the waste. "That was a lot of work," said Cook, who had made the jam herself.

"When will breakfast be sweet again?" asked Ali-Asghar sadly, for we all knew that Gordiyeh wouldn't buy any for our bread.

I followed my mother, head bowed, until we reached our room. "A potato is smarter," I heard Cook saying.

"It's her bad star," added Shamsi.

In our room, my mother didn't look at me or berate me, even

though I knew she thought I had lost my reason. She put her chador over her head and began praying, touching her head to the *mohr* — clay tablet — she had placed on the ground. After praying, she sat on her heels and called for help. "Please, God, protect us. Please, God, don't let us become beggars in the street. I call on you, Ya, Imam Hossein, Ya, Hazrat-e-Ali, you who know what it means to be martyred, please save my daughter, who has made a child's mistake."

I wished I had considered my mother's concerns about our future before I had removed the rug from the loom. When, at last, she finished her appeals, I crawled over to where she sat, staring straight ahead.

"Bibi," I said, touching her arm. "I beg your forgiveness with my whole heart. If I had known how angry everyone would be, I never would have made such a bad decision."

My mother's arm was stiff, and she didn't look at me. She moved away from my grasp. "How many times have your father and I told you not to be rash?" she asked. "How many times?"

I sighed. "I know," I said.

My mother looked up to the ceiling as if appealing to God for a better daughter. "You don't understand how lucky you have been," she replied. "But this time, I am certain that your luck has ended."

"Bibi, I was only trying to make it better," I whined.

"May your throat close!"

I turned my face to the wall and sat there, my eyes dry, my agony all inside. I would have given the life that pulses through my heart to relieve my mother's suffering. She went right back to praying out loud, as if the stream of her words could wash away my error.

THE MONTH THAT I spent fulfilling my punishment seemed as vast as the desert. I began my day by collecting and emptying the pots full of night soil, which made me green with nausea. Then, after Gordiyeh consulted with Cook and Ali-Asghar about the tasks at hand, she assigned me the ones no one else wanted to do. I washed the greasy kitchen floor, chopped slimy kidneys, stomped filthy laundry in a basin and wrung it until my arms ached. Even in the afternoons, when everyone was sleeping, Gordiyeh loaded me with tasks. My hands became as rough as goats' horns, and I fell on my bed every evening weak with exhaustion. I bitterly regretted what I had done, but I also felt that my punishment was more severe than I deserved, and that Gordiyeh was enjoying her power over me.

One morning, when my month of labor was nearly finished, a servant summoned me and my mother into the birooni at Gostaham's command. My legs were trembling as we walked through the courtyard, for I was certain they were going to tell us that we were no longer welcome in their home. In the Great Room, I was surprised to find Gostaham seated in the place of honor, near the top of the carpet, with Gordiyeh on his right. He beckoned to my mother to join him on a cushion at his left. I sat alone facing them on the other side of the carpet.

"How are you, Khanoom?" Gordiyeh asked my mother, using the polite term for married women. "Is your health good?" Her sudden courtesy was unexpected.

"Why, yes," said my mother, mimicking the same tone of politeness. "I am very well, thank you."

"And you, my little one," continued Gordiyeh. "How are you?"

My skin prickled with surprise at the endearment, and I answered that I was in good health. I looked at Gostaham to try to understand the meaning of the meeting. Though normally able to sit cross-legged for hours without moving, his back straight as a loom, now he kept shifting his weight and rearranging his legs.

When the coffee arrived, Gordiyeh made a great show of passing it to us and offering us dates to accompany it. An awkward silence fell over the room as we sipped our coffee.

"Khanoom," Gostaham finally said, addressing my mother, "it is my duty to tell you about a letter I received this morning from

Fereydoon, the horse merchant who commissioned a carpet from us some months ago."

My mother looked surprised, for she had only heard the name once before, when I told her about my contributions to the dangling gems design. What had I done wrong now? I wondered. Was there something in my design that had upset him?

"It is obvious that Fereydoon is pleased with the carpet, judging by what he said after seeing it on the loom," said Gostaham. "But the letter he wrote made very little mention of it, in fact, almost none at all."

My hand shook so much that I had to put down my cup for fear of spilling coffee on the silk rug, leaving behind a large brown stain that could never be removed.

"There is really only one other thing a wealthy man like that might desire," continued Gostaham, "and that is your daughter." He was speaking in a straightforward, businesslike tone similar to the one he used to negotiate the price of a rug.

My mother pressed her palms to her cheeks. "There is no God but God," she said, as she always did when she was surprised.

Gostaham put both hands on his turban and readjusted it as if he could no longer bear its weight. I knew him well enough to be able to read the fidgety marks of his distress. But why? What could be more flattering than the offer of a wealthy man?

Gordiyeh jumped in, unable to hide her excitement. "He wishes to make your daughter his wife," she said breathlessly.

Gostaham gave Gordiyeh a warning look, which my mother didn't see. She leapt to her feet, her coffee cup teetering and almost spilling. "At last!" she cried, opening her arms to the sky. "A match sent from the heavens for my only child! After all that we have endured, our fickle fortunes have finally changed! Praise be to Mohammad! Praise be to Ali!"

Gordiyeh looked amused by her outburst, but her reply was kind. "My mother's heart knows how yours must feel," she said.

"Few are the women blessed with such good fortune, as welcome as rain."

"Daughter of mine, spring of my heart," cried my mother, opening her arms toward me. "Since the moment of your birth, you have brought wonders to our humble family. You're the light of my eyes."

My heart began to swell with hope. As the wife of a rich man, I would become one of those fat, pampered ladies the women of my village had teased me about. In the year of the comet, could such good fortune be possible?

Once my mother had calmed herself, she had questions. "How does Fereydoon know he desires my daughter?" she said. "Outside the house, she's always covered from head to toe!"

I kept my silence; the last thing I wanted the family to know was that I had uncovered myself in the presence of a stranger.

"I understand that Homa was singing your praises at the hammam," Gordiyeh said to me. "One of Fereydoon's woman servants happened to be there, and she told him of your charms."

I breathed with relief. He had waited to make the offer until he had found a proper excuse. Then I blushed, wondering whether the woman servant had described how I looked without my clothes.

My mother must have assumed that my silence grew out of modesty. "When shall we hold the ceremony?" she asked Gordiyeh. "As soon as we can, I think."

"I agree," said Gordiyeh, "although I don't believe he will require a grand wedding. Your daughter and Fereydoon would only need to meet with a mullah to make everything legal."

I had no experience of wealthy weddings, but in my village, weddings were celebrated for three days, if not more. What Gordiyeh described sounded more like signing a contract.

"I don't understand," said my mother, looking puzzled.

"The proposal I have here," said Gostaham, showing us the elegantly written letter, "is not for a lifetime marriage contract. It's for a *sigheh* of three months."

I had heard the word *sigheh* but didn't know all that it meant, except that it was short.

"A sigheh?" said my mother, looking puzzled. "I know that pilgrims to Qom may contract a sigheh for an hour or a night—but these are arrangements for pleasure. You want my daughter to marry for that?"

Gordiyeh must have read the dismay on our faces. "It's true that it won't last forever," she said, "but nothing on this earth is permanent by God's own design. The important point is that it will bring you financial benefits you could never claim elsewhere."

My mother's instincts as a tradeswoman had stayed sharp. She straightened her back, and a fierce expression entered her eyes. She looked just like she had on the day she squeezed high prices out of the harem women.

"How much?" she asked, a steely tone in her voice.

Gostaham unfolded the letter and read out the sum. It was the same amount Fereydoon had offered to pay for the carpet he had commissioned from Gostaham. It would be a tidy sum of money for us but insufficient to buy our independence.

My mother clicked her tongue against her teeth. "It's not enough. Once my daughter's virginity is gone, who will want her then? It's far better for her to marry a man for life."

Gostaham looked as if he were about to agree, but Gordiyeh cut him short. "You mean you'd rather give her to a baker's son with hairy, flour-coated arms than to a man of wealth?" she asked. "Don't forget that the sigheh is renewable. If your daughter pleases Fereydoon, he may wish to keep her indefinitely. Each time he renews, he will pay the agreed-upon sum. He may also grace her with gifts of jewelry or even a house. If she is lucky and clever, the alliance could make your fortune."

Gostaham shifted again on his pillow, looking much less opti-
mistic. "Let's not forget it could also end quickly," he said. "The only
guarantee is three months. Beyond that, it's entirely his decision."

Gordiyeh spoke to my mother in a sugar-coated tone that
made her husband's words seem slight. "Why wouldn't a fine girl
like your daughter please Fereydoon? Such a moon would shine on
him all night, every night!"

"Yes, she would," said my mother. "But if he likes her so much,
why doesn't he make us a proper offer?"

"He can't," said Gordiyeh. "His first wife is dead, carried off by
the cholera that wasted his daughter. As the son of a wealthy man,
he is bound to marry a highborn woman who can bear his heirs."

I knew that a village girl like myself would not do.

"Homa is already looking for a suitable young woman," said
Gordiyeh. "But I imagine that Fereydoon is craving companionship,
now that he has mourned his first wife. He could have anyone in the
land for the purpose — and yet your daughter is his choice."

I felt a surge of excitement. He had taken notice and made me an
offer — me, a village girl whose fingertips bore calluses from carpet
making and cleaning!

"Your dangling gems carpet must have made him take a fancy
to you," Gordiyeh said to me as if she could hear my thoughts.
"Above all other women, he has fixed his attention on you. That
must be more than you had ever hoped for — to catch the eye of
such a wealthy man!"

"True," I said, blushing.

"Really, there is no way you can err," said Gordiyeh. "Any children you conceive will be legitimate offspring, and will be supported. No man in his position would let the mother of his children
go hungry. And just imagine what might happen if you keep him
happy and satisfied!"

Gostaham held up his hands as if stopping the flow of Gordiyeh's
words. "Remember, Khanoom," he said to my mother, "although

any children would be legitimate, they'll never have the same status as the offspring of his permanent wives."

Gordiyeh made a chopping movement with her hand as if to push his words away. "Only God knows what will happen," she said. "It's not for us to decide."

Gostaham looked at my mother. "It behooves you to think very carefully about this offer, Khanoom. You can't predict whether he will leave or stay. You don't know if you and your daughter will live in luxury or be reduced to begging. And even if your daughter has children, she will have no inheritance rights — none."

Gordiyeh sighed in exasperation. "Many odd twists of fate could also occur if she marries a baker," she said. "From one day to the next, he could fall sick and die. The Shah could accuse him of cheating on the weight of bread and cook him in his own oven. He could be thrown off a mule and crack his head."

"No doubt," replied Gostaham. "But then she would have a legitimate family to rely on — her husband's parents, brothers, and cousins. She would be less likely to be alone and sorry after only three months."

"Sorry?" I asked.

"Well, really, there is nothing to worry about," said Gordiyeh. "A sigheh is a legal union."

"Legal, yes, but some people consider it beneath them," rejoined Gostaham. My face burned for a moment, although I didn't know exactly what he meant.

Gostaham turned to my mother. "If he were offering a regular marriage, I wouldn't hesitate to urge you to accept," he said.

"Still," said Gordiyeh quickly, "there's much cause for celebrating. It would be best if you accepted the offer and used it as another source of income, especially since our finances here at home are so unstable."

"Unstable?" said my mother, looking around at the well-kept room. Following her gaze, I observed thick bouquets of red and yellow roses, mounds of honeyed sweets, platters heavy with sweet melons and cucumbers, and bowls full of roasted pistachios. "You're worried about money?" she asked.

"My husband's salary from the royal rug workshop is hardly enough to meet our expenses," Gordiyeh said. "The Shah permits him to perform extra commissions in his own time, which are what keep us comfortable, but they come and go with the wind. A new silk carpet is the first thing a financially troubled family can do without."

She turned to Gostaham. "And isn't it true that even the royal family can't be trusted as patrons? I remember the stories about how the late Shah Tahmasp fired hundreds of miniature painters, gilders, calligraphers, and bookbinders after he became pious. Such a calamity could happen again."

Gostaham looked disgusted for a moment. "Shah Abbas is nothing like his grandfather. He has no reason to stop supporting the royal rug workshop, which is very profitable."

"Still," said Gordiyeh impatiently, "who can predict what will happen? Of course, a mother and daughter on their own should always be cautious about their financial future."

My mother rocked back at those words as if battered by a fierce desert wind. Nothing could have terrified her more than the thought that we might have to struggle on our own again, as we had in the months after my father's death.

"Fereydoon and his relatives have dozens of houses in Isfahan and throughout the country," Gordiyeh continued. "Every house they buy and every tent they pitch in the desert needs carpets—good carpets. Such a family orders silk, not wool."

She turned to me. "Think how such an alliance would benefit our family!"

It was the first time I had heard her say "*our* family" in a way that included my mother and me. Although the sigheh money would be ours to keep, I began to understand that Gordiyeh had her own reasons for promoting the union.

"I would do anything to aid *our* family," I replied.

"And I, too," added my mother. "What does he say about providing a house for my daughter?"

"He hasn't offered one," said Gordiyeh. "But if your daughter is pleasing and obedient, that may come."

My mother sighed. "It's certainly not the offer I thought it was at first."

"I understand," said Gordiyeh in a soothing tone. "Of course you want the best for your daughter. But what better offer could a young woman with no dowry expect?"

My mother's brow furrowed, and I saw a look of helplessness in her eyes. "I'll have an answer for you in a few days," she finally said.

"Just don't keep him waiting too long," replied Gordiyeh.

"And do not say a word about the offer to anyone," added Gostaham. "We'll want to keep quiet about it even if your daughter does marry Fereydoon."

"Why?" I asked.

Gordiyeh looked away. "It's perfectly legal," she repeated, and then there was a long, uncomfortable silence during which Gostaham cleared his throat. My mother looked at him, waiting for an answer.

"It's not the type of thing a family like ours would advertise," he finally said.

I had another concern that felt like salt under my skin. "What about my schooling?" I asked. "Gostaham is still teaching me about carpets."

For the first time that morning, Gostaham looked pleased, as if I were truly the child of his heart.

"No matter what your mother decides about the marriage, I will continue to instruct you for as long as you want to learn," he said.

It was as though a light had passed from his heart to mine. "I want to keep learning," I said. "What if I have to live far away?"

"Since Fereydoon hasn't offered a house, you will remain here," said Gordiyeh.

"Won't he insist on shutting her away from the eyes of strangers?" my mother asked.

"He's rich, but he's not from a high-class Isfahani family," Gordiyeh said. "The only women he's likely to sequester are his permanent wives."

She turned to me. "Don't worry—I'm sure it won't matter to him what you do during the day."

AFTER THE MEETING, I went to the chamber where my mother and I slept and looked around without seeing anything, then climbed the stairs to the roof as if to check on laundry, although there was none, then visited Cook to see if she needed help. I chopped onions for a few minutes until I spilled a bowl of cleaned fenugreek onto the floor, after which I was thrown out of the kitchen and told not to return.

It was not that I objected to Fereydoon's person, for even though he was not as handsome as Iskandar, he was erect, well muscled, and gave off the appealing smell of horses. But his proposal was not the respectful offer I had hoped to receive from a suitor. If Fereydoon wanted me, why didn't he offer to marry me forever? And if he required a highborn woman to bear his heirs, why not marry her first and then offer to make me his second wife?

I fretted at my chores, knowing that my fortunes might change in a single day. If I married, I would give up my virginity, once and always; and I might bear children. I would be forever changed. I imagined the days of leisure and nights of love, the bowls of honey and dates, the growing rolls of flesh on my belly. But what if I was no longer married after only three months? I would hardly have time to grow fat.

I wished I could go to Naheed's and ask her and her mother what they thought. But Gostaham had instructed us to remain silent about the offer. If the sigheh ended after three months without a pregnancy, so much the better for my later prospects if no one knew. That seemed odd to me, since every marriage I had ever heard about was announced and celebrated with great joy. Why was there a veil of secrecy over this one?

"Daughter of my heart," said my mother when we met in our room that evening, "what have you been thinking?" There were dark circles under her eyes, and her feet were red again. The work in the kitchen had been very hard that day.

I took a cushion and put it under her feet as she stretched out on her bedroll. "You and my Baba always told me you would marry me to a good man," I said. "How can Fereydoon be that man, if he only wants me for a few months?"

My mother sighed. "From everything we've heard, his reputation is upstanding," she said. "There's no reason to believe otherwise."

"I feel as if he wants to buy me cheaply," I replied. "You and my Baba raised me to expect better."

My mother took my hands in hers. "We cannot have the same hopes we once had," she said. "This offer surpasses what I thought possible."

"What else is possible?"

"Nothing," my mother replied darkly. "Gordiyeh is right. How can two penniless women expect more?"

I adjusted the white cloth that covered my hair and returned my hands to my mother's warm ones. "If it were my decision, I would say no. After all, Hajj Ali said that marriages made in this period would be full of passion and strife."

My mother withdrew her hands from mine. "It's not your decision," she said with iron in her voice.

"I have the right to tell the mullah no if I object," I replied angrily, remembering what Goli had once told me.

"If you do that, you will forever estrange yourself from this family, and that includes me."

My heart was chilled by her reply. "You mean you would have me marry Fereydoon against my will?"

"Our position in this household is unsound," she replied.

"I'm sorry," I said, knowing that I was much to blame.

"That's why I am asking you not to be so imprudent for the first time in your life," said my mother more gently. "This decision is best left to your elders, who have your interests at heart."

The merest allusion to my mistake made me want to hide my face in shame. Having acted rashly, I longed to show that I could learn from my misconduct.

"*Chashm,*" I said meekly, using the word of obedience that soldiers give their commanders. "I submit to your will." And with that, I touched my head to my mother's swollen feet, determined to do whatever she asked of me.

THE NEXT MORNING, my mother gave her consent to the proposal. Gostaham wrote a letter of acceptance to Fereydoon and offered his congratulations to us without enthusiasm. Almost immediately, we received a note back from Fereydoon proposing to formalize our union the next day, the first of Ramazan.

We slept late that morning because we knew we would be observing the fast until nightfall. My mother helped Cook chop vegetables and fry meat, while I picked bugs and stones out of the rice and soaked it to remove its starch. Even that simple task seemed to take longer than usual because I was hungry and parched. My thoughts wandered often to Fereydoon as I worked. Since I had not seen him for several months, I wondered how he would look and whether I would regret bowing to my mother's decision.

By midafternoon, my tongue was sticking to the roof of my mouth and it was difficult to speak. The days had become hot, so everyone was thirsty and had to struggle not to think of water. The days were also long, which meant an endless wait until nightfall, when we were permitted to eat. Every moment required strength of will.

By early evening, we were all enervated from lack of food and drink. Gordiyeh's children and grandchildren gathered at the house, giddy with anticipation. As the thick aroma of Cook's lamb and chicken stews permeated the air, I began salivating in a way that hurt my tongue. The adults fed the children who were too young to keep the fast. Tension built in the house as the moment of satisfaction drew near. Cook, who seemed especially nervous, barked orders at us as if we were soldiers. She wanted all the food to be ready on time, but not so soon that it would grow cold. I felt as if I might snap from the cloud of feelings that hung over me.

At last, the great cannon's boom stirred everyone to life. I helped Shamsi and Zohreh carry the food to the Great Room. Gostaham's family descended on the meal like leopards tearing into deer. There was no other sound than that of chewing. Gostaham, who could scoop rice into his bread and lift it to his mouth without dropping a grain, now let the rice fall where it may. No one said a word until bellies had been filled and throats soothed with drink.

In the kitchen, my mother and I and the servants were equally quiet as we served the food. Normally we would have waited until the family had finished eating, but not during Ramazan. We were too depleted. I could hardly decide whether to eat or drink first, but I started with a cup of Cook's thirst-quenching sharbat, a mix of fruit juices, sugar, vinegar, and the essence of roses. The drink was sweet and sour at the same time, which enlivened my appetite. But when I sat down to eat, I couldn't swallow a morsel.

While we were drinking our tea, Fereydoon arrived at our door with his accountant and the mullah. Gostaham escorted them into the Great Room and treated them to drinks and sweetmeats before calling us in. I was fully covered in my chador, as was proper in mixed company. I peeked at Fereydoon, who was sumptuously dressed in a brown velvet robe patterned with golden steeds topped with horsemen like himself. Gostaham read the marriage contract out loud to verify its duration and the amount we would be paid. When the mullah asked for my consent, I gave it right away, as I had promised my mother. Fereydoon signed the document, and my mother, Gostaham, the mullah, and Fereydoon's accountant were the witnesses.

Fereydoon was very businesslike about the proceedings, but when no one was looking, he gave me a long, frank stare of appreciation that made me tremble. His gaze made my body feel heavy and ripe, like a date bathing in its own juices. I shivered at the thought of what it would be like to be alone with him for the first time. I knew I would have to shed my clothes, but I had very little idea what would happen after that. I hoped I would like it, and I prayed that he would like me. I drew comfort thinking of Goli's words. "Everyone likes it," she had once said.

My mother collected a sack of coins from the accountant. Fereydoon and his entourage thanked us and departed. As we returned to our room, I heard the silver clinking within my mother's clothes, which made my wedding seem more like a matter of trade than celebration.

Because it seemed odd to stay at home quietly on my wedding day, my mother and I walked to the Image of the World for amusement later that evening. The shopkeepers had festooned their alcoves with lights so that people could examine merchandise until the early hours. Jugglers and storytellers amused the crowd with their tricks, and boys sold honeyed almonds and sugar crystals infused with saffron. Families bought sticks of grilled lamb and ate them while walking from shop to shop. It was lively, but it felt peculiar to be lost in this nameless crowd rather than celebrating my marriage as I would have in my village. Well-wishers would have surrounded me for a day and a night. Together, we would have danced, sung songs, told stories, and recited verse, and after we were all sated on rice with chicken, orange peel, and sugar, my husband would have arrived to claim me for his own. I thought about how proud my father would have been, and I missed him with all my heart.

It was nearly dawn before we walked home again. My mother and I ate a meal of curds, herbs, nuts, sweets, and bread to keep us going through the day. I had a final glass of sour cherry sharbat before sinking into sleep not long before the sun's first rays appeared. As I pulled the blankets around me, I hoped I would not awaken before the sun reached its zenith. But I tossed on my bedroll, for my body was not used to sleeping while it was light. I felt dizzy and unsettled by the changes that had occurred so suddenly. It reminded me of the time when my father had left us alone forever during the course of a single night. The very ground I walked on then had seemed to tremble, as if an earthquake were about to reduce our village to rubble.

I DIDN'T HAVE to wait long for my first summons from Fereydoon. It came on the fourth day of Ramazan in the form of a letter that directed me to be bathed, dressed, and ready to meet him before the cannon went off the following evening. I was finally going to become a mature woman: Like Goli, I would know everything.

The next afternoon, my mother and Gordiyeh took me to the elegant hammam in our district. For the first time, my mother directed Homa to take me into one of the private cubicles. She spread a thick, sour-smelling cream made from the lemon-colored orpiment plant on my legs and underarms. After a few minutes, she poured a bucket full of water over me and the hair melted away, leaving my legs and underarms as smooth as a little girl's. Then she tilted my head back and groomed my eyebrows, not as strictly as if I had been a mature woman, but just enough so that they curved like crescent moons.

"You're looking prettier and prettier," said Homa. I blushed, for I was not used to thinking of myself that way.

When I was smooth, I rejoined the other women in the main part of the bath. I felt the new sensation of my hairless thighs whispering to each other as I walked. Returning to where my mother and Gordiyeh were lounging and laughing, I stretched out beside them. They prepared a batch of henna paste in a bowl, and Gordiyeh painted my palms to the wrist and half the length of the tops of my fingers. My mother did the bottoms of my feet and half the length of the tops of my toes. Many hours later, when they removed the paste, my toes and fingers looked like ornaments. They didn't joke with me or tease me, which is what happened to most brides, for they were determined to keep my marriage a secret.

Then it was finally time to bathe. As Homa scrubbed my back, she said, "Hair and henna, it's as if you're getting married!"

"You'd be the first to know about it, Homa-joon!" I said, in what I hoped was a lighthearted tone. I was unaccustomed to lying, and the words seemed to stick in my throat.

Homa laughed and poured a vessel of water over my head to rinse me. After that, we made the Grand Ablution in the hammam's largest tub. The hot water usually made me sleepy and indifferent, but this time, I fidgeted until the other women begged me to stop.

When we arrived home, Gordiyeh led me and my mother into her dressing room, a small chamber in the andarooni. It was filled with trunks containing garments for special occasions. As they pulled out the precious silks, Gordiyeh asked my mother about her own wedding.

"I thought I was the luckiest girl in the village," she replied with a smile, "because I was marrying the comeliest man."

"Ah, but beauty comes and goes!" replied Gordiyeh. "I was a lovely thing once myself, not heavy and sagging the way I am now."

My mother sighed. "I wouldn't have minded if his beauty had fled, if only his life had remained! But if God is willing, my daughter's future will be sweeter."

After I shed my clothes, Gordiyeh helped me into a transparent white silk sheath. I shivered, wondering how it would feel to show myself in that attire to Fereydoon, for I could not imagine revealing myself to him fully unclad.

Next came a loose silk tunic, as red as an apple, matching trousers, and sparkling golden slippers with pointed toes. The jewel of the outfit was a golden robe patterned with red rosebushes, which looked as fine as if painted. Each bush sprouted a tender bud, a half-opened flower, and a rose at the height of its beauty. A butterfly stretched its wing toward the heart of the blossoming rose, eager to feed.

My mother held open the robe for me, and I slipped it on. "Daughter of mine, see how these roses have no thorns," she said. "Let that guide you when you are with your husband."

Suddenly I felt dizzy, probably because I hadn't eaten anything since before the sun rose, out of respect for Ramazan. I sank onto a stool to steady myself. Gordiyeh painted my eyelids with kohl and darkened my eyebrows. Then she dabbed a bit of rose-colored paint on my lips, making them look smaller, and created a tiny black beauty mark below the outside corner of my left eye. My mother covered my hair with a bit of white lace, allowing a few stray locks to decorate my face. A string of Gordiyeh's pearls went under my chin, outlining my face from temple to temple. Gordiyeh fastened another strand of pearls around my head. I could feel each jewel resting on my forehead, as cool as a stream.

"Stand up, *azizam*—my dear," said my mother. I arose and they looked at me. They seemed transfixed, as if they were gazing at a beautiful painting I had never seen.

My mother put a hand on each of my cheeks. "You are as lovely as the full moon," she said.

Once dressed, I was afraid to move for fear of disturbing their fine work. My mother led me to a container of burning incense, bidding me place one foot on either side of it to perfume my clothes. "And everything under them," Gordiyeh said with a lusty laugh. The sweet, strong smell of the incense clouded my thinking and made me feel dizzy again.

Next, Gordiyeh covered me in a white silk chador and a picheh so that I wouldn't be recognized. My mother put her own black chador over her mourning clothes. As it was Ramazan and too early to eat, they did not feed me a sweet dripping with almonds and rose water, but instead brushed it against my lips and wished me sweetness in my married life.

My mother and I had been directed to meet Fereydoon at one of his homes near the old Friday mosque. We left Gostaham's and walked away from the river in the direction of the North Gate, following the bazaar until we arrived at the city's old main square. From there, we passed four caravanserais, three hammams, and two religious schools before reaching the old Friday mosque, which had been built some five hundred years before. The mosque was made of brick that was neither painted nor tiled. While the Shah's square and his Friday mosque were magnificent beyond compare, this area of town had a quiet grandeur born of endurance. Even the Mongols had not destroyed it.

"Let's go in the mosque for a moment," I said.

We passed through its immense doorway into a dark corridor with solid brick walls and thick columns. I thought of all those who had prayed here before me, especially women who had been virgins one day and married the next. It seemed to me as if I were now in the darkness of ignorance, but soon I, too, hoped to pass into the bright light of knowledge. I stepped from the dim corridor into the mosque's outdoor prayer space, which basked in the sun's radiance. I stood for a moment in the light, uttering prayers, and my mother let me be until I was done.

"I'm ready now," I told her.

We left the square and turned down a narrow street where the only visible sign of homes was their tall gates. The cannon was about to fire, and the streets were full of people hurrying to the places where they planned to consume their next meal. Their faces looked strained and full of anticipation.

My mother asked a boy for directions to Fereydoon's, and he led us to a carved wooden door. We used the women's knocker, which made a high-pitched sound. Almost immediately, an older woman servant opened the door and introduced herself as Hayedeh. I recognized her, for she had joined in the festivities the day that Homa had sung my praises.

We stepped inside and removed our chadors. She paid us her respects, yet, with a clear sense of her superior position, told my mother that she would take charge of me from that moment. I hadn't expected to say good-bye so quickly. My mother put her palms against my cheeks and whispered, "Don't forget you are named for a woman of strength and wisdom. I know you will live up to your name."

As she turned to go, I saw a flood rising in her eyes, and there was a matching one in mine. I don't think I've ever felt more alone than in that moment. Noting my distress, Hayedeh said simply, "You will like it here."

The house had four rooms arranged around an open courtyard with a pretty fountain that sounded like music. Hayedeh collected my outdoor wraps and scrutinized my attire. She must have deemed it suitable, for she led me into one of the chambers and told me to remove my shoes and wait.

The room was like a treasure chest. Its walls had numerous niches, which were painted with a design of orange poppies and fanciful turquoise flowers. The ceiling was decorated with a sunburst pattern like a carpet's carved out of white plaster. It had been inlaid with small mirrors, which shimmered like stars. A very fine silk rug with a floral pattern covered the floor. Two smaller carpets that showed birds singing together in a flowering tree hung on the walls, too precious to be walked upon. Within arm's reach lay bowls filled with melons, grapes, and tiny cucumbers, as well as tall ewers containing water and red wine.

I have no sense of how much time passed before Fereydoon arrived. Each minute seemed as long as a year, and I hardly moved for fear of ruining my appearance. I think I must have looked as frozen as a princess in a painting. Every detail was as perfect, yet I was not myself. I examined my hennaed hands and toes as if they belonged to another, for I had never been decorated before. I thought of my friend Goli, and of how much I had longed to know the mysteries she had known for years. Now I wished I didn't have to know them.

The cannon fired, and within moments the door to the room opened and Fereydoon strode in, trailed by a half dozen servants bearing platters of steaming food. "Salaam," he said, sitting down on a cushion close to mine. He was wearing a lavender robe over a green tunic, and a white turban shot with silver thread. Two servants whipped open a dining cloth and placed it in front of us, while others laid out platters with enough food for twenty people. Then they all respectfully withdrew.

Fereydoon seemed as comfortable as when he had first seen me uncovered. "You must be famished," he said. "Let's break our fast together."

He tore a piece of bread, scooped up a morsel of lamb and rice cooked with dill, and offered it to me. I looked at it in alarm. I had never before accepted food from a strange man's hand.

"No need to be shy," said Fereydoon, leaning toward me. "We

are man and wife." When I recoiled, he laughed. "Ah, virgins!" he said, with a smile of delight.

I took the food from his fingertips and placed it in my mouth. It was as savory as any I had ever eaten, and there were mountains of it. We had also been served two stewed chickens, the haunch of a roasted lamb, rice with fava beans and onions, and a sweet rice dish made with saffron, barberries, orange peel, and sugar. I couldn't consume much, but Fereydoon ate magnificently of everything, as might be expected of one in his position. From time to time, he stopped and prepared a choice morsel for me. Just as at home, we didn't speak as we ate, the better to appreciate the gift of food.

When we had finished, Fereydoon called for the servants and ordered the dishes to be removed. I could see them assessing how much food remained on the platters and calculating whether or not they'd be eating well tonight. Having done the same thing myself, I knew they would.

Now Fereydoon called for a water pipe and a musician. A large glass pipe with a burning ember on top of the tobacco appeared at the same time as the smooth-skinned young player, who still didn't have his first beard. Fereydoon took a pull on the pipe and offered it to me, but I declined, never having smoked before. The musician seated himself across from Fereydoon and waited until he commanded him to play by lifting his hand. Then the musician began moving his bow over his *kamancheh,* whose melodies seared my heart. As I watched the duo, so in harmony with one another, I felt a piercing loneliness. The kamancheh and its player called out to me about a life of closeness I had never known, and perhaps never would. I suddenly began missing my father. I took a breath to try to calm myself, but my expression caught Fereydoon's eye.

"What's this?" he said. I couldn't reply, as I was fighting my feelings. The musician kept playing. Fereydoon signaled him to stop, but he didn't notice. Finally Fereydoon said loudly, "Enough! You may go." The young man played a bit longer before he finally looked up. I noticed a strangely flirtatious smile at the corners of his lips as he thanked his master and departed.

I felt wretched, as if I had already made a terrible blunder. But rather than being angry, Fereydoon reached over to me and began stroking the top of my hennaed hand. His hands were twice as large as mine, and his skin was the color of brewed tea against my red fingertips. His hand was softer than any I had ever felt before. He lingered over my callused fingertips, smiling as if he liked the way they felt.

While Fereydoon was looking at my hand, I glanced at his face. He had a thick black mustache and a closely cropped beard that reached all the way to his ears. I could smell tobacco in the vicinity of his lips, which were as red as my tunic. I had never been so close to a man's face before, except for my father's, and I must have looked frightened. Fereydoon drew me into his arms and stroked the hair near my face and each of my hands. The warmth of his skin started to make mine glow in return.

"So," he said, "this is my little mountain girl from the south, so tough and hard on the outside, yet so buttery underneath! Who would have thought?"

I wouldn't have described myself that way, yet it must have been true. After my father's death, tenderness had seemed an emotion for other people to enjoy.

"From the day I saw you shed your coverings, I wanted to have you," he said.

"And yet, I snapped at you," I replied, remembering how I had told him to stop looking.

"As you should have!"

"Why did you wait until now to ask my family for me?" I asked.

"You weren't ready," he said. "But things had changed when Hayedeh saw you at the hammam."

I blushed, and Fereydoon kissed my forehead right underneath the string of hanging pearls. My body flushed. It was a wonder to be the one person who mattered to someone, if only for a moment, more than anyone else.

I wanted to talk more, but Fereydoon took my hand and led me into a small bedchamber located through a carved wooden door. Light flickered from a few oil lamps placed in niches in the walls. A large bedroll with a pillow big enough for a couple filled most of the room. It was a chamber made for just two things: sleep and love.

We sat down on the bedroll, and my heart began to beat so fast I could see the silk tunic respond to its thuds. Fereydoon removed Gordiyeh's precious golden robe, tossing it aside with the casualness of a person accustomed to things of value. Then he gently lifted the tunic over my head. I shivered in the sheer silk undergarment that revealed almost everything. Fereydoon put his hands on my waist for a moment, and their warmth calmed and stilled me. I could feel him waiting for that. When I relaxed, he began caressing the front of my body very, very lightly with just the tips of his fingers, which were hot through the silk.

I wanted him to continue, but Fereydoon removed the last of my garments rather quickly and gazed upon my naked body, while I tried not to twist away like a worm on a hook. A look of delight filled his eyes. "Breasts as firm as pomegranates, hips like an oasis! Somehow, I always know!"

I was blushing from his words of praise. "Red roses are blooming on your cheeks," he said gently. He cast aside his own garments, the precious fabric twisting up like rags. When Fereydoon removed his turban for the first time, I drew in my breath. His hair fell to his shoulders in thick black shining waves. I wanted to touch it, but didn't dare.

The wiry hairs against his body looked like velvet patterns on brocade. Though I didn't look directly at his middle, I glimpsed something that made me think of sheep organs for sale in the meat bazaar: kidney, liver, and tongue.

When Fereydoon took me in his arms, with nothing between us, I smelled fresh apple-flavored tobacco at his lips and felt the bristly hair on his face and chest. His body felt deliciously warm against mine. I was so innocent I didn't know what to expect next. I had seen animals rutting in the fields, and I knew men and women did something similar. But when Fereydoon joined his body to mine, I held on to the bedroll to brace myself, for it seemed violent. As his passion flowered, I knew it was inspired by me, but I felt far away from it. I was indeed like a princess frozen in a painting, watching Fereydoon as he devoured me. When he ascended the seven heavens and shouted with joy, I observed him curiously through a half-open eye. After he fell asleep, I felt thwarted and confused. Why was what we were doing the source of so many jokes among the women of my village and, no doubt, among the men? Why had Goli looked rapturous when she talked about it?

Sometime in the early hours, Fereydoon woke up and took me in his arms. It seemed he wanted to do the same thing again. I complied, although I felt like a raw sore. Inspired by his actions, I began moving my hips against his as if I knew what to do, increasing my efforts when I saw his eyes flutter like the wings of a butterfly. As I continued, he reared up out of the bedclothes and squeezed my back fiercely with his soft hands, as if he were trying to crush his body into mine. After a few long moments, his arms relaxed and he slid onto one side of the bed.

"That was beyond compare," he said, kissing one of my breasts. Before he slept, he smiled at me, and I had the feeling I had done just the right thing.

I had a dream that night about polo. The rival horsemen were pursuing the ball fiercely and blocking each other from it. When one of them finally drove the ball through the goalposts, I expected the crowd to leap and roar, but no sounds emerged from their throats. I awoke with a start, thinking about Fereydoon's thighs shooting between mine, and wondering why the feeling hadn't been as delightful as I thought it was going to be.

AS I WALKED home that morning, everything I saw—the old Friday mosque, the bustling bazaar, the plane trees sheltering the road through Four Gardens—seemed newly born under the hot sun. My skin tingled with the memory of Fereydoon's embrace. My heart raced, like the day I had stood on the bridge looking into Isfahan and had longed to unlock the city's mysteries. Yet I felt a hollowness inside as if something were missing, something I could not name.

As I passed through Four Gardens, my eye was caught by a wealthy man's pleasure grounds, which were planted with bright pink dog roses and lilies in an unearthly shade of blue. I wondered what it would be like to recline in the thick green clover under those shady poplars, with a picnic of bread, almonds, and sheep's cheese — and a husband. A couple of lusty young men noticed I was dawdling and began begging for a sign from me. "She's as plump and as pliable as a peach," one of them whispered loudly to the other. "You can tell from the shape of their ankles."

As I turned toward Gostaham's street, ignoring them, I smiled secretly under my picheh. Now I knew exactly what bothered them so much beneath their robes. I looked around at other women, delightfully hidden behind their veils. We were a surprise to be unwrapped layer by layer.

My exhilaration was not pure. Something had been missing in my night with Fereydoon; something that caused others to celebrate the act in countless songs, poems, and knowing looks. "It is like a fire that catches dry grass and joyfully consumes it," Goli had once said. But what did that mean?

When I arrived home, my mother greeted me with affection and asked how my health was. I replied that I was well, thanks be to God.

"And how was your evening?" she asked, anxious to know everything.

I stretched out on my bedroll, suddenly tired. "I believe that everything happened as it was supposed to," I replied.

"Praise be to God!" she said. "Was Fereydoon pleased?"

"As far as I could tell," I said flatly, remembering how important his pleasure was to our future.

My mother stroked the hair away from my face. "You sound as if you didn't enjoy yourself."

It was as if she could read my thoughts. "How did you know?"

"Don't worry, my child," my mother said. "It will improve from one time to the next. Just have patience."

"Why will it improve?"

"You'll get used to each other, and you'll do things to please each other."

"Truly?"

"I promise."

I longed to talk with a married friend like Goli about what had happened, but I knew no one like that in Isfahan.

Naheed came to visit me that afternoon, knowing nothing of where I had been. I had not seen her in more than a month, for I had been punished most of that time and not allowed to leave the house or have visitors. When she arrived, I was sleeping. I arose to greet her, yawning. She hardly noticed my tiredness and didn't even remark on my hennaed hands and feet. Naheed was in love, and she was unable to think of anything else. We kissed each other on both cheeks and sat on my bedroll while my mother went to the kitchen to have her tea.

"I'm so excited," Naheed said. There was a red blush on her cheeks, and her lips seemed full and soft. I had never seen her looking so beautiful. Compared with her, I knew I looked fatigued, with circles under my eyes from lack of rest.

"Has anything happened lately?" I asked. I glanced at her hips, which looked thicker than usual. She was keeping his letters inside her clothes, tied up in the sash that hung low.

"Yes," she said, "I've brought his latest missive, which I've already read a thousand times over." She pulled it out of her sash. "It is full of beautiful sentiments, but I will read you the line that is the most important."

Unfolding the letter, she read:

> Give me assurance that your eyes, as green as emeralds, will shine
> their love on me, and be assured that I will be as eternally true to you as
> a diamond.

"That sounds like a marriage proposal!" I said.

"That's exactly what I thought," she replied, "although he would have to make a formal offer to my family." She sighed and leaned back into the cushions, her face a picture of bliss.

I wished I could tell her that in the last few hours, while she was exulting over a letter, I had revealed my most secret parts to a man — and seen all of his. But then I would have had to tell her it wasn't as wonderful as I had hoped it would be.

Naheed sighed. "I can't stop thinking of his eyes. They are so black and shiny, even from far away."

I thought about Fereydoon's eyes. They were a warm brown color, and they had been so close to mine that I had seen the pupils contracting in response to the light of the oil lamps.

"He is as handsome as Yusuf," I said, "the pearl of his age."

"And his lips!" she said, as if she hadn't heard me. "They are

so thick and red." She blushed, her creamy cheeks going pink all at
once. "I wonder what it must be like to kiss him!"

I could have told her what a kiss was like. When Fereydoon first
put his tongue in my mouth, it seemed as fat as a worm, and he had
pushed it between my lips and crushed my nose against his without
giving me room to breathe. But I liked the way his tongue felt when
it darted in and out of my mouth. Naheed, I believed, was imagining a kiss that would stop chastely at the lips.

"I think of nothing but being wrapped in his embrace, feeling
his chest against mine and the muscles in his arms."

How could she know of the strangely pleasant roughness of a
man's wiry chest against her breasts, as I did? But the other things
we had done had been less pleasing: the strange hot pressure when I
opened my legs, the sharp pain, and his exploding wetness later. I
grew uncomfortable thinking about it.

"You're blushing," said Naheed. "Do these things embarrass
you?"

"Perhaps," I said, willing myself to bring my mind back to her
concerns. If Fereydoon and I had been as deeply in love as Iskandar
and Naheed, would I have conquered my shyness and enjoyed my
night with him more?

"I have only you to thank, dear friend, for my happiness," Naheed continued. "This never would have happened if you hadn't
agreed to come with me to polo."

"It is nothing!"

"My heart is yearning to hear from him again," continued Naheed. "I need to hear more words of love to know if his feelings
match mine."

I longed to tell Naheed about my sigheh, but Gordiyeh and Gostaham's demand for silence made me fear that my new situation
would diminish me in her esteem. Even if I had been able to confide
in her, I wouldn't be able to describe Fereydoon with the joy with

which she discussed Iskandar. My marriage had been one of necessity; hers would be one of choice.

"You aren't listening to me," said Naheed with a frown. "What is it? You look sad today."

I had been trying to keep my feelings out of our conversation, but it was impossible.

"I just wish . . . that I was married to someone I loved!" I said abruptly, but it was more than that. Why couldn't I have a fairy face, with creamy white skin? Why couldn't my father be alive, to rain his blessings upon me? And why couldn't I be with a man who wanted me so much that he would marry me forever?

"It will happen for you, too," said Naheed. "When you discover love, you will see that it is the most exalted feeling of the heart."

She threw her arms around me before we parted, unable to contain her emotions. I wondered if she was right. Naheed seemed to be swept away by the force of her own desires. Was that love? I didn't know, but I was happy to see her blooming like a rose garden, even though my own heart felt hollow.

FEREYDOON CLAIMED ME by night, but by day I still belonged to Gostaham. Shortly after my first night with Fereydoon, he summoned me to his workroom. Now that I knew the ways of men, I felt shy around him, but he treated me just the same, as an apprentice with a job to complete.

My mother and I had already repaid Gordiyeh for the wool I had squandered using part of the sigheh money; the rest of the silver paid off the debts we had incurred in our village. After I promised to take Gostaham's advice in choosing colors, he agreed to purchase the wool for another rug. I swore by the Holy Qur'an that I would not remove the rug from the loom until it was completed.

Gostaham had drawn a new design in black ink and offered to

tutor me as to how he chose his colors. I tried to keep my attention on our work rather than on my night with Fereydoon as he spread out the design in his workroom. It portrayed a vase surrounded by a garden of large fanciful blooms.

"Shah Abbas favors this design so much, it has been named after him," Gostaham said with a chuckle. "The design is not particularly complicated, which means that the colors become most important of all."

The vase had a narrow mouth and a body curved as generously as a woman's. Was my own made as fine? I blushed to think of myself naked before Fereydoon, and of how generously he had praised my breasts and hips.

Gostaham pulled out his tray of powdered pigments from a niche in the wall behind him. "Now watch carefully," he said.

At the very center of the vase was a rosette. Dipping his brush in water, he colored the rosette black with a cream center. The poppy holding the rosette became a bright orange, which he made float in a creamy sea of milk. The blossom enclosing the poppy became black, and the sides of the vase surrounding it, magenta.

"Tell me the colors you see, in order."

I started at the vase. "Cream, black, orange; cream, black, magenta," I said, becoming excited as I spoke. "It's a pattern!"

"Correct," said Gostaham.

The three large blossoms surrounding the vase contained succulent interior worlds of flowers, leaves, and arabesques. The first he colored mostly orange, punctuated with green; the second was mostly green with touches of black, orange, and pink like spots on a butterfly's wings. It was no surprise that the third blossom was largely pink.

"Watch the colors again," he said.

The third blossom began as a tiny pink flower with a cream center surrounded by black petals, which exploded into a mature magenta rose in a black sea punctuated by tiny orange flowers. It was like seeing a flower blossom through all the phases of its life. It reminded me of how Fereydoon's middle had seemed to unfold, stand tall, burst forth, and come peacefully to rest.

"You didn't answer my question," said Gostaham.

I hadn't even heard his request for me to name the colors. "Cream, pink, black; magenta, orange, black," I said, with more excitement than before. There was the pattern again, but in a different arrangement.

"Good. Now look at all the blossoms as a group. Since I'm using the same colors repeatedly, why is it that the eye does not grow bored?"

The answer was plain. "Although the blossoms are related, like members of a family, each is an unparalleled treasure."

"Just so."

Gostaham sketched ropes of smaller flowers around each of the large blossoms, encircling them loosely but affectionately, in much the same way that Fereydoon had first held me around the waist. From Gostaham's pen emerged the wild red tulip, with its black center, purple-black violets, red-brick pomegranate flowers, black narcissus, and pink roses.

"Now I have a test for you," Gostaham said. On another piece of paper, he sketched a blossom from the side and colored it with a green-and-black center and blue leaves. "Where shall I put this in the design?" he asked, handing me the paper.

I held the new drawing against the design, but it seemed to quarrel with the magenta and orange. Finally I said, "I can't find a place for it."

Gostaham smiled. "That's right," he said. "The colors don't fit, even though they are beautiful on their own."

"Unity and integrity," I murmured, remembering his last lesson.

"Praise God!" said Gostaham, his face lit by one of his rare smiles. "Now copy this design and its colors until you understand it with your own eyes and fingertips. Then, and only then, will I give you permission to begin knotting."

I did as I was told. After Gostaham gave his approval, we went to the bazaar together and looked for shades that matched the ones he had selected. Had we been working on a carpet for the royal rug workshop, he would have had those shades dyed to his specifications. Still, Isfahan's wool sellers were so well stocked that we were able to find hues close to the ones he recommended. I was jubilant, for now I could knot a carpet that would make both of us proud.

A FEW DAYS LATER, Fereydoon summoned me again. After receiving a letter from him in the morning, Gostaham found me in the courtyard working on the new carpet and told me, "You'll be wanted tonight." It took me a moment to understand what he meant, and then I colored with embarrassment at the thought that he and everyone else in the household knew what I'd be doing that evening. But after Gostaham left me to myself, I felt happy that Fereydoon wanted to see me, for I did not feel certain of how well I had performed as a wife.

When I finished my knotting for the day, I covered myself in my wraps and walked to the small, elegant home where I had given my virginity to Fereydoon. On the way, I thought about how affectionately my mother and Gordiyeh had prepared me for him, and how my bathing and dressing had taken all day. This time, and from then on, I was to be prepared by the women of Fereydoon's household. I worried about how it would feel to be handled by women I didn't know, women who served him instead of me.

When I arrived, Hayedeh greeted me and led me into the small hammam in Fereydoon's house. She had a firm, no-nonsense manner, as if she had done this many times before. The hammam was in a pretty white room with a marble floor and two deep marble tubs.

I began to disrobe, as I did when I visited Homa's hammam, until I noticed that Hayedeh and her fat assistant, Aziz, were looking at me with something akin to scorn.

"I can do it myself," I said, thinking to save them effort.

Hayedeh would hear nothing of it. "We would be in great trouble if you were found to have bathed without our help," she said, making a noise that sounded like a snort.

Chastened, I allowed the women to finish disrobing me. They removed my clothes gently and folded them with care, although they were just the simple cotton garments I wore at home. When I was naked, they guided me into the hottest tub, as if I couldn't get there on my own. Because I had cared for myself in many ways since I was small, it felt peculiar to be treated like a vessel made of glass.

While I was resting in the water and letting the heat seep into my skin, Aziz offered me cool water and fragrant cucumber. As it was still Ramazan, I told her I would wait until after I heard the cannon. I wanted to get out of the hot water after only a few minutes, but they insisted I stay until my body felt limp. When my skin was soft all over, they helped me out of the tub, scrubbed me with soapy cloths, and examined my legs, underarms, and eyebrows for stray hairs. After making sure I would not offend Fereydoon with any forests of growth, Hayedeh washed the hair on my head and anointed it with a sweet-smelling oil made of cloves. Aziz massaged my shoulders and neck with her large, fat hands, and I pretended to fall asleep. If these servants knew any gossip about Fereydoon, I was sure they wouldn't be able to resist talking about him.

I have always known how to feign sleep, as that was the only way I could eavesdrop on my parents at night. My leg gave a sharp spasm and my mouth fell open. When a trickle of drool spilled down my cheek, I knew I would have convinced even those closest to me that I was as good as dead.

"What else is there to do?" asked Aziz in a whisper.

"Just dress her."

"Pity to cover her up," replied the heavy one with a sigh. "Look at her!"

Look at what? I wondered. I couldn't see where their eyes were looking, and I began to feel heat rising on my cheeks and chest.

"It's as if he can see right through their clothes," replied Hayedeh. "He'd never have been able to tell just by looking at her face."

"Yet she's so dark: almost the color of cinnamon."

"True," replied Hayedeh, "but look at what she hides beneath those old clothes!"

The heavy one laughed. "I was like that once, I'm sure!"

"No doubt you were, but have you ever seen such tiny hands and feet, as delicate as a child's?"

Aziz sighed. "Then again, her fingertips are as rough as a goat's horn," she said. "I'm sure he doesn't like that."

"It's not her fingertips he's going to mount," replied Hayedeh, and the two women cackled together as if it were the funniest joke they had ever heard.

"Yes," said the heavy one wistfully, "summer figs don't get as ripe."

"And summer roses fade within a week. Wait till she gets pregnant; then the curves of her body will burst and sag."

"You mean *if* she gets pregnant," said Aziz, and the two women laughed again, even harder this time. "After all, she only has three months."

"The day is waning; we'd better wake her up," said Hayedeh, and she began massaging one of my feet. I started and stretched as if I were just emerging out of a fast sleep. Despite all their ministrations, I ached as if I had been poked in the liver. How long would Fereydoon continue to want someone that even two old servants had found ways to pity?

"Look: She's cold!" said Aziz to Hayedeh. She seemed to have forgotten that I was awake and could hear what she was saying.

The attendants sat me on a wooden stool and began dressing me in clothing that a woman can wear only for her husband. They guided my legs into sheer trousers and my arms into a silk undergarment that tied only once at the neck. Over those I donned a pale pink sheath and a turquoise robe, which fell open to reveal my sheer tunic and the place where breast joined breast. On my hair, I wore a delicate wisp of white silk, more for adornment than for modesty, and a string of pearls across my forehead. The silks swished softly against my body as the women led me into the small chamber, the same one where I had met Fereydoon the first time. They lit braziers of frankincense, which I stood over to perfume my clothes and skin. They also brought in flasks of red wine and milk in vessels made of porcelain. I slipped off my shoes and placed them side by side on one of the tiles that adorned the floor. The strong, smoky incense seemed to catch in my throat. I hoped my mother was right, and that things would be different this time.

I didn't have to wait very long, for Fereydoon arrived just after dusk. He entered the room, removed his shoes, and sat heavily on a cushion near me. The dagger at his waist glittered in the light of the oil lamps, which I wished had been less bright.

"How is your health?" he asked in an abrupt tone.

My skin prickled at his sharpness, but I answered as calmly as I could, "I am well, thanks be to God." When I asked in turn how he was, he merely grunted in reply. I thought we would have food and drink first, for neither of us had consumed anything all day, but Fereydoon led me into the bedchamber and briskly pushed the turquoise robe off my shoulders. Off it came faster than a rose petal falls to the ground, followed by my pink tunic. Fereydoon pulled off my sheer trousers and cast them aside. I remained in my thin silk shift, which tied at the neck but opened to reveal all else. "I think I'll have you just like this," he said.

Fereydoon shrugged off his clothes and doffed his turban, sending it spinning across the room like a skipping ball. Without bothering to remove my hair covering, he parted my shift and crawled on

147

top of me on the bedroll. Unlike our first time together, he thrust into me without delay. I winced, but he was not looking at me, and so, remembering what I ought to do, I began moving my hips in the way I had learned the last time, although I ached. It was only moments before Fereydoon shuddered and collapsed on my chest. I lay there beneath him, disappointed again, listening as the sound of his breathing quieted to normal. Was this the way it was to be with us? I felt a strong desire to caress his thick, wavy hair, which he revealed to my eyes only. But he was already nearly asleep, and I didn't dare rouse him. I lay there sleepless, my eyes wide open. This was nothing like what I had expected of marriage. It didn't remind me at all of how my father had adored my mother, or how Gostaham treated Gordiyeh.

After a while, the cannon boomed and Fereydoon stirred, stretched, put on his clothing, and told me to do the same. He clapped for the servants, who returned hastily with food and with the impertinent musician I remembered from our first evening. We ate another sumptuous meal of roasted meats, saffron rice, and fresh greens while the musician entertained us. I thought he was the prettiest young man I had ever seen. He had large almond-shaped eyes, thick brown curls, and the coquetry of a dancing girl. He couldn't have been much younger than I was, but the skin on his beardless face was smoother than mine. Fereydoon looked transported by his playing. When he reached high notes that shivered with beauty, Fereydoon nearly seemed to swoon. I thought I caught the musician sneering at the sight of Fereydoon's pleasure, but when Fereydoon opened his eyes, the young man's face was carefully neutral.

When Fereydoon had had enough of the musician, he sent him away along with the servants. Pouring milk into a large vessel of wine, he bade me drink it. I had never had any wine, as many of the women of my village refused to drink it for religious reasons (although I know some of them tasted it privately). The beverage had the aroma of a ripe grape and the comforting froth of fresh milk. I drank it very quickly and lay back on the bedroll, stretching out my arms and letting my legs part in a way that was starting to seem natural. I felt as relaxed and limp as I had in the bath. I imagined that Fereydoon might hold me in his arms and kiss my face, and that, after joining our bodies, he would listen as I told him stories about my life at home. But Fereydoon's eyes began to glitter, and without a word, he tore off all my garments again, this time with violence—I was alarmed to witness the fate of such costly clothes—and lifted me in his arms. He had me against the inlaid wooden doors that led to the room, which banged loudly with his every thrust. I cringed as I imagined what the servants must be thinking of the banging, as rhythmic as a drum, for they were right outside the door, listening for Fereydoon's quietest handclap. But that was not all. Fereydoon dragged me away from the doors and threw some cushions on the floor so that he could have me kneeling in the way that dogs rut, and finally, as the sky lightened, he took me standing up and supported in his arms, with my legs wrapped around his back. That night, I had no reason to worry about whether Fereydoon wanted me—whether my skin was too dark or whether I delighted him as a wife.

Diligent though I was in his arms, my body didn't soar with pleasure. Where were the raptures everyone had promised? I was even more disappointed than I had been after our first meeting, for nothing had changed. But I did whatever Fereydoon told me to do, mindful that he could say good-bye to me after a few months, and leave my mother and me dependent on the kindness of Gordiyeh and Gostaham. I could not imagine enduring ever again the winter of deprivation we had suffered in my village. Here in Isfahan, we were warm, comfortable, and well fed. So if Fereydoon told me to leave my clothes on or take them off, to go here or there, or to bend over like a dog, I felt I must obey.

Fereydoon seemed well pleased by our evening together. He reached for me again in the morning, groaning quickly, and then hummed to himself as he wrapped his body in a robe before his bath. I put on my cotton clothes to wear home. The servants appeared with coffee and bread, averting their eyes from me. I thought I caught Hayedeh smirking as she collected the cushions Fereydoon had arranged on the floor, for she could tell exactly what we had done and in which corner of the room.

DURING THE FIRST few weeks of my sigheh, I worked hard on the carpet. As it grew on my loom, I became more and more happy with it. The colors were felicitous; Gostaham had seen to that. There was no doubt that the rug outshone the last one. Even Gordi-yeh couldn't deny it. Having endured her fury, I rejoiced about that.

One afternoon, I was in the courtyard knotting the rug when a servant came by to tell me that Gostaham had returned home with a Dutchman. That was my signal to go upstairs to the secret nook and peek through the white carvings. Gostaham and the Dutchman were sitting on cushions in a semicircle with the accountant Parveez, who was present to write down any agreement the two might achieve. Although I had seen foreigners before, I had never seen one from the Christian lands to the west. All I knew was that the faran-gis believed in worshipping idols, and that their women thought nothing of displaying their hair and their bosoms in public.

The Dutchman had hair like straw and blue eyes like a dog's. Rather than wearing a long, cool tunic, he was attired in a tight blue velvet jacket and short blue pants that formed pouches near the tops of his thighs, as if he had buttocks both front and back. His legs were covered with white stockings, which must have been hot. When he raised his arm, I saw that sweat had bitten white rings into his coat.

"It is a great honor to have you as a guest in my home," Gos-taham was saying to him.

"The honor is very much mine," replied the Dutchman in fluent

Farsi. Like children, he had trouble making *kh* and *gh* sounds, but otherwise he was very easy to understand.

"We don't see foreigners like yourself very often," Gostaham continued.

"It's because the journey is long and arduous," replied the Dutchman. "Many of my colleagues have died in their pursuit of business here. But we are grateful that your esteemed Shah Abbas has opened your country so warmly to trade. Your silk is far cheaper than China's, and just as good."

Gostaham smiled. "It's our biggest export. Every family who can afford it has a shed for silkworms."

Gostaham had one of his own near his house. I loved to go inside the cool, dark shed and stroke the soft white fibers that grew a little rounder every day.

"The silk certainly makes some of the finest rugs I have ever seen," said the Dutchman, who seemed eager to steer the conversation to business.

"Indeed," said Gostaham, but he was not ready for that discussion. He changed the subject to a friendlier topic. "I imagine that if you have been traveling for more than a year, you must miss your family," he said.

"Very much," said the Dutchman, sighing heavily.

I was eager to hear something of his wife, but he didn't elaborate. "It's kind of you to ask about my family," he said, "but what I wanted to talk about today was carpets, and the possibility of commissioning one from a great master like yourself."

I stiffened in my nook. Didn't the Dutchman have any manners? It was rude to begin discussing business so quickly. I could tell Gostaham was offended from the way he looked away without speaking. Parveez stiffened; he was embarrassed for the man.

The Dutchman's forehead creased with heavy folds, as if he realized he had made a mistake. Fortunately, the awkward moment was interrupted by Taghee, who entered the room bearing vessels of sour cherry sharbat. It was stuffy in the nook, and I craved a taste of the tart drink.

"Please tell us about your country," said Gostaham, demonstrating his unerring hospitality. "We have heard so much about its beauties."

The Dutchman took a deep drink of his sharbat and leaned back into the cushions. "Ah," he said, smiling. "My land is a land of rivers. You needn't carry water when you travel, as you do here."

Parveez spoke for the first time. "Your land must be very green, like an emerald," he said. He was an accountant in training who liked to imagine himself as a poet.

"Green everywhere," replied the merchant. "When spring comes, the green is so piercing it hurts to look at it, and it rains almost every day."

Parveez sighed again, no doubt at the thought of so much water, and his long eyelashes fluttered like a woman's. I don't think the Dutchman noticed.

"We have cows that get fat from the rich green grass, and dairies that make the creamiest cheese. We grow yellow and red tulips, which require much water to thrive. Because we are a nation of water, we are also sailors. We have a saying: 'You must never turn your back on the sea.' We are always finding ways to tame her."

"You have blue eyes," said Parveez, "like the water."

I giggled quietly. I suspected that Parveez was thinking of attaching himself to this fellow, perhaps as a traveling companion whose poetry would be inspired by the sight of foreign lands.

The Dutchman smiled. "Even our houses sit on the sea. My own is built on one of the canals that run through the city. Because of the damp, my people like to warm their floors with your rugs. On top of them they put many items made of wood — things to sit on, things to eat on, things to lie on at night. We don't like to be near the floor, where it is moist and chilly."

"We have no need for that here," Gostaham said. "The ground is dry and comfortable."

"Where do you find so much wood?" Parveez asked the merchant with astonishment. "Your country sounds like a paradise."

"Our forests grow thick all over the country. A man can walk in with an ax and cut more wood than a horse can carry."

"Does it look like the countryside around the Caspian Sea, which is the greenest in all of Iran?" asked Parveez.

The Dutchman laughed. "What you call green, we call brown," he replied. "We have one hundred trees for every one of yours, even in the most luxuriant part of your land."

I thought back to the single cypress in my village. People who lived in a land as fertile as the Dutchman's must never have to experience the pain of a hungry belly.

The Dutchman wiped away the sweat on his forehead and drank the last of his sharbat. Gostaham and Parveez were drinking hot tea, which of course would cool them down more quickly, but the Dutchman didn't seem to know that.

"With so much water, you must have hammams beyond our understanding," Parveez said. "I can imagine huge pools of water, hot and cold, with fountains and cascades streaming from on high. You must be the cleanest people in all the world."

The farangi paused. "Well, no. We have no hammams."

Parveez looked surprised. "How do you keep clean?"

"Our women heat up a basin of water over the fire at home for special occasions, but we never bathe in the winter when it is cold."

Parveez's face twisted in disbelief, and I myself felt a disgust almost as deep as when I had had to empty the pans of night soil. "All winter — without a bath?"

"And all fall, and all spring, too. Usually, we bathe at the beginning of summer," said the merchant nonchalantly.

I thought of the rings under his arms. Without a bath, he would sweat over and over into his clothes until they smelled as rank as fields covered with dung. I was glad I wasn't sitting near him. The room fell quiet for a moment. The Dutchman scratched his head, and flakes of dandruff drifted onto his shoulders.

"I will miss your baths when I return home," he conceded. "The land of Iran is the paragon of pure, the baths are the promised land of purging, and the rose water is the perfume of paradise!" His expressions in Farsi were flawless and I could see that Gostaham and Parveez were delighted by his poetic words of praise.

A servant brought in trays of food and laid them in front of the guest. "Really, there is no need to go to so much trouble," said the Dutchman. "I simply wanted to inquire if we might do business together."

Gostaham twitched as he tried to contain his anger at this display of rudeness. He looked down at the carpet as he said, "Please, my friend, eat. We won't allow you to leave with an empty belly."

The Dutchman ate a few morsels grudgingly, with an unconcealed air of obligation. I was astonished by his barbarous manners. He seemed like an animal, incapable of normal human pleasantries.

It was very hot in the nook, but Gostaham probably wanted me to wait and hear what the Dutchman desired. When he had finished eating, he invited the Dutchman to explain why he was honoring us with his visit.

"I need to commission two matching rugs for an owner of the Dutch East India Company," he replied. "They are to be made with his family's coat of arms, and prepared with the finest of silk and the tightest of knots."

Gostaham quizzed him about the size, the colors, and the knots, and proposed a price so high it made me gasp. The Dutchman looked pained. The two began negotiating, but when neither would budge, Gostaham asked Samad to bring in coffee and sweetmeats, and broached another topic.

"It seems that the Dutch East India Company is making forays into every corner of the globe these days," Gostaham said. "What is the latest from the New World?"

"A fledgling concern has been established called the Dutch West India Company," replied the Dutchman, "which is developing a lucrative trade in furs. The firm is also trying to buy a vast island from the savages to make it easier to do business."

"Indeed!" Gostaham said, with a brief, shrewd smile. I knew that he would not be offering a bargain price to the Dutchman now that he had learned how well his patron's business was doing.

I went back to my loom. Before long, Samad appeared and told me to cover myself quickly, and I retrieved my chador from my room, wrapped it around myself, and returned to my knotting. After a few moments, Gostaham led the Dutchman into the courtyard. I spied Gordiyeh in the kitchen, where she could listen without being seen.

"This girl is a part of my family," Gostaham said to the Dutchman, "and she is a fine knotter and designer. What you see on the loom is all her own."

That wasn't true, of course.

"What I can see is that talent runs in the family," replied the Dutchman graciously. "Will the carpet be for sale?"

"Yes, as soon as it is done," Gostaham said.

"It is very beautiful," said the Dutchman. "Your fingers are so fast, I can hardly follow them."

That pleased me. I had become faster in the last few months because Gostaham had shown me how to save time with each knot.

"Husband," called Gordiyeh from the kitchen, where she remained hidden from view, "why don't you include her carpet as a special gift for our esteemed Dutchman? Then perhaps he will pay us the price you asked for the other two."

I froze.

"Now you're sweetening things!" said the Dutchman immediately, no doubt realizing he could charge his patron for two silk carpets while rolling up a free one for himself. "Let's sign an agreement!"

I hoped Gostaham would object, but he said nothing. The men returned to the Great Room so Parveez could commit the agreement to paper.

I sat at my loom, too dazed by disbelief to continue my work. After the Dutchman left, I thought I heard Gostaham and Gordiyeh arguing at the entrance of the house. Gordiyeh was saying something about how the Dutchman would be paying twice the Iranian price for the commissioned carpet, anyway. Gostaham's voice was too low for me to hear. If he thought his wife had erred, he didn't say anything to me. But how could he? He loved her too much to cross her.

Gordiyeh came into the courtyard and said, "I'm sorry I had to do that, but I was sure the Dutchman would not be able to resist such an offer. And you know how much we need the money."

It never looked to me like the family needed money, at least not the way my mother and I did. But beyond that, there was the matter of fairness.

"Gostaham promised that we could sell the carpet, and that the money would be ours after we paid him for the wool," I said.

Gordiyeh shrugged. "You can always make another carpet," she said lightly, as if my work didn't matter.

That was all I could bear. I went to our little room and stayed there for the rest of the day. When my mother learned what had happened, she uttered a string of curses on Gordiyeh's head that I thought would strike her down that minute. But she held back from saying anything to her, fearful of her sharp tongue and of how she might exact revenge.

I suspected our black luck was due to the comet. Everyone was talking about its malevolence and how it caused chaos such as earthquakes and lapses in behavior. Ali-Asghar had told us about a royal groom who invited a fellow groomsman to share the bread and salt of his table, only to be stabbed out of envy over his higher rank. Although I didn't dare say so, I wondered if Gordiyeh's actions could be ascribed to the same disruptive source.

I WAS SO ANGRY that night, I couldn't sleep, and the next day's work was more taxing than usual. I washed the laundry with the servants, drawing water from the well and beating the clothing with the strength of my whole body, wringing it out with my hands, and hanging it in the sun to dry. Then I had to peel and slice a hill of potatoes for Cook and pick all the stems out of the dried barberries she planned to use in a stew. Gordiyeh told me I needed to work faster, for she was expecting a houseful of guests that day. I had never felt more like a servant.

When the kitchen work was done, I knotted the carpet until my neck was sore and my legs were cramped beneath me, for now I wanted nothing more than to finish it so I could finally begin one of my own. I had no chance to rest, and before my afternoon chores were finished, I received an unexpected summons from Fereydoon. Normally, he sent a note in the morning or the day before, allowing me time to make myself ready. Fatigued beyond reason, I had to hurry to his house to be prepared for him, although it was the last thing I desired that day.

In the late afternoon, I rushed through the streets, which were deserted because it was so hot. A veil of dust seemed to hang in the air, and even the Friday mosque's blue dome looked dulled by the heat. When I arrived at Fereydoon's house, I was hot, thirsty, and tired, but the women gave me no respite. They pulled hair out of my eyebrows, which brought tears to my eyes, and removed it from my legs, which hurt even more. I fell asleep while I was in the tub. By the time they had finished with me, I hardly cared that Fereydoon had arranged for me to have a new silk tunic as blue as the Eternal River, with a brilliant yellow sheath underneath, nor that they were binding the ends of my hair with matching yellow ties embroidered with golden birds. I didn't even look at myself in the metal mirror. When the women led me into the room where I awaited Fereydoon, I tried to fight sleep, but my head was nearly on my chest when I heard him at the door.

Although I had been with Fereydoon more times than I could count, nothing had improved for me in our bedchamber. That filled me with regret, but at least I had stopped worrying about whether I was appealing to him. He seemed to take all his pleasures with great zest, whether food, wine, tobacco, or me.

Fereydoon burst in that evening as if he were bringing the wind with him, so quick were his movements. With twice his usual vigor, he pulled me into his arms and said, "I couldn't wait until tomorrow, so I summoned you on short notice. I had a long sleep this afternoon, just so I could be awake with you until day chases away night."

I tried to smile. I wanted nothing more than to rest, yet now I must be lively until dawn. When the evening meal arrived, he passed me tender pieces of lamb and chicken. I ate little so as not to be heavy with sleep. When he offered me wine mixed with milk, I refused it for the same reason. He looked disappointed as he poured it for himself.

After the servants cleared away the plates and departed, Fereydoon asked me to show him my new clothes. I stood and twirled, so that my wefts flew wide and I could see their yellow tails brightening the air and wrapping around my face and body.

"Sweet child of the south!" said Fereydoon, rising to join me and placing his hands on my waist. "You curve just like the moon."

He raised his hands to my face and smoothed my eyebrows with his fingertips, making me glad the women had shaped them, and said, "Crescent moons." Then, sweeping his hands over my breasts, he smiled and said, "Half-moons." And finally, grabbing my buttocks in his two hands, "Full moon."

I laughed at being so admired, which was a welcome change from the rest of my daily life. Fereydoon was teaching me that although my skin was not fair, I had curves beneath my clothes that could stir a man, even one as privileged and experienced as he was. I also felt something different in his manner, something softer than before. I didn't believe it had anything to do with me. Perhaps he had made a fine deal on an Arabian mare and wanted to celebrate with me in his bed.

Fereydoon cupped his hand on my belly and slid it lower, holding it there. "But this is what I like to see most of all—this plump mound rising from your body and swelling over your belly like the moon over the earth."

Fereydoon removed all my clothing and his and for a few moments he continued running his hands over the moons of my body. I loved it when he played with me this way and made my skin warm beneath his touch. I became heated and eager, craving more. But all too soon, he slid his thighs between mine, nudged my legs open, and began the work of sowing his seeds. I closed my eyes and panted a little because I knew that excited him, and I moved my hips in time to his. Maybe we would finish quickly tonight, I thought, imagining how delicious it would feel to close my eyes and sleep. My limbs felt as leaden as the heavy weights that athletes lift in the Houses of Strength. Perhaps I even fell asleep for a moment, because I believe I stopped moving. Rousing myself with a start, I quickly began thrusting my hips again to meet Fereydoon's while peeking at his face. His eyes were closed, and he seemed to be concentrating on something. There was a trickle of sweat at his temples. I shut my eyes and kept at my work. After what seemed like a long time, he stopped moving and sprawled on top of me as if he were exhausted. I didn't move, hoping that we were done.

"Lift your arms," he instructed.

Dutifully I put my arms overhead. He bit my breasts and began moving his hips again, and I made sure to concentrate on the task before me. We continued that way for a while, but Fereydoon was failing to meet his moment of bliss. He sighed — a short, frustrated exhalation — and paused again.

"Grab my back with your arms — grab me!" he said with longing in his voice. I put my arms around his back lightly as he thrust with what seemed like desperation. I began to feel dry and sore between my legs and wished that he would hurry. This act had never taken so long before. I glanced at Fereydoon's face again and was alarmed to see a look that reminded me of a man and his donkey I had seen earlier that day at a mill. Around and around they walked, pushing the heavy stone that crushes the grain, man and beast stupefied by the repetition of the task.

Was Fereydoon tired of me so soon? I lay rigidly in his arms, not knowing what to do. When nothing seemed to be happening, Fereydoon pulled his body away from mine and lay on his back, staring at the ceiling. Out of the corner of my eye, I was surprised to see the stiffness between his thighs, like a pole holding up a tent, just like on the first night we had shared together. But in his eyes was a look of dullness that seemed as endless as the sky. Minute after minute passed, so many that I became aware of the sound of people walking by the house in the dark.

"Roll onto your side," Fereydoon said finally, sounding annoyed. I obediently turned so that my back was facing his body and remained there with my legs closed, wondering what would happen next. He sighed again before lifting my right leg with his arm and bending my knee so my leg slid over his right hip. By then I was as dry as the desert sands, and when he tried to put himself inside me, he could no longer slide in. Sleep began creeping up on me again, with its soft, insistent pull.

Fereydoon pulled away from my body and lay on his back. He grabbed my hand and put it between his legs, showing me how to move it up and down.

"Faster," he said at first. Then: "Not so hard." And later: "Up near the top." And finally: "Never mind!"

Fereydoon turned away, and I heard the sound of skin slapping against skin, a noise that became louder and louder as the speed of his hand increased. Before long, he began to pant with pleasure and within just a few minutes he groaned and shed tears into his own palm. I had never known him to handle himself this way before. Why hadn't he found his pleasure with me? I thought I had done everything he had instructed me to do.

Without Fereydoon's body close to mine, I began shivering, but he didn't move. I rolled myself in the bed covers, feeling alone. We spoke together for a few moments, but our conversation left me even more confused. Before long, I heard Fereydoon snoring softly like a child. Though I was fatigued, sleep would not come to relieve me. I lay awake for a long time, trying to understand why I had failed. I knew I should have behaved as though I were delighted by Fereydoon's presence. But I had been tired beyond thought, and pleasing him felt like just one more task I had to do for someone else. I was weary, weary and worn. The last thing I heard before I finally fell asleep was the sound of donkeys braying as their masters led them to market. It seemed like the saddest sound I had ever heard.

When I opened my eyes the next morning, Fereydoon was gone. It was the first time he had left me without saying good-bye. The room seemed empty and lusterless without him. After donning my clothes, I rushed out the door and hurried home.

THAT AFTERNOON, after I finished my chores, I left Gostaham's house for Naheed's. Now, more than ever, I needed a friend. I longed to unburden my heart and hear her advice, but I knew I could not reveal myself to her. All she would have to do was tell Homa too

161

much one afternoon at the hammam, and the town would know my story before nightfall. If Fereydoon wasn't going to renew my contract — and now I had reason to believe he was dissatisfied — it would be better to let the sigheh die quickly.

All the way through Four Gardens, the sun beat on my head and the ground seemed to burn through my thin shoes. The light was so bright it hurt my eyes through my picheh. Even the river glinted sharply in the heat. Someone was grilling liver kebab, and the dirty smell of it seemed to catch inside my picheh. The thought of eating in this heat nauseated me. My belly churned. I stopped and bent over, longing to vomit, but nothing would come out.

When I arrived at Naheed's, she ushered me into her rooms and asked the servants to bring in lemon sharbat right away. "You look hot," she told me.

After I had refreshed myself and the servants were out of earshot, Naheed removed the latest letter from its hiding place in the sash around her waist. "You won't believe this," she said. "Just listen to what he writes."

Light of my heart, in recent months, I have come to know you better than any woman except those in my own family. God gave us the blessings of the word and the pen, but never did I expect that a woman could wield both with such beauty. Your alefs *are like a cypress tree, straight and tall; your* behs, *with their sweet dot beneath, are like the beauty mark on a lover's cheek. They have taken me captive; with every letter you write, my heart is more and more deeply ensnared. So completely have your words imprisoned me that I have begun seeing them in your face — glimpsed only once, alas, but enough beauty seen in that moment to last a lifetime. The locks around your face are like the letter* jim, *curling without regard to the way they hook a lover's heart. Your rosebud mouth, which is piercingly red, is tiny and precious like the letter* mim. *But most of all, when I dream of you I imagine your emerald eyes, as pretty and elegant as the letter* saad. *I am in a state of longing for your every word. Leave me in this state of distress no more! Consent to be my wife, to share every moment of your days and nights next to me, and I will promise to cherish you until the last letter of our lives is written.*

When Naheed finished reading, her eyes overflowed with tears and she sat still without wiping them. I had never seen a woman fall in love before, and I envied the purity of her feelings.

"Voy, voy!" I said. "What a gem, what a prince among men." But even as I said that, my heart was shedding the tears that Naheed was able to shed openly with her eyes. No one loved me the way Iskandar loved Naheed. I had not learned how to make Fereydoon's heart soar with love and longing, but, despite my grief, I must remain silent. I could not share my sorrows and dip into the sympathy and comfort I knew Naheed would have showered on me. That was the worst of all.

"Yes, Iskandar loves me," said Naheed, the words like honey on her tongue. "And my heart has been lost to his. I want nothing more than to spend my hours by his side, listening to his sweet words of love."

Now that I knew more about men and women, I didn't believe the polo player would only whisper words of love. He would want to nuzzle Naheed and to part her thighs, like Fereydoon had parted mine.

"Insh'Allah, he will love you with his words, but also with his body," I blurted out.

Naheed's eyes seemed to get clearer for a moment. "I have never heard you speak that way," she said. "What do you mean?"

I shouldn't have said anything, but it was too late. I thought back quickly to the things I had heard in my village. "Back home, after my friend Goli got married, she told me how important it was to her husband to take her at night," I said.

"Oh, that!" said Naheed with a look of disdain. "I suppose he will do whatever he wants to — that will be his privilege when I am his wife."

I took a sip of coffee. "You're not worried about that, not even a little?"

"Why should I worry? I just want him to hold me in his arms and utter the honeyed words he writes in his letters. If I have that, I will be content."

The last few weeks had taught me that things had to work between a man and a woman in the dark, things that had nothing to do with words. Would it be different for Naheed and Iskandar because they loved each other already?

"We will be just like Shireen and Khosrow, the happiest of lovers once they were finally united!" said Naheed exultantly, and to me she looked like a woman in the middle of a happy dream.

I smiled. "Iskandar didn't see you bathing naked in a stream, but I believe he saw enough of your face to be as entranced as when Khosrow surprised Shireen without her clothes."

"I knew I could ensnare him! I knew it!" said Naheed.

The more I thought about it, though, the more Naheed and Iskandar reminded me of Layli and Majnoon, for those two lovers had loved without the benefit of being together. What did they know about each other? Majnoon had starved himself in the wilderness, composing poetry about Layli that found a home on every Bedouin's lips. Layli had been sequestered by her family, who were certain he was mad. The two had gone to their graves filled with longing, yet what would have happened if they had been united? What if they had fumbled in the dark, and what if Layli had had to listen to the lonely sound of skin slapping against skin? Naheed couldn't know if being with her beloved was a taste of paradise until they shared the same pillow.

I knew I must stop getting lost in my own sad thoughts and try to help Naheed conclude her quest. "How will you get your parents to approve the marriage?" I asked.

Naheed's crafty smile lit up her face, and I was glad to see her back to her plotting self.

"Iskandar wrote to me that his mother and his sisters always bathe at Homa's hammam on the first day of the week. He told them to start looking for a pretty girl for him to marry, and he described someone exactly like me."

"That was clever," I said.

"I wish I had the ripeness that Homa praised you for at the hammam. I've been trying to eat more, but it doesn't help."

I protested. "Naheed-joon, you are the prettiest girl I've ever seen. There will be no doubt of their interest!"

Naheed smiled, secure after all in her beauty. "I will try to get them to notice me. If they like me, and if an offer is made from his family to mine, my parents will never know that Iskandar and I have secretly corresponded all this time."

"And what about his family—will your parents approve of them?"

Naheed put on a brave face. "His father tends horses for a governor in the provinces," she said.

I was astonished that he came from such humble stock. "Won't your parents insist on a rich man?"

"Why should they, when I have money enough for two?"

"But Naheed—" I said. She looked away, and I didn't have the heart to continue. "May God grant your every wish!"

I prayed for her happiness with all my heart, but I felt much older than her, and wiser, too. While Naheed was singing the blessings of love from afar, I was mired in the problems of a marriage unfulfilled. And although I had arrived wanting to unburden my heart to her, I was beginning to understand that it probably would have been of no use. She was caught in the web of her dreams, and they were much prettier than the truth of married life that I had come to know.

Naheed put her arms around me and laid her cheek against mine. I smelled the sweet musk she used to perfume her clothes. "If I couldn't unburden my heart to you, I'm sure I would die," she said. "Thank you for being such a loyal friend."

It was good to feel the strength of her affection, for I had suffered a crimp in my heart ever since we had been caught at polo. I returned her embrace, but then sat upright and alone.

"For a while," I confessed, "I thought you wanted to be friends just so that you'd have a companion for the games."

Two pink spots appeared on Naheed's cheeks, and she looked away.

"Perhaps that was true at first," she admitted, "but not anymore. You are the kindest friend, the most unaffected, and the most true. I'll always be grateful you took the blame for me at polo. If it wasn't for you, my love for Iskandar would have been discovered and destroyed."

"It was nothing," I mumbled, blushing.

Naheed's eyes were bright and happy. "I hope you and I will share our secrets and our hearts forever," she said.

"I hope so, too," I said, and a much-needed spring of joy welled up in my heart, although it was quickly followed by melancholy, for I ached to confide in her as she had confided in me. But I didn't mind taking the blame for polo now that she had revealed how much it had meant to her. Naheed's love for Iskandar had softened her, like Layli's for Majnoon.

First there wasn't and then there was. Before God, no one was.

When Layli's mother told her about the man she was to marry, she responded with neither anger nor tears. Bowing her head, Layli replied obediently, "I am yours to command, Mother." For what did it matter?

Layli's parents had chosen a wealthy man from a respected Bedouin tribe. For her wedding day, the families erected tall black tents in the desert and furnished them with soft carpets, bowls of fruit, braziers of incense, and oil lamps. Layli wore a red gown embroidered with silver thread and silver shoes. Around her neck were fine silver chains with carnelian stones inscribed with verses from the Holy Qur'an.

When Layli's husband greeted her for the first time, she felt nothing but indifference. He smiled at her, revealing a gap where he had lost a tooth. As they exchanged their wedding vows, Layli could think only of the man she loved, Majnoon.

Majnoon was part of her tribe, and they had played together in the desert as children. He had once brought her a blooming yellow desert flower and dropped it shyly in her lap. Even when she reached the age of ten, had been veiled, and could no longer play with boys, she thought about Majnoon and loved him. He grew into a handsome young man, tall and thin in his long white tunic and turban. He could not suppress a smile when she walked past. And although he could not see her, her beauty was something well known about the tribe, as accepted as the light of the moon.

When he was old enough, Majnoon begged his father to approach Layli's parents for their daughter. They refused, for Majnoon had strange habits. He had already taken to spending days by himself in the desert. He would return thin, wasted, clad in nothing but a white turban and white loincloth, and it took time before his senses returned. That was how he had earned his nickname Majnoon, which means "crazy."

"What is wrong with your son?" asked Layli's father.

Majnoon's father could not answer, for he did not know what drove his son into the desert, or why he returned shattered, as if he had glimpsed the Divine.

After Layli's parents refused him, Majnoon fled to the desert and lived alone, surviving almost without food or water. Whenever he saw a gazelle or another animal in a trap, he released it, and soon the animals began gathering around his camp and lying down beside his fire. Predators became friends in his presence, and one and all protected him from harm.

With his beasts around him, Majnoon began composing poetry that mentioned the name of his beloved, verses so beautiful that passing strangers memorized them and brought them to other Bedouin camps. Soon Layli's name was heard everywhere and her parents decided she must marry, for the sake of her honor. Knowing she had no hope of marrying her true love, Layli accepted her parents' choice, for she must not defy them. And one man was just as unsuitable as the next if it was not Majnoon.

After the wedding festivities, Layli sat quietly on her marriage bed, waiting for her husband, Ibn Salam. Delighted to claim her as his prize, he entered and offered her a plate of the sweetest dates, carefully selected from the date palms he owned. She tasted them politely and spoke with him amicably, the very picture of an obedient wife. But when he touched her hand, she withdrew it. Even as the night fled, he did not dare approach her lips with his or put his sun-browned hands on her small waist. At dawn, he fell asleep beside her, fully clothed, and she curled up near him and did the same.

Life continued in this fashion for months. Layli greeted Ibn Salam with respect, prepared his tea and his meals, and even massaged his feet when he was tired, but would never allow him near her flawless treasure. For he was an ordinary man. He could ride a horse, hunt with a falcon, and earn enough from his date palms to keep them in comfort. But he would never compose poetry like Majnoon, nor make her heart soar with longing. Layli respected her husband and even admired him but felt no stirrings of desire.

Despite her indifference, Ibn Salam was falling more and more in love with Layli. That she should refuse to open her heart hurt him deeply. He once considered taking her against her will, for after all, she was his. But what good would that do? Layli was a woman who would come to him herself, or not at all. He resolved to wait and hope that she might one day soften, and that made his heart grow bigger with each passing day. Although she was as closed to him as a shell, he became as wide open to her as the sea. No man treated his wife with more tenderness or loved her more completely.

As months turned into years, and still Layli remained chaste, she at last began to wonder about her decision. All her friends had married and were bearing children. She alone knew nothing of a man's body or of holding her own child in her arms. *Didn't she deserve the same life as others? Shouldn't she, the glory of her tribe, offer her husband all of herself, and hope that her love would one day blossom to match his?*

In the market a few days later, she heard a new verse about Majnoon's love for Layli on an old man's lips.

> My foot welcomes pain,
> For it reminds me of my beloved.
> I would rather walk in Layli's field of thorns
> Than in another's garden of roses.

Layli drew in a breath. "Where is he?" she asked the man, knowing Majnoon must be near.

"He has returned," replied the man, "and looks for no one but you."

"And I him," she replied. "Tell him to meet me this evening, in the grove of palms." For she had to test her love to see if it remained pure and strong.

Layli told her husband she was going to her mother's tent to drink tea. She arrived at the palm grove, wrapped in her veils, after dark. Majnoon sat in a patch of moonlight, clad only in a loincloth. He looked taller and thinner, for he had wasted away; she could see all the ribs jutting out of his body. He seemed like a creature of the wild now, naked before God and the sky.

"At last, my beloved!" he cried.

"At last!" she echoed. She had not seen him for more years than she could count.

"My Layli! Your tresses are as black as the night; your eyes as dark and lovely as a gazelle's. I shall love you always."

"And I you, life of mine!" She sat down just outside the circle of moonlight that bathed him.

"Yet now I must question your love," Majnoon added, his eyes full of sorrow. "Why have you betrayed me?"

"What do you mean?" she replied, drawing back with surprise.

"You have a husband!" he said, shivering, though the night air had not grown cool. "Why should I believe that you love me still?"

"I have a husband in name only," she replied. "In all these years, I could

have given myself to him a thousand times over, yet my fortress has remained unvanquished."

"For me," he replied, and there was joy in his eyes.

"For you," she answered. "For what is he compared to you?"

She wrapped her garments more closely around her, as if to protect herself from prying eyes. "Yet, truth be told, lately I have come to wonder about the life I have chosen," she added. "You are free. You may go as you please, live with your animals, and compose your verse. You may sing out what ails you, and all will repeat your sorrow. But I am confined here, alone, and may tell no one for fear of losing my honor. Now tell me: For whom is it harder to be faithful?"

Majnoon sighed. "For you, my beloved. For you. That is why, with my whole heart, I abandon you to your husband's love, if you choose to give yourself to him. For you deserve love as much as any woman. For my part, I shall always love you no matter what you do."

Layli remained silent, for she was deep in thought.

"Layli, my beloved, I am your slave. When I see a cur that has passed near your house, I kiss its dirty paws with reverence, for it has been close to you. When I look in the mirror, I no longer see myself, but only you. Don't call me by my name anymore. Call me Layli, for that's who I have become!"

Layli felt her heart blossom. What was the good of the love of a man like Ibn Salam—what was the use of his tired feet, the stink of his tunic after a day at the hunt, the stories he had spoken a thousand times? Yet how could she promise herself to Majnoon, who would never belong to her?

"How do you keep the faith of your love?" she asked. "Do you not shiver with disappointment and dry up with yearning? Do you never wish to abandon me?"

Majnoon laughed. "What good would my love be if it were so easily disturbed by obstacles?" he asked. "When I was younger, I suffered so much disappointment over your parents' refusal that I thought my heart would burst. But the more I thought of you and wept over you, the deeper and clearer my love became. Suffering has revealed to me the depths of my own heart. What is ordinary love compared to that? It ebbs and flows and is easily swayed. But *my love for you has become so deep and strong it will never wane. There are few certainties in this world, but such love is one of them."*

Layli wanted to melt into Majnoon's thin, wasted body, to live with him and his animals under the clear desert sky, to hear the verses on his lips. But there could be no honor in such a life, for all good people would shun her. There was no hope of ever living with him on earth.

But perhaps that was not the most precious thing. Even if Layli could not have Majnoon by her side, she could always have his love. She felt her heart expanding, growing bigger and bigger until it encompassed nothing but him. That was love, she thought, not the everyday fare that Ibn Salam was offering her. That was what loosened tears from her eyes and made her wild with ecstasy. "My beloved, my heart is yours!" she exclaimed. "When I see my reflection in a basin of water, I shall see only you. We are so close it matters little whether we are near or far."

"My Layli," he replied, "you are like the blood circulating in my veins. If I cut myself, I rejoice, for I feel your warmth."

It was late, and Layli dared not stay any longer. She walked back to her tent alone, her heart bursting with joy. She would remain Ibn Salam's wife, but in name only. Her love for Majnoon was so deep it needed nothing but itself. From now on, he would always be Layli, and she would always be Majnoon.

CHAPTER FOUR

A week went by with no word from Fereydoon. Perhaps he had gone to the south on business, I thought, knowing his father often sent him to examine costly steeds to determine their worth. Or perhaps he had gone to visit his parents or his sister, or taken a hunting trip for pleasure. Every evening, I asked Gostaham and Gordiyeh if any letters had arrived that pertained to me. At first they simply said no, but as the days passed, they began to answer my question with pitying looks. After another week, I started to jump when I heard the knocker and scurried to the door on any excuse.

Although he had been angry with me the last time we parted, still I hoped he would want me for another three months. My mother and I needed the money. And although I wasn't in love, at least not the way Naheed loved Iskandar, there were mysteries I still hoped to understand. Perhaps if we had more time together, I would learn to love him. And there was always the hope that he would make me a permanent wife, or that I would get pregnant.

I had already bled twice since I had married Fereydoon. Before each time, my mother had watched me closely for signs that I was carrying a child. After I began bleeding, my mother said, "Don't worry, azizam. There is always next month." But I knew she was disappointed and worried that I would be as slow to conceive as she had been.

In the third month of my marriage, my mother made me a special medicine that was supposed to encourage pregnancy, a green brew that reminded me of brackish water. She also commented on everything I ate and did.

"Praise be to God!" she said one day when I had consumed a mound of sour fruit torshi with my meal. "That's just what I craved when I was pregnant with you."

I was delighted, for I hoped for a child as much as she did. Then it would be certain that we would have a home of our own, and would be taken care of by Fereydoon for the rest of our days.

That evening, my mother spent a long time on the roof reading the stars. When she returned to our room, she told me the child would be a boy, for Mars was in ascendancy. "He will have your father's good looks," she said, more pleased than I had seen her in a long time.

Gordiyeh encouraged my mother's hopes. "You're looking very round today," she said to me one morning, staring at my face and my stomach. And then, turning to my mother, she said, "Being a grandmother is even better than being a mother."

"I hope I will hold my grandchild soon," she replied. But I didn't feel any different. I began counting the time remaining until the end of my contract, feeling more restless with each passing day.

THE AFFECTIONATE TIES between Gordiyeh and Gostaham never ceased to baffle me. I had seen my father perform kindnesses for my mother—massaging her feet when they were weary, or surprising her with new leather shoes—but I had never seen a man give as much as Gostaham gave to Gordiyeh. He was always bringing her gifts, such as date cookies, bolts of velvet, or flasks of perfume. Why did he love her so? What did she do to bind him to her like a moth circling a flame? From the outside, she had little to offer. Her face was doughy like unbaked bread, and she moved heavily, her flesh lumpy and dimpled. She often wielded a sharp tongue, especially when she was worried about money. And yet Gordiyeh was like a diamond, hard but with a flash in her eyes that made her desirable.

One afternoon at the midday meal, Gordiyeh came into the Great Room dressed in a fine silk tunic the color of a lake, the curve of her large breasts visible beneath the fabric. A single emerald on a gold chain drew the eyes there. She had covered her hair with embroidery, drawn a line of kohl on her eyelids, darkened her lush eyebrows, and put a touch of color on her cheeks and lips. When Gostaham arrived, she told him she had spent the morning helping Cook make one of his favorite dishes, rice with lentils and lamb. As I brought hot bread into the Great Room, I watched her offer him the most tender bits of lamb and refill his drinking vessel with sweet pomegranate sharbat. She even brought out some wine, closely guarded in her storerooms, and served him a few glasses with his food. Gostaham's eyes softened and his round body relaxed into the cushions. Before long, he began telling jokes.

"Once there was a woman who married three times and was still a virgin," he was saying to her as I brought in some of the candied almonds we had made earlier that year. "The first husband was a Rashti who couldn't do anything because he was as limp as old celery. The second was a Qazvini who liked boys, so that's the only way he took her."

"And the third?" asked Gordiyeh, with a teasing smile.

"The third was a language teacher who only used his tongue."

She laughed deep in her belly, and I saw Gostaham's eyes alight on the opulent flesh that trembled around her emerald. She was courting him! But why? It was not something I imagined that older couples needed to do. And what did he mean by the teacher who only used his tongue?

By the end of the meal, the air around Gostaham seemed heavy with desire. When he suggested it was time for an afternoon nap, Gordiyeh arose and followed him out of the room with a long, husky laugh. I watched her go with him into his rooms rather than her own, which was peculiar. I had never seen her behave this way before.

My mother and I helped Cook clear the dishes from the Great Room and put them into buckets for washing. After I cleaned the serving plates, she rinsed them and stacked them to dry. It wasn't long before I began to hear Gordiyeh make a noise that sounded like small repeated screams. I strained to hear what she was saying, bracing myself for bad news, but her cries were wordless.

"What's wrong with Gordiyeh?" I asked Cook.

She was putting away the leftover rice. "Not a thing," she replied, avoiding my eyes.

My mother and I continued washing in silence. After we finished the serving spoons and vessels, we began scrubbing the oily pots used to cook the meat and rice. All was quiet for another half hour, at which point I heard the same loud cries again.

"Voy!" said my mother. "Even after all these years!"

"That's how she gets what she wants," replied Cook. "Just wait and see."

"It doesn't sound real."

Cook laughed so hard she began coughing and had to put down the pot she was scrubbing.

"You may be right, but it still works," she said when she had finally recovered.

What exactly was making her scream with such abandonment and pleasure? With Fereydoon, I had had occasion to pant, but nothing I had ever done with him had made me feel like howling like that. I wished I knew why.

Early the next morning, Gostaham sent a servant to summon me to his workroom. He looked better rested than I had seen him in weeks; even the bags under his eyes were less dark than usual. I wondered if that was because of what Gordiyeh had given him the afternoon before.

"Sit here," said Gostaham, patting the cushion beside him. "I need your help on a sewing project."

He unrolled a scrap of carpet about two handbreadths long. It had a coarse pattern of wild red tulips and had been abandoned before its fringes were finished.

"I bought this yesterday evening for Gordiyeh," he said.

I must have looked surprised, for surely she would not appreciate such an ordinary carpet when her husband was a master of the craft.

Gostaham laughed at my expression. "Here's the real gift," he said, pulling something out of his sash. It was a heavy gold chain with rubies set in square mounts, each of which was surrounded by hanging pearls. I caught my breath.

"I want you to sew this onto the surface of the carpet, trying your best to conceal the rubies among the humble tulips," he said.

Gordiyeh would unroll the carpet, thinking it was nothing, and would have to search for a moment to uncover the hidden gems.

"She will be dazzled," I said. "Wouldn't it be a wonder to knot a whole rug with jewels like these!"

"It happened once," replied Gostaham. "The most famous treasure of the last Sassanian shah, Yazdegerd, was a jewel-studded carpet. That's what gave me the idea, although my approach is necessarily more modest."

"Where is it now?" I asked, eager to see it.

"Destroyed," Gostaham replied. "Nearly one thousand years ago, the Arab general Sa'd ibn Abi Waqqis marched to Yazdegerd's white stone palace and stormed it with an army of sixty thousand men. When they entered the palace to loot its booty, they were awestruck by its wondrous carpet, a lush garden whose roses gleamed with rubies and whose river sparkled with blue sapphires. Even its trees were knotted in silver, with white blossoms made of pearls. Sa'd and his looters slashed the carpet into parcels of booty—according to their own accounts!—extracting the jewels to sell and using the remaining scraps as trophies."

"It is an outrage," I said softly.

Gostaham smiled. "But what a story!" he replied. He left me to go to the royal rug workshop, and I returned to the andarooni to borrow a thick needle and some red thread from Shamsi. Back in Gostaham's workroom, where I knew I would not be disturbed, I held the necklace against my own bosom. The stones were deliciously heavy and cool on my chest. I wondered what it would be like to be so admired that a man would want to please me with such a costly gift.

Threading my needle, I pushed it through the back of the carpet in the middle of a tulip and lightly affixed the first ruby in place. It almost seemed to vanish, except for its sparkle. I continued that way with every gem, arranging the gold chain so it looked like vines spiraling through the carpet's surface.

I had a lot of time to think as I sewed Gordiyeh's gift. She was not beautiful, and she was often ill-tempered and capricious. Yet with a single afternoon of love, she had made her husband's heart soar and loosened his purse strings. Perhaps it was because she was a *seyyedeh:* The descendants of the Prophet were known for having sexual powers beyond those of other women. After years of marriage, Gordiyeh was still getting her husband to do exactly what she wanted, while I could hardly keep my husband's attention for three months. I longed to know all the things Gordiyeh knew so that I could bind Fereydoon to me.

*   *   *

WHILE I WAS waiting to hear from Fereydoon, I was not idle. To keep myself from thinking about him, I worked long hours on the Dutchman's carpet. Sometimes, when I was stiff from knotting, my mother helped me. She'd sit beside me in the courtyard and I would call out the colors for both of us, since the pattern was complicated and unfamiliar to her. It was then that I had a bold idea: What if I could find a few women knotters and hire them to make my designs? That's exactly what they did in the royal rug workshop and in the rug factories that dotted the city.

I even knew who I would ask. On one of my trips to the bazaar, I had noticed a woman selling her own rugs among the other peddlers at the Image of the World. She had made several woolen carpets in the Isfahani style, with a sunburst in the center radiating out to a starry sky or to a garden bursting with flowers. I had stopped to look at her work.

"May God praise the blooms of your hands!" I said. "Your work is very fine."

The woman thanked me but looked uncomfortable. I asked her if she had been selling carpets in the bazaar for a long time, knowing that most women would prefer it if male family members peddled their wares.

"No, only recently," she replied, again looking uneasy. "My husband is ill and can't work. I have two boys to feed —" And here her face crumpled, as if she might burst into tears.

I pitied her. "May your luck soon be brighter!" I said. "With such fine work, I know it will."

Her shy smile made her face look radiant. From then on, whenever I went to the bazaar, I stopped and said hello to Malekeh. Her carpets did not sell until she offered one of them for almost nothing. She nearly wept when she told me about it, for she had barely recovered the cost of the wool.

"But what could I do?" she asked. "My children had to eat."

She was in an even worse position than my mother and me, and I wondered if there might be some way to help her.

The first thing I had to do, though, was finish the Dutchman's carpet. I worked on it steadily with my mother's help, and now that I was a much faster knotter, it grew quickly. Although I still burned with rage that Gordiyeh had given it away without consulting me, I also felt comforted by the beauty of the pink, orange, and magenta flowers that were blossoming on my loom. In the future, I would use what Gostaham had taught me about color for my own gain.

The day that my mother and I lifted the rug off the loom and made the fringes was a happy one for everyone in the household. For Gordiyeh and Gostaham, it meant they could satisfy an important client with a fine gift. For my mother, it meant that I could start another carpet that might help us earn our independence. For me, it marked the end of a long, bitter apology.

When the Dutchman came to claim the carpet, I hid myself in the nook off the stairwell to observe events in the Great Room. Gostaham called for coffee and melon, batting away the Dutchman's eager requests to see the rug until the proper amount of conversation had occurred. Then he had Ali-Asghar fetch it and roll it out before the Dutchman's feet. From my perch, I had a view of the carpet that allowed me to see it in a new way. If I had been a bird flying overhead, that's what a garden might have looked like, with its wealth of blossoms in joyful shades.

The Dutchman's eyes opened wide for a moment. "It makes me think of the gardens of heaven," he said. "May we all hope to see them when our time on earth has expired!"

"God willing," replied Gostaham.

The Dutchman fingered the carpet. "I am certain that even Queen Elizabeth of England never possessed a carpet that could rival such fine work," he said. "Please accept my thanks for such an unparalleled treasure."

My heart overflowed with joy to hear my work described as better than anything owned by a great queen, even if the Dutchman was exaggerating. Perhaps now Gostaham and Gordiyeh would see my value.

"I am delighted that you are so satisfied with the product of my looms," Gostaham said, and he beamed his broad smile toward the carved plaster, where he knew I was listening.

The men began discussing the carpets that the Dutchman had commissioned on behalf of the wealthy merchant, which were being made by workers at the royal rug workshop. They arranged an appointment for him to see them, and then a servant showed him to the door.

THEY SAY THAT the glorious Prophet Mohammad, who wiped the sweat off his brow while ascending to the throne of God, spent seven lifetimes in each of the seven heavens, yet returned to earth before his sweat reached the ground. How is this possible? They say it's possible for time to expand into years for one person, while for another it consumes only an instant.

Indeed, each day that I didn't have word from Fereydoon seemed to stretch longer than the last. As I squatted in the courtyard two days before the expiration of my marriage, cracking walnuts and pulling out the tough dividers that kept the two halves of the flesh apart, I felt as if I were living out a lifetime in every breath.

Not long after dawn, the sun was already hot, and I paused to wipe the sweat off my face. More out of distress than hunger, I put half a walnut in my mouth without looking at it. It was so rotten my tongue curled. Just at that moment, before I could swallow my theft, Gordiyeh came out of the kitchen, crossing the courtyard in the direction of the storerooms.

"Are they flavorful?" she asked, making it clear she had seen me eating.

I swallowed with difficulty and smiled at her as if I hadn't understood her meaning.

"*Salaam aleikum,*" I said.

"Cook is making pomegranate-walnut chicken — isn't that your
favorite?"

"All except for her lamb with sour lemon," I replied, knowing
that Gordiyeh liked to remind me where my bread and salt were
coming from.

Gordiyeh peered into the mortar, which was full of nut meats.
"Be careful — you've got a shell in there," she said.

It was so jagged it could have cracked a tooth. I was not usually
so clumsy at my work, yet perhaps it was no surprise, since my mind
kept straying. I tossed the shell away, but now Gordiyeh was dipping
her fingers into the ground nuts to check their size.

"Make them more like powder," she said. "They need to almost
dissolve in the syrup."

Cook was distilling it right now, boiling the juice of pomegranates with spoonfuls of sugar. The air was heavy with the tart-sweet
scent, which normally made my mouth water, but not today.

"Chashm," I said. Gordiyeh looked satisfied, for she liked me
to be obedient. Under my breath, I muttered, "They're better
crunchy."

I launched my pestle at the nuts, grinding them into nothingness. The sweat rose again on my forehead, and I began to feel sticky
under my clothes.

A few minutes later, Gordiyeh emerged from the storerooms
with her hands full of onions.

"Ay, Khoda!" she said as she came out. "The way everyone has
been eating, there's nothing left in there."

I tried to look sympathetic, although I knew the storerooms
were packed with pyramids of costly red saffron, fat dates from the
south bathing in their own sugary juices, casks of strong wine, and
enough rice to feed a family for a year.

"Shall I pound fewer nuts?" I asked, hoping her concern about wasting food might save me work.

Gordiyeh paused, as if she couldn't decide whether more work or less wasting would be better. "Go ahead and pound them — we'll save them for later if we don't need them," she finally said.

I tipped out the nuts I had finished pulverizing and scooped up others, trying to behave as though this were any other day. Gordiyeh paused for a moment longer, her eyes on the walnuts. "Still no word?" she asked.

If there had been a letter, with Fereydoon's signature swooping like a bird in flight, she would have heard about it from Gostaham. There was no need to ask, other than to remind me that my status was falling in the household. I already felt it in the type of tasks Gordiyeh assigned to me, like the nut pounding, which was normally Shamsi's job. Perhaps she had already given up on him, and indeed, if I didn't hear from Fereydoon today, I probably never would. I was too overcome for a moment to continue my work.

"Poor animal!" said Gordiyeh, as she returned to the kitchen. "Insh'Allah, you'll receive a message from him soon."

Whenever I thought about the last time I had been with Fereydoon, it was like touching a pot that had been stewing over a fire. I drew back quickly, blistered to the core. When he had wanted to talk, I listened, and when he wanted my body, I let him do as he pleased. I didn't understand how I had failed him.

I continued slamming the pestle into the nuts. How much had changed since my mother and I had moved from my village to Isfahan! I had been as protected as a silkworm in its cocoon. I longed to be a fifteen-year-old virgin again who knew nothing of the impetuous shifts of the stars.

At the midday meal, I couldn't eat much, which surprised Cook, who knew how I relished her pomegranate sauce. "Akh!" I cried out when I crunched on a sharp shell hidden in the sauce. Otherwise, the meal was quieter than usual, and my mother looked worried whenever our glances met.

Afterward, I helped clean up and scrubbed the burnt rice out of a pot until my fingers were raw. Before everyone went to take their afternoon rest, I asked Gordiyeh whether any errands needed to be done. With a pleased expression, she told me to go to the bazaar to buy *gaz,* the sticky nougat with pistachios that her grandchildren loved. I left Gostaham's house, wrapped in my chador, with my picheh covering my face, and walked quickly to the gaz shops in the Great Bazaar. I made my purchase and then, instead of going home, I traversed the Image of the World and entered the bazaar at its south end. Taking a long route to the river to avoid seeing anyone I knew, I walked past tunic makers, fruit and vegetable hawkers, and pot and pan sellers until I was outside the bazaar near the Thirty-three Arches Bridge. I looked around quickly to make sure no one recognized me before I crossed it and walked upstream to the new Armenian part of the city.

I had never ventured alone among so many Christians. Shah Abbas had moved thousands of Armenians to New Julfa—some say against their will—to serve him as merchants in the silk trade. Many had become rich. I walked by their ornate church and peeked inside. The walls and ceiling were covered with images of men and women, including a painting of a group of men eating together. They had halos around their heads, as if they were meant to be worshipped. I saw another painting of a man carrying a piece of wood on his back, with a terrible look of suffering in his eyes, followed by a woman who looked as if she would give her life for his. So perhaps it was true that the Christians worshipped human idols as well as God.

Gostaham had told me that the Shah graced the Armenians with his presence during religious celebrations twice a year, yet when an Armenian architect had designed a church that was taller than the tallest mosque, his hands had been cut off. I shivered at the thought, for what could an architect—or a rug maker—do without hands?

Leaving the church, I turned down a small alley and continued until I spotted the sign that Kobra had once mentioned: a page of writing affixed to a door painted spring-green. I couldn't read much of it, but I knew this was where I was supposed to be. I knocked, looking around again anxiously, for I had never gone on an errand like this before.

The door was opened by an older woman with startling blue eyes and long honey-colored hair lightly covered with a purple head scarf. Without a word, she beckoned me inside and shut the door. I followed her through a small courtyard and into a house with low ceilings and whitewashed walls. The room we sat down in was full of strange things: animal bones in ceramic pots, ewers of red and golden liquids, baskets overflowing with roots and herbs. Astrological symbols and cosmological charts were pinned to the walls.

I removed my coverings and sat against a cushion. Rather than ask me anything, the woman lit a clump of wild rue, closed her eyes, and began reciting poetry in a singsong voice. Then she opened her eyes and said, "Your problem is a man."

"Yes," I replied. "How did you know?"

The charm maker didn't answer. "How did you come to Isfahan?"

No doubt she could tell from my accent that I was from the south. I told her my mother and I had left our village after my father had died and we had almost starved, and that I was embroiled in a three-month sigheh with a wealthy man.

The charm maker's blue eyes looked troubled. "Why didn't he offer to make you his full-fledged wife?" she asked.

"I'm told he must marry a woman who can bear him suitable heirs."

"In that case, why didn't your family wait to find you a proper marriage?"

"I don't know." I didn't want to tell her about how I had destroyed the rug.

The woman looked puzzled. She eyed my attire, a simple red cotton tunic and orange cotton robe, bound with a red sash. "Are there money problems in your household?"

"My uncle and his family are very comfortable, but his wife always worries about the burden of feeding my mother and me."

"So they were gambling that your husband would keep you a long time, and perhaps shower you with gifts."

"Yes," I replied, "but my marriage ends the day after tomorrow."

"Voy!" replied the charm maker, looking alarmed. "We don't have much time."

"Can you make a charm to make him want me?" I asked.

"It's possible," she said, but she seemed to be searching my face for clues. "What is your husband like?"

"He has a lot of energy," I said. "He tells everyone around him what to do. He is often very impatient."

"Does he love you?"

"He has never said so," I replied, "but last time, he bought me new clothes, and it was almost as if he liked me." I said this in a tone full of wonder, for I had only just grasped it myself.

"Yet you are not speaking like a woman in love, her eyes shining bright with joy."

"No," I admitted with a sigh.

"Do you love your husband?"

I thought for a moment before answering. "I don't tremble the way one of my friends does when she talks about her beloved," I said. "Being with him is something I've had to do."

"In that case, do you have any idea why he might not have sent for you?"

"No," I said miserably.

Her blue eyes seemed to pierce mine. She fanned the rue, whose sharp smell made my eyes water. "How have your nights been together?"

I told her how shy I had felt, yet how Fereydoon had often kept me up until dawn, taking me in the four corners of the room.

"That's what might be expected in the beginning," she said.

"I suppose so, but now it seems as if the fire of his passion is dying."

"Already?" She paused and again seemed to be striving to understand something. "What happened the last time you saw him?"

"I don't know," I said, trying to avoid the question. "I always do what I'm told, but I sense his weariness."

"As if he was bored?"

"Yes," I said, shifting uncomfortably on my cushion and looking away. There was a long silence, broken only when I admitted in a halting voice that Fereydoon had pleased himself without me.

"Did he say anything to you afterward?"

I had not allowed myself to think about this for many days. "He asked me if I enjoyed being with him. I was so startled by the question that I said, 'I am honored beyond my years to be in your world-brightening presence.' "

The charm maker smiled, but it was not a happy smile. "That was very formal of you."

Now that I had begun, I thought I might as well tell her everything. "Then he lifted his eyebrows and said, 'You needn't talk with me like that when we're alone.' "

"So then you told him the truth about how you felt?"

"Not exactly; it was the first time he had given me permission to speak my mind. What I said was, 'My only concern has been pleasing you.' He bent his body over mine, stroked the hair away from my face, and said, 'Child of the south, I know that. And so far, you have. But there's more to this than pleasing me, you know.' Then he asked me if I liked what we did together at night, and I said yes."

"Is that the truth?"

I shrugged. "I don't understand why people talk about it so much all the time."

The charm maker looked at me so sympathetically I thought I might weep.

"Why don't you like it as much as he does?"

"I don't know," I said again, shifting on my cushion and wishing I had not come. The charm maker took one of my hands and held it between hers to comfort me. I felt just the way I had right before my father's death, as if I were about to lose everything at once.

"I can't endure the way things unravel," I said all of a sudden, not knowing why.

The charm maker looked as if she understood. "My child, you can't stop what God gives and takes away, but you, too, can end things. Promise me you'll remember that."

"I promise," I said, though it was the last of my worries.

"Now that I understand your problem, there are a few things I can do to help you," said the charm maker. "But first I want to know this: Isn't it possible that your husband will take a permanent wife?"

I paused for a moment, remembering that right before I got married, Gordiyeh had said that Homa was already looking for a girl suitable to be the mother of his heirs.

"Of course," I said.

"Then let me make you a charm to knot their path," she said. She reached into a basket that contained many balls of thread. Choosing the seven colors of the rainbow, she knotted the threads together in seven places and then bound the cord around my throat.

"Wear it until it falls off," she said. "And don't tell your husband what it's for."

"If I see him again," I said miserably.

"God willing, you shall," she replied. "And if you do, you must try harder to please him."

I was taken aback by her suggestion. "I thought I was already doing everything he wanted."

The charm maker stroked my hand as if she were soothing a difficult child. "I don't think so," she said gently.

My cheeks flushed with shame. "I wish I knew the things my mother knew when she was my age," I said bitterly. "My father loved her every minute of their life together."

"What do you think her secret was?"

I told her that my mother's ability to tell stories had magnetized my father's love, even though he was once the most handsome man in the village. I did not have such gifts.

The charm maker stopped me. "Imagine for a moment that you were the one telling a story instead of your mother," she said. "Let's say it's the one about Fatemeh the spinner girl. At the beginning, you captivate your listeners by telling them how Fatemeh's father drowns in a shipwreck, leaving her to fend for herself. But what if, rather than waiting until the end of the story to tell them how she fares, you tell them right away?"

"That would be silly," I said.

"Indeed," she replied. "So how do you think a story should be told?"

"When my mother tells tales, she puts the beginning, the middle, and the end in their proper place."

"That's right," said the charm maker. "The storyteller teases you with a little bit of information here and a little there. She keeps you in a state of wonder until the very end, when she finally sates your desire."

I knew exactly what she meant. My mother's listeners became entranced, staring at her with glazed eyes and open mouths as if they had forgotten where they were.

The charm maker smoothed back her honey-hued hair. "So think of your evenings with your husband as a time when you tell him a story, but not with words. To him, it's an old tale, so you need to learn to tell it in new ways."

I blushed again, but this time it felt like a burn starting deep within my liver and spreading until even my toes were tingling. "I've already had a few ideas," I admitted, "but I've been too ashamed to try them out."

"Don't delay," said the charm maker with an edge of warning in her voice that let me know she believed I was in peril.

"Yet I don't know where to start," I said, in almost a whisper.

"There is a clue in the question your husband asked the last time he saw you," replied the charm maker. "Is there anything you like doing with him?"

"I like his kisses and caresses," I said, "but they always end when he joins his body to mine. Then he forgets all about me and pushes toward the moment of his greatest pleasure."

"And what about you?"

"I try to do everything I can to help him."

"He doesn't need help," said the charm maker. I stared at her, hoping she would continue, but she remained silent. The moments passed slowly, while I twisted on my cushion with anticipation and hope.

"Tell me," I pleaded.

She smiled. "So now I have your full attention."

"Yes," I replied.

"And you won't be satisfied until I give you what you need."

My head felt light from the acrid smell of rue lingering in the air. "I must know."

"You are in thrall, and if I wanted to keep you there," she said, "I might tell you a side story, perhaps a quick one about Fatemeh's mother and the circumstances of her birth."

190

"I wish you wouldn't," I said, hearing a begging tone in my voice. My heart was beating faster than usual and my hands felt moist.

The charm maker was watching me carefully. "So now you understand," she said with a smile.

"Yes," I replied.

"In that case, I shall not frustrate you any longer," she said. "The ending is always necessary, though it is never as exciting as the climb."

Then she asked if I had ever seen a certain part of my body, one that was usually kept hidden.

"Of course not!" I replied, recoiling in surprise. In my village, I had always shared a room with my parents. At the hammam, I had always been surrounded by other women. The only private place I ever visited was the latrines, which were too dark and smelly to linger in.

"And yet, you must know what I mean."

Despite what I had just said, I thought I did. I could feel it, after all.

"Before your husband moves too far up the mountain of bliss, place yourself in a pinnacle-pleasuring position, and join him as he climbs. Some of the positions you can try are the frog, the twisting scissors, the Indian, and the nail in the shoe."

To make sure I knew what she meant, she demonstrated the positions with her fingers. I began imagining how they would feel with Fereydoon and wondered if I could arrange myself so he thought they were his own plan.

"I can do what you suggest," I said. "But I never thought my husband cared much about my pleasure."

"Perhaps he doesn't," she said. "But imagine how you would feel if every night you met him, he failed to ascend."

It had been agonizing not being able to please him. I had been like a stuffed doll that doesn't move until the child playing with her puts an arm or a leg in a new place. No wonder Fereydoon had become bored.

"I bend my head low before your knowledge," I said to the charm maker.

She smiled. "When you are as old as I am, you will know just as much, and probably more," she replied.

I paid the charm maker with money my mother had given me from the sigheh, for she had done her best for me. It was only when I arrived home that I realized she hadn't given me a charm to make Fereydoon want me, but rather one to prevent him from wanting someone else. That seemed very odd to me, until I understood that I must discover ways to charm him myself.

THAT NIGHT, I could hardly bear to be near my mother, Gostaham, or Gordiyeh. Whenever I met their eyes, it seemed as if they were looking at me with pity, confirming with their silence that no letter had arrived from Fereydoon. My mother didn't say anything, but at night she patted the blankets around me gently and told me one of my favorite tales, the one about Bahram and his slave girl Fitna. I loved that story, for Fitna had won Bahram through a clever trick that revealed to him his own weaknesses. I only wished I could do the same with Fereydoon.

I fell asleep and began dreaming that we had returned to our old house in my village. When we opened the front door, the whole room was filled with snow. My mother and I had no choice but to burrow into it. We tried to insulate our burrow with scraps of clothing and carpets, but we were piteously cold. The whiteness of the snow hurt my eyes and its wet cold penetrated my fingers and toes. I felt as if I had been buried alive in a bed of white. I woke up shivering, with sweat on my forehead and chest.

Lying in the dark, I wondered what fate held in store for us.

How long would Gordiyeh and Gostaham be willing to keep us if we didn't get more money from Fereydoon? We would be hungry again; we would have to accept the generosity of others, which would sometimes mask sinister desires. And I wanted to stay in the city. I liked the way my body had filled out in the capital, becoming womanly and rounded because we ate well every day. I loved what I was learning from Gostaham, who was now teaching me how to draw lions, dragons, birds of paradise, and some of the other fanciful animals I had seen in the Shah's hunting rug.

But more than that, my mind was filled with ideas about how to win Fereydoon if I should have another chance. If I were a peacock, like the one I had been trying to draw recently, I would rub my soft, iridescent feathers all over his back. If a fox, I would blindfold his eyes with my tail while licking him with my quick tongue. Now *that* would rub the bored look out of his eyes!

The next morning, I was awakened by the sound of a vendor with a nasal voice advertising his barley soup, and I went to ask Cook what she needed me to do. As we were speaking, I heard the knocker for women. Shamsi fetched me and led me to Gordiyeh and Gostaham, for a letter had arrived for me at last.

"What does it say?" I asked, forgetting to greet them properly, for I feared the letter would confirm the end of my alliance.

"Good morning to you, too," Gordiyeh replied, reminding me of my manners, and I quickly returned her greeting.

Gostaham broke the letter's wax seal, which bore Fereydoon's unmistakable signature. As I watched his eyes move back and forth, I had an urge to seize the letter and try to read it myself.

"Well?" Gordiyeh said.

Gostaham continued to read. "If only he would stop using so many flowery expressions and get to the point," he said, scanning the lines of handwriting. "Ah—here it is at last. Fereydoon is requesting her this evening. Praise be to God!"

I was speechless with relief.

Gordiyeh smiled. "Such good fortune is a sign of favor from heaven," she said.

I didn't want to make the mistake of being fatigued, the way I had been during my last visit. "I will need time to prepare for him," I said.

Gordiyeh seemed to understand. "You are excused from all your duties," she replied. "I'll tell Shamsi to work in the kitchen today in your place."

Her generosity surprised me, until I remembered she had her own reasons for desiring this union. From time to time, she would ask me if Fereydoon had mentioned that he wanted new rugs and would suggest that I prompt him to commission one from us. I never had.

I asked my mother to let me be alone the whole morning, and she left to gather herbs for her medicines. Shutting myself in our little room, I hennaed my feet and hands and decided to surprise Fereydoon by applying the designs to a place only he would see. It took several hours and I had to remain very still while the paste was drying, which was difficult because I was so restless. I also had to keep myself lightly covered out of fear that my mother would return and discover the daring thing I had done.

In the afternoon, I walked to Fereydoon's house for what I thought might be the last time. Since our contract expired the next day, I didn't know whether he wanted to enjoy me only once more or if he had other plans for me. Naturally, I was at pains to conceal what I had done from the sharp eyes of Hayedeh and Aziz. When they saluted me, they seemed more nonchalant than before. I began removing my own clothes. They didn't stop me, which made me suspect that they didn't believe I would ever return. Before I descended into the tub, I said, "Don't you want to inspect me for stray hairs?"

Hayedeh made a pretense of looking for them while continuing her conversation with Aziz. "Anyway," she said to her, "the wedding takes place in a week at the home of the groom's father, who is a pistachio farmer." She casually scrubbed my back with a kisseh as she described what her daughter was going to wear. Without her help, I immersed myself in the tub.

After they had dressed me, I went into the bedchamber I had shared with Fereydoon so many times and sat in my usual place, but I was restless and couldn't keep still. I arose and walked into the adjacent room, where we took our meals. What exactly would I do? I approached the silk rugs hanging on the wall that showed pairs of birds singing together in a tree. Their knots were so tight that their surface was sleeker than skin. A sudden impulse seized me to remove one of them. I took it into the bedchamber and spread it on the floor at some distance from the bedroll. Then I returned to the main chamber and waited.

When Fereydoon arrived, he was in a dark mood. He barked at the servants for wine and a water pipe before even coming through the door. Within seconds, he noticed that the rug had been removed from the wall, leaving a blank space next to its mate.

"What mule removed that rug?" Fereydoon growled. The servants cowered and protested their innocence with flowery words. I was afraid, but I said, "It was me."

"It looks terrible like that."

"I have a reason," I replied.

Fereydoon ignored me, lifting his arms so that a manservant could remove his robe and sash and unbuckle his pearl-studded knife. Another servant tiptoed in with the wine and pipe and backed away, bowing. Fereydoon pulled his turban off his head and consumed his libations without offering me any. When the food arrived, he ate it quickly, almost angrily. I hardly dared to put a morsel to my lips.

195

The coffee arrived in two delicate green vessels. Fereydoon tasted it before the coffee boy had left the room and grumbled, "It's not hot enough."

The coffee boy returned to remove the cups, but he didn't look apologetic, nor did he offer words to soothe Fereydoon's anger.

"Wait a minute," said Fereydoon. The coffee boy, who was probably no more than twelve, stood before him with the cups on the tray. Fereydoon grabbed my cup and threw the liquid in the boy's face. He staggered, the tray nearly dropping out of his hands.

"You see?" Fereydoon roared. "It's not even hot enough to hurt you. Now bring me something that is!"

There were scalded patches near the boy's eyes. He stammered a few words of apology and backed out of the room with tears streaming down his face.

"Donkey!" Fereydoon cried after him. I had never seen him behave this way. His anger had been as sudden and unpredictable as a hailstorm, and just as indifferent.

Another servant returned minutes later with coffee so hot it burned my throat. Fereydoon drank his in a gulp, strode into the other chamber, and threw himself onto the bedroll, closing his eyes. It wasn't long before I heard loud snores. Was this how my final night with Fereydoon must pass, with no chance of saving myself? I was filled with turmoil, yet frozen in place as if I were stuck in the bed of snow I had dreamed about the night before. I remembered the slow, chilly death I had almost experienced in my village and suddenly I leapt to my feet, knowing I had to do something.

Night was falling and the room was becoming dark. I lit an oil lamp and placed it near the silk rug before tearing off my clothes except for my pink silk trousers. Crawling on top of the bedroll beside Fereydoon, I did my best to be clumsy and awaken him. It worked: His eyes fluttered open.

"I have something to show you," I whispered, my voice a desperate hiss.

"What?" he mumbled, sounding annoyed.

I was quiet for a moment, and then I said, "It is for you, and only you, to find."

"Find what?" he asked, half asleep.

"The secret I have prepared for you," I said. He rolled onto one elbow, blinking his eyes to wake up. I rolled away a little, and when he reached for me, I rolled away again.

"Let me see you," he said.

I got on my hands and knees, but turned around slightly to show him a view of my trousered hips and bare breasts. Then I began crawling toward the oil lamp. With a surprised look, Fereydoon got on all fours and followed. I let him grab my hips, but I wouldn't turn around. From behind, he began exploring my bare chest with his soft hands. When I liked what he was doing, I leaned back against his chest, covered his hands with mine and kept them there.

"What's the secret?" asked Fereydoon softly. He was awake now, his eyes more alive than they had been in months.

I wrested myself from his embrace and crawled away again as fast as I could. He grabbed at my trousers but missed, then came crawling after me again, laughing. When I was ready, I let him catch the edge of my trousers and press me down with my stomach on the ground.

"Turn over," he said. I lay still, teasing him with a smile and resisting him as he tried to flip me.

"Ah!" he said, in a delighted tone, when I refused to budge. He didn't force me, but rather lifted the waist of my trousers and tore the fabric off my body. The silk made a loud ripping sound, and satisfaction illuminated his face. Then he shrugged off his own clothes.

I still refused to turn over. "You haven't found it yet," I teased.

Fereydoon became wild then. He searched my naked back in the light of the oil lamp, caressing me with his hands and lips. His caresses were different this time; they seemed intended to inflame me. When he tried to turn me again, I still wouldn't let him: I liked what he was doing too much. Fereydoon became wild, kissing and biting my shoulders and lifting up the front of my body to stroke my breasts from underneath. I began to feel as liquid as hot pomegranate syrup, and when I was panting and could no longer bear to hold myself back from him, I rolled over to allow him to explore me further.

"Where is the secret?" he asked impatiently. I teased him with a smile, and Fereydoon dragged me into the light of the oil lamp, kissing and caressing me until he came closer and closer to my treasure.

I kept my legs tightly closed and wouldn't let him open them, indicating parts of my body as if to say, first touch me *here,* then kiss me *there.* It was as though he were discovering me for the first time. His mouth and hands crisscrossed my body like a caravan, making stops at oases along the way. When I was boiling with pleasure, my legs fell open, for I no longer desired to be separate from him. That's when he saw what I had done. With a "voy!" of surprise, he moved his head between my legs to look more closely.

Rather than just darkening the bottoms of my feet and my hands with henna, as women usually did, I had borrowed one of Gostaham's single-haired brushes and painted my thighs where the flesh was heaviest and softest. My design was of pointed petals like those that would encircle the inmost center of a carpet. In between each petal, I had painted sprays of tiny roses, lilies, and narcissus.

Fereydoon dragged me closer to the lamp to see better, and then he couldn't keep his hands or his tongue away from my thighs. I remembered Gostaham's joke about the language teacher, and it was only moments before I understood that the woman in his story had found a pearl beyond price in husband number three. Now, with Fereydoon's lips in a new place, and his hands reaching all over my body, I began to breathe harder and faster. Too quickly, he stopped what he was doing, opened my legs, and sank his hips into mine. "Wait!" I wanted to shout. I looked into his clouded eyes and felt that he had forgotten all about me, for he was lost in his own ecstasy.

I began breathing normally, even as his grunts started to come faster. I don't know what emboldened me to do this, but as his hips were moving away from mine, I closed my knees, twisted around quickly, and crawled away.

"Vohhh!" he said in frustration.

He cursed and pleaded and called my name, but as I refused to return, he followed on all fours. I let him chase me around the room, and then I made haste to the silk rug I had laid on the floor, with his breath practically at my ear. He grabbed my hips as if he were still master, but I could sense that he was waiting for me to do something. I turned around and pushed him very gently back onto the silk rug, and there he lay staring up at me, waiting to do my bidding. I put my knees on either side of him and began rubbing the length of my body along his. He reached his hands to my breasts, at last, and I moaned as the passion returned to my body. For the first time ever, I caressed his beautiful hair, which fell in shimmering black waves around his head. The softness of his hair in my hands, the slippery silk under my knees and feet, and the bristly hairs on his chest stirred a warmth in my groin I had never felt before. I took him this time, gluing my hips to his and rocking back and forth, slowly at first and then faster, until we were no more separate than warp and weft. Fereydoon followed along at my speed, meeting me this time as I had so often met him. The world, which I had always thought of as solid, suddenly began to lose its substance. I screamed and perhaps roared, and Fereydoon roared with me, and I felt myself dissolve in an instant the way the moth is consumed by the flame, with nothing remaining but a puff of smoke.

Our roars must have alarmed the servants, for they banged on the door, asking if Fereydoon was well, and he barked at them to give him peace. The two of us didn't speak at all, but stayed panting on the rug. As soon as his breath had quieted, Fereydoon could not keep his hands separate from my body. He began caressing me again, and I reached down and touched his middle. It was as stiff as a pole, even though we had just finished. We began sporting again like animals. Thinking of the fox's tail, I grabbed my sash, tied it around Fereydoon's eyes, and nibbled him with my tongue until he began making small cries of ecstasy that had never issued from his lips before. We continued that way for the rest of the night.

In the morning, I awoke with Fereydoon's face close to mine, his eyes open. Though he had business to attend to, he didn't seem to want to leave. Even after he had bathed and dressed, he could not stop himself from parting my legs again to see the design I had drawn, and dipping his fingers there.

For my part, I could hardly believe what I had learned to do. At last I understood the rapture that Goli had described! Now I, too, could smile knowingly to myself when women joked about relations with men, for my body had finally grasped the joy of it.

Not long after I returned home that morning, Gostaham received a letter from Fereydoon renewing my sigheh for another three months. He must have written it right after we said good-bye. With jubilation, we sent back a letter of agreement. Gordiyeh congratulated me, surprised that I had succeeded. "I thought he had done with you," she said.

Gostaham gave us another sack of coins from Fereydoon's accountant, after taking his share to pay for our keep. My mother put both her hands to my cheeks and told me I was like the moon. I glowed with triumph. Unlike Gordiyeh, my mother, and all the other women I knew, I had had to prove myself after marriage or risk losing my husband. I had succeeded with only hours remaining, and I vowed not to make the same mistake again. Right away, I began planning what I would do the next time Fereydoon summoned me to his bed.

THAT AFTERNOON, a messenger from Naheed knocked on Gostaham's door to tell me that I was invited for coffee. Although my eyes were burning with fatigue and I longed to rest, I had to go with her to avoid being rude. Naheed had sent for me several times during the last few days, but I had returned my apologies, for I had been too perplexed by my own problems.

I already knew what Naheed was going to tell me. Only a few days before, she had probably met Iskandar's mother and sister at the hammam, and they would have exchanged pleasantries all afternoon as they bathed. At the end of the day, his mother would have been enchanted enough to reveal that she was searching for a good match for her son. Since Iskandar was already in love, I suspected that his family's offer had come quickly and that Naheed's had already accepted. Girls like Naheed were destined to marry wealthy men; but her fate would be even better, for she would be marrying someone she had chosen herself.

I hummed to myself as I walked through Four Gardens. Rosebushes were blooming in a garden near the river, and I stopped to admire them. Small yellow buds with delicate petals were planted near fat red blossoms that had already spread their petals wide. The song that I loved to sing with my father came to me:

I shall plant roses at her feet,
For I am drunk, drunk, drunk on love.

If a girl like Naheed could get what she wanted, perhaps so could a girl like me. I had won Fereydoon as a lover; maybe with more cleverness I could ensnare him as a permanent husband.

When I arrived at Naheed's, we greeted each other with a kiss on each cheek. As her mother's birds chirped merrily in their cages, I looked at Naheed for signs of the good news. But as soon as the servants left us alone, Naheed's face twisted into grief, and she collapsed onto a cushion, crying.

I was astonished. "Naheed, my dear, my life! What has happened?"

She looked up for a moment, her green eyes beautiful through her tears. "They said no," she said, before choking on more sobs.

"Who said no? Iskandar's parents?"

"No, no. My own parents!"

"Why?"

Naheed sat up and tried not to choke on her own sobs. "They found the letters," she said when she finally recovered. "There were too many for me to keep them in my sash. I hid them underneath my bedroll, but I must have been careless. One of my mother's maids betrayed me. She is a wealthy woman now, I'm sure."

"You poor animal!" I said. "Did they even consider Iskandar as a husband for you?"

"No."

"Why not?"

"He's too poor!" said Naheed, sobbing even more. I reached forward and put my arms around her waist, and she leaned toward me and cried on my shoulder. When she had stopped for a moment, she looked at me with so much pain in her eyes that my heart felt heavy with grief. "I love him!" she burst out. "I will always love him! Whatever happens, he and I will always be as close as a cloud and its life-giving rain!"

I sighed, though I was not surprised that her parents had refused a poor man. "Have you heard from Iskandar?"

"He sent me a letter through Kobra, but we have to be very careful now because my parents are watching me. They said I had shamed the family name by having a secret romance, and that people would

202

talk. They have instructed the head servants to pat down the others for missives when they come in the door."

"What did he write to you?"

"That even if I am old and sickly, if my hair is gray and I walk with a limp, he will love me always."

"I'm so sorry," I said. "I know how much you love him."

Naheed clicked her tongue against her teeth. "How could you know? You have never been in love," she said almost angrily.

I admitted that was true, although now that I had enjoyed an evening of newly awakened delights with Fereydoon, my feelings had begun to change. I wondered if they could be considered love.

"Naheed-joon," I said, "on my way here, I was so certain you were going to tell me you were engaged to Iskandar and were about to obtain your heart's greatest desire that I was singing to myself with joy."

"I thought so, too," she replied.

I considered for a moment. "What if Iskandar does well for himself? Is it possible that your parents will change their mind one day?"

"No," she said darkly. And just when I thought her tears had started to dry, she bent over and moaned like an animal in a trap. I hadn't heard keening like that since my father had died, and the sounds tore at my heart.

I tried to comfort her. "Naheed, my life, you must have hope. Let's pray to God, and trust that He has a compassionate fate in store for you and Iskandar."

"You don't understand," Naheed replied, and returned to her low, guttural wailing. A servant knocked at the door with our coffee. I jumped up and took the tray from her hands so that she wouldn't enter and see Naheed's tear-streaked face.

"It's all right," she said, "they all know about my engagement."

I was puzzled. "What do you mean?"

Naheed's tears flowed even faster, like a heavy spring rain. "If I had renounced Iskandar, my parents probably would have done nothing, but I wept and told them I would never forget him. For that reason, they have contracted a marriage for me with another man. I am to be married when the moon is full again."

This news was even crueler than the last. How could Naheed's parents, who had loved and spoiled their girl all her life, throw her at a man while she was still mourning her first love? I felt very, very sorry for her. I put my arms around Naheed again, inclining my head toward hers.

"And whom are you to marry?" I asked, hoping it was a good choice who would make her happy.

"My mother called on Homa, who she said knew of just the man," said Naheed bitterly. "Of course, I have never seen him in my life."

"Do you know anything at all about him?"

Her parents would have been able to choose from among thousands, for Naheed had money and beauty in equal measure. Perhaps he would be her match in those things and unveil the nighttime pleasures that I now had learned to enjoy.

She shrugged. "He's a horseman, which my parents thought would make him a good substitute for Iskandar."

The hair on my arms stood on end suddenly, as if there was a draft in the room.

"What else?" I asked.

"Just that he is the son of a wealthy horse breeder who lives in the north."

I stared at Naheed. I knew I had to say something, but I couldn't get my lips to form words. Instead, I began coughing and gasping for breath. I bent over at the waist, head bowed, trying to find air.

"Voy!" said Naheed. "Are you all right?"

It seemed as if the attack would not end. I coughed until tears ran out of my eyes, and then I remained wordless.

"You look miserable," Naheed said as I was wiping my eyes.

"If you only knew how much," I replied. I forced myself to hold my tongue, since I had been hasty many times before. Weren't there hundreds of wealthy horse traders? Or at least dozens? And didn't most of them have sons? Surely it must be another man.

"Your parents must have told you more," I said encouragingly.

Naheed paused to think for a moment. "He lost his first wife, but that's really all I know," she replied.

I felt a chill inside that made me want to wrap my arms around myself to dispel it.

"What's his name?" I asked abruptly, my voice tight in my throat.

"I don't know why it would mean anything to you," Naheed replied, "for it doesn't to me." She sighed. "He could be Shah Abbas himself, and I wouldn't care."

"But who is he?" I insisted, feeling as if I might burst out of my skin.

Naheed looked surprised at my persistence. "I hesitate to say his name—I dislike the very sound of it," she replied. "But if you must know, it is Fereydoon."

I had another fit of coughing which felt as if I might lose my vital organs. I could have told her everything about her husband to be, of course; how his hair looked when released from his turban, how he closed his eyes in rapture at the sound of the kamancheh, the way he smelled when he was excited. Now I even knew how to please him, yet only she would have the right to become his proper wife for the rest of her days. A hot surge of jealousy coursed through me. At the thought that he might prefer her, I started sputtering so hard, it was a wonder that she didn't suspect what was wrong.

Naheed looked very moved by my outburst. "My dearest friend, I'm sorry that my plight has disturbed you so deeply. Please don't allow my bad luck to dim your life's blood."

I thought quickly about how to explain myself. "It's just that I wanted you to be happy," I said. "All the things you have told me have torn my heart."

The tears slid out of her eyes, and mine too were veiled with mist. But while Naheed's tears were mixed with gratitude for my friendship, mine sheltered a guilty secret.

The last call to prayer erupted in the air, signaling that it was time for me to go home. I left Naheed with her grief and walked back slowly with mine. Alone on the street, I could finally stop pretending why I was heartsick. No wonder Fereydoon had ignored me for so many weeks; he must have been busy discussing the marriage contract with Naheed's parents and arranging the details of the wedding.

And what about our night of pleasure? He had let me gratify him until the cocks crowed, taking all my gifts as if they were his right. My blood began to seethe, and I walked faster and faster through Four Gardens until I bumped into a hunched old woman with a cane and had to excuse myself for disturbing her.

I heard a cat yowl in the bushes, probably in search of a mate, just like me. I had never desired anything but to be married to a good man. Why must I be the pleasure girl, while Naheed, who already had everything, could be the permanent wife? And why, of all the men in Isfahan, did her intended have to be Fereydoon?

When I arrived home, Cook heard my steps and called out to me from the kitchen. "You're late," she complained. "Come help us clean the dill."

"Leave me alone!" I snapped. Cook was so surprised, she dropped her knife.

"I don't know how you manage such a mule," she said to my mother. I ignored her and stormed through the courtyard to our little room. How could Fereydoon have contracted a marriage without telling me? He didn't know Naheed was my friend, but concealing such a momentous step showed how little I mattered in his eyes.

WHEN FEREYDOON SUMMONED me the next day, I went to his house but refused to let Hayedeh and Aziz bathe me, perfume me, or brush my hair. Now that my status had been restored, they were afraid of me again. They begged and pleaded until I yelled at them to retreat, and they left, cowed. I sat in the little room where we usually frolicked and waited for Fereydoon, still wearing all my street wraps. I was so angry I could feel the air getting hot around me, and my cheeks burned.

When Fereydoon arrived, he noticed my unusual attire but didn't say anything. He removed his shoes and his turban and told his servants to leave. Then he sat down beside me and took my hand in his. "Listen, joonam," he began, as if he were going to explain something. It was the first time he had ever used the term "soul of mine."

I didn't let him continue. "You don't want me anymore," I said.

"Why wouldn't I want you anymore? Especially after that last night." He smiled and tried to push open my knees. I kept them squeezed shut.

"But you're getting married."

"I have to," he said. "Don't worry: Nothing else will change."

His answer implied only one thing. "You mean, you intend to keep us both?"

"Of course."

"You don't know what problems that will cause."

"Why?"

"Naheed is my best friend!"

He looked truly surprised. "Of all the women in Isfahan —"

"And she doesn't know about my sigheh with you."

207

"Why not?"

"My family told me to keep it quiet."

Fereydoon shrugged. "Your family is concerned about their social standing," he said, "but people do this kind of thing all the time."

"Doesn't it affect *your* standing?"

"A man can marry the way he likes," he replied.

I looked at his costly blue velvet robe patterned with falcons, and in that moment he seemed to possess everything, while I had nothing.

"What does it matter what people think, anyway?" he said. "Wives who like each other can help each other with children and other womanly matters."

"I'm not even your real wife!"

"That doesn't matter, either."

I remained silent, for it certainly mattered to me. Marriage to a wealthy man like Fereydoon would ease all my worries. I waited, hoping he would pledge to marry me, but he did not.

Fereydoon wrapped his arms around me, but I did not yield. "This is what my father wants," he said, his breath warm on my ear. "He has always craved an alliance with one of the established families of Isfahan. This will aid his chances of being appointed a governor one day."

He sighed. "But don't think for a minute that I don't want you. If I didn't, I would have let you go the way a tree sheds its leaves in autumn."

I didn't reply. He never would have made a proposal to Naheed's family if their daughter had not been as radiant as the five fingers of the sun.

"She's very pretty," I said, almost peevishly.

"That's what I hear," he replied. "I'll be meeting her in a day or two to see for myself."

Fereydoon began stroking my cheek with his soft hands. "I don't know anything about what she's like. But from the moment I met you and you ordered me not to look at you, I liked you. Most women would have pretended to be polite and slithered away; you showed me your sharp tongue. I admired your black hair and brown skin, so like two rich, dark velvets. I thought you were too young to be one of Gostaham's daughters, and when the servant boy returned, I paid him to tell me who you were. When I hired Gostaham to make the carpet, I asked him to include the talismans because I wanted your fingers in the design. Once I saw the rug on the loom, with its shimmering jewels, I decided to have you."

His words made my heart soar for the first time. "I never knew why you wanted me," I said.

Fereydoon sighed. "My life is full of people who sing my praises so they can win a larger coin. Before she died, even my first wife used to coddle me to win the things she wanted. You don't do that, and I like it."

This surprised me, for I did everything I could to please him with my body. Yet it was true that I withheld the honey from my tongue.

Fereydoon smoothed his hands across his face as if wiping off the dust of the day. "I can't change the facts of my position," he said. "My father needs me to marry well-connected women, and I will. But that doesn't mean I don't want you—like this—and often."

Fereydoon pulled my body between his legs, my back against his chest, and began stroking me although I was swathed in clothes. I didn't want to let him please me, but his touch made my knees part, especially when I remembered what I now knew how to do. I allowed him to remove my street garments as if he were stripping off the layers of an onion.

"After last night," he said, "I thought all day about what new surprise you might be preparing for me tonight."

"I did nothing," I said with iron in my voice.

"Ah, well," he replied. "You were upset. It doesn't matter."

He began caressing my legs, and I pushed away his hand, but he didn't mind. I saw right away that he would enjoy the novelty of taking me unprepared—unbathed, in my street clothes, resistant to his touch. I pushed him away again, but I didn't mean it; he quickly saw that it was a game and courted me as if he were the courtesan, and I the one who had to be satisfied. He stroked my body until I could not keep myself away from him. Then he let me have him in any way I chose. He watched in wonder as I swooped over the mountain not once, but three times. He delighted in turnabout, the surprise this time being that he must devote himself to my pleasure. I took it and took it from him that night, until I was as sated with him as he had ever been with me.

Before I fell asleep, I thought back to the story my mother had told me a few days earlier about the slave girl Fitna and how she had tested and tamed her shah. He had not understood her value until he believed her to be gone forever. I wondered if I, too, could find a clever way to make Fereydoon declare me the most treasured affliction of his heart.

First there wasn't and then there was. Before God, no one was.

Once there was a shah of Iran named Bahram who was known far and wide for his bravery. He had once slain a man-eating dragon and rescued the child inside its belly, and he had wrenched his own gold crown from the jaws of a lion. But in his moments of leisure, his greatest love was the hunt.

Bahram had a slave girl named Fitna who joined him on every hunting expedition. Fitna was lean and strong, and she could ride a horse as fast as her master. They used to gallop together for miles, searching for wild asses and other beasts of prey. At night Fitna feasted at his table, and he delighted in her above all others. Even his two sisters, whose arms were adorned with bracelets of gold, didn't shine in his eyes like Fitna, whose bare arms were as white as pearls.

210

One day they were hunting deep in the desert, where prey was scarce. The shah's men fanned out far and wide, forming a human net to drive the beasts toward him. Bahram and Fitna rode together, conversing, until the shah spotted a wild ass. With a shout, he spurred his horse and chased the animal, aiming an arrow at its heart. The ass dropped to its knees and relinquished its life to the shah. Seeing that Fitna watched but failed to utter a word of praise, Bahram spoke.

"Didn't you see how well I aimed?" he inquired. "Here comes another beast now. How shall I kill this one?"

Fitna smiled, knowing how well he loved to be tested. "I can think of a fine way to strike it down," she replied. "Why not pin its paw to its temple?"

Bahram thought for a moment until a plan formed in his mind. Placing a metal ball within his sling, he launched it at the ass's ear. Stung, the beast pawed at its temple to clear away the headache. The shah swiftly drew his bow and with a single arrow fastened the animal's paw to its head. Pleased with himself, he turned to Fitna for the expected praise.

In an even tone, she said only, "You are well practiced at the hunt, sire. He who works at a skill will one day master it."

The shah was surrounded by courtiers who fawned upon him when he merely breathed. How could this slave be so bold? Knowing it would be wrong to strike her down, he withheld his blows. Secretly, he called an old, grizzled officer to his side and issued a command. "That woman has troubled the royal peace," he said. "Destroy her before I do it myself."

The officer swept Fitna onto his horse and galloped to a distant city, where he owned a palace with a tall tower. As they traveled, his heart was heavy with the thought of the task that lay ahead. He had killed many men in battle but could not bear the thought of destroying an unarmed slave girl.

When they arrived, he led Fitna up sixty steps to the top of his tower, where he planned to fulfill the shah's command. But before he could draw his weapon, she stopped him with these words. "Do not forget that I am the shah's favorite," she said, her eyes filling with tears. "Stay your hand from killing me for a few days, but tell the shah you have followed his orders. If he is satisfied, you may take my life without fault. But if he is not, you will one day earn his blessings."

The kind officer considered for a moment. He had always been loyal, but this time the shah's order seemed unjust. What did he have to lose by waiting? If the shah's heart was hardened, he had only to return and carry out the deed. And if it wasn't, then he would be shielding his leader from his own error.

He left Fitna in his tower and returned to Bahram's palace. When he was received by that lion of lions, he reported that he had sent the girl to her grave. The shah's eyes filled with stinging tears, and he turned away to hide his grief. The officer returned to his tower to tell Fitna the news. She was happy but not hasty, knowing the shah well enough to let time do its work.

Fitna spent her days at the officer's palace befriending a calf, who became her main companion. Since the calf would not climb the sixty stairs to the tower, she used to carry it all the way up on her back, where it would graze in the green grass that grew on the roof. Every morning she brought the calf there, and every evening she returned him to the animal pens below, whispering to herself, "May I be worthy of this trial." At the end of six years the calf had become a full-sized ox, and Fitna's muscles were as strong as a wrestler's.

One day, Fitna pulled the ruby earrings from her ears and gave them to the officer. "Take these gems and sell them, and buy supplies for a fine feast," she said. "We'll need incense and candles, rice and lamb, pastries and wine. Bring all these things here, and then invite the shah to dine with you after the hunt."

The officer, who had grown fond of his prisoner, refused to take her jewels. Instead, he opened his own bags of treasure to purchase the things she had requested. The next time he saw the shah, he begged the favor of his visit. "It would do great honor to your humble slave," said he, "if you would drink and sup with me on top of my tower."

Hearing this fine speech, Bahram granted his request. While the shah went off to hunt, the officer returned to his tower and helped Fitna prepare a grand celebration. Together, they unrolled his finest carpets on the roof and arranged pillows for reclining. Then Fitna cooked a beautiful meal, singing *as she stirred a bit of amatory musk into the shah's favorite dish of lamb with dates.*

Toward evening, Bahram arrived with his men, and the officer ate and drank with them until they could consume no more. While they were smoking their water pipes, the shah said, "You have a fine palace here, my friend, and a lush garden. But these sixty steps are a long way to go, I should think, for a man of your age. Is it not one step for every year?"

The officer concurred that his age was indeed near sixty. "For a man used to the military life, the steps are no trial," he added quickly. "But I know a woman who can mount all these steps with the weight of an ox on her back. I don't think there's a man in the empire who could do the same."

"How could a woman lift such a beast?" the shah asked. "Bring her here so that we all may witness this feat."

The officer descended to find Fitna, hoping that when the evening meal was over, both of them would still be in possession of their lives. He trembled a little as he searched for her. But when he lifted the curtain leading to her quarters and beheld her, all his nervousness dropped away. She wore layers of white Chinese silk, which she had scented with incense. A white veil hid everything but her eyes, and a scarf lined with seed pearls covered her hair. Her almond eyes were lined with kohl. She was ready for battle.

Fitna loaded the heavy ox onto her back and mounted the stairs one by one. When she reached the top, she saluted Bahram and laid the ox at his feet. "O shah of shahs," said she, "please accept my gift of this ox, which I was able to offer to you here through my skill alone."

The shah looked awestruck, but his reply was full of reason. "This thing you call skill," he said, "is just repetition. You've borne the burden of this ox so many times that now it seems easy."

Fitna smiled and bowed down to the ground. "Sire, you are right," she said. "I have borne this ox every day for six long years. But should someone who shoots a wild ass be celebrated for skill, while someone who lifts an ox be known only for repetition?"

Now the shah was speechless. He looked from Fitna to the officer and back again as if he were seeing the dead. Then he sprang to his feet and lifted

Fitna's veil. When he saw her moonlike face, he cried out with joy. Tears streamed from his eyes, matched by those that flowed from hers. For a few moments they were like two river spirits, speaking only through water.

The shah cleared the tower of all his men, including the officer. Then he seated Fitna on the carpet beside him and said, "I humbly request your forgiveness. In a moment of weakness I coveted your praise, but now I see that your wisdom is an even greater gift."

"My dear shah," replied she, "the sorrow I have felt in your absence is so great it could reduce a town to rubble. Loving you too much, I almost lost you forever."

The shah asked for Fitna's hand in marriage. "You are truly a desirable trial!" he said teasingly, for "trial" was the meaning of her name.

The next day, the two were married at a sumptuous wedding, and the kind officer was rewarded with a thousand pearls for the one he had sheltered. But that was only the beginning. Fitna, true to her name, continued to test the shah for the rest of his days.

CHAPTER FIVE

As I walked home from Fereydoon's the next morning, I felt a convulsion in my belly followed by a steady pain. Could I be pregnant? I held my chador with one hand while holding my belly with the other, as if to feel for a baby. That was the only thing that might tie me to Fereydoon forever. Why would he continue to want me otherwise, when he was soon to be bound to a green-eyed beauty?

Wanting to get home quickly to check myself, I rushed through the old square near Fereydoon's and into the bazaar connected to it like a long spine. I hurried past a cluster of gold shops with gleaming piles of bracelets on display and wealthy women crowded around them like hungry crows. I wasn't even slowed by the meaty aroma of a breakfast soup made of lamb parts, although every vendor called out to me, swearing his "paws and brains" tasted the best.

When I arrived home, breathless, I greeted my mother before rushing to the latrines. Shortly after I loosened my tunic and removed my trousers, I knew. Even though it was too dark to see, I could feel a trace of the slick blood, which would soon rush forth like a river. I placed a thick cloth between my legs and returned to the room I shared with my mother. Without a further word, I stretched out on a bedroll and closed my eyes.

My mother took my hand in hers, saying, "Light of my eyes, what ails you?"

I couldn't bear to reveal what I had learned from Naheed, so I decided to tell her what I had discovered.

"I'm not pregnant," I said. "Even after all this time."

My mother began stroking my hand. "Azizam, it has been less than three cycles of the moon. You must be patient."

"Patient?" I said. "Goli got pregnant in the first month of her marriage. Why is it taking me so long?"

My mother sighed. "It took a long time before God granted you to me," she said.

I was unconsoled. I hadn't thought my mother's problems with conceiving would become my own.

"What if I'm barren?" I said. I could barely spit the words out of my mouth, so fearsome was the thought.

"You are young, with plenty of years ahead of you," said my mother. "If many more months go by without a child, I will make special charms to help you. May God grant that you conceive quickly!"

I wondered if my mother understood how different it was for me than it had been for her and my father.

"Bibi, I don't have fifteen years to try, the way you did," I replied.

My mother averted her eyes as if she didn't care to be reminded that my marriage could end at any moment. Then she patted my hand with resolution. "We will make a *nazr* together, and slaughter an animal for the poor once your wish is granted," she replied.

I turned my head away. My mother looked surprised that I didn't feel a nazr would be enough.

"Did something happen?" she asked. "Has he told you he no longer wants you?"

"No," I said, but my lips trembled so much that she knew there was more to say. I drew in a breath.

"He is taking another," I added. "A permanent wife."

"No wonder you are so distraught!" said my mother. "But perhaps that doesn't mean anything, as far as your marriage is concerned."

"If I were to get pregnant, I would worry less."

"Yes, of course," said my mother. "When did he tell you?"

"Naheed told me."

"Naheed?" she asked, drawing back in surprise.

Instead of answering her unspoken question, I lay silent. My throat closed and my face compressed until it felt as small as a polo ball.

"Ay, Khoda!" my mother said when she understood. She looked at me, hoping for a denial, but there was nothing I could say.

My mother began praying. "Lord of the Universe, remember us in your infinite mercy. Blessed Mohammad, listen to our prayers. Ali, prince among men, grant us your fortitude and strength."

"Bibi, I can't bear it," I said. "Now at least one of them is sure to hate me."

"Did you tell Naheed?" my mother asked, looking worried.

"No."

"Thanks be to God," she replied. "You are right—we must do something quickly. For now, you must quiet yourself. In the morning, we will have plenty to do and you will need to be fresh."

She layered the blankets over me and put a pillow under my head. Then she gathered my hair behind the pillow and began combing it very gently, while she told me about the adventures of a sly mouse and the large, dumb cat who wanted to eat it. Her soothing words, combined with the feeling of the comb massaging my scalp, quickly carried me away into a restful sleep.

It was fortunate that the next day was Thursday, because we were at liberty in the afternoon. We waited in the courtyard until

Shamsi crossed from the kitchen to the storerooms. My mother followed her, speaking honeyed words so that she would allow her to fill her pockets with walnuts in the shell and a handful of raisins. In exchange, she had to promise her a bottle of her best black medicine for raspy throats.

"What a miserly household," my mother grumbled.

We put on our pichehs and chadors and walked arm in arm toward the Seyyed Ahmadioun district to visit the mosque with the famous brass minaret. Along the way, we passed a young mother shepherding her four children home. It looked as if she had borne them one right after the other, for they were close in age. I wondered if a fertile woman like her had ever had to go on an errand such as mine.

Even from far away, we spotted the brass minaret blazing like a flame in the afternoon sun. This beacon guided us through unfamiliar districts until we arrived at the doorway of the mosque. In the women's section, we prayed together, touching our heads to disks of clay. When I was done, my woes seemed lighter.

The minaret was wrapped in gleaming sheets of brass inscribed with holy words. Inside, it was narrow, cool, and dark, and its stone steps were worn smooth from supplication. I stood on the bottom step while my mother handed me a small, flat board and a walnut.

"Break it," she said.

I put the walnut on the step in front of me, placed the board on top of it, and sat on it with all my weight. The nut shattered with a satisfying crack, and I smiled at this first success. The crushed nut went into my pocket.

"Praise be to God," said my mother, handing me the next nut. I ascended and continued cracking, praying with each crack that my womb would split open to receive a seed and spit out a tender nut meat of its own.

Higher and higher I rose in the tower, with my mother behind me cheering my progress. Other women began their ascent below us. About halfway to the top, I heard a woman sobbing. I clutched at my mother, and we listened until we understood. The woman's nuts had been too hard to crack, a sign that she would be barren forever. I pitied her.

We continued up the stairs. As I sat on the board and cracked another nut, I thought of Goli and wondered if she was pregnant again. I imagined bringing a child of my own to my village and showing it to her proudly. What would everyone think when they knew that in my child's veins ran the blood of a wealthy man!

My mother tugged at my chador. "Azizam, there are women behind us who are waiting to ascend. You should keep going."

I continued my ascent. All the nuts kept cracking as if they were waiting to split open at my touch. When I reached the top of the staircase, we turned and descended the way we had come, murmuring wishes of good fortune to the other women, especially to the one whose red, swollen eyes told me her luck had been bitter. Outside, we cleaned the nut meats and my mother gave me a palmful of raisins to mix with them.

"Now don't be shy," she said, as we began walking home.

I took a deep breath and chose the first man because he looked as if he might be my father's age, and had the same fine spider's web of lines at the corners of his eyes.

"Ey, graybeard!" I said, showing him the nuts and raisins. "May I offer you the fruit of my hands?"

His eyes softened with tenderness, just as I hoped they would. He opened both of his hands, palms wide.

"Blessings upon you, little mother-to-be!" he replied. "May you bear seven healthy sons, one every year!"

I smiled and gave him a handful of the nuts, wishing him bountiful blessings in return. His kind words filled me with hope. Surely this was a sign of God's grace and mercy, to have a man who reminded me of my father wish me seven sons!

As we continued walking, it seemed as if every man we met had a kind word.

"May you bloom like a summer rose!" said a young fellow mounted on a mule, stooping to accept my offering.

"May you be as fruitful as a pomegranate!" said an old man with a hump, who looked as if he could use a good meal. I gave him an especially large handful.

"May your belly swell to the size of my turban!" said a fellow whose head wrapping was so white and clean it must have just been laundered.

Only one handful of nuts remained when I spotted a young man with a friendly face who was seated on his heels. His long arms and legs reminded me of Fereydoon's. I stretched out my hand and begged him to partake of my last handful of nuts. He ignored me, scanning the street as if he were waiting for a friend. I tried again.

"Please, kind sir, taste a morsel of my offering," I said.

This time he looked at me, his eyes hard. "I don't want any," he said. "Why don't you eat them yourself?"

I recoiled; it was an act of deliberate cruelty. My mother took my arm and led me away, saying "Shame! Shame!" The man didn't care; he never looked in our direction again. As my mother pulled me away, the nuts fell out of my hand and scattered, and a couple of pigeons descended to claim them.

My mother tried to make light of it by reminding me of our good fortune until that moment. "One bad man can't confound the will of God," she said, but I could not be consoled. As we walked home in the twilight, I thought of the woman with the swollen eyes whose labors had come to nothing, and how her piteous sobs had made the minaret a temple of sorrow.

IN THE AFTERNOON, after serving Gordiyeh and Gostaham tea and sweets in the Great Room, my mother told them about Naheed's engagement. Gostaham said, "Ey, Baba!" in surprise and asked us if we were sure it was the same Fereydoon. Then there was a long silence, broken only by Gordiyeh's annoyed exclamation.

"Why did he have to choose Naheed! What terrible luck!"

Gostaham motioned to us to join them on the cushions. My mother and I sat side by side and watched them drink their tea. Gordiyeh did not call for refreshments for us.

"Perhaps we should break the new contract, since it has barely begun," my mother said.

"I don't know if we can," said Gostaham. "It's a legal agreement now that we have accepted the money."

"That doesn't mean we couldn't ask Fereydoon, as a man of honor, to release us," said my mother.

"Why would he? He made the renewal offer even though he knew he was getting engaged to Naheed," said Gostaham.

"But he didn't know we were friends," I protested.

"You never told him?" asked my mother.

"I mentioned that I had a friend, but I didn't ever say her name. Now I wish I had."

"I'm not sure it would have mattered, anyway," said Gostaham. "He can marry whomever he wants."

Gordiyeh sighed loudly. "What a shame he didn't choose you," she said. "But at least he renewed the sigheh. He must like you well enough."

I twitched with irritation. Like most women, Gordiyeh had married secure in the knowledge that she had gained a lifetime contract. How could she understand what it was like to have a marriage that expired after only three months?

"Let's look at the possibilities," Gostaham said to my mother. "You can either accept the contract or beg for release. It would be better to go along with it, I think, especially now that your daughter is no longer a virgin. You might still have something to gain."

"Especially if there's a child," said Gordiyeh, and I thought of the young man with the hard, handsome face who had refused my final offering of nuts.

"But everybody would have to know about it then," said my mother.

"That's true," replied Gordiyeh, "but the advantages to you would be so great that it wouldn't matter."

"But what would Naheed and her parents think?" I asked. Gordiyeh looked away; Gostaham looked down, and a long silence followed that inflamed my greatest fears. If it had been some other family, nobody would have cared, since every family strives for its own advantages. But this situation was as sticky as naphtha.

"You must think of yourself," said Gordiyeh. "Naheed has everything in the world, and you have nothing."

I began seething like a pot of boiling water. Whose fault was it that we still had so little of our own? They had sold the most precious thing I had — my virginity — without reaping lifetime gains. My carpet had been given away with no profit to myself. Every day, my mother was afraid that we'd have to fend for ourselves again. Surely we deserved more than that!

My mother turned to me. "What do you desire, daughter of mine? After all, Naheed is your closest friend."

Before I could say anything, Gordiyeh broke in. "Because of who Fereydoon is, I wouldn't do anything without thinking about it carefully," she said.

I had the feeling that she was being very cautious with me, knowing how hasty I could be.

"I'm not sure what to do," I said honestly.

"What's your advice?" my mother asked Gordiyeh.

"Since you already have a contract, fulfill its terms," she said. "Then you can let it end without any risk of offense, or reconsider it if he renews again."

"But what if Naheed's family learns the truth? Won't they despise us?" I asked.

222

"There's no reason for them to ever know," Gordiyeh said quickly. "No man would mention such an entanglement to his in-laws or to his virginal fiancée."

My mother turned to me. "Well?" she said.

Without thinking, I had begun to stroke the rug under my fingertips. It was as velvety as the one I had removed from Fereydoon's walls, and I was reminded of how my back had glided against it while Fereydoon's body was on top of mine. My face began to flush. Now that my body had opened to Fereydoon's pleasures, I wanted to return to those places of delight as often as I could. And though I loved Naheed, Gordiyeh's words had been correct: She had everything, and I had nothing—except for a few months with Fereydoon.

"I'll do what you say," I told Gordiyeh.

She looked well satisfied, probably because there was still a chance that Fereydoon or his family would commission a carpet.

"Your wisdom is large beyond your years," she replied.

My mother was pleased, too, knowing that we need not worry about our keep for at least another three months.

THERE IS NOTHING sadder than a bride who is miserable on her wedding day. To see a girl who has been raised in one of the leading families of Isfahan, who has been treated as tenderly as a lily, and who is beautiful as well, to see that girl with red-rimmed eyes in her red-and-gold wedding dress, and to hear a sniffle that charitable guests assume results from a chill—that was too much to bear. I was grateful that I was not a member of Naheed's family, for then I would have had to attend the 'aqd—the wedding ceremony held just for relatives of the bride and groom, led by a mullah. That afternoon, he had asked her three times if she consented to marry Fereydoon, and she had remained silent until the third time, when she said yes. She and Fereydoon had signed the lifetime contract, after which the men and women separated to go to their respective parties.

My mother and I and Gordiyeh had to go to the party for women in the evening, for there could be no excuse for missing it. It was held in the Great Room of Naheed's home, which was illuminated by delicate green oil lamps and decorated with large bouquets of flowers. When we entered, servants offered cold fruit drinks, hot cups of tea, and trays of sweetmeats. Naheed sat by herself on a divan inlaid with mother-of-pearl. Guests streamed in, having removed their outdoor wraps, to greet her and display their finery. I wore the pretty purple robe Naheed had given me with the fur cuffs, and an orange tunic underneath.

"How well that suits you!" she said after I kissed her on both cheeks.

"Naheed-joon, you look more beautiful than you could ever know," I said. For it was true. Her dark hair was decorated with pearls, and her eyes seemed even greener than usual because of her red silk dress, which was embroidered with gold-wrapped thread. She was so lovely I couldn't bear to look at her for too long, so I looked away.

"Don't be so sad for me," she whispered. "I can't endure it."

"All this time, I have believed urgently in your happiness!" I replied. I meant with Iskandar, not Fereydoon.

"You are the only true sweetness in my life," Naheed said. "I shall always be grateful to you for nourishing my secret." She turned her head aside to conceal from others the tear that was leaking onto her cheek.

Guests were still arriving, and I had to make way for those who wanted to greet her. I rejoined my mother, who was on her own while Gordiyeh spoke to friends. Naheed's mother, Ludmila, joined us for a moment.

"Congratulations to you and your family," said my mother. "May your daughter's blessings be eternal."

"Isn't it wonderful?" said Ludmila, her green eyes exactly like

224

her daughter's, except that they looked clearer and happier. "It's just the match I'd hoped for. I'm relieved this day has finally come."

I had to struggle to make my face look as delighted as hers. "I hope from the wellsprings of my heart that they will be happy," I said, but my voice was dull.

I couldn't have felt more like a traitor than I did at that moment. Ludmila looked at me as if she knew something was wrong, but then a friend called out to her, and she moved away.

The servants began to scurry around, unrolling tablecloths on top of the rugs in preparation for the food. They rushed in all at once with platters of whole roasted lamb, oven-cooked squabs, wild game, including the flesh of onager and hare, thick vegetable stews, and steaming platters of rice. My mother and I claimed two cushions and ate our meal together. The meat from the lamb's haunch was as soft as butter. My mother lifted some off the bone with a piece of bread and urged me to eat it. "It melts," she said.

I put it in my mouth but didn't notice how it tasted. The din of the women rose higher and bothered my ears. I wished I could go home and do something quiet, like work on a carpet. I thought of my own marriage and how it had involved no celebrations, only the clink of silver.

After the food was cleared, two female musicians began playing their drum and kamancheh and singing rousing songs about marriage. Groups of women stood up and danced together, repeating the refrains. Naheed had to sing with them and smile, although her heart was in the grave. "Look at the happy bride!" shouted a guest. "May your future always be as bright as today!"

As the evening grew later, the lyrics became more bawdy. A group of women began singing about finding just the right fit between a knocker and its door. Naheed's face became ashen, even when others assured her that she would soon enjoy it as much as they did. I hoped she didn't, for her husband was mine; and yet I hoped she did, for she was my friend.

The party continued deep into the night, even as the town around us grew silent. I drooped, craving my bedroll. But it was not over yet. Near dawn, the servants brought out another meal of lamb, liver, and kidney kebab, fresh hot bread, and yogurt with mint. The excitement began to mount, for we knew that Fereydoon was due to arrive. Ludmila and the women of her household wrapped Naheed in a white chador embroidered with gold, covering her face with a picheh so she would not be seen on the street.

The knocker for men boomed through the house, and Fereydoon swept into the courtyard, dressed in a purple velvet robe with a sky-blue tunic underneath. The women made a show of throwing their wraps around their bodies, without real concern about being seen, for the usual rules were relaxed at a wedding.

Everyone but me and my mother shouted blessings at Fereydoon: "May your marriage be fruitful!" "May your wealth increase!" "May your sons take after their father!" Fereydoon turned to the women, grinning and basking in their good wishes. Although he saw me, he did not acknowledge my presence. A pang of jealousy invaded my body as he took Naheed's hand and led her through the house and out the door, while the rest of us surged behind her into the quiet street. A pair of dappled Arabian horses awaited her. Fereydoon lifted her by the waist so that she could put her foot into the stirrup and mount the mare. Then he hoisted himself onto the steed and flashed a triumphant smile.

I imagined how he would lift Naheed's picheh and look on her beautiful face, and I tried to crush the thoughts that kept arising about what they would do once they were alone. I wondered if he would admire her long, slender body, so different from mine, and if they would fit together the way he and I did. As they began to ride away, the women shouted blessings to the new husband and wife. All of us trotted behind the horses, which, in their excitement, left dark, heavy droppings in our path. The women's cries grew so high-pitched I wanted to cover my ears. I grabbed my mother's arm for fear I would collapse in the street. Then, at last, the animals gained speed and disappeared, and we could go home.

THE NEXT MORNING, Gordiyeh stopped into the kitchen while I was mixing flour and water to make bread. I happened to be alone, for my mother was in the courtyard boiling herbs, and Cook had gone to the latrines.

"Good news!" she said. "Naheed's parents have commissioned a large silk rug from us as a gift to celebrate her marriage. It is to be made with saffron dye."

"That's wonderful," I said, feeling as heavy as the dough.

Silk loved saffron, but the cost was beyond compare. Workers would harvest thousands of lavender-colored flowers when they bloomed in the fall and remove the three stigmata — so thin as to be almost weightless — from each flower. The bright red stigmata would be dried and powdered, and a dye brewed to create the dearest of yellows.

"It's a sign from above that it was wise to keep the sigheh secret," Gordiyeh said. "You did right, you know."

I must have shown my unease, for Gordiyeh leaned toward me and said in a whisper, "The consequences will be very grave if Naheed's family ever learns about your sigheh. Do you understand me?"

I thought I did; she meant she would put us out. But I also realized that the commission made Gordiyeh vulnerable. If Naheed's family ever found out about the sigheh, they would believe she hadn't told them out of greed.

"I will not speak of it," I said coolly, "under one condition."

"What?"

"I need to be excused from kitchen duties so I can make a rug."

227

"For how long?"

"A few months. And I need to bring some women here to help me."

Gordiyeh laughed. "You *are* a crafty little thing. The city has changed you."

"Perhaps it has," I said. "But as you have said yourself, a mother and daughter on their own should always be cautious about their financial future."

Gordiyeh snorted as I threw her words back at her, and her eyes were cold. "You drive a difficult bargain," she said.

"But well worth its price to this household."

She couldn't deny that. "I agree," she said reluctantly, "but let me hear your promise."

"And let me hear yours," I replied. Her eyebrows jumped at that, but she had little choice.

"I promise," we said together.

It was the first time that Gordiyeh had not bested me. I would no longer be docile under her orders if I could think of a way to get something in return. She didn't like it, but she had to take note of it.

WHEN WOULD I hear from him again? How long before he would tire of her and want me in his bed? The days came and went with no word. He would be spending a lot of time with his pretty new wife. There was only one thing I could think of to do to soothe myself, and that was to pick up my pen and draw. I spent hours working on a design in the new Shah Abbas style that Gostaham had shown me, but I thought I'd try something a little different, inspired by the foliage in the Four Gardens district. I drew long, tapered leaves that looked like scimitars, which would cross the rug horizontally. Once I had the pattern for the leaves, I drew small bouquets of flowers and arranged them vertically above and below. The design led the eye in both directions, left to right and back again, using the leaves; and up and down and back again, using the blossoms.

When I showed Gostaham the design, he studied it for a long time. He made a few corrections and changes before giving me his approval. Then he sighed and exclaimed, "If you had only been a boy . . . !"

I sighed, too.

"You take after me more than my own daughters — you have a natural gift. If you had been a boy, you could have risen through the ranks and learned to make carpets that would be treasured forever and cited by the masters after you. Perhaps, as a sign of recognition from the Shah, you might even have been permitted to inscribe your name on one of your finest works. I know you would have made me proud. As it is, you have made a very good design."

I flushed, imagining my name knotted in silver thread on an indigo carpet, identifying me as a master for hundreds of years to come. No one in my village ever signed their rugs.

He continued studying my design. "What are you going to do for the colors?"

"I thought I'd ask for your help," I said, having learned my lesson on the last one.

"Choose your color samples yourself, and then show them to me," he replied.

I spent entire afternoons in the bazaar looking at balls of wool and thinking of how the hues would fit together. I brought Gostaham fourteen color samples and my design, which I had outlined on a grid, and described which colors I thought would go where. I planned to use a grassy green on the long leaves.

"You could make this rug," he said, "but it wouldn't be as beautiful as you had hoped."

"Why?"

"The colors don't sing together," he said. "That's the difference between an adequate rug and the rug of a master. It's also the difference between making a good profit and a vast one."

I went back to the bazaar and tried again. Although my pattern was based on leaves, the long, tapered shapes that crisscrossed the rug also looked like feathers. They made me think of the lightness of birds and the coolness of wind. I decided to make the feather shapes as white as a dove against a cerulean blue, with a background of deep wine and a dark blue border. The deeper colors would make the paler feathers appear to be light, as if floating from the sky.

Gostaham approved the main colors but felt that the contrasting hues weren't quite right. He told me to find slightly different ones: a darker gray-green for the flower stems, a brighter shade of red for accents within the blossoms. I went back to the bazaar, asking impossible questions. "Don't you have a gray-green that looks like the stem of a flower in the shade?" "How about a richer red, like sour cherry jam?" The merchants soon tired of me. "This is all I've got," one of them told me, waving his arm at his wares. "If you need more precision, pay someone to dye the wool for you." I didn't have that much money, so I persisted until I found samples that seemed right.

After Gostaham approved all the color choices, he told me to paint a copy of my design and show him. I colored it in painstakingly, trying to demonstrate that I had learned his lessons well: Delight the eye with patterns, but refresh it; surprise the eye, but don't overwhelm it.

Even so, Gostaham still didn't like my plan.

"You have large blotches of color without enough complexity. Paradoxically, more detail makes the design lighter. Try again."

It was the hardest thing to achieve as a designer yet the simplest and clearest thing to see as a viewer. I tried three more times. By the time I colored the last copy, I felt I had found the balance I needed among the parts. I begged my mother to give me some of my sigheh money to hire workers. Alone, it would take me a long time to make a rug as tall as I was. But with two workers, it could be done in a few months. My mother didn't want to part with the money because it was all we had, but she changed her mind after she saw my design. "Mash'Allah!" she said. "That is more beautiful than any pattern you've ever made."

As soon as she gave me the money, I went to the bazaar and bought all the wool, and I hired Malekeh to help me. Her husband's health had not improved, and she was grateful for a chance to earn money without having to sell her wares on the street. She had a young cousin named Katayoon who was a fast knotter, and I hired her, too. Neither one knew how to follow a design on paper, so I promised to call out the colors for them.

Before we started the carpet, I showed my final design to Gostaham and asked for his approval. It took him only a few moments before he smiled and said simply, "You have understood."

There was something like wonder in his eyes. "Although you are not a child of my own, you are indeed a child of my heart," he said. "I have always wished to share the secrets of my work with a son. Although God never granted me a boy, He has brought me you."

He fixed a look on me that was so tender, I felt as if I could see my father's bright eyes shining through his.

"Thank you, dear *amoo*," I said, bathing in his love. It was the first time I had dared to address him as "uncle."

NAHEED HAD MOVED to one of the many homes Fereydoon owned, this one located close to the Eternal River with a view of the water and the mountains. After she was settled, she sent a messenger asking me to visit her. I didn't want to go, but I knew that I must, to make things look right.

As I walked through Four Gardens toward the river, I was glad her house was far from the old Friday mosque and the jewel-like home where I met Fereydoon. I turned onto a street near Thirty-three Arches Bridge. The air was fresh, for it was cooled by the river. I understood that the houses were large from the vast distances between one tall gate and the next. Naheed's messenger had told me to look for a new house with a lot of wind catchers on its roof. They sucked air inside and cooled it over pools of water in the basement, keeping its occupants fresh on even the hottest days.

When I stepped through the tall gates that guarded the outside of Naheed's home, I was taken aback. It was a small palace, as if Fereydoon hoped to populate it with a dozen sons and daughters. A deferential servant took my chador and led me into a guest room with silk carpets knotted with rosettes so small they could only have been made by children. The vessels for flowers and libations were all of silver. The cushions sparkled, for they were woven with silver thread. I tried to quell the envy that surged in my heart.

When Naheed entered the room, I was surprised at how quickly she had assumed the role of a woman of wealth and power. She wore thick gold armbands with hanging turquoise and pearls, and the same combination of stones on her forehead, strung on a gold band that held her lacy white head covering in place. Her pale blue silk robe and tunic were subdued, making her look older. Her face was quiet and composed. Her eyes seemed larger than ever, but they were not red. She now reigned over a domicile with twelve servants who attended only to her needs.

"Naheed-joon!" I said, kissing her on each cheek—"though I suppose now that you're married, I should call you Naheed-Khanoom! How are you?"

"How do I look?" she asked wearily.

"Like the moon," I said, "but older than before."

"And sadder."

"Yes, and sadder," I said. We looked at each other, and the sadness in her eyes found a reflection in my own. We sat on cushions close to each other, and Naheed called for coffee and sweets.

232

"How is married life?" I asked, trying to sound nonchalant.

"It's as good as can be expected," she said with a shrug. "I don't see him much."

That seemed odd for a new bride, yet I couldn't help hoping that the reason was me.

"Why not?"

"He is very busy with his land, his horses, and his duties to his father."

"But surely he spends time with you."

"Only at night," she said.

That was not what I wished to hear. I searched her body and face for signs of satisfaction that I hoped not to find. I couldn't bear to know if they were enjoying each other, so I said quickly, "I suppose you can't forget Iskandar."

Her eyes became bigger and sadder, but she retained her composure. "Never," she whispered.

She beckoned me closer. "I must speak quietly. I cannot show myself here until I know who is loyal to him and who is loyal to me. I must pretend that everything is exactly as I want it to be."

"I'm sorry you are so unhappy," I whispered back.

"How can I be happy?" she said. "He is nothing like Iskandar. He is neither handsome nor kind."

In my eyes, Fereydoon had become more handsome than Iskandar. I thought about his muscled thighs wrapped around my hips and his warm wiry chest pressed close to my own. I wanted to protest, "But what about his beautiful hair? And what about when his tongue is drawing patterns on your thighs?" Instead, I began speaking of other things—the carpet I was working on, the wedding presents Naheed had received, her calligraphy—but the conversation kept returning to Fereydoon.

"I could almost stand being married to him—any man is as bad as the next if he isn't Iskandar—except for what happens at night," she said, and then she stopped speaking abruptly.

She took a sip of coffee from a fine blue porcelain cup. "I wish you were married so I could tell you all about it."

Even as she said this, I knew Naheed would tell me everything because she needed to talk, and I was the only woman she trusted. But I didn't want to hear.

"Have you gotten to know his daughter?" I asked quickly, trying to change the subject.

Naheed looked surprised. "Who told you about her?"

For a moment I didn't know how to answer. I had to be very careful now not to reveal too much.

"Ahhh—the carpet," I sputtered. "Remember the carpet he commissioned with talismans to thank God for his daughter's return to health?"

"You mentioned that carpet long ago, when you were helping Gostaham," said Naheed. "But you never told me that Fereydoon commissioned it."

I breathed with difficulty. "I didn't put him together with the man you were marrying until recently," I lied.

"Oh," she said. "I would have expected to be told everything you knew about the man I was marrying." Her tone was sharp.

"I'm truly sorry," I said. "I must have forgotten."

"How strange," she replied. "Is there anything else you know about him?"

My heart was turning blacker than ever, like a lamb's heart roasting over a fire. "Only that Gostaham hopes for more commissions!" I said quickly, trying to sound lighthearted.

Naheed raised her eyebrows, for as the wife of a wealthy man, it was now in her power to offer them. I ducked my head, embarrassed by what I had said.

"I didn't mean anything by that," I said quickly.

She waved her hand. "I know."

Naheed took another sip of coffee while I felt sweat leak down my back.

234

"I'm glad your home is so beautiful," I said.

Naheed looked around herself with dead eyes. "I would have preferred a hovel, if it could be one I shared with Iskandar," she said, and then her face tightened around her eyes. "Remember when the women were teasing me at the wedding? I was afraid, but I never thought having a man in my bed would be as bad as this."

I felt a thrill in my black heart. The better part of me wanted to tell her: It will improve.

Naheed shivered, and the pearls hanging from her upper arms shivered, too. "During the day, he exhibits good manners and good breeding. But at night, he transforms into an animal. When I feel his hot breath at my neck, I want to scream."

That was exactly what I liked about him. He was like an animal in the dark, and being with him allowed me to be the same way. At home, with Gordiyeh, I had to be deferential and show myself to be a good worker; with Gostaham, I tried to be a good pupil; with my mother, to show respect; with visitors, to prove myself a well-mannered daughter. Only with him could I show the truth of my flesh. It had taken me a long time to discover that, and on the nights I didn't see him, it was what I longed for.

I cleared my throat, embarrassed.

"You're blushing," said Naheed with a smile. "I suppose that's only natural, for a virgin."

"Do you think you'd like it better if he were Iskandar?" I asked.

"Of course," she said. "The sight of him without his clothes makes me long for my beloved. His hands on my body feel as rough as a cat's claws. Even his beard scratches my face. I want to throw him off, but I must lie there and wait until he is done."

"How does he like *that?*" I blurted out. I had felt shy when I had first lain with him, but never repulsed in the way Naheed described. The one time I had failed to please him, he had punished me for weeks. What would he do to her?

Naheed looked at me with an odd expression, the corners of her mouth turning down. "He doesn't seem to notice very much. It's as if he's just doing his duty as a husband."

Was it possible that he went to her bed because it was required, but saved himself for me? I wanted to believe it.

"What if you praised him?"

"I tell him that he's as fierce as a falcon and as strong as a lion. I give him honey all the time, but it doesn't matter."

Fereydoon disliked such hollow words, I knew. She would have to do better than that.

"But you don't believe those things about him?"

"No."

"Perhaps, in time, you could learn to like it."

"I doubt it," she said. "But I could live with it, if not for having lost the one thing I cared about."

"Iskandar?"

"Not just him, but also his letters. Right before I got married, he and I agreed it would be too dangerous to continue."

"You were right," I said. "But Naheed, now that you are married forever, do you think you can try to like your husband after all?"

I could hardly believe I had uttered those words. I was caught between wanting my friend to be happy, and wanting her husband—and mine—for myself.

"Never," she said.

"But then, how will you live?" I asked gently.

"I don't know," she said, looking as if she were going to cry. But rather than sobbing in my arms, as she had done before her marriage, she quickly gained control of her face, though I could see how painful it was for her to hold herself back.

"Naheed-*joon!*" I said sympathetically.

"I cannot show myself here," she whispered, and only then did she grind her teeth together to prevent her tears from rising. Her lips pulled back from her teeth, and frown lines etched themselves

236

near her mouth. When she had assassinated the tears, she looked as beautiful as ever, but the grief in her eyes was terrible to see.

As I was leaving, I remembered with a pang of guilt the twist of rainbow-colored threads hidden under my clothes, at my throat. The charm maker had been right: It had knotted up her love. I should have pulled the threads off my neck, but I could not bear to relinquish Fereydoon.

THE DAY AFTER I saw Naheed, Fereydoon summoned me again. As I sat in the little room anticipating how Fereydoon and I would come together, I shivered with pleasure. While Naheed recoiled from him with her whole body, mine opened up pore by pore at the thought of him. How different it was from when I had first lain underneath him! Then I had been the slave, and he the master. Now he was sometimes slave to me. I waited for him that afternoon with the foreknowledge of where we would go together, yet with luxuriant uncertainty about how we would travel there. Fereydoon, I knew, did not plow a groove in the same way twice.

When he arrived that day, it was with a large bundle that he told me promised heavenly delights. After the servants departed, Fereydoon asked me to remove my clothes on my own. I did so slowly in the semidarkness, while he sat cross-legged on a cushion with the bundle beside him. I started awkwardly, but by the time I reached my undergarments, I began to enjoy his gaze.

When I was bare, he arose and lifted me into his arms, twirling me gently around the room. I felt giddy with my long hair swinging behind me and the air stroking my body. When we were close to the bedroll, he lowered me on top of it and told me to close my eyes. I lay there, warm and waiting. I could hear him untying the bundle; then he stood above me quietly. After a moment, I felt a delicate pitter-patter on my belly, the gentlest of showers. I smiled and arched my back. He crouched, pulled another handful from the bundle, and let the rain fall again. Still above me, he rubbed his hands together and the scent of a rosebush filled the room. I opened my eyes: my whole body was patterned in rose petals. Some were pale pink, others bright red, and still others mauve, a multicolored carpet of flowers. A hot red wave started at my toes, surged up my middle, bloomed on my cheeks. I reached for his waist and drew his hips to mine.

"I want your dates in my milk," I said, quoting a poem I had heard at the hammam but probably wasn't supposed to know.

He rubbed against me, crushing the rose petals between our bodies. Their sweet hot perfume filled the air, mingling with our musk. He covered my eyes with rose petals and, with me so blinded, did everything I hoped for and everything I demanded. We surmounted the peak together that night, blending our cries, as if entwined in the fragrant gardens of paradise.

Judging from what Naheed had said about the dullness of her nights with Fereydoon, it was no surprise to discover that he wanted me more than ever. Every time I was summoned, I felt remorse over Naheed, but then when I imagined what I would do with Fereydoon, my knees went slack beneath my clothes, and I couldn't stop myself from going to see him. And every time I went, I dreamed up new ways to please him, and to stop him from bringing our time together to an end. Sometimes it was the way I designed my body for him. Once I strung some blue ceramic beads on a cord and tied it around my hips. They rattled and marked the rhythm of our movements together, teasing his ears. Another time I told him he could not have me until he removed all my clothes using just his mouth. He did what he could, untying the strings that held my clothes with his teeth, pushing fasteners out of their loops with his tongue, pulling off my trousers with his lips. He had a sore jaw afterward, but I have never seen him happier.

The secret I was keeping from Naheed was even worse than I

had thought. Not only was I married to her husband, but I understood how to give him pleasure in ways she couldn't even imagine.

IN THE MORNINGS after I left Fereydoon, I returned home and worked with Malekeh and Katayoon. They came every day except Friday to work on a loom we had set up indoors. Both of them desperately needed the work. Malekeh's husband's illness continued to linger. Katayoon's father, a bricklayer, had recently died after falling off the dome of a mosque he was helping to build. "Straight to God," she had said, her lip trembling. I felt special sympathy for her because she was only fifteen, about the same age I had been when I had lost my father. Now that I was almost seventeen I felt much older, as if I had lived seven lifetimes since leaving my village.

Despite their problems, the women went about their work like an army of ants. Both of them knotted as quickly as I did. Malekeh was shy, but when she became more comfortable, she liked to tell me about her children's antics. Katayoon was like a colt who just wanted to run wild. She kept herself tethered to the loom through an act of will. If I had not been her employer, she would have made a wonderful friend.

Every morning when they arrived, they seated themselves at opposite ends of the loom. I sat behind the loom as I had seen the men do at the royal rug workshop, my design in my hand, and tried to call out the colors at just the right moment. If the chant was "red, red, beige, blue, beige, red, red," they could easily lose the sequence if I didn't make each call right before they had finished the previous knot. Katayoon was a little quicker than Malekeh; I had to tell her to slow down so they could knot the same colors at the same moment. Malekeh, on the other hand, had stronger arms, and when she compressed her knots with a comb, she made them tighter than Katayoon's. I had to ask her to bear down more gently so the rug wouldn't come off the loom with a shorter side.

Every day, we worked from mid-morning until it was time to eat and then resumed again until the middle of the afternoon. I made sure they had plenty of tea and sweetmeats so they would work with ease; and at midday, we all ate together. I suspected it was the only meal they could be sure of. It made me feel good to help them, for I had once felt the ache of hunger myself.

One morning Katayoon had a question about which color to use, for my design was not clear in that spot and I had stumbled in calling out the colors. I thought for a moment and said, "Use the red! And we'll use it in that flower from now on."

"Chashm!" she replied, and did my bidding. I discovered that I liked the feeling of having authority, especially after so many months of doing what others had told me.

Even though I had often spent the night before sporting with Fereydoon and had not slept, I made myself stay awake until Malekeh and Katayoon departed, and then I had a rest. If it was still light when I awoke, I continued knotting the carpet on my own. I wanted to finish it as soon as I could. Gordiyeh had no claim on this one, so whatever I earned would belong just to me and my mother.

ONE MORNING, a stooped old woman knocked at our door and told me that Naheed wished to see me. I asked her to give Naheed my apologies, for I was busy with Malekeh and Katayoon, but she replied that she had been ordered not to return until I was within her care. With that, she sat down heavily in the courtyard and wrapped her shawl around her curved back, as if preparing for the night. I wondered why Naheed had decided to summon me so urgently. The thought that she might have discovered my secret made sweat break out on my neck.

I returned to my knotters, hoping the messenger would get tired and go away. We worked through the morning, and after eating lunch and knotting a few more rows, Katayoon and Malekeh departed. I went to my room and slept. When I arose, the messenger was emerging from the kitchen wiping her mouth, and she asked if I might be ready. Sighing, I donned my picheh and chador, for I knew she would not leave without me.

The streets were bitterly cold, despite a clear sky. The harsh sun seemed to examine all that lay beneath it without pity. The roasted-nut seller who sold his wares near Gostaham's house had lines so deeply engraved near his lips they looked like the slashes of a knife. When the messenger turned to make sure I was still with her, a trace of green oil from our fenugreek and fava bean stew gleamed like a disease on her cheek. I was glad to be able to hide under my picheh from the glare of the sun.

We passed the Seminary of the Four Gardens, where boys studied to become mullahs. I was still taking weekly writing lessons with Naheed, and the calligraphy on the building that had once just looked like beautiful decorations now called out to me the names of God: "The Kind—the Just—the Compassionate—the Fierce—the All-Seeing—the Implacable."

When we arrived at her house, Naheed pressed a coin into the hunched woman's hand and sent her away. I kissed Naheed on each cheek and removed my wraps. I was thirsty, but she did not offer me any of her mint tea. Her face looked pale, and I suspected that her life had become bleaker than before. Fereydoon had begun to lose interest in her bed; he was already spending more nights with me. As the end of my second contract approached, I was certain that he would renew it again, so great was our mutual pleasure every time we joined together.

"I would have come sooner, but I couldn't leave my work," I said. "Why did you send for me?" I had trouble forming the words with my dry tongue.

"I just wanted to see you," Naheed said, but her voice was cool.

I shivered and shifted uncomfortably on my cushion.

"You look cold," Naheed said.

"I am," I replied. "May I have some tea?"

"Of course." She called for her servants to bring tea, but no one came. Usually her women were sitting right outside the door, ready to fulfill her smallest wish. I wondered if she had instructed them not to reply.

"I saw Homa a few days ago," Naheed said abruptly.

"Really?" I said, trying to sound calm. It wasn't common for Naheed to bathe in her old neighborhood now that she had a hammam and bath attendants of her own.

"Did you bathe?" I asked.

"I did," she replied. "It was nice to see familiar faces again. Here it is just me and my women."

"I'm sorry I didn't know," I said, nervously rearranging my legs. "I would have met you there."

Naheed made a face. "Homa told me you had just been there, even though it wasn't your usual day. She said she sees you at the hammam often—sometimes three times per week."

"Yes," I said, "I go there a lot." I didn't explain further, fearing she would catch me in a lie. Every time I gave myself to Fereydoon, I had to make the Grand Ablution to purify myself in the eyes of God. In the morning, Fereydoon used the bath at his home, so I had to go elsewhere.

"Why do you go so often?"

"I like to be clean," I mumbled.

"You used to go just once a week."

I didn't know what to say.

Naheed looked angry all of a sudden. "You're behaving as if you have a secret," she said. I felt pinpricks of sweat under my arms, and I avoided her eyes.

I put my right hand on my heart and lowered my eyes to give myself time to recover.

"I beg your forgiveness," I said, feeling my heart hammering against my chest.

"For what?"

I couldn't think of a believable excuse for visiting the hammam so often. I glanced up, my eyes pleading for understanding.

A hard light came into her eyes. "Tell me the truth," she demanded.

I twisted miserably on my cushion while she held me in her blazing gaze. I felt as exposed as if I had wandered onto the street with no clothes.

"Well?" she prompted. Her voice was sharp and cold.

Looking into her eyes was like staring at the noonday sun. I raised my hands to shield myself, for I could no longer bear her scrutiny.

She could not know it was Fereydoon. Surely not, or her face wouldn't look so calm.

"It's true," I confessed.

"So you *are* married."

"Yes," I replied.

"All this time, when I said you didn't know what it was like to be with a man, you were laughing at me."

"Not laughing," I said, "just trying to keep the promise I made."

"Why would you keep your marriage a secret? It's not a crime."

"It's not a regular marriage," I said. "It's a sigheh."

Naheed looked as if I had spoken a filthy word. "A sigheh?" she said. "But why would your family do that to you?"

I sighed. "When you got married, your family gave your husband a huge dowry of gold and silk. For me, it was the reverse: My husband gave *us* money. That's why."

Naheed looked petulant; I still couldn't tell how much she knew. "You should have told me and my mother. We would have advised you and found you a proper marriage — maybe with a carpet maker like yourself."

A carpet maker! So Naheed didn't think I would be suitable for someone like Fereydoon. Why should her fate bring her so much privilege, while mine did not? Every soul was equal in the eyes of God.

I could hear anger tightening my voice. "I wish I had," I said, but it was only partly true, now that Fereydoon and I were like warp and weft.

"My dearest friend, I'm sorry for you," Naheed said, in such a scornful tone that I knew the marriage lowered me forever in her eyes. "If I still lived at home, my mother wouldn't have allowed me to see you once she knew about your sigheh."

"I couldn't help it," I said bitterly. "Remember when I cut the rug from the loom because I wanted to do better? Gordiyeh raged at me about the loss of the wool. The sigheh offer arrived right after that, and my mother felt we had no choice."

I stopped there, wishing we could talk about something else.

"So whom did you marry? Now you must reveal everything," she said, smiling to encourage me, but I noticed her eyes looked harder than emeralds.

"Naheed, you must already know," I said miserably, the words clotting in my mouth.

"How would I know?" she replied in an innocent tone.

I hesitated. I knew that Gostaham, Gordiyeh, and even my mother would have advised me to make up a story to keep peace among the families. All I had to say was that my husband was a successful groomsman or a petty silver merchant—someone with modest success, but not enough status to make Naheed suspicious.

"Don't you wish to take me into your confidence?" Naheed asked, looking offended. "Or has our friendship ceased to matter to you?"

"Of course it matters!"

"Then tell me. Whoever it is, I'll be glad for you."

"Do you promise?"

She didn't answer, but put her hand reassuringly on mine. I

longed to unburden myself of my secret, which had weighed on me
for too long. Naheed had valued me once for telling her the truth
about her spoiled dates; perhaps she would value the truth again,
and it would bring us closer.

"It is Fereydoon," I whispered, so softly that I hoped she wouldn't
hear.

Naheed released me and jumped up out of her cushion. "I knew
it!" she cried, her eyes angry again. "I sent Kobra to his little house
on an errand, and she thought she heard your voice. I hoped it wasn't
true."

I looked away, ashamed.

"I trusted you! I thought you always spoke the truth!"

"I always tried to," I said. "Naheed, it happened months before
your engagement to Fereydoon. How could I know that your parents would select him, of all the marriageable men in Isfahan? Our
fates have been tied together, just as Kobra predicted when she read
our coffee grounds."

Naheed was staring down at me in the cushion; she would not
spare me. "How long is your sigheh?"

"Three months."

"And when did you first make the agreement?"

"Almost three months before your wedding."

Naheed pointed an accusing finger at me. "That means you renewed it!" she exploded.

I sighed. "When you told me about your engagement, my mother
and I had already accepted his renewal offer and his money. We
were afraid to cancel the agreement for fear of offending Fereydoon
or our hosts. We have no one else in the world to protect us, and no
money of our own."

"Money!" said Naheed in a tone of disgust. "Everything's about
money, just as it was with my Iskandar."

"But Naheed," I pleaded, "we were afraid of having to beg on the streets. You don't understand. How could you know what it's like to fear that your next meal will be your last?"

"I don't know what that's like," she said, "and I thank God. All I know is that you have been disloyal; you have sat beside me, listening to my stories about my husband, pretending he was nothing to you. And you probably told him all the awful things I said about him. No wonder he has been ignoring me."

"I never told him anything you said," I replied. "We don't talk much."

"Oh," she said, understanding more than I had intended. "How can you even stand it — to submit to him in bed?" Then, musingly: "Of course, you are paid and must do what you are told. He would expect that with a woman like you."

"That's not the reason," I said, wanting to hurt her back. "At first it was for the money, but now I do it because I love it."

She put her hands over her ears like a child. "I don't want to hear any more," she replied. "But don't think you're the only one — he also takes that young musician into his bed whenever he pleases."

A sound of revulsion escaped my lips as I thought of the pretty, impudent boy with the smooth cheeks. He had always felt free to flirt in my presence, as if I didn't matter.

When I recovered myself, I looked at Naheed for help, wondering if we could become allies. "In that case, we are all his to use as he wishes," I said. "What shall we do?"

"I don't know about *we*," she said. "You know that *I* can do nothing about his wives or sighehs. The only thing I can do is bear him proper heirs. That's something the musician can't do."

I looked at her closely; she seemed a little rounder in the face and belly, and I guessed she was pregnant.

"Naheed," I said, "I beg you most humbly to forgive me. I know I should have told you sooner, and I regret my error. But now that fate has thrown us together in such a peculiar way, can't you and I both be his wives, and raise our children together?"

Naheed laughed out loud. "You and I?" she said. "You say that as if we're two chickpeas in a pot."

"Aren't we?" I said. "I have always loved and admired you. When I met you, I thought you were like a princess in a tale."

"And I thought of you as a simple village girl who would accompany me to polo," she replied in such a dismissive tone that I felt stricken to the heart. But then she was silent for a moment. Her face softened, and I saw moisture in her eyes.

"Everything changed when I began to know you," she continued. "I grew to care for you because of your honesty, loyalty, and loving heart. But now I see that I was wrong, for you have hurt and betrayed me, and treated me worse than an unclean dog on the street."

I felt great remorse, for I cared for her and had never wanted to cause her grief. But before I could say anything, Naheed shook her head as if to banish her tears, and her anger reared up stronger than before. "I should have known better than to befriend a girl like you," she said.

"What do you mean?" I asked, feeling my own anger start to boil. "Because I was raised in a small village?"

"No," she said.

"Because I work with my hands?"

She hesitated for a moment, and I suspected that was part of it, but then she said, "Not that, either."

"Then why?"

"A respectable married woman like me does not associate with someone who sells sex for silver."

I jumped to my feet, anger scorching my cheeks, for she made it sound as if I were no better than a prostitute. "Respectable, perhaps, but a rose never had so many thorns," I shouted. "That's why your husband turns to me, and groans with pleasure in my arms."

Naheed arose, approached me, and bent her face so close to mine I felt her breath against my lips.

247

"I can't force you to relinquish him, but if you bear his children, I shall curse them," she said softly. "If a cherry sharbat seller poured them a poisoned drink, no one would ever be the wiser."

Her eyes and her jewels glittered like knives in the late-afternoon light. I began backing away. Naheed's hands curled into claws, as if she wished to grab and wound my organs of conception. I ran toward the door and pushed it open. A woman servant, who had been crouching nearby, fell over, surprised at my graceless departure. "Where's my tea?" I shouted at her as I grabbed my outdoor garments from a hook and rushed outside, where I knew Naheed would not follow.

It was cold, but I could not bear to go home. I walked to Thirty-three Arches Bridge and ducked into one of its pointed archways. Clouds were gathering over the mountains, and the water looked like sharp green glass. I stared at rich women with silk chadors strolling slowly over the bridge in their wooden-heeled shoes, which raised them above the ground, while poor women shuffled along in dirty cotton rags wrapped around their feet.

I remembered how quickly Naheed had first offered her friendship, which meant that my usefulness was on her mind when we first met. But that didn't explain all the time she had spent with me after we had been caught at polo, and all the attention she had lavished on me during my writing lessons. Naheed had trusted me with her most precious secret, and she had even told me that she hoped we would always be friends. But now I understood what she believed about poor village girls like me: that we should content ourselves with making the velvety carpets under her feet.

It was starting to drizzle. A man opened his palms to the sky to feel the rain, uttering his thanks to God for the gift of water. As I quickly retraced my steps over the bridge, the drops got bigger and began to sting. I imagined Naheed safe in her home. She'd be watching the rain fall in the courtyard from a heated room, and not even a drop would darken her blue silk robe. If her feet became cold, a maid would warm them with her own hands. I clutched my chador tightly to try to protect myself from the rain, but it was no use: I arrived home wet and chilled to the marrow.

When my mother saw me, her eyes opened wide with alarm. She stripped off my wet garments and wrapped me in a thick wool blanket. I shivered so fiercely that she had to drape her body around mine to keep the blanket in place. My tremors did not cease until well after the last call to prayer.

DURING THE NEXT FEW DAYS, I felt weary inside. My body seemed too weighty to carry around, my eyes burned, and I sniffled from time to time. My mother fussed over me and fed me her thick black herbal concoctions, believing that I was ill. When Fereydoon summoned me again, I went to him with so much heaviness in my heart, I could not conceal it.

"What's the matter?" he asked as soon as he walked into the room. He sat on the cushion next to mine and stroked my face, and I leaned my head against his shoulder as if I were a sick child.

"I'm sad," I said.

He pulled off his turban and sent it spinning across the room to make me laugh. I managed a weak smile.

"Sad about what?"

"Everything." I didn't want to tell him about what had happened with Naheed, for fear he would hurt her in return.

"Why?"

I wasn't sure I could make him understand. "Don't things ever happen that make you sad?"

"Not really," he said. "I've been worried at times that I might be killed in battle, or that my father might turn against me, or that I might die too soon."

"I'm always afraid of that."

"What, of dying too soon? Not a young woman like you."

"No, that other people will die or that things will end."

Fereydoon looked away for a minute; I could see that he wasn't going to make me any promises about our future, even about our sigheh.

"I know what to do to make you feel better," he said. He put his arms around me and kissed my face, then held me quietly for a long time. When I became thirsty, he lifted a glass of milk and wine to my lips, which I drank slowly. I basked in his tenderness, which I experienced so rarely.

He asked if I wanted him, or just wanted to be held in his arms. I wanted both, so he gave me one and then the other. It was so slow the first time that the lamps burned all their black oil and extinguished. We twined together like silk and velvet, and when we were finished, I lay quietly in his arms, and he stroked my hair. Then we both slept a little.

I was the first to wake because my mind was so full of thoughts. Of how I had come to Isfahan, and how Naheed had seemed like one of the heroines in my mother's tales. How the first time I had met her, she had said about her parents, "I'll get them to do what I want." How I had believed that a girl like her could always obtain what she desired. How I had hoped to be friends with her forever, and how I loved her and wished for her forgiveness.

Although he was still asleep, Fereydoon put his arms around me. The guilt I felt about hurting Naheed evaporated for a moment with the joy of being encircled in his arms. I began kissing his neck, and when he awoke, I was hungry. I flung myself at him, wanting to taste and bite. We were like lion and lioness together, fierce and playful, and Fereydoon's eyes were heavy with gratitude.

"I never know what to expect with you," he said, "except that I will be suffused with pleasure, and that every time it will be different."

"I never know, either," I replied, feeling proud of what I could do. Perhaps I learned slowly, but unlike Naheed, I had finally understood how to do this thing well. And now, in the dark of night, with our bodies wet with each other's sweat, my heart was opening to Fereydoon. I rolled onto my side and looked into his face.

"Do you know why I was sad earlier tonight?"

"No," he said, sounding sleepy.

"I went to see Naheed. She knows."

He opened his eyes and looked at me. "About the sigheh?"

"Yes."

I expected him to be shocked, but he yawned and rubbed his beard, and then his hands traveled down his chest in the direction of his thighs. When he found what he was looking for, a small smile appeared at the corners of his lips.

"What did she say?" he asked while rubbing.

"She wasn't very happy," I replied.

"And so?"

His words weren't even cold; they were just indifferent. They sent a shudder through my body as if I had swallowed ice on a hot day. Before I had time to reply, Fereydoon grabbed my hands to help him with his task. I was reluctant and tried to pull away, for I wanted to tell him more. We wrestled for a while until finally I broke free, falling back onto the bedroll. Fereydoon rolled on top of me, and I saw a hardness in his eyes that reminded me of Naheed. There was a demand for silence within them and an insistence that I please him, right now, without another word.

I think my eyes must have shown my resistance, and that was the worst thing I could have done because Fereydoon viewed it as a game. He pushed my knees open with his and took me without another word. I grunted miserably, unprepared, and watched with pained surprise as Fereydoon's eyes fluttered with extra pleasure.

I decided to show him I was angry. I allowed exaggerated noises of pleasure to escape my lips, although my eyes wore a bored look, and I thrust my hips into his with false enthusiasm. I expected that my feigned delight would give him pause, even shame him. Instead, to my astonishment, he stiffened until he became as hard as a tent pole. I moved my body around wildly, hoping to bend him or throw him off, but my fury only fanned his ardor. Just as in our earliest days together, it didn't matter to him what I thought or how I felt. If I received pleasure from his body, he enjoyed that, and if I resisted him, he would find a way to enjoy that, too. The only thing that bored him was impassivity. Within moments, he squeezed my back with his hands and roared like a lion, making sure I understood the imperviousness of his pleasure.

As he rolled off me, his body glistening with sweat and his eyes soft with satisfaction, he tapped the heel of his palm against my cheek. It was the way a horseman might cuff a mare that had succeeded in jumping a difficult hurdle but still needed to be reminded who was in charge.

"Good girl," he said. Within moments, he was snoring.

I lay beside him, my scalp burning with humiliation. Was my only role to please Fereydoon, whether or not my mind was troubled? I rolled out of bed, not caring if I woke him, and sat alone on a cushion on the other side of the room.

Fereydoon snorted and stretched out his arms and his legs, taking up the whole bedroll. The pillows flew off until only his remained. There in the gloom, I saw my marriage for what it was: a way for Gordiyeh to try to sell rugs, for my mother to feel calmer about our future, and for me to have a man without having a dowry.

I rubbed my face where Fereydoon had cuffed it. I had longed to love a man as deeply as Naheed had loved Iskandar, until I realized that her love was built on nothing but dreams. I had searched myself for signs of love for Fereydoon but had not found any deep roots. Now I knew I never would.

An owl cried out near the house, claiming the dark. I couldn't even claim half of Fereydoon's bed. I leaned against the wall and wrapped my arms around my body, holding myself in the night. Fereydoon never noticed that I had left. At dawn, I forced myself to curl up on the bedroll, for I didn't dare anger him with my absence. When he awoke, I feigned sleep until he was gone.

THE NEXT AFTERNOON, I walked to the hammam in search of Homa, not knowing who else to confide in. It was a gusty day, and the wind blew my chador around my legs and threw grit into my eyes through my picheh. The weather was still chilly, and the clay houses near the hammam seemed to huddle together against the wind. A child's head wrap flew by, chased by an anxious mother and her little boy. The wind made a low, lonely sound as it pursued them through the alley.

It was a relief to go inside. I shook the dust out of my chador and searched for Homa until I found her in the clothes-changing section of the hammam, which she was cleaning before it opened for women. I must have looked as green as fenugreek, because she immediately opened her arms to me and kept me enclosed while I confessed everything. I don't think I've ever talked so much. When I was done, it was very quiet, and Homa was still cradling me like a child. She led me to some cushions, stretched out my legs, and fitted a pillow under my head. Then she dotted my body with rose water to give me strength.

"Did you know?" I asked.

"I suspected," she replied, her eyes sympathetic, "but I didn't guess the man."

"Did I do wrong?"

"In the eyes of God, you were legally married," she said calmly.

"But did I?"

"What do you think?"

I sighed and looked away.

"Poor child!" she said. "I can see how sorry you are. If you had

253

been my daughter, I would have told Naheed and her parents about your sigheh before her wedding. They probably would have married off their daughter all the same, for what wealthy man does not have his concubines? But then they would not have blamed you, and perhaps you would have retained your friendship."

Deep in my heart, I knew she was right. "Homa, what should I do?" I asked.

She sighed. "What is there to be done now? Everyone will know the truth, so you might as well stay married."

"Why?"

"Because you no longer have your virginity. Before, you were poor, but at least you had that to offer. Now what do you have?"

She was right, of course. "What if Fereydoon doesn't renew?"

"Then you must be alone."

I was too young to imagine spending the rest of my days on my own, with no children by my side. That was even worse than what my mother had endured. "I don't want to be alone," I said bitterly.

Homa stroked my hand. "My child, do not fear. If your sigheh ends, you will have some advantages all the same."

"Advantages?"

Homa smiled. "If God is with you, and may He always be, then you will find a better man and marry again. If not, you can still contract your own sighehs. No one can tell you who to marry from now on."

I hadn't thought about that. "But Naheed told me her mother would have forbidden our friendship after my sigheh."

Homa closed her eyes for a moment and dipped her chin in agreement. "It is not the most honorable of situations. That's why most divorced women who contract sighehs do it in secret."

"Why do it at all?"

"For money, for pleasure, for children, or in the hope that a man may someday make you his real wife."

"But would people consider me low class?"

"They may."

No one I trusted had told me so plainly that my reputation had been blackened. My expression must have shown my distress, for Homa took my face in her hands.

"Azizam, you must never tell, but I did it once myself," she whispered.

"Why?"

"I fell in love with a boy when both of us were young, but our families married us to other people. After my husband died and my children were grown, my first love and I still wished to be united. Since he could barely feed his wife and eight children, we could not marry in the usual way."

"Did anyone know about it?"

"No, we thought it wise to keep it silent."

"Did he give you money?"

"Only if I needed it," she replied.

"How long did it last?"

"For ten years, until the day he died," she said. "I thank God for giving us the right to sigheh, for it was my only experience of love."

"Then why couldn't you tell anyone?"

"Many people from good families think it is indecent for women," she said. "After all, wouldn't you rather be a permanent wife and the queen of your household?"

"Of course," I said, "but I didn't have that choice."

"Often, we must live with imperfection," she said. "And when people worry about a stain on their floor, what do they do?"

Despite how I felt, I had to laugh, for I knew what she meant. "They throw a carpet over it," I replied.

"From Shiraz to Tabriz, from Baghdad to Herat, that is what Iranians do," she said.

I was quiet for a moment, for that was at the heart of it. I looked up at Homa, who took my hand and warmed it between hers.

"Homa, what shall I do?" I asked again. "What will happen to me?"

"Azizam, it is too soon to say," she replied. "For now, recognize that you have had bad luck, and that you have also made your mistakes, like Haroot and Maroot. Those two wanted something so badly that they succumbed to temptation and betrayed the Greatest Master of All. You wanted something, too, but have understood that it's not always possible to obtain your desires. And now you long to make amends. Make them in whatever way you can, and be like the date that grows sweeter and sweeter, even though the soil that nourishes it is rocky and harsh."

Before anyone else came into the hammam, Homa washed me and massaged me like a mother, combed my hair, wrapped me in a towel, and fed me strong poppy seeds to make me drowsy. I stretched out on a bedroll in a cubicle and fell into a deep sleep. The old story of Haroot and Maroot came to me in my dreams, along with the determination to be nothing like them.

First there wasn't and then there was. Before God, no one was.

Once there were two angels named Haroot and Maroot. One of their favorite pastimes, when their heavenly deeds were done, was to spy on humankind. Knowing that the earth was bountiful, they believed that living in accordance with God's laws should have been as easy as pulling fish from the waters of the Gulf. Yet everywhere they looked, they saw humans stealing, lying, cheating, fornicating, and killing. Look here: see the man in Constantinople plotting to force his neighbor's daughter into his foul embrace. Look there: see the woman in Baghdad concocting a poison to stir into her wealthy father's stew. Haroot and Maroot watched such conflicts unfold over months and years. Every time a human being had a fall, they made a sound together like the tinkling of bells.

One day God summoned Haroot and Maroot into His presence and announced that they were to be sent to earth on a special assignment. "You will assume the bodies of human beings," He said, "and you will show all the angels in heaven, and all of humankind besides, how to live just and honorable lives."

Haroot and Maroot's wing tips glowed with the honor. Within moments, they assumed human forms and materialized in the holy city of Mashhad, which was always full of pilgrims. Haroot had become a tall, handsome bearded fellow with empty pockets. Maroot was shorter and squatter, with a flat nose, but his purse jingled with gold abbasi coins.

They found themselves in the courtyard of the most holy site in all of Iran, the shrine of Imam Reza, which glittered with small mirrors cut like jewels. Sensing their spiritual natures, pilgrims formed a circle around them and asked questions. Since they were angels well versed in God's ways, their service came easily to them. Their thoughtful answers were like sweet rain from heaven, soothing and fruitful.

Toward nightfall, Maroot began to feel a stabbing pain in his middle. Not knowing what it was, he marveled at the strangeness of the sensation. Had God sent him to earth on a mission like that of Jesus? Would he, too, have to die? The thought of experiencing more pain in his body made him shiver and clutch his abdomen.

Noticing his distress, his friend Haroot stood up too quickly, saw black, and crashed to the earth. The devoted pilgrims lifted the two men and carried them into one of the mosque's shady arcades. "All day those two forgot to eat and drink," said one of the pilgrims. "It was as if they had already left their bodies behind and ascended into one of the spheres of heaven."

The sensible pilgrim had brought her own food. She scooped a morsel of roasted eggplant onto a triangle of bread and placed it gently in Maroot's mouth. His eyes fluttered and he began nibbling on her fingers. He tugged the remaining bread and eggplant from her hands, eating with a piggish abandon that surprised and disgusted her. When the pilgrim gave water to Haroot, he consumed it all with loud slurping sounds and demanded more. "What are these men?" she wondered.

At nightfall, most of the other pilgrims returned to their lodgings. As an act of charity, the woman determined to stay behind until the two men had *regained their strength. Having eaten and drunk, Haroot and Maroot were feeling better. By the time the moon rose, they began to notice more about the woman who had ministered to them. Her face was white, and she had apples blooming on her cheeks. Her dark eyes were fringed with lashes as pretty as a doe's. Haroot longed to lift the cloth that covered her hair. Maroot wondered about the mystery of her belly, no doubt round and soft like freshly baked bread.*

Seeing that the men had returned to health, the woman rose to return to her lodgings. "Wait, O merciful pilgrim," said Haroot in a pleading voice he didn't recognize as his own. "Please share your company with us for a few moments more. We need you."

They are like children, the woman thought, but she sat with them again, vowing to leave as soon as they regained their calm. Where could two such strange fellows have been raised? To make the time pass, she asked, "You are children of which town?"

Haroot and Maroot burst into laughter they couldn't control, gasping and snorting, she thought, like wild pigs. It was as if they had never laughed before. Maroot was on the ground with his face in the earth before his laughter finally subsided. He arose with his cheeks and nose streaked with dirt.

"If we told you, you'd never believe us," said Haroot, while Maroot gestured toward the heavens.

Perhaps they are from a religious order where men become so deeply spiritual they forget their earthly roots, the woman thought, but there was doubt in her eyes. "Originally, when your mothers gave birth to you, where did you live?"

Haroot and Maroot knew they were being treated with the patience shown to simpletons. A new sensation arose in each of them, as unfamiliar as all the others. Maroot's cheeks burned, and Haroot's back and jaw stiffened.

"We're from the greatest sphere," said Haroot, gesturing upwards again.

"And we can prove it," Maroot added.

The woman looked skeptical. "How can you prove it?"

"Earlier in the day, you listened with great attention to every word we uttered," said Haroot. "Didn't we seem different than other men?"

The woman reflected on how she had perceived them that morning. "Some hours ago, I might have believed you," she admitted. "You hardly seemed to inhabit your bodies."

Haroot and Maroot watched her lips linger over the word "bodies." Each was stricken with a desire to reach for her and stroke her warm belly and thighs. Perhaps, if they kept her near, she would be generous with them, the way pilgrims could sometimes be.

"Our bodies were new to us," confided Maroot.

The woman waved her hand as if to dismiss him. Once again, she rose to go.

"Wait!" said Maroot. "I have proof."

"You said that before."

"I can tell you something known by no other being on earth."

The woman waited quietly, looking unconvinced. Haroot put his hand to his heart, feeling regretful about what he knew they would do. To his surprise, he found a way to quash that feeling as quickly as it arose.

"The price of what we know is a kiss," said Maroot.

Haroot became angry because he thought his friend was trying to exclude him. "One for each of us," he said with a fiery glance.

The woman shifted her weight from foot to foot. "What is it that you know?" she asked.

"We know about God," said Maroot.

The woman had traveled many farsakhs on foot to reach Mashhad. Every day, she prayed five times and tried to open her heart to the divine. Could the message of the heavens be right in front of her, in the form of these child-like men?

"Is it a bargain?" prompted Haroot.

"Perhaps," she said with a small smile.

Remorse had been growing again in Haroot's breast, but a glimpse of her small white teeth between her red lips helped vanquish those feelings.

"Sit beside us," he said, patting a blue tile, "and we will tell you the thing that only we know."

She sat between Haroot and Maroot, who pressed close against each of her hips. Haroot felt an ecstatic surge in his loins. For a moment he imagined throwing Maroot in a well, just so he could be alone with the pilgrim.

"Speak," said the woman. "What can you teach me about God, the Compassionate, the Merciful?"

"His ninety-nine names are already well known," said Maroot. "The only man to know the hundredth name was the holy Prophet Mohammad — that is, until the two of us arrived on earth."

"You think you know the Great Name?" said the woman. "I don't believe you."

"First, a kiss," said Haroot and Maroot together.

"Oh no," said the woman. "I've heard promises like yours before. First, the name."

Haroot and Maroot leaned in close, putting their lips near each of her ears. After drawing in a breath, the two men whispered the Great Name. The woman's mind filled with the majestic sound, which reverberated between her ears. Had she been able to think of Haroot and Maroot, she would no longer have doubted them. But all of her thoughts had become echoes of the sound, and her body began to feel as cool and as light as air. All her desires were fulfilled in a single instant, and she became a planet in the third sphere beyond earth, from which she now glows eternally as pure light.

Haroot and Maroot were transported, too. They found themselves suspended by their ankles inside a deep well, their heads pointing toward the water. By day, the sun beat down, blistering their lips and burning the soles of their feet. Their throats dried and cracked as they stared into the cool water, which was just out of reach of their hands. By night, they shivered in the cold, their flesh puckering with goose bumps. If they spoke at all, it was to remember what it had been like to be angels and feel nothing.

Sometimes, when the stars were positioned in the skies just so, they could see her. She beamed the light of her beautiful, compassionate eyes onto the earth, and they loved her and longed for her through their misery.

CHAPTER SIX

The next day, I was standing in the kitchen helping my mother clean herbs for her medicines when the knocker for men boomed twice. "Go see who it is," Cook said, so I covered myself in my chador and picheh, opened the door, and saw one of Fereydoon's menservants, who handed me a letter for Gostaham. Knowing that he couldn't recognize me in my wraps, I concealed the letter and told Cook it had been a merchant selling mountain roots for stew, which I knew we didn't need.

I went to the room that my mother and I shared and looked at the seal: It was Fereydoon's. My heart beat faster. I had shown Fereydoon my displeasure, and now perhaps he was writing to say he was done with me. I held the paper to an oil lamp in a vain effort to see the writing it concealed. I told myself to take the letter directly to Gostaham, but I couldn't force my feet to move. Even if the letter was not mine, the news it contained certainly was. I hesitated, and then I broke the seal.

It took me a long time to read the letter: My skills were still poor, and I couldn't understand many of the words. But I found my name mentioned a few times, and I understood that Fereydoon was offering a sigheh for another three months, in consideration of the fact that he was pleased with me.

Having committed an unforgivable deed by opening a letter addressed to Gostaham, I hid the letter in my sash. I needed to think about the offer this time without the advice of my family. Now that I was no longer a virgin, it was my turn to decide what I wanted. Homa had said that was my right.

KATAYOON AND MALEKEH arrived a little later than usual that morning. Katayoon looked as fresh as ever, but Malekeh had deep circles under her eyes.

"How is your husband?" I asked.

"Still ailing," she replied. "He was coughing all night."

"How about some coffee to lift your spirits?" I asked. She gratefully accepted the steaming vessel I put beside her.

When we sat down to work, I called out the colors while considering Fereydoon's offer. I felt my body saying yes to it. Not even one day had gone by and I was already craving Fereydoon's arms, despite the way he had cuffed me; and I had already thought of a dozen new ways to please him and myself. I had become like the opium eaters who fret until they get their daily dose of the sticky black drug, after which they relax against their cushions, their knees parted, a look of bliss in their eyes.

I told myself it was a fine idea to go on with things as they were. Now that Naheed knew everything, I didn't need to keep the sigheh a secret anymore. She would hate me and hate my children, but I would have Fereydoon's attention, and perhaps I could live a happy, separate life. Maybe I would conceive boys, and although I would have no rights of inheritance, they would take care of me in my old age.

If I accepted Fereydoon's offer, it would also be a sweet form of revenge. I would be like a thorn, reminding Naheed that Fereydoon had married her not for love, but for power. When her husband was absent at night, she would think about how much he was enjoying me, and suffer.

Such were my thoughts until the midday meal, when Gordiyeh came to talk to me. She was smartly dressed in a new yellow robe and green tunic, with the emerald Gostaham had given her long ago shining like a small sea above her breasts.

"I have just received an invitation to visit Naheed's mother," she said.

"May your visit be charmed," I replied, concealing a smile. Rather than tell her what had happened, I decided to leave that to Ludmila.

"Would you like to accompany me?" Gordiyeh was pleased with me lately and was showing it with small favors. "We'll probably discuss the carpet commission, which I know will interest you."

"You are kind to think of me," I replied, "but I must attend to Katayoon and Malekeh, who need me here so that they can do their work."

"All right, then," she said, smiling. I know she liked it when I stayed with my chores.

I continued singing out the colors for my knotters until it was time to stop for a moment so that Malekeh and Katayoon could compress the knots with a wooden comb. Malekeh pressed down so hard on her side that the comb broke, and then she looked as if she, too, might snap. I could always see how she felt by looking at her eyes, which spoke far more than she did.

"No matter," I said, although I could ill afford the loss. "I'll buy a new one."

Malekeh said nothing, but I knew she was grateful that I did not make her pay for the comb.

When she and Katayoon departed, I began knotting on my own. I wanted to be there when Gordiyeh returned so I could see her face. She came back an hour later looking white and scared, the kohl smudged around her eyes. She shook a letter in my face.

"What do you know about this?" she asked, her voice like a shriek.

"What is it?"

"Kobra told me to wait outside, and then Ludmila handed me this letter and slammed the door in my face."

I feigned surprise. "Why would she do that?"

Gordiyeh sat down beside me on a cushion. "They must have found out," she said, tapping the letter against my shoulder. "This cancels the order for the rug. Do you know what that means to us?"

Gostaham had spent a mountain of money on the design and on ordering a roomful of silk to be dyed to his specifications. The carpet would be impossible to sell elsewhere, for it was designed with motifs particular to Fereydoon and Naheed. I had not thought about its fate when Naheed and I were arguing.

"What a calamity!" I said, and meant it. I knew everyone in the household would pay if Gordiyeh felt worried about money. We had only just started eating jam again.

Gordiyeh poked me with her finger. "When was the last time you saw Naheed?"

"Just a few days ago, but she didn't mention anything about the carpet," I said. That much was true.

"Then how did her parents find out?"

"I don't know," I said, trying to look scared. "I wonder what Naheed will think . . . Will her parents tell her?"

"Of course they will," said Gordiyeh. Her voice became cajoling and almost gentle. "Surely you or your mother must have told someone."

"I have never opened a discussion about my marriage," I said, keeping my voice even. Gordiyeh looked as if she didn't believe me.

"I'm frightened," I added, hoping to engage her sympathy. "I hope Naheed doesn't ask me to visit her."

"I don't think you have to worry about that anymore."

Gordiyeh went to her rooms with a headache. I thought I would be gloating over how she had been disgraced, but my thoughts turned to Ludmila. She had always been kind to me, and now she despised us. I regretted that my desire for Fereydoon had made me agree to keep silent. What should I do now about his offer? That morning, I had wanted to accept it. Now I wasn't sure. My heart turned first one way, then the other.

AS SOON AS I had a free moment, I went to the bazaar to replace the comb that Malekeh had broken. I walked by the rug sellers and wool dyers to get to the part of the bazaar reserved for rug tools such as surface-shearing blades, fringe separators, and combs. The alleyways were dim and narrow in this section of the bazaar, and they were littered with trash.

As I looked in the shops, I heard someone playing a searing melody on his kamancheh. I hummed along, for it was strangely familiar. When I realized why, I retraced my steps and found Fereydoon's young musician sitting alone on a stone, playing his instrument. The ends of his turban looked ragged, and his face was streaked with dirt.

I approached him and said, "Salaam. It's me."

"Who is 'me'?" he asked in a surly voice without looking up from his bowing.

I flipped up my picheh to show him my face.

"Oh," he said. "You're one of his."

"What do you mean by that?" I asked, surprised by his rudeness.

"Nothing," he replied, as if the subject bored him.

I concealed my face again. "What happened to you? I thought you were one of his favorites."

He bowed a note on the kamancheh like a cat yowling, and his lips formed a sarcastic smile. "He threw me out."

"Why?"

"I gave him too much cheek," he said. "He loves it until you say the wrong thing."

The sour notes he was playing hurt my ears. "Stop that," I said. "What will you do now?"

"I don't know," he replied. "I have nowhere to go." I saw fear in his pretty, long-lashed eyes, and his smooth chin trembled. He was still hardly more than a child.

I pulled out the coin I had intended to use to buy the comb and put it in his begging bowl. "May God be with you," I said.

He thanked me and bowed a sweet, melancholy melody as I walked away. It reminded me of the music he had played the first night I had spent with Fereydoon. How much had changed since then, both for me and for the young musician! How abruptly he had been abandoned to the street!

Having lost my heart for shopping, I turned my steps toward home. On my way out of the bazaar, I passed a small mosque that I knew well. I entered it and sat quietly in one of its carpeted side rooms, listening to a woman read aloud from the Qur'an. She had arrived at one of my favorite passages, about how there are two seas, one with water that is sweet and nourishing, while the other is salty, yet from both emerge big, beautiful fish. The words calmed my heart, and when I heard the call from the minaret, I arose and prayed, touching my head to the mohr. After I finished, I sat down again on the carpet, listening to the woman's smooth voice with my eyes closed. I thought of Fereydoon and Naheed and the knots of our friendships, which stayed knotted in my mind like tangled fringes. I still didn't know what to do about Fereydoon's offer, and my sigheh was due to expire soon.

Whenever I used to be tormented by a problem in my village,

my father would always relieve me of it with an observation. What would he say to me now? In my mind I could see him clearly as he looked on our last walk together, his walking stick in his hand. He lifted it and pointed it like a sword. "Open your eyes!" he said, his voice booming through me.

I obeyed, and it was as if I were seeing the carpet under my feet for the first time. Its flowers began to flicker as if they were turning into stars, and its birds seemed to take flight. All the shapes I was so used to, like the yellow tiled walls of the mosque, the dome reaching heavenward, even the ground itself, now seemed as changeable as particles of sand in the desert. The walls began to wobble and buckle—an earthquake? I wondered—but no one else seemed to notice, and nothing was certain anymore, neither the ground nor the walls or ceiling. I, too, seemed to lose my physical form, and for a blissful moment a feeling of surrender came over me, dissolving me into perfect nothingness.

"Baba," I cried silently. "What should I do?"

He didn't reply, but his love rushed through my body. I felt joy in his nearness for the first time since his death. I remembered the day he had shown me the waterfall and the woman with the strong arms concealed behind it, despite his weariness. His love had never sprung from his own interests, nor did it depend on my pleasing him. To have known his love was to know what love should be. It was as clean and as pure as a river, and it was how I wanted to feel inside from now on. Khizr, a prophet of God, showed lost pilgrims the way to water in the desert; now my own father was showing me my way.

The pulsing around me slowed and stopped. The walls became solid; the carpet just an ordinary one. I touched the rug to tether myself to earth, then arose on unsteady feet. The woman reading the Qur'an noticed my wobbling and offered me assistance.

"Take care, for you look shaken," she said.

"Thank you, but I feel much better now," I replied. When I left the mosque, my step was firm, and a decision about Fereydoon had flowered in my heart.

I FOUND MY mother and told her what had happened at the mosque. My father's voice was still booming inside me.

"He told me, 'Open your eyes!'"

"And gaze upon the truth," she added, finishing the poem he liked to quote.

She beamed with joy. "How wonderful that he is still so much with you," she said, her eyes misting. "He is with me, too."

"Bibi, he has helped me make a decision," I said, knowing she would listen if it came from him. "I am finished with the sigheh."

Despite what I had told her, my mother looked shaken. "What! And ruin our future?"

"He won't always want me, Bibi. One day he'll grow tired and find another."

"Well, why not just take the money until his attention flags?"

"Because of Naheed's parents. They despise us now. They've made that clear by refusing the rug they ordered."

My mother sighed. "They know a man will have his sighehs. They'll learn to bear that burden."

I paused. "You sound just like Gordiyeh."

My mother drew back, offended.

"There's one thing you don't know," I added gently. "The last time I saw Naheed, she threatened to hurt any children I might bear. How could I live with such a fear?"

My mother knew as well as I did that Naheed had it in her power to arrange such treachery. "What a scorpion," she said. "I always wondered if she was truly your friend."

"I know," I said. "You were right about her."

"But then what will we do?" my mother asked, looking panicked now that she saw how serious I was. "Gordiyeh and Gostaham have already been embarrassed and suffered a costly loss. If you offend Fereydoon, they may lose even more. What if they become so angry they throw us out?"

My mother's hair had become streaked with gray since my father's death, and her face etched with lines. Her words tugged at me, for I knew she loved me beyond all others. After my father died, I was her only concern — and her only comfort. She poured out the cup of her life for me.

"Don't let us starve," she said helplessly, and I knew she wanted me to change my mind.

I tried to soothe her. "Bibi, nothing else will change," I said. "I will be their carpet slave as I was before, and make and sell carpets of my own."

"You made a fine carpet in our village and we almost starved anyway."

"But now I know how to hire others to work for me, and how to get a fair price."

"How?" she asked. "You're not a man."

"I can find a man to help me."

"You'll get cheated."

"Not if I find a *good* man."

"It's too dangerous. We can't eat a rug."

"But I will put aside some money, and then we will always have something even if my carpets don't sell right away."

My mother moaned. "If only your father were still alive. Ali, prince among men, help us, save us," she began, calling on the Prophet's son-in-law as she always did in times of distress. "Ali, king of all the believers, I beg for your blessings and your protection . . ."

As I listened to her pray, I felt prickles of irritation. My mother was disappointed in me, without even admitting it to herself. Had I been a beauty, I might have married well and saved her from hardship. Marrying me to Fereydoon was the way she showed her despair. Since I would not fetch all that much, we had better take what was offered. But I had been born with one thing my mother hadn't expected. My skills as a knotter and designer had been tested in the city, and I had surprised everyone.

"Bibi," I said, interrupting her, "listen to me. We can't rely on others for our protection. Let us try together to make our lives sweeter. I believe in my heart that's what my father would have wanted."

My mother considered this for a moment, then clicked her tongue against her teeth. "Not at all," she said. "He would have wanted you to marry well, and for me to live contentedly by your side, a grandchild in my arms."

"But I didn't marry well," I said angrily. "And whose fault was that?"

It was the last weapon I had, and I used it.

My mother put her hands to my cheeks, looking remorseful. "Well, then," she said, with an air of defeat. "You are a grown woman now."

I knew by her answer that the decision was mine to make. I sent a prayer of thanks to my father for being my ally that night.

"But I will only agree to your decision to leave the sigheh," my mother continued, "if you do one thing. The next time Fereydoon summons you, tell him you love and desire him, and ask if he would ever consider making you his wife."

I felt humiliated by the idea. Wasn't he supposed to ask for *me?* Who was I, to ask a wealthy man for a permanent knot?

"If he married you, our lives would be sugar," my mother added. "That's the only certainty we have."

I sighed. "Don't you think that if he wanted me, he would have asked by now?"

"As you said, we must try every way of making our lives sweeter."

She was right: I had said so myself. "I will do as you say," I replied, even though my womanly pride smarted at the thought.

ALTHOUGH FEREYDOON HADN'T received a communication from us about his offer, he summoned me a few days later. He was so eager to see me that he banished all the servants before we had eaten, and began by catching my ear between his teeth. I didn't feel amorous, but I made a show of pleasing him. Thinking of how Gordiyeh had gotten Gostaham to do her bidding, I groaned more loudly than usual in his arms, for I wanted him in a good mood for what I had to say.

We dressed again and the servants brought the food. After we had eaten, he relaxed contentedly with a vessel of wine in one hand and a tobacco pipe in the other. I pretended to be looking for someone. "No music tonight?" I asked, expecting to hear what had happened to the boy.

"Not tonight," Fereydoon replied, sounding indifferent.

As if to forestall further questions, he turned toward me and untied my sash with a practiced hand. "I had some peculiar news recently," he said, his breath near my ear.

"What's that?"

"Naheed told me that her parents have canceled the rug commissioned for our wedding gift," he said. "She didn't explain why."

He looked puzzled, as if he had no idea why such a thing could happen.

"I know why," I said, watching him.

"Really?" said Fereydoon. He removed my trousers, rolled them up, and flung them across the room. "Why?"

"They've discovered the sigheh, and they wish to punish Gostaham and Gordiyeh, as well as me."

"So that's it," he said lightly. "It's a shame they're so angry, but they will get used to it. After all, I'm their son-in-law."

"I suppose you could buy the carpet from Gordiyeh and Gos-taham," I said.

"Not if Naheed's parents don't want us to have it," he replied. "Think of how insulting it would be if they saw the carpet in our hallway!" He laughed as if charmed by the thought.

Fereydoon's nonchalance made me bristle, but I knew better this time than to show my anger. I thought I'd test him further, though. "Naheed is very wounded," I said. "I believe she hates me now."

He lifted off my tunic and my sheer undergarment, leaving me naked except for the cloth covering my hair.

"That's unfortunate," he replied, "because she is saddled with you for as long as I say. And I won't have such defiance from a wife."

I felt goaded by his words and by the unfairness of things between us. The charm maker's words came back to me: "You have a right to end things, too."

I squashed my feelings and tried to begin moving the conversation to what I needed to discuss. I began lightly stroking his chest.

"When you were a child, did you ever imagine you'd marry two close friends?" I tried to sound playful, as if it were a great joke we all shared.

"I often thought about women and how I should like to bed them," he said. "My father sent me my first when I was thirteen. But I spent most of my time working with his horses, learning how to ride and break the savage ones."

"That sounds exciting," I said. I imagined him out in the wild, stroking the animals and mounting their backs at will.

"And when I was a little girl," I added, feeling as if those times were a long way off, "I imagined that I would be married to a husband who would pave my path with rose petals. That's what my father always said."

"And didn't I do that?" Fereydoon snorted with laughter.

"My father never would have guessed how," I replied, for Fereydoon had in fact paved *me* with rose petals. He laughed again and began opening my thighs.

I continued to talk. "I always wanted to marry and raise as many children as God would give me, with my husband by my side," I said, feeling light-headed at my own audacity.

"God willing, you shall," he replied, but he said nothing about with whom. He opened my thighs further. "Let's start making them."

I rolled myself on top of him, to try to ensnare his attention for a moment. "It must be nice to have a daughter," I said.

"She is the light of my eyes," he replied, grabbing my buttocks and squeezing them. "I, too, hope for many children, daughters and especially sons."

"What if I had your sons?" I said, rubbing my breasts against his chest, and grabbing his center of pleasure.

"That would be a blessing," he said, his eyes becoming clouded. I continued stroking him with my hand, for I finally had learned where he was most sensitive, and he began groaning softly.

I took a breath and stopped moving. "But would that mean a permanent knot of marriage?"

His back stiffened, and he began softening in my hand. "I don't know," he said carefully. "It depends on who else my father wants me to marry, and if I had any other sons."

He rolled me over so that now he was on top of me. "What if my son was your only one?" I asked quickly.

"Perhaps," he said in a tone that didn't convince me. He stroked my breasts and began kissing me, as if to change the subject. I opened my legs and moaned encouragingly, but my mind was else-where. How likely was it that a son of mine would be the only one? He could marry four wives, and I wasn't even pregnant yet.

When Fereydoon had finished kissing me, he paused for a mo-ment. "I know what you want," he said. "But I can't promise any-thing."

My heart sank. "And in the future?"

"Only God knows about the future," he said. He pressed against my thighs to open them. "Let us drain our cup of wine right now, as the poets say, before we become clay vessels smashed upon the ground."

Was I to be such a vessel? I didn't have time to ask. For the next several hours, I was lost in sweet blackness and warmth. He was especially tender with me, as if to make up for not offering me a permanent knot. I loved to feel his arms around me, for I felt safe at that moment. But when we were done, I recalled bitterly that he had promised me nothing.

In the morning, I awoke before he did and watched his face in sleep. It had become more plump since I had met him, as had his belly. His thick red lips exuded the smell of wine, tobacco, and me. The lines near his mouth were sharp. Why would he ever marry me? If he tied a knot with me, he'd have to pay my expenses, and my mother's, for the rest of our lives. As it was, he only had to pay for three months at a time. He had always been a clever businessman, and the bargain he had made for himself was a good one.

AFTER MY CONVERSATION with my mother, I was eager to show her that I could sell my carpet for a good price. During the next few days, I drove Katayoon and Malekeh to finish it, and together we worked as hard as a team of donkeys. As soon as the last knot in the upper left-hand corner was in place, the three of us clustered around the carpet and beheld it in awe, thanking God for His blessings. What a feeling that was, to knot the last of thousands upon thousands of knots! How astonishing to see how each tiny speck of color had its essential place, just like the humblest moth in God's creation!

I hired an expert rug cutter from the bazaar to shear the top of my carpet. When he was done, the surface was like velvet and the design seemed even sharper than before. It reminded me of a crisp spring day, when suddenly a pure white dove soars across the sky, as light as thought. Although I had seen hundreds of rugs in the bazaar, I believed mine could stand well against the finest home-knotted pieces.

When the fringes were finished, I paid the women with the last of the money my mother had given me from the sigheh, and we said our farewells. I told them that as soon as I sold the carpet, I would hire them to make the next one. Then I gave them a little extra money for their good work.

"My boys will eat well today because of you," Malekeh said.

I took the carpet to Gostaham and asked him to tell me what he thought of my work. We unrolled it in his workroom so that he could look it over from end to end, and he praised it briefly before pointing out its flaws.

"Some things are hard to see until a carpet is done," he told me. "A brighter red would have made the feathers look even lighter. Next time, I would also suggest smaller borders, for the same reason."

He talked me through every color, every pattern, and every choice I had made. Although disappointed by his criticism, I knew he was right. He was truly a master, and I was humbled by all he understood about the craft.

"You mustn't be dismayed," he said. "What I have told you is for your rug maker's ears alone. A buyer will never even notice what I've talked about, for his eyes will be enchanted by the rug's beauty, and he'll understand that it is one of the splendors of its age. Do not sell it cheaply, for now you must begin to understand your own worth."

I thanked him for molding my clay into a finer form.

"If you hadn't already had the clay for me to work with," he said with a smile, "it couldn't have been done."

That was high praise indeed from a master like Gostaham, and it filled me with joy. Then he offered to help show and sell the carpet, but I wanted to do it on my own. When I told him so, his face took on a baffled look.

"Are you sure?" he asked.

I was very sure. That was the best way to convince my mother I could make good money from my craft.

Gostaham continued to look perplexed that I wanted to proceed without his help, but he gave me his blessing and told me to get the highest price I could.

MY HAPPINESS over the rug dispelled quickly, for the mood in the household was becoming more and more dark. Several of Naheed's parents' friends wrote letters to Gostaham canceling their carpet commissions, giving excuses that we all knew were false. With the disappearance of these projects, Gostaham and Gordiyeh began to feel afraid. They still had their income from the royal rug workshop and owned their fine home, so they would never starve, but now they worried about losing their luxuries and their status. Suddenly there was bickering in the house. Gordiyeh hounded Gostaham to get more commissions, and he complained that all their misfortunes wouldn't have happened if she hadn't been so greedy. When he reached for her, she pulled away, and her screams of joy no longer filled the house. Even the servants looked morose. I heard Shamsi singing softly as she wrung out the laundry, "Ey, wind, blow the bad luck out; Ey, rain, pour the good luck in."

One afternoon after the midday meal, Gostaham and Gordiyeh summoned my mother and me to the Great Room. We entered and paid our respects to them, but their responses were curt. The very air seemed sour as we removed our shoes and assumed our places on cushions.

Gostaham began speaking, as he usually did before Gordiyeh took over. "Yesterday I sent a servant to Fereydoon's residence," Gostaham said. "He was never admitted to see him."

"How impolite," replied my mother.

"It's not just impolite," said Gordiyeh. "It's unprecedented." She turned to me. "We wondered if you and Fereydoon might have had a dispute. Even a little thing that might have made him angry." She smiled at me encouragingly.

"He seemed very well pleased with me the last time I saw him," I replied. "Was this matter about me?"

"We still haven't been paid for the dangling gems carpet," said Gostaham. "It seems as if Fereydoon doesn't wish to part with his money."

"Perhaps he was occupied with business matters," said my mother.

"I doubt it," said Gostaham. "More likely, he is angry."

"Might Naheed's parents have shown him their displeasure?" I asked, trying to put the blame where it belonged.

"They'd never do that," said Gostaham. "He's a grown man who can marry as he likes. That's the law."

"What happened the last time you saw him?" asked Gordiyeh, looking hungry for information.

"The only new thing I can think of," I said, inventing a memory, "is that he told me I delighted him more than any other woman."

"Imagine that!" said Gordiyeh, as if such a prospect had never occurred to her.

"And that he was eager to see me again," I added.

"That's good," said Gordiyeh, sounding as if she didn't believe me. "What about Naheed — could she have poisoned her husband's ear against us?"

"I don't know," I replied. "She no longer invites me to visit."

Gordiyeh turned to her husband. "The best we can hope for now is that Fereydoon renews the sigheh. Remind me: When does the contract end?"

"Tomorrow," I said.

"Do you think he will renew it?"

"I don't have any doubt about it this time," I said, feeling his letter pressed against my hip.

"That's a relief," replied Gostaham, stretching out his legs. "If Fereydoon is allied with our family, I'm sure he'll pay for the rug."

Gordiyeh brightened. "We'll all be happier when we have his letter of renewal in hand, won't we?"

"All except for me." I said this in a louder voice than I had intended.

Gordiyeh drew back into her cushion. "What could you possibly mean?"

"I intend to refuse him."

"That's not possible!" Gordiyeh turned to my mother almost pleadingly. "It doesn't matter what your daughter says in this room," she said. "I know fate has surprised her lately. Perhaps she needs time to listen to your words of wisdom."

My mother's back remained unbowed. "It is entirely my daughter's decision," she said. "She is a married woman and old enough now to know what is right and what is wrong."

She didn't betray the slightest sign of weakness, which would have given Gordiyeh room to persuade her.

"You do wrong," Gordiyeh said to me.

I felt the blood rushing to my cheeks. "Not I!" I replied in a voice that sounded loud to me. "Gostaham says I have skills enough to join the royal workshop, if only I had been a boy. But rather than let me ply my craft and find a virtuous marriage, you sold me for next to nothing."

My mother pressed the edge of her sleeve to her face. "By Ali, she is right," she said. "I accepted the offer because I thought it was the only way to keep us safe from want."

It was the first time I had ever seen Gostaham looking sheepish. He avoided my eye, yet he would do nothing to quiet his wife. As a carpet maker, he was a master, but as a husband, he was as weak as a newborn lamb. Now that I was no longer a virgin, I understood how things worked between him and his wife. Despite her faults, he loved her, and there was no happier day for him than when he brought home a new commission. She would fill the house with her husky laugh and invite him to her bed. For that, Gostaham would do whatever was necessary to keep peace in the household.

"We *all* hoped for more for you," Gordiyeh said. "Your luck may improve if you try again."

"It's too late," I said.

Gordiyeh's voice became icy. "May your tongue be stung by bees," she said. "If you receive a renewal offer, you will say yes. Do you understand?"

I jumped to my feet, angrier than I had ever been in my life. Although I am not tall, Gordiyeh, Gostaham, and my mother all looked small to me.

"I will not," I said, planting my feet.

"You ungrateful child!" Gordiyeh yelled so loudly that the whole house could hear. "Don't forget we have lost money because of you!"

"And I have lost my virginity because of you!" I yelled back.

Gordiyeh was seething with rage. "You viper! After all we've done to help you!"

"You can always make another carpet," I said coldly. "My virginity is something I can never restore."

I didn't regret the time I had spent in Fereydoon's arms; after all, I had become a true woman there. But my value had diminished since I had lost my virginity, and with no dowry to offer, no man had any reason to take me as a permanent wife.

"You traded me for the hope of future gains," I said, my voice rising again. "You owe me something for that."

"We owe you nothing," Gordiyeh shouted back. "We can dismiss you tomorrow, and no one would think we had done wrong."

Gostaham looked as if he wished he could be anywhere but in that room, yet he didn't utter a word.

I glared at Gordiyeh without speaking. Finally, the silence was too much for Gostaham to bear.

"Azizam, we can't afford to incur Fereydoon's wrath," he said gently.

I gazed down at him for a moment, my heart full of gratitude for all he had taught me. "Revered amoo," I said, calling him "uncle" out of affection and respect, "you are my teacher, the brightest star of my eyes. Would you have me continue to hurt others for the sake of money?"

Gostaham looked pleadingly at his wife. "These are women's matters, really," he mumbled.

"Yes, they are," said Gordiyeh, wresting the conversation away from him. "We will watch for a letter from Fereydoon, and then we will renew. There is no more to be said. And now, you may return to your work."

She pressed her hands against her temples, as she always did when she felt the threat of a headache. As we left, she said to Gostaham, "What do you expect of someone who would rip a rug off the loom?"

On our way to the kitchen, I muttered the worst insult I knew. "Her father is frying in hell," I said.

We began helping Cook slice vegetables, but after a few moments, my mother said she felt ill. "Go and lie down," I replied. "I will do the rest." I chopped the celery with so much force that the pieces jumped and scattered on the floor, and Cook scolded me for wasting food.

BY THE END of the afternoon, I had made a bold plan. I gave a coin to Taghee, whispering that I needed him to find out when the

280

Dutchman liked to have his hair barbered or where he bathed (however infrequently), so that I would know where to find him.

"He goes to the bazaar every Wednesday afternoon to look at carpets," said the errand boy, slipping my coin into his sleeve with a saucy look.

"Wait!" I said, trying to get it back, but Taghee slipped away into the birooni. He was a sly one, indeed.

Since it was Wednesday, I went to the bazaar, pretending I had an errand, and walked from stall to stall, feigning interest in carpets for the better part of the afternoon. While admiring a Qashqa'i carpet in indigo, I spotted the Dutchman across the alley conversing with a young merchant with a close-cropped beard. I watched until he took his leave and then darted from one alley to the next until I had reached the top of the road he was walking down, and could meet him as if by accident.

I lifted my picheh so that my face was visible and strolled down the alley. The Dutchman was looking at carpets hanging from a shop's alcove when he saw me.

"Salaam aleikum," I said, boldly saluting him. "Are you shopping for carpets today?"

"Indeed I am," said the Dutchman, surprised at being addressed. I reminded him of my family and of the wool carpet I had made.

"Ah!" he exclaimed. "Never have I found another carpet as fine as yours, which I admire above all others."

I smiled; his facility with polite speech was unusual in a farangi, but I enjoyed it all the same. He was peculiar to look at up close. His blue eyes were as translucent as a cat's, and his movements just as unpredictable.

"I'm always looking for fine pieces to sell in Holland," he said.

"Then perhaps you'd like to have a look at a carpet that I've just finished?"

"Certainly, that would be a pleasure."

"May I invite you to come and see it?"

"I would be most grateful if you would have it sent to me," he replied. "My wife is due to arrive soon, and I'd like to show it to her, too."

"I would be honored," I said.

"With your permission, I will send a boy to your home and he can bring the carpet to where I live."

"Please have your boy ask for me, and for no one else," I said.

The Dutchman considered me for a moment. "Wouldn't your family be able to help him?"

I hesitated. "I want to surprise my family," I replied.

An eager look came into his eyes. "What a good idea," he said. "May I send the boy today?"

I was surprised by his haste, but I thought it best to proceed. "I am at your service."

The Dutchman bowed and took his leave. He paid the highest prices I had ever heard of. If he desired my carpet, I would earn well for it.

When I arrived home, the Dutchman's boy was already waiting for me. Hoping for a quick sale, I relinquished the carpet to him, giving him a good tip to make sure he would help me if I needed him.

CONFIDENT THAT I would soon have a purseful of money from the Dutchman, I continued with my plan. Covering myself so that nothing at all of my face was visible, I went to the Image of the World in search of a scribe. I found one near the Friday mosque, and I instructed him to write a letter addressed to Fereydoon on his best paper and in his most careful handwriting. He was to explain that he was writing on behalf of Gostaham, for whom he worked, and to

say in the finest language he knew that the family thanked Fereydoon graciously for the offer of the sigheh, but that I had refused it
of my own will, and that it was not the family's decision but mine
alone.

"Where is your family today?" asked the scribe, who had a scrag-
gly beard and a wart near his nose.

"At home."

"How strange that they sent you out all alone," he said, "especially on a mission of the heart."

"They're not well today."

"All of them?"

When I did not reply, he beckoned me toward him and said in a
whisper, "I'll do it, but it will cost you three times the normal
rate."

What could I do? He made a good living by determining how
desperate his clients were.

"I will pay," I said.

"And if you ever reveal me as your scribe, I will swear by the
Holy Qur'an that it was someone else."

The scribe wrote the letter and read it in a whisper so that only
I could hear. It didn't sound as smooth as the letters that Fereydoon
and Gostaham wrote, although it was full of flowery, flattering language. I puzzled over it, for I could not tell what was different about
it. But I was in a hurry, and I thought it would do.

I took the letter home and waited until Gostaham was out of the
house, and then I went into his workroom and removed his seal
from its hiding place. I knew he was often careless about locking it
up, never dreaming that anyone in the house would dare to imper-
sonate him. I melted some red wax on the back of the letter and
quickly pressed the seal into it. Now there could be no doubt it came
from Gostaham's household.

When I was finished, I felt clean inside for the first time in

months. No matter how severe the penalty, I could no longer endure the sigheh. I knew that Gordiyeh and Gostaham would be very
angry and that I would be punished, but I thought they would forgive me as they had before.

I saved the hardest thing I had to do for the afternoon. Sitting
alone in our little room, I crafted a letter to Naheed. My handwriting was as ungraceful as a child's, but I wanted her to get a letter
from my own hands, telling her exactly what was in my heart. She
had taught me to write, and I wanted her to see how much I had
learned from her and how I valued her instruction, knowledge, and
friendship. I knew Naheed would understand the honesty of the
feelings behind the clumsily written words.

> *Naheed-joon, my dearest friend,*
>
> *I am writing to beg your forgiveness. I have loved you better than*
> *any other friend, and I have hurt you. At first, before I knew of your*
> *engagement, the sigheh hurt only me, but when it was renewed and I did*
> *nothing to stop it, I broke faith with you. I wish I had made the right*
> *decision by telling you about it before your marriage. I hope you will*
> *pardon me for my error in judgment. I will always love you; but I see that*
> *you can no longer love me. And so I have decided to give you and*
> *Fereydoon your peace. I have refused his second renewal and therefore*
> *our sigheh is over. I wish you a joyous life, and hope you will one day*
> *remember me with all the love I feel for you.*

Then I ripped the twist of rainbow-colored threads off my neck
and untied the seven knots one by one, murmuring a blessing with
each release. Once the threads were smooth, I enclosed them in the
letter. Naheed wouldn't know exactly what the twist had meant,
but she would understand that I had renounced a charm and done
everything I could to unknot her love.

*   *   *

THE NEXT DAY, my mother and I were pitting dates when we heard Gostaham shouting in the birooni. As the sound grew louder, I caught the words "carpet" and "sigheh." I wiped my hands and tried to prepare myself.

"Bibi-joon, my sigheh is over," I said, trying to keep my voice steady.

"May God protect us!" my mother replied. She continued digging seeds out of the sticky fruit, and I noticed that her hands were shaking.

Gostaham charged into the courtyard with a letter in his hand, with Gordiyeh at his heels pleading to know what was wrong. His turban was askew, and his purple tunic was soaked with sweat. Remembering the time the two of them had yelled at me for removing the rug, I began flushing and sweating, although I knew I had done the right thing this time. I stood up to face them.

Gostaham threw the letter at my feet. "Where did this come from?"

I pretended not to know what it was. "I can't read or write," I said.

Gostaham's face was red with rage. "I went to Fereydoon's residence today to plead for the money he owes us," he said, as if he hadn't heard me. "What a surprise to be told I had written him a letter rejecting the sigheh!"

"What?" Gordiyeh asked, bewildered.

"When I saw my own seal on the letter, it was useless to deny it. I told Fereydoon I had hired a new scribe who would be thrown out of my employ. I begged his forgiveness for the letter's gracelessness, and praised his generosity and his name."

Gordiyeh covered her face with her hands as if the shame were unbearable.

I was quaking now. Although I had listened to the letter before sending it, I didn't read well enough to know that the scribe had done such a poor job. My silence and flushing face made my guilt obvious.

"How dare a woman of my household put me in such a humiliating position!"

He grabbed my tunic and pulled me toward him. "You have no excuse for this," he said. He smashed one hand into my temple and cracked the other against my jaw. I dropped to the ground.

My mother threw her body in front of mine. "Hit me first!" she cried. "Only don't touch my child again."

"I don't suppose Fereydoon paid you," Gordiyeh said to her husband.

"Pay me?" Gostaham snorted in derision. "I was lucky he didn't order someone to poison me. The only way I could gain his forgiveness was to invent more stories. I told him we had found a permanent marriage for her and that it was in her best interest to accept it while she was still young, unless he wanted her for himself."

"What did he say?" my mother asked, unable to conceal the hope in her voice. I put my hand to my cheek to stop the pulsing pain in my jaw. The taste of blood was like iron on my tongue.

"He said, 'She is used, and I have had my fill of her.' And then he brushed one hand against the other as if to clean them of dirt."

It was just as I had expected. I might have been able to please Fereydoon a while longer, but one day he would have rid himself of me.

Gordiyeh's face seemed to compress into knots as she peered down at me. "Your very tread is evil!" she said. "If it weren't, your father wouldn't have died at such a young age, Naheed wouldn't have discovered the sigheh, and our friends wouldn't have canceled their commissions."

There was no way to get rid of an evil tread. It would always bring misfortune on the household and taint everything it touched, at least in her eyes.

"Naheed found out from Kobra," I argued, the blood leaking out of my mouth. My mother ripped off her head scarf, her long gray hair falling around her shoulders, and soaked it up with the cloth. "All I did was admit it was true."

"You should have lied," Gordiyeh said.

"I couldn't bear it any longer!" I cried, although the pain when I opened my lips was fierce. "How would you feel if every three months you had to worry about whether your husband still wanted you? Or if your best friend threatened your children?"

"May God always keep my daughters safe," Gordiyeh replied, ignoring my questions.

I picked up the letter Gostaham had thrown at my feet. Of that, I was ashamed. No one had taught me more than he; and though he hadn't extended as much protection as a father, he had been a loving teacher.

"Nothing can excuse the fact that I took your seal without asking," I said to him. "It was only because I saw no other way of leaving the sigheh."

"You should have told me how unhappy you were!" Gostaham exploded. "I could have announced your decision to Fereydoon with apologies and professions of thanks for his generosity. No doubt he is so angry because he did not expect to be dismissed so gracelessly, and with such poor grammar."

I sighed. Once again I had made the mistake of acting too quickly, yet this time I had had good reasons. "But Gordiyeh told me I had to say yes."

"If you had admitted your plans, I would have seen the danger and found a better way."

I didn't believe him, for he had never gone against his wife's wishes before. "I deeply regret my error," I said nonetheless. "I know I haven't always done things the right way, for I am not of Isfahan. I kiss your feet, amoo."

Gostaham opened his palms to the sky and looked up, as if forgiveness had come to him from above.

"Haven't they caused trouble enough?" Gordiyeh said. "We've

lost the commissions for several carpets because of her. They no longer deserve to live here."

I tried again; I had nothing to lose. "I beg your permission to stay under your protection," I said to him. "I will work like a slave on your carpets, so much so that it won't cost you an abbasi for us to live here. I will do everything you say without complaint."

"That was what she said the last time," Gordiyeh said.

Gostaham remained silent. Then he said, "Yes, it is. It's too bad, really too bad."

That was all Gordiyeh needed before pronouncing the words she had been yearning to say for weeks. "You are banished from this household. Tomorrow, you must go."

Gostaham cringed but did not tell her to hold her tongue. He walked away and Gordiyeh followed, leaving me bleeding there. My mother tilted my head back and used her scarf to swab at the soft flesh inside my cheeks, which was ripped and bruised. I winced from the pain.

It wasn't long before we heard Gordiyeh's moans throughout the house, Gostaham's reward for letting her get her way.

"That is a filthy sound," I muttered.

My mother did not reply.

"Bibi," I mumbled, for I could hardly open my mouth, "I'm sorry about the way I did this."

My mother's face became stony. She arose abruptly and went into the kitchen, leaving me alone. "Not her again," I heard Cook say. I lay on the ground, bleeding and bewildered. I stood up slowly and made my own way to bed, moaning with pain.

Shamsi, Zohreh, and my mother finished pitting the dates for the meal. The rich aroma of lamb stew with dates filled the air, and I heard all the servants eating together. I remained on my bed, occasionally dozing, holding my jaw to quell the pain. My mother did not ask how I felt when she came in to sleep. In the middle of the night, I arose to use the latrines and ran into Shamsi, whose eyes grew large when she looked at me. I put my hand to my face and discovered that my cheek had swelled to the size of a ball.

THE NEXT MORNING, I could not open my mouth enough to eat, and my lower lip was numb. Ali-Asghar, who knew about horses and sheep, felt my jaw for fractures. "I don't believe it is broken," he said, but just in case, he wrapped a cloth around my chin and tied it on top of my head, instructing me to leave it on until the pain had gone away.

"How long?" I asked between closed teeth.

"At least a week," he replied. A look of pity entered his eyes. "You deserved to be punished," he said, "but not like that. I wouldn't hurt even a cursed dog the way he hurt you."

"And all for the sake of his wife!" said my mother.

"As always," said Ali-Asghar, who had been their servant for many years. "That will never change."

We put our few clothes into bundles and awaited Gordiyeh and Gostaham in the courtyard.

"Where is your carpet?" my mother asked, looking worriedly at my small bundle.

"I think the Dutchman is going to buy it," I replied, although I hadn't heard from him. I wondered with a pang why his boy hadn't returned with an offer.

Just then, Gordiyeh and Gostaham came into the courtyard dressed in their crisp tunics, hers pink and his like wine. Neither one said anything about the cloth around my head or my swollen face. Gordiyeh offered me her stiff cheeks to kiss good-bye and then resolutely looked away. I thought that Ali-Asghar must have spoken to Gostaham about my injury, for he took my hand and left a small purse of coins in my sleeve when Gordiyeh wasn't looking.

"Thank you for all you have done for us," said my mother to them both. "I apologize for the ways we have been a burden."

"May God always be with you," replied Gordiyeh, in a tone implying that we would need help.

"And with you, too," my mother replied. She looked hopefully from one to the other, as if they might relent, but they turned away and walked back into the birooni. I did not say anything other than good-bye, for my face ached from Gostaham's blows, and my heart ached even more.

Ali-Asghar escorted us into the street, and we watched the tall gates of the house close behind us. From the outside, Gostaham's house now looked like a fortress. Nothing could be seen of the comforts within, not even a light. The other houses on the street were just as blank and unsmiling.

We walked to the top of the road that penetrated Four Gardens. The beggar was at his usual post near the cedar tree. His alms bowl was empty, and he shivered in the wind, the end of his stump blue with cold. At the sight of him, my mother leaned over and began wailing from the depths of her heart.

"Kind Khanoom, what ails you? How can I help?" the beggar asked, waving his stump. To have such a ragged fellow offer assistance only made her wail more loudly. I tried to put my arms around her, but she evaded my embrace.

"Bibi-joon, we'll find a way," I said with my teeth clenched to protect my jaw. But I didn't sound convincing, for I hardly believed it myself.

"No, we will not," she said. "You have no understanding of what you have done. We are on the streets now, and we may die."

"But—"

"We should go back to our village," my mother said. "At least we have a roof there."

I imagined leaving the city the same way we had come, over the bridge built for the Shah. But I knew I could no sooner take my first steps on that bridge than I would turn around to look at the city again, if only to see its turquoise and lemon domes basking in the morning light. And then I imagined continuing a few more paces, only to stop at one of the bridge's archways to embrace the view of the city with my eyes. I had become the nightingale to the rose of Isfahan, singing an eternal love song to its beauties.

"I don't want to leave," I said.

"Don't talk to me anymore," snapped my mother. She began walking away and I followed, while the kind beggar begged us to make amends with one another.

Her steps led us to the Image of the World, where a bitter wind was whirling the dust in the square. A man passed us, rubbing his hands together and shivering. The vendors were like mosquitoes, buzzing around our ears with no respite. A knife seller kept thrusting "blades as sharp as Solomon's" under our noses.

"Leave me alone — I have no money," I finally growled. It hurt my jaw to say that much.

"That's a lie," he said rudely as he walked away.

A gust of cold wind blew dust in our faces. My mother caught some in her throat and began to cough. I called out to a coffee boy to bring us two steaming cups and paid him with one of my precious coins. The knife seller saw my silver from across the square and caught the sun on one of his blades, flashing it into my eyes.

I filled my lungs to hurl a curse, but my mother stopped me. "May your throat close, for a change."

Chastened, I sipped the coffee between barely parted lips. I had no idea what we were going to do. I knew I had to think of something before my mother started looking for a camel driver to take us back to our village.

"I have an idea," I said. When I stood up, my mother followed, and we picked our way among the vendors until I spotted a cluster of women who had spread out their humble wares near the gateway to the bazaar. One offered a hand-embroidered tree of life, probably the best thing in her household. Another was selling blankets she had woven herself. I looked for Malekeh and found her squatting on her two carpets. When she saw me, she sprang to her feet in horror.

"May God keep you safe!" she said. "What happened to you?"

"Malekeh," I whispered, "can you help us?"

She drew back for a moment, considering my bruised and swollen face. "What have you done?"

I wasn't surprised that she blamed me, for I knew how I must look. "Gordiyeh decided that we were too much of a burden," I said.

Malekeh's eyes narrowed. "Did you bring shame on your family?"

"Of course not!" snapped my mother. "My daughter would never do such a thing."

Malekeh looked contrite, for my mother was obviously a respectable widow in black mourning clothes.

"They became angry after I made an error of judgment on a carpet," I said, which was at least partly the truth. I didn't want to tell her about my sigheh, for fear it would make me low in her eyes.

"Malekeh, do you know anyone who would take in two poor women? We have money to pay."

I shook the little bag of coins hidden in my sash. I knew that Malekeh needed the money, and we needed to be under the protection of a family.

She sighed. "My husband is still ailing, and we have only one room for the four of us."

"I beg you," I replied. "We can care for him while you're out."

Malekeh hesitated, looking as if she was about to say no.

"I know how to make medicines," offered my mother. "I'll try to cure him."

Hope made Malekeh's face pretty for moment. "What can you do?" she asked.

"I can make a concoction of dried mountain herbs that will cure his lungs," my mother said promptly. She pointed to her bundle. "Here are the plants that I collected during the summer."

Malekeh sighed. "You helped me when I was very needy," she said. "I will not leave you to freeze or starve."

"May God rain His blessings on you, Malekeh!" I said. She had every reason not to believe my story, but she chose to help anyway.

My mother and I squatted with her, trying to help her sell her wares. Malekeh called out to passersby, enticing them to look at her carpets. Many men stopped to look at her instead, for she had lips like a rosebud and a pearly smile. My mother tried to distract them by detailing the carpets' merits, but the honey had left her tongue. I thought back to the way she had enticed the traveling silk merchant to buy my turquoise carpet, bargaining coyly until she got her price. Now she just looked tired, and no one stopped to banter with her for very long. I sat on the carpets while she worked, holding my hand against my jaw to quell the pain. The only person who was selling anything on that frozen day was the blanket maker, for her wares were irresistible.

Late in the afternoon, Malekeh still had not made a sale, and most shoppers had gone home. She rolled up her rugs, and she and I each slung one across our backs. My mother carried our small bundles, and we followed Malekeh through the bazaar, toward the old square and the old Friday mosque.

My mother walked ahead beside Malekeh, her body stiff. She did not turn and look at me or ask me how I felt. The pain in my jaw tore through my body, but I suffered even more deeply from her neglect.

As we traversed the old square I had walked through so many times on my way to see Fereydoon, I began thinking about him and the small, tree-lined street where his jewel-like pleasure house was located. He might be there right now, preparing to greet another musician or some other sigheh. I felt an involuntary gripping of my loins as if I were holding him there, and a surge of heat blossomed from my belly to my cheeks. I must renounce those pleasures now, and I might never have them again.

We kept walking until we were almost outside the city. I had never known that so close to Fereydoon's pleasure palace was a warren of streets where servants lived. Malekeh turned down a dark, twisting alley wet with mud. Piles of garbage lay in the street, with flies buzzing around them. Puddles of night soil stank even more, for there were no night-soil collectors here. Filthy wild dogs lunged at the piles of garbage, halted only by the rocks hurled at them by little boys with dirty hair.

Although it was still light outside, the streets became darker and darker as we twisted through the alleys, and the smells more rancid. Finally, after too many turns to count, we arrived at Malekeh's broken door. We passed into a tiny courtyard floored with broken tiles, where a gang of children were playing and fighting. Two of the boys rushed at Malekeh, their dirty hands outspread. "Bibi, is there chicken?" "Is there meat?"

"No, souls of my heart," Malekeh said gently. "Not today."

Disappointed, they rejoined their friends, and the squabbling continued.

"Those are my children, Salman and Shahvali," she said.

Malekeh pushed open the door to her room. "Welcome," she said. "Please be comfortable while I make tea."

We left our shoes near the door and sat down. At one end of the room was a tiny oven for heat and cooking, with a few blackened pots nearby. There were two baskets on the floor, which probably contained the family's possessions and clothes. The ceiling was brown in places where the rain had leaked through. I pitied Malekeh for having to live in such squalor. When I employed her, I had never realized how badly she needed the money.

Malekeh's husband, Davood, was sleeping on a bedroll in one

corner, breathing heavily as if something were stuck in his lungs. She touched his head to see how hot he was and wiped away the sweat from his brow with a cloth.

"Poor animal," she said.

We drank weak tea together, barely speaking. I took care not to hurt my lips on the rim of my vessel, which was chipped. Before long, Malekeh called in her children for their evening meal, though she had only bread and cheese to feed them. My mother and I refused the food, claiming we were not hungry. I would not have been able to force bread into my mouth or to chew it, in any case.

"You need soup," Malekeh said to me sympathetically.

"With your permission, I'll make soup for everyone tomorrow," my mother replied.

"Ah, but with what money?"

"We still have some left," I croaked. The pain in my jaw was fierce.

When it grew dark, we spread the family's blankets on the floor. Davood slept near one of the walls, with Malekeh beside him and her children in the middle. Then came my mother and finally, me. When our bodies touched by accident, my mother moved away and kept her distance from me.

With all of us stretched out on the ground, there was just enough room for one person to arise and use the night-soil vessel, crouching near the oven for privacy. Davood wheezed loudly throughout the night. The children must have been having dreams, for they cried out from time to time. Malekeh often sighed in her sleep. I know I moaned, for I awoke to that terrible sound and realized it was mine.

It was a rainy night, and I was awakened by a drop of cold water that struck my face from a leak in the roof. As I wiped it away, I thought of Gostaham's Great Room, with its ruby-red carpets, its vases of flowers, and its perpetual warmth. I shivered and pulled the thin blanket around me. When I finally arose with the dawn, I was more tired than I had been the night before.

IN THE MORNING, my mother and I offered to stay behind to care for Malekeh's husband and children while she tried to sell her carpets. But before she departed, to make us honest in the eyes of God and her neighbors, she asked us to contract sighehs with Salman and Shahvali. They were only five and six, so the sighehs were not real marriages, of course. We simply pronounced our acceptances of the contracts, and suddenly we were family and would not have to cover ourselves around Davood.

"You are now our daughters-in-law," said Malekeh with a smile, "even you, Khanoom." It was peculiar to think of my mother as the daughter-in-law of a woman who was half her age, and yet necessary.

After Malekeh left, my mother asked the children to take her to the nearest bazaar, where she bought a bag of cheap lamb bones. She threw them into a pot full of water on top of the oven and boiled them with a few vegetables. Davood woke up, looked around the room in confusion, and asked who we were. "Friends," said my mother, "here to make you a healing soup." He grunted and rolled over to sleep again.

I stayed on my bedroll in a daze. From time to time I fell asleep, only to awake to the pain in my jaw and the ache of hunger in my belly. I had trouble sleeping, for Malekeh's home was noisy. Six other families lived in rooms right off the shared courtyard, including Katayoon, her brother Amir, and their mother, so there was constant traffic. I felt assaulted by all the smells: night soil, cooking oil gone rancid, the frightening odor of chicken's blood after slaughter, the acrid smell of boiling beans, the reeking shoes left in the courtyard, all the everyday stink of close living. And then there were endless sounds: a mother shouting at her child to do his lessons, a husband yelling at his wife, neighbors fighting about money, wheels creaking in the uneven mud alley, vegetables being chopped, mumbled prayers, moans of pain and distress—I heard it all. Gostaham's house had been as quiet as a fortress.

The only thing that kept me from despair was the knowledge that I owned a costly rug. When I recovered, I would seek out the Dutchman and complete the sale. As soon as I held the silver in my hands, I wanted to start a new carpet with Katayoon and Malekeh. My dream was to be able to hire others so that we would have many carpets on the looms at once, just like at the royal rug workshop. Then maybe my mother and I could finally earn enough money to keep ourselves and live as we pleased.

It took more than a week for my jaw to heal enough for me to seek out the Dutchman. I hadn't wanted to visit him while I was feeling so bruised and broken, for it would have been easy for him to think I would take any price for my carpet.

When I told my mother of my plans to find him, she said only two words: "I'll cook." She was still not speaking to me very much. Her anger seared me, and I hoped that the money from the Dutchman would soothe her.

My mother took the last of our coins to the small bazaar near Malekeh's house and bought a chicken. In the courtyard, she slashed the artery in its neck while all the other people's children looked on enviously, then cleaned the bird and cooked it in a pot with fresh greens. Malekeh came home that night to the smell of stew, a delight she had not had in a long time. We all feasted together, and even Davood sat up and ate a few bites of stew, proclaiming it "the food of paradise."

The next day was Wednesday, the Dutchman's day at the bazaar. My mother heated the leftover stew and bread for me late in the morning. I ate my fill before putting on the last of my good clothes—Naheed's pink tunic and purple robe—although I knew no one would see them. "I'll be back soon, with silver, I hope," I said.

"Good luck," replied my mother dryly without looking at me.

I left off my picheh so the Dutchman would recognize me and walked through the bazaar toward the Image of the World. After only a short time with Malekeh's family, I no longer felt as if I belonged in the Great Bazaar with its view of the Shah's palace and his lemon-colored mosque, so bright against the blue sky, for now I lived in a place where even keeping clean was a struggle.

In one of the alleys, I came across the young musician playing his kamancheh. He looked more dirty and disheveled than before. I hurried past, for I had no coin to give him. How many beggars there were all over the city! I had barely noticed them when I had first come to Isfahan.

When I arrived in the carpet sellers' section of the bazaar, I pretended to look at the wares on display while hoping to hear a familiar foreign voice. To pass the time, I examined a prayer rug that showed a shimmering expanse of sable-colored silk between two white columns joined by an arch. Its knotting was so fine, and its vision so pure, I forgot the ache in my jaw.

Though I spent many hours in the shops, I didn't see or hear any sign of the Dutchman. Still hopeful, I began asking the merchants if they knew of him or where he lived. One of them, a portly fellow who was hard to see clearly because of the thick haze of opium in his shop, said, "I haven't seen him for days." I must have looked alarmed, for he leered at me and told me he'd give me money for whatever I needed. I clutched my chador under my chin and ran out of his shop.

The day was getting colder. I blew on my hands to keep them warm, squatting for a moment near one of the shops. A coffee boy went by with a tray full of steaming vessels, singing out how his liquid would stir the blood. I looked longingly at the hot drink but did not have the coin.

Remembering that I had seen the Dutchman speaking with a young merchant the first time I had found him, I walked slowly to that man's shop. He was alone, sitting on a cushion with a wooden desk on his lap, on which he was reading a ledger of accounts.

"Salaam aleikum," I said.

He returned my greeting and asked how he could help.

"Do you know the farangi with the blue eyes?"

"The Dutchman," said the merchant, standing up to assist me. My heart lurched for a moment, for his close-cropped beard and thinness reminded me of Fereydoon. I blushed and averted my gaze.

"I'm seeking him on an urgent matter of business," I said. "Might you tell me where to find him?"

"You can't find him," said the merchant. "He has left."

"Left Isfahan?"

"Left Iran."

My heart began beating so quickly I feared it might jump out of my mouth, and I had to brace myself against the side of the alcove.

"What ails you, Khanoom?" asked the merchant, addressing me respectfully as if I were married.

"I am . . . unwell," I said, trying to hold myself up. After all that had happened to me and my mother, I could not bear the thought that my one remaining hope for the future had been stolen.

"I beg you to sit and rest," he said. I sank down into his cushions, trying to recover myself, while he called out to a passing coffee boy and paid him for a cup. I drank it quickly, grateful to feel the familiar warmth in my blood.

I had stirred the merchant's curiosity, of course. "What is your business with the Dutchman?" he asked, still standing at a respectful distance.

"He was thinking of buying a rug I made," I said. "His servant fetched it weeks ago, and I haven't heard from him since."

I had trouble concealing the pain I felt. I thought of Naheed, and how she had forced her face into a look of composure. I did the same by sinking my nails into my palm.

"I'm so sorry, Khanoom," said the merchant. "You must know that farangis only come here to get rich, and many of them don't have the manners of a dog."

I thought about how poorly the Dutchman had comported himself with Gostaham.

"I heard that he even obtained a carpet from one of Isfahan's carpet-making families for free. It takes skill with the tongue to do that," said the merchant.

"What great fortune," I replied bitterly, remembering how Gordiyeh had betrayed me. I looked around and noticed that some of the other merchants were beginning to stare. I rose to go; I could not linger alone in a man's shop without people making remarks about my honor.

"If you see him, will you tell him that a woman is looking for him? Perhaps he has forgotten."

"Of course," he said. "God willing, he will return and pay you all that you deserve."

"May I come here again to ask after him?"

"Think of my shop as your own," he replied.

The expression of pity in his eyes told me that he didn't believe I would ever see the Dutchman again. I thanked him for his kindness and began the long walk home. It was nearly evening, and the weather had turned cold and sharp. As I trudged through the old square, the first snowflakes of the year began to fall. By the time I arrived at Malekeh's, they were sticking to my chador. My jaw was aching in the cold, and I had to warm my face in front of the oven before I could talk. Malekeh and her boys clustered around me, and even my mother looked hopeful that I was bringing good news.

When I told them to expect nothing, Davood broke into a fit of wet coughing that sounded as though it would never end. Malekeh looked weary, as if her bones no longer had enough weight to carry her body. And my mother's face seemed even more deeply etched with worry than before.

Malekeh gave me a puzzled look. "You let his boy take your carpet—without any security?" she asked.

"He was doing business with Gostaham," I said. "I thought that would protect me."

My mother and Malekeh exchanged a glance.

"Your designs are so beautiful," Malekeh said musingly. "You have great conviction when you call out a rug's colors. It's easy to forget that you are still very young."

My mother sighed. "Younger than her years," she said darkly, and she remained silent after that. We sat there together, drinking pale tea and eating cold bread, for that was all we had, and listening to the sharp, angry cries of the children in the courtyard.

I WANTED TO start a new rug, but we didn't have enough money for wool. The only thing we could do to earn coins was brew medicines and sell them. Having noticed that many of the district's residents were already coughing and sneezing in the cold, my mother decided to make a concoction for diseases of the lungs, nose, and throat. "You can try," said Malekeh doubtfully, "but most people here are too poor for such luxuries."

I asked if I could help. "I believe you've helped enough," said my mother in a sharp voice.

I sat quietly while my mother built a hot fire in the oven and put the roots and herbs she had gathered during the summer on to boil. The tiny room filled with a bitter smell, and the air became clouded with steam. My eyes watered so much from the fumes that I had to go out in the courtyard from time to time. Only Malekeh's husband seemed to improve: The steam cleared his throat and allowed him to breathe more freely for a while.

In the afternoon, my mother sent me to the small local bazaar to buy several dozen cheap clay vessels, undecorated, with clay stoppers. I looked at the thin coins she put in my hand, which were so few that only someone more miserable than we were would even bother to take them. But I went to the bazaar, anyway, lifting my chador from time to time to keep it from dragging in the wet garbage that lay uncollected. This bazaar served the poorest residents of the city by offering things like crude pots, shoes made out of old clothes, tattered blankets, and used turbans.

The first clay merchant I approached scoffed at what I had to offer. "I'm not a charity," he said.

I sought out the most run-down shop in the bazaar, but when I offered the merchant my coins, he, too, laughed at me. Hearing a child wail from the back of his shop, I offered to bring him two bottles of medicine that would calm children and treat coughs. When he agreed, I knew it was partly out of kindness, for with my sunken face I looked undernourished. I had caught a glimpse of it in the metal pans for sale at the entrance to the bazaar.

After my mother finished brewing the medicine, she poured it into the vessels and stoppered them. I took two of the bottles back to the clay merchant, who thanked me for the prompt return of my obligation. Then we told all the families in the courtyard that we would trade medicine for coins or food. But Malekeh was right: No one had the means. It was not like in Gostaham's neighborhood, where families kept supplies of medicine in the house. Here, sickness was a costly tragedy, and only when it was dire would a doctor be summoned and a woman sent to the druggist to buy the things he had prescribed and prepare a medicine.

After failing with the neighbors, we made plans to peddle the medicine elsewhere. Because all the respectable peddlers were men, we asked Katayoon's brother Amir to come with us and help us sell our wares in the wealthier parts of town. He was a tall, gangly boy with a friendly manner and a voice that rumbled as if it came from a grown man.

The first day, we left early in the morning and went to a prosperous neighborhood near Four Gardens, far enough from Gostaham's house to avoid meeting him by chance. Amir took eagerly to his role. "May you breathe as easily as the wind!" he shouted, his warm breath freezing in the air. "Made by an herbalist from the south with proven powers!" From time to time, a servant would come outside to inspect our wares. If it was a man, Amir would grab a bottle and try to sell it to him. If a woman, my mother and I would go. By the afternoon, we had sold two vessels of the liquid, enough to buy bread and grilled kidneys for the three of us.

"Shall we try to sell our wares near the mosque with the brass minaret?" I asked my mother. She did not reply. I sighed and followed her home.

For the next several weeks, we peddled our medicine every day but Friday in the city's richer neighborhoods. The weather had become colder and more people were getting sick. We were not earning much money, but it was enough to keep us fed and to add a small amount of food to Katayoon's table.

One day, my mother awoke with glassy eyes and a damp feeling in her chest. I told her I would go out alone with Amir, but she said that would not be proper. Although I begged her to stay home and rest, she forced herself to her feet, and we made our rounds that day in the Christian part of town across Thirty-three Arches Bridge.

It was bitterly cold. An icy wind blew off the Eternal River, and the tops of the Zagros Mountains were white with snow. The river looked as if it might freeze. As we walked across the bridge, a great gust of icy wind trapped us in its embrace. My mother and I held on to each other to avoid being blown away. "Akh!" she exclaimed, her voice thick with fluid. We continued over the bridge, passed the huge church, and began walking down a street that looked prosperous.

Despite the cold, Amir had lost neither his enthusiasm nor his shouting power. He called out the merits of our medicines, his deep voice like an invitation. Women in particular responded to his call. A pretty young servant emerged from one of the homes and opened her gates to inspect our bottles. When my mother and I ran to greet her, she looked disappointed that Amir did not approach.

"Breathe easier, and may you stay well!" said my mother.

"How much?"

My mother broke into a fit of coughing so severe that tears ran out of her eyes, and she choked and snorted before she managed to recover herself.

The servant drew back and slammed the gates in our faces.

My mother squatted against that grand house and wiped her eyes, promising that she would soon recover, but we had no heart to continue that day. We returned to a cold, dark house. My mother wrapped herself in a blanket, shivering, and slept on and off until the next morning. I put a pot outside our door to signal that there was illness within our house so that neighbors who had means might drop in an onion, a carrot, or a squash. I planned to make a thin soup out of whatever we received. But when my mother awoke, she refused all food, for she was burning with fever.

FOR THE NEXT FEW DAYS, I did nothing but tend to the family. I fetched water from a nearby well and offered it to my mother and Davood. I placed cool cloths upon my mother's head. I tied string around an egg brought by Katayoon and suspended it from the ceiling, for new life has curative powers. When Salman and Shahvali became hungry, I mixed together flour and water and made them bread. I did everything that Malekeh was too tired to do, from washing the boys' clothes to sweeping the house.

When my mother's fever came, in the afternoons, the pain was almost too much for her to bear. She held the blankets to her eyes to try to shut out the light. She twisted on her bedroll and shivered, although sweat glistened on her forehead. Then, after the fever had fled, she lay on the bedroll with lifeless limbs, her face drained of color.

I gave the last of our vessels of lung medicine to Amir, who sold them and brought us the money. My mother had planned to use it to buy dried roots and herbs to make the next batch, for she could not collect fresh plants during the winter. But I was unable to put aside any money, since Malekeh still had not sold a carpet.

I spent the coins as slowly as I could, buying only essentials such as flour to make bread, and vegetables for soup. The food did not last very long. When the money was gone, we all endured the first day of fasting with few complaints. But the second day, Salman followed me while I was at my chores, begging me for food. "He needs bread!" he said, pointing to Shahvali, who was so tired he sat quietly near the stove, his eyes dull.

"I would give you my life, but I have no bread," I said, pitying him even more than I lamented over my own empty stomach. "Take Shahvali to Katayoon's house and beg them for a morsel to eat."

After they left, I looked around at the dim room in dismay. My mother and Davood lay on stained bedrolls. There was dirt near the door where we left our shoes, and the room smelled of unwashed bodies. I hadn't had time to bathe myself. I could not believe that I had once been anointed by my own bathing attendants, washed clean and plucked until I was as smooth as an apple, dressed in silks, and sent to minister to a man who changed houses the way others changed clothes.

My mother opened her eyes for a moment and called out for me. I rushed to her side and stroked the hair away from her face. "Is there any soup?" she asked in a rasping voice.

The despair I felt was as wide as the sky, for I had none to offer her. I was silent for a moment, and then I said, "I'll make you some, Bibi-joon. Something hot and healing."

"God willing," she said, closing her eyes.

I could not sit still, knowing that she was hungry; I must do something to help her. Wrapping myself tightly in my picheh and chador, I walked to the carpet sellers' section of the Great Bazaar.

The young merchant was at his usual post. Hardly daring to breathe, so great was my hope, I asked if he had seen the Dutchman. He clicked his tongue against his teeth, his eyes sympathetic. Disappointed, I thanked him and took my leave.

The Dutchman's blue eyes had seemed so innocent of guile. How could he have done such a thing? I had believed he would follow the rules of honor. I had not considered that, as a farangi, the Dutchman might leave whenever it suited his cold merchant's heart.

His treachery would be judged by God, but that thought didn't release me from my sorrows. What could I do? How could I help my mother? I thought of the young musician and the beggar with the stump. If they could make their living on the streets, I must try to do the same. My heart pounding, I walked through the bazaar until I reached the Ja'far Mausoleum, where crowds came to pay their respects to a religious scholar who had died more than a century before. It seemed like a respectable place for a woman on her own to ask for charity. I stood outside and watched an old, blind beggar man whose alms bowl gleamed with silver. After listening to him at work, I removed my sash, put it on the ground for coins, and began to repeat what I remembered hearing others saying.

"May you have eternal health!" I whispered to a group of women who were leaving the mausoleum. "May your children never go hungry. May Ali, prince among men, keep you safe and well!"

The blind beggar man gestured in my direction. "Who's there?" he barked.

"A woman only," I said.

"What ails you?"

"My mother is ill, and I have no money to feed her."

"What about your father, brother, uncles, husband?"

"I have none."

"What ill fortune," he said gruffly. "Still, I don't share my corner."

"Please, I beg you," I replied, hardly believing that I must now beg a beggar man. "My mother will starve."

"If that's true, then you may stay for now," he replied. "But speak up! They'll never hear you if you mumble that way."

"Thank you, graybeard," I said, using the term of respect for a wise old man.

When I saw a smartly dressed fellow, in a clean white turban, leaving the mausoleum, I cleared my throat and began my pleas in what I hoped was a clear, but sorrowful, voice. He passed without dropping a coin. Shortly afterward, a young woman paused and asked me to describe my plight. I told her about my mother's illness and how hungry I was.

"Are you married?" she asked.

"No."

"You must have done something shameful," she concluded. "Why else would you be here alone?"

I tried to explain, but she was already walking away.

The blind beggar man was earning well. He had been begging there since he was a child, he told me, so people knew him and his great need. "May all your prayers be fulfilled!" he said to them, and they felt comforted by their own charity.

"How are you faring?" he asked me at midday.

"Nothing," I replied sadly.

"You need to change your story," he said. "Look carefully at the listener before you start speaking, and then tell them something that will open their heart."

I thought about that for a few moments. When an older woman passed me, I noticed that her beauty had been great but was fading.

"Kind Khanoom, please help me!" I said. "My fate is very hard."

"What troubles you?"

"I was once married to a man who owned more horses than there are mosques in Isfahan," I said, trying to sound like my mother when she was telling a story. "One day, his second wife invented a tale about how I planned to poison him for his money, and he cast me out. I have no one to go to, for all my family is dead. I have been left with nothing!" I cried.

"Poor animal," she replied. "Those second wives are the real poison. Take this, and may God remember you." She dropped a coin onto the cloth.

When two young, well-muscled soldiers approached the mausoleum, I was emboldened to tell them something different.

"My parents died when I was very young, and my brothers have been killed," I moaned.

"By whom?"

"By the Ottomans, in a battle to protect our northwestern border."

"What bravery!" said the men, leaving me two small coins.

Men stopped far more often than women to talk to me. "I'll bet you're as pretty as the moon," said a boy who was just getting his first beard. "Why not lift your picheh so I can have a look?"

"Your father is frying in hell!" I said, between gritted teeth.

"Just a peek!"

"Hassan and Hossein, O saints among men, protect a poor woman from cruel strangers!" I cried in a loud voice, and he sped away.

A fat man who had dyed his beard with henna was even more brazen than the boy. "I don't care what you look like under that picheh," he said. "How about a quick little sigheh, just for an hour?"

He held out his palm, which was gleaming with silver. His thick fingers were knotted with calluses.

I grabbed the cloth containing the few coins I had earned and rushed away. Behind me, the fat man said, "I have a meat shop in the bazaar. Look for me if you're ever hungry!" And then he threw a few small coins at my feet, which scattered around me. I turned my back, but then I thought of my mother's wan face and stooped to gather them. The butcher was laughing as he walked away.

"I'm leaving, graybeard," I said to the beggar man, for now I had enough money for the soup. "Thank you for your generosity."

"May God reverse your bad fortune," he said.

"And yours, too," I replied, but then I felt ashamed, for I knew nothing would remove his blindness.

I went to the food section of the bazaar and spent all my coins on onions and lamb bones. As I returned home with my bundles, the price I had paid for them weighed on my heart. To have to invent stories to earn the pity of strangers, and to endure solicitations from foul-minded men — it was all I could do to keep myself upright as I walked through the bazaar toward Malekeh's squalid neighborhood. But I suppressed my keening, for it would not help me now.

WHEN I ARRIVED HOME, my mother was curled up on her thin cotton bedroll, the blanket knotted around her legs. She was in one of her calm moments between fevers, but her eyes frightened me. It was as if they had died in her face. I rushed to her side, laying my parcels around her.

"Bibi, look! I have onions and bones! I will make a soup to infuse you with strength."

My mother shifted slightly on her bedroll. "Light of my eyes, there is no need," she said.

I took her cold hand in mine and felt the sharp bones in her fingers. Her body had wasted away since she had become ill.

"I cannot eat," she added, after a pause.

I thought of the young man's taunts and the fat butcher's leer. I would have gladly endured them again if only my mother would eat a morsel or two. "Please try, Bibi-joon," I begged.

"Where did you get money for food?"

She knew I had spent the last of our coins from the sale of her herbal cures, so I had to admit I had gone begging at the Ja'far Mausoleum. She closed her eyes as if she could not bear my answer.

"Did men ask you for favors?" she whispered.

"No," I said quickly.

I plumped up the pillow around her head and smoothed her long gray hair away from her face. It was matted and stiff from days of not being washed. My mother turned her head; she hated not being clean.

"You're looking much better today," I said brightly, trying to convince myself it was true.

"Am I?" she replied. Her skin was yellowish, and the circles under her eyes were darker. "I feel better," she said, in a thin, weak voice.

I dipped another cloth in cool water and wiped her face and hands. She sighed and said, "Ah, how good it feels to be fresh."

"As soon as you get better, we'll go to the hammam," I said in my cheerful voice, "and we'll spend all afternoon soaking and scrubbing."

"Yes, of course," said my mother, in the voice she used to indulge a babbling child. She turned carefully onto her side and said, "Akh! Akh!" Her illness had attacked her hips, legs, and back.

"Shall I massage you?" I asked. She dipped her chin in assent, and as I began releasing the muscles, her face slowly became more calm.

"While you were gone, I had a wonderful dream," she said, her eyes closed. "It was about the day you and your Baba brought home the ibex horns."

My mother touched my cheek. "That was the most blissful day of my life, except for the day you were born."

"Why that day?" I asked.

"After you fell asleep, your father and I joked about how we had never needed any aphrodisiac like the horns. Then he took me in his arms and told me how thankful he was that he had married me and no other."

"Of course, he loved you," I murmured soothingly.

"There is no 'of course' to love," she replied. "Not after fifteen years without a child!"

The sharpness in my mother's tone startled me and made me wonder how my parents had fared in the years before my birth. I knew that every month, my mother had gone to Kolsoom for herbs to make her pregnant, until in desperation she had visited the stone lion in the Kuh Ali cemetery and rubbed her belly against it, praying for a child. I understood now how she must have felt. I had tried only for a few months and had been saddened at the sight of my own blood every time.

"Was my father angry?" I asked, pressing my fingers into the spongy muscles of her calf.

"He was desperate," she replied. "All the men of his age were already teaching their young sons how to ride and how to pray. Bitterness grew between us and sometimes we would pass a day and a night in silence. I wrestled with myself for a year until finally, I decided I would sacrifice myself to relieve his misery. 'Husband,' I said to him one day, 'you must take a second wife.'

"He looked surprised, but couldn't conceal his hope for a son. 'Could you truly accept a life with another woman by my side and under our roof?' he asked.

"I tried to be brave, but my eyes filled with tears. He was such a loving man that he never raised the subject again. Soon after that, I became pregnant and our world was bright again."

My mother placed her hands on her middle. "The day my belly began to cramp, your father was hard at work on the harvest," she recalled, her face soft. "I was surrounded by my women friends, who massaged my feet, gave me cool water to drink, and sang to you. But try as I might, you would not come out. I labored all through that long day, and all through the night. In the morning, we sent a boy to Ibrahim and begged him to set free one of his sparrows, so that you, too, would be released from your bondage. The boy came back and reported that the bird had flown like the wind. Once I heard that news, I turned myself toward Mecca, squatted, and gave a final push. There you were at last!

"In the years after that, your father still longed for a boy," she continued. "But on the day he brought home the ibex horns, he told me he was thankful he had married me and no other. That's how much he loved us. And you — you were more precious to him than any son."

My father had loved me like the light of his eyes. It had seemed natural to me to be blessed with such love. Now that I was older, I could easily imagine how different things might have been.

My mother's face radiated joy, and she looked beautiful despite her pale, wasted body. "Your father is gone, but I will never forget how he made his peace with God," she said, "and now I can do the same. Daughter of mine, I accept our fate — yours and mine — just as it is."

Knowing how deeply my mother disapproved of my behavior in Isfahan, her blessing made my heart shed tears of blood.

"Bibi, I would sacrifice myself for you!" I cried. My mother opened her arms, and I curled up beside her on the stained bedroll. She put a thin arm around me and stroked my forehead. I breathed in her maternal smell, sweet to me even in her illness, and felt her gentle hand on mine. It was the first time she had caressed me in weeks, and I sighed with contentment.

I wanted to stay curled up with her, but as the afternoon waned, I knew I must arise and attend to the cooking. Perhaps my mother would eat some soup, after all. I tried to slip away, but she tightened her grasp on my hand and said in a whisper, "Daughter whose face I love, you must promise me one thing."

"Anything."

"After I am gone, you must go to Gordiyeh and Gostaham and beg for their mercy."

I turned my body to face her.

"My child," she continued, "you must take the news to them with my dying wish: that they find you a husband."

The ground beneath me seemed to quiver, just as it had when my father had died.

"But—"

She tapped my hand with her finger, demanding silence. It was like the touch of a feather.

"And you must promise me that you will bow to their will."

"Bibi, you must live," I pleaded in a whisper. "I have no one else but you."

The pain in her eyes was visible. "Daughter of mine, I would never leave you, unless called by God."

"No!" I cried out. Davood awoke and asked what was wrong, but I could not speak. He had a coughing fit as wet and foul as the weather outside before falling asleep again.

"You haven't promised," said my mother, and again I felt her birdlike touch on my hand. I thought of how strong her hands used to be from years of knotting rugs, wringing out laundry, and kneading dough.

I bowed my head. "I swear by the Holy Qur'an," I said.

"Then I may rest content," she replied, closing her eyes.

The boys burst into the room, complaining that they were hungry. I had to leave my mother's side to attend to my work. As I thought back to her words, my hands began quivering, and I almost cut myself as I chopped the onions. I threw in the lamb bones, salt, and dill, and stoked the fire with dried dung to make the soup boil. The boys sniffed the air hungrily, their faces pinched and weary.

When the soup was ready, I served my mother, the children,

Davood and Malekeh, and myself. It was little more than hot water, but after fasting, it seemed like a princely meal. As the boys drank their soup, their cheeks became as red as apples. I looked at my mother lying on the bedroll. Her soup was steaming beside her, untouched.

"Bibi, I beg you to eat," I said.

She put her hand over her nose as if the smell of the lamb bones sickened her. "I cannot," she replied weakly.

Salman burped and held out his vessel for more soup. I served him again, praying there would be leftover broth for my mother. But then Davood said, "May your hands never ache!" and emptied the pot into his bowl.

Shahvali said, "I want more, too!"

I was about to tell him that none remained, but then Malekeh's eyes met mine. "I'm sorry your mother can't eat her soup, but we should not waste her portion," she said gently.

I fetched the soup sitting beside my mother and handed it to her son without replying. When I returned to my mother's side, I tried not to listen to Shahvali's slurps, for my nerves were as frayed as the threads in an old carpet. I held my mother's limp hand and began praying in a soft voice.

"Blessed Fatemeh, esteemed daughter of the Prophet, grant my mother perpetual health," I begged.

"Fatemeh, wisest of women, hear my prayer. Save a blameless mother, the brightest star in her child's life."

MY MOTHER WAS hungry the next morning, but I had nothing for her. I was angry at Malekeh for giving away my mother's soup and avoided her eyes. After she had departed, and my mother and Davood had fallen asleep again, I put on my picheh and chador and walked quickly to the Ja'far Mausoleum. I was glad I lived far away from the Great Bazaar, for I did not want anyone to know I had become a beggar. On the way, I thought of new stories to tell passersby so that the rivers of their generosity might flow.

The beggar man was already there with his bowl. "May peace be upon you, graybeard!" I said.

"Who's there?" he asked gruffly.

"The woman from yesterday," I replied.

He thrust his cane in my direction. "What are you doing here again?"

I drew back, frightened of being struck. "My mother is still very ill," I said.

"And I'm still very blind."

"May God restore your sight," I said, trying to answer his rudeness with kindness.

"Until he does, I need to eat," he replied. "You may not come here every day, for we'll both starve."

"Then what am I to do? I don't want to starve, either."

"Go to one of the other mausoleums," he said. "If your mother is still ill next week, I will permit you to return here."

My cheeks began to burn. How dare a bedraggled beggar refuse me the few small coins I could earn! I walked away from him, taking up my place near the entrance to the octagonal shrine. Setting down my cloth, I began asking passersby for help.

Before long, a tall, older woman who must have been one of the beggar man's regular benefactors arrived and inquired about his health.

"Not too bad, by the grace of Ali!" he replied. "At least I'm better off than her," he added, gesturing in my direction. I thought he was being kind again and trying to send coins my way.

"What do you mean?" asked the woman, eager for gossip.

In a loud whisper, he replied, "She uses the generosity of esteemed people like you to buy opium."

"What!" I said. "I've never touched opium in my life! I'm here because my mother is ill."

My protests only made me sound guilty. "Then you should spend your money on her instead of yourself," the woman replied.

"God knows what is right," said the beggar man sagely.

The two began conversing loudly about the perils of addiction. People who were walking by stopped and stared at me as if I were an evil jinn. I could see it was useless to stay, for they trusted the beggar man's word. No one would give coins to an opium eater.

"Good-bye, graybeard," I said, with resignation. I hated to be cordial to him, but I might have to return. "I'll see you next week."

"May God be with you," he replied, in a kinder tone. Now I understood how he had survived at his corner for so many years.

I visited two other mausoleums, but each had their regular beggars, who hissed at me when I tried to claim a corner. Too tired to insist, I turned my steps toward home. The sky was heavy with clouds, and there was a thin layer of snow on the ground. By the time I reached the old square, the cold had driven away all the vendors and shoppers. The few beggars who remained outside were shuffling to the old Friday mosque to take shelter. In the wan light, the dome of the mosque looked hard and frozen. I felt frozen, too. By the time I arrived at Malekeh's, my fingers and toes were stiff with cold.

My mother was asleep on her dirty bedroll. The bones of her face looked frighteningly visible through her skin. Her eyes fluttered open and searched my person for parcels. Seeing I had nothing, she closed them again.

I pressed my cold hands against my mother's face, and she sighed with relief. She was burning from the inside. Afraid that the fire in her body would vanquish her, I went out, collected some snow, wrapped it in the arm of one of my tunics, and laid it on her forehead. When she moaned for something to drink, I gave her sips of a strong liquor mixed with the juice of willows, a tonic for fevers that Malekeh had bartered for in the bazaar. My mother drank it under protest, then vomited it up right away along with green bile. I cleaned up the lumpy, smelly mess, wondering why the liquor seemed to be making her worse.

There was no food for the family that night. Malekeh came home and drank some weak tea before going to bed. The boys were enervated from hunger and whined about their aching bellies before curling up on either side of her. The sight of them together filled me with longing for the times I had gone to sleep with my mother's arm around me and her reassuring stories in my ear.

As the moon rose, my mother's fever rose with it. I gathered more snow to cool her and laid it gently on her forearm. This time, she inhaled sharply and drew back from the snow as if it burned. When I tried again, she crossed her arms over her chest in a weak attempt to protect herself. I was anguished about hurting her, but I continued to apply the tunic of snow to her body, for this was the only treatment that cooled her. Before long, she stopped moving her limbs and began to keen softly. Had she cried out and screamed, I would have rejoiced, for I would have known there was vigor in her. But this sound was as weak and pathetic as the cries of an abandoned kitten. It was all that her poor, tired body could force out.

As I tended to my mother, I listened to the household's nightmarish chatter. Salman cried out in his sleep about a terrible jinn chasing him under a bridge. Davood wheezed as if his lungs were half filled with water. A woman who lived in one of the rooms off of the courtyard wailed and called on God for protection as she endeavored to give birth.

I don't know how much time passed before my mother began trying to speak. Her lips were moving, but I couldn't make out the words. I tried to smooth her hair away from her face. She stopped my hand and mumbled, "First there wasn't."

"Sleep, Bibi-joon," I urged, not wanting her to waste her energy telling a story.

She released my hand and rolled restlessly on her bedroll. "Wasn't," she mumbled again. Her bottom lip cracked and began to bleed. I felt around in the dark until I found a vessel of lamb's fat and herbs, which I applied to her mouth to halt the bleeding.

Her lips worked fruitlessly as if she were still trying to finish the invocation. To help her, I whispered gently, "And then there was."

My mother's mouth curved into something like a smile. I hoped she would be calm now. I held her hand and stroked it, as she had stroked mine so many times before. Her lips began working again. I had to bend my face close to hers to hear what she was saying.

"Was!" she said insistently. "Was!" Her eyes were glazed and looked joyful in the strange, unhealthy way that an opium addict's do.

Sweat streaked her brow. I brought her some water and tried to lift her head so she could drink it. Excitedly, she averted her face and kept trying to speak. The words sounded as jumbled as vegetables in a stew. I thought of how she used to tell stories in a honeyed voice that entrapped listeners in her spell.

"Bibi-joon, you must drink something—you are as hot as a coal!" I said.

She sighed and closed her eyes. I soaked a cloth with water and offered it to her. "Will you suck on this, just for me?" I pleaded.

She opened her mouth and allowed me to insert a small corner of the cloth. She made a sucking motion to please me, but after a moment or two, began to try to talk again. The cloth fell out of her mouth. She grabbed her belly and mumbled a few incoherent words.

"What is it, Bibi-joon?" I asked.

She massaged her stomach. "Pushed and pushed," she whispered, her words like susurrations. She took my hand again and pressed it faintly.

"And then there was . . . ," she mouthed, and I could make out the words only because I knew them so well.

"Please, please keep yourself still," I said gently.

Her arms and legs tightened, and her forehead knotted. Her mouth opened, and finally she breathed, ". . . *you!*"

She reached up and touched my cheek, her eyes tender. Of all the tales she had ever created, I was the one written in the ink of her soul. I held her fingers against my face, wanting desperately to infuse her body with the strength of mine.

"Bibi-joon," I cried, "please take the life that pulses through my heart!"

Her fingers became flaccid and slid away from my face. She lay motionless on her bedroll, her energy spent.

I would have given my very eyes to go back to the moment that Gordiyeh and Gostaham had told me I must renew the sigheh. I would have begged Gostaham to remove me from that tangled knot in a suitable fashion, and if he had refused, I would have acceded to his demands to stay with Fereydoon until he tired of me. Anything at all to prevent my mother's suffering.

My mother was speaking again. Her words came out one at a time, at great cost to her. "May God . . . keep you . . . from need!" she whispered slowly. Then her body seemed to go limp.

"Bibi, stay with me!" I cried out. I squeezed her hand, but there was no response. I shook her arm slightly, then her shoulder, but she didn't stir.

I rushed to Malekeh, who was still curled up with one child on either side of her. "Wake up, wake up!" I whispered urgently. "Come and look at my mother."

Malekeh wiped her eyes, sighing, and arose sleepily. She crouched beside my mother's bedroll, and when she looked closely at her sallow, sunken face, she drew a frightened breath. She placed her fingertips near my mother's nostrils and held them there. I stopped breathing, for if my mother was not drawing breath, neither could I.

The first call to prayer from the Friday mosque pierced the air.

People were beginning to stir. Outside, a donkey brayed and a child wailed loudly. Salman awoke and called to Malekeh, pleading for bread. She positioned her body in front of my mother's, as if to shield Salman from the sight of her.

"She is barely tethered to earth," Malekeh finally said. "I will pray for her — and for you."

SHORTLY AFTER DAWN, I covered myself in my chador and picheh and ran most of the way to the meat sellers' section of the Great Bazaar. The sheep had already been slaughtered and skinned. A moneyed crowd buzzed around carcasses hanging on hooks and displayed on countertops. The marbled meat made my mouth water, and I thought of how much strength a fresh lamb stew would give my mother. Perhaps someone would offer charity. I put my sash on the ground and began to beg.

I watched a small errand boy, no doubt from a wealthy family, order almost more meat than he could carry, while next to him a woman in a tattered chador bartered fiercely for feet and bones for her stew. An older man who was buying kidneys reminded me of my father, who loved kidney kebab and used to char it expertly over a fire. In the bustle, no one paid attention to me.

Time was passing and I could not wait. I threw myself to the ground and cried out to passersby to remember the gifts God had given them and share them with others. People stared at me with curiosity, but my outburst did not soften their hearts.

Wracked with worry about my mother, I abandoned my post and began searching through the meat bazaar for the fat man with the knotted fingers. I found him in his shop alone, hacking at a lamb's haunch. His belly bulged against his pale blue tunic, which was spattered with blood, and his turban was smeared with long red streaks.

"How can I serve you?" he asked.

I shuffled my feet. "I'm the one from Ja'far," I murmured.

The butcher smirked and said, "Let me give you some meat."

He offered me a stick of kebab that had just been grilled. The rich smell of the lamb, which was dotted with coarse salt, sapped all my vigilance. I lifted my picheh and bit into the dripping meat. Passersby stared, surprised to see a veiled woman revealing her face, but I was too hungry to care.

"Ah, nice and tender," he said. I ate the kebab without speaking, the juice dripping down my chin.

"And now I have been permitted to see your pretty lips."

I did not reply. When I had finished eating, I said, in a pleading voice, "I need food for my mother, who is ill."

The butcher laughed, his belly shimmying under his clothes. "Yes, but can you pay?"

"Please," I said. "God will reward you with fatter lambs next year."

He gestured around him. "There are beggars in every section of the bazaar," he said. "Who can feed them all?"

He was an ugly man, I thought. I turned and began walking away, although it was just a pretense.

"Wait!" he called after me. He grabbed a sharp knife and slashed the haunch, which fell open to the bone. He chopped the meat into chunks the size of my hand and threw them into a clay vessel.

"Don't you want this?" he asked, offering me the bowl.

I reached toward it with gratitude. "Thank you for your charity!" I said.

He drew back before I could touch it. "All I ask is for an hour after the last call to prayer," he whispered. His lips dropped into a leer that he seemed to think would entice me like a bee to a poppy. The thought of lying under his big belly and feeling his large bloody hands sickened me.

"I need more than that," I said haughtily, as if I were used to such filthy bargains. "Much more."

The butcher laughed again, for he thought he understood me now. He grabbed the haunch and cut me twice as much again. Throwing the meat into the vessel, he pushed it at me. I grabbed it out of his hands.

"When?"

"Not for a week," I said. "Not until my mother is better."

The butcher laughed. "A week, then, until we sigheh!" he said in a whisper. "And don't even think about losing yourself in the city. No matter where you live, I can find you."

I took the vessel, shaking with revulsion. "I'll need more meat in a few days," I said, still trying to play my part.

"As you wish," he replied.

"Well, then, in a week," I said, trying to sound coquettish as I walked away. Behind me, I heard the butcher's greasy laugh.

I took the meat to the pharmacists' section of the bazaar and traded some of it for the best medicine I could find for fever. Then I ran home to check on my mother. When I arrived, she called my name weakly and I thanked God for sparing her for another day. I gave her water and spooned some of the medicine gently into her mouth.

There was still so much meat that I was able to trade a small portion to Katayoon's family for celery and rice. I made a large stew that would last, if kept cold at night, for several days, as well as a thick meat broth for my mother.

Our feasting that night was beyond imagining. Malekeh, Davood, and their sons had not tasted lamb for a year. Davood sat up throughout the whole meal, which he had never done before. My mother was too ill to eat the stew, but she sipped the broth and took more of the medicine.

"Where did you get this meat?" Malekeh asked.

"Charity," I replied, not wanting to tell her the truth. Rich people often sacrificed a lamb to fulfill a nazr, but they never offered such fine cuts. Had my mother been less ill, she would have suspected my answer.

I sent my prayers of thanks to God for the food, begging for His forgiveness for the promise I had made to the butcher. I had no intention of ever seeing him again. I decided to walk a wide arc around the meat sellers' section of the bazaar from then on.

For the next few evenings, I heated the stew and served the family. The boys ate as much as they were given as fast as they could; Malekeh and Davood ate slowly and gratefully, while my mother barely wetted her lips with the broth.

When the stew was nearly gone, a small, dirty boy entered our courtyard and asked for me. He beckoned me outside and thrust a large vessel full of shiny red meat toward me. I drew away from it, frightened.

"Aren't you pleased?" he asked. "It's from the butcher."

"Ah," I said, trying to behave as if it were expected.

"The butcher is anticipating your visit," the boy said, "after the last call to prayer."

Even in his young eyes, I could see contempt and disgust for what he thought I was.

"How did you find me?" I asked, my voice unsteady.

"It was easy," he said. "I followed you home the other night."

I grabbed the meat and said good-bye in a curt voice. Inside, I put the meat in a pot with some oil and made another stew. When my mother asked where the meat came from, I told her the obvious: "From a butcher."

I didn't know what to do. If I eluded the butcher, he would come to Malekeh's house and degrade me in front of everyone. Then we would be called shameful and thrown out on the street again. I thought of the pretty, young musician and how he had been reduced to begging and to rags. As the meat began sizzling, I could feel myself perspiring, but the heat of the stove had little to do with it.

That night I dreamed that the butcher led me into a small, dark room and broke all my bones with his thick hands. He put me on display on one of his bloody hooks, naked, and when someone wanted meat, he carved me while I was still alive. I screamed and screamed in horror, waking everyone in the house. When they asked what was wrong, I couldn't tell them. I lay awake, agonized about what to do. My appointment with the butcher was in two days.

GORDIYEH AND GOSTAHAM had cast us out and left us to our doom, and now I must return to them as a beggar, in disgrace. It was as if God himself wished to make my humiliation complete.

Well into the chilly afternoon, I covered myself in my chador, not thinking about the condition of the tunic and robe I was wearing, and walked to their house. It was difficult to knock at Gostaham's grand gates, and even more difficult when Ali-Asghar answered the door.

"What are you doing here?" he asked, as if he had seen a jinn.

"I've come for charity," I replied, bowing my head.

He sighed. "I don't think anyone will see you."

"Can you try?"

He looked at my face closely. "I'll remind them of your jaw," he said finally, and disappeared for a few moments.

When he returned and summoned me in, my heart began to pound. I removed my coverings and followed him to the Great Room, where Gordiyeh and Gostaham were seated on cushions drinking their afternoon coffee. Gordiyeh wore a velvet robe she had commissioned out of the fabric patterned with red and yellow autumn leaves, and her matching yellow shoes were placed neatly near the door. She was eating a rosewater pastry, which made my mouth water with hopeless longing.

"Salaam aleikum," they said together. They did not invite me to sit down, for I was just another supplicant now.

I knew that nothing but complete submission would work with Gordiyeh. I bent to kiss her feet, which were hennaed bright red on the bottom.

"I throw myself on your charity," I said. "My mother is very ill, and I need money for medicine and for food. I beg you, by the love of Fatemeh, for your help."

"May Imam Reza restore her health!" said Gostaham. "What happened?"

Gordiyeh peered at me, her sharp eyes understanding everything at once. "You've become as thin as a sheet of bread," she said.

"Yes," I replied. "We are not eating the way we did here."

"What a surprise!" she replied, with satisfaction in her voice.

I controlled my temper, although I believed Gordiyeh was pushing her advantage too far.

"I beg you to place us under your protection again," I said. "I would do anything to see my mother safe, warm, and well fed."

Gostaham looked pained; Gordiyeh triumphant. "I wish that were possible," Gordiyeh said, "but the bad luck melted away after you left. Fereydoon paid for the dangling gems carpet and for the rug that Naheed's parents had commissioned. I believe Naheed persuaded him to do that."

"I think I know why," I said. "I told her I was relinquishing her husband and begged her forgiveness. Perhaps she encouraged him to make amends on my behalf."

"That was good of you," said Gostaham. "It helped us a great deal."

"Leaving Fereydoon was not to your advantage," said Gordiyeh, interrupting her husband. "Look at you now."

I looked down at my stained, tattered tunic. It was more unsightly than anything a maid in Gordiyeh's house would ever wear.

"When did you see Naheed?" Gostaham asked.

"I didn't see her," I replied. "I wrote her a letter."

He looked astonished. "You wrote her — by yourself?"

I could see no reason to conceal my skills any longer. "Naheed taught me to write a little," I said.

"Mash'Allah!" Gostaham exclaimed. "My own daughters can't even hold a pen." Gordiyeh looked embarrassed, for she herself could not write.

"I am no scholar," I said quickly, "but I wanted her to learn from my own hand how sorry I was."

Gostaham raised his eyebrows in wonder. "You are always surprising me," he said. He still loved me; I could feel it in his gaze.

"There are more surprises," said Gordiyeh. "You probably haven't heard that Naheed has birthed her first child. It is a boy."

I had suspected she was pregnant during my last visit to her. To forestall Gordiyeh from reminding me again about all I had lost, I said, "If only I had been so lucky."

"Luck has not favored you," Gordiyeh agreed.

"But it has favored *you*," I said, for I was getting weary of thinking of the comet and hearing about my evil tread. "Can you help a little, now that my mother is ill?"

"Haven't we done everything we could?" asked Gordiyeh. "And didn't you throw our generosity in our faces?"

"I deeply regret my actions," I said, for it was true.

Gordiyeh didn't seem to hear. "I don't understand why you are so poor," she said. "What happened to your rug? That should have brought you an armful of silver."

I started to answer, but Gordiyeh began waving at the air as if she were batting at a fly.

"I don't even know why I'm asking you," she said. "We've heard your explanations too many times before."

"But I've had to beg for food!"

"I know," said Gordiyeh. "Cook saw you in the meat market pleading for coins."

I shivered at the thought of the butcher. "We hadn't eaten for—"

"What do you mean 'beg'?" interrupted Gostaham.

I tried to speak again, but Gordiyeh wouldn't permit it. "Never mind," she said sharply.

"Wait a minute," Gostaham said. "Let the girl tell her story."

"Why should we?" asked Gordiyeh, with a whip in her voice. But this time, her boldness raised Gostaham's ire.

"That's enough!" he roared, and Gordiyeh looked chastened for a moment. I was astonished, for I had never heard him stifle her before. "Why didn't you tell me Cook saw her begging? Do you expect me to let a family member starve?"

Gordiyeh fumbled for an answer. "I—I forgot," she said weakly.

Gostaham stared at her, and it was as if he saw, in that moment, every one of her weaknesses written on her face. There was a long silence, during which she did not have the courage to look at him.

Turning to me, Gostaham said, "What happened to your rug?"

"I sent the rug to the Dutchman," I replied, my voice becoming thick with grief. "But then I had to nurse my jaw, and when I went to find him, he had left Iran."

Gostaham winced; I couldn't tell if it was the mention of my jaw or my carpet. "He never paid?"

"No," I said sadly.

"What a rotten dog!" said Gordiyeh in disgust, as if she realized she must now treat me more charitably in front of her husband. "He picked up the rugs he had commissioned soon after you and your mother left. It's a good thing we demanded the money first. You should have done the same."

"Indeed," said Gostaham, "those farangis will take anything they can grab! They have no honor."

I shifted from one foot to the other, weary of standing. "I would not have asked for your help otherwise," I said.

Gostaham looked at me with pity and called to Taghee to fetch his purse.

"Take this money," he said, handing me a small bag of coins. "Do everything you can to make your mother well."

"I will try not to trouble you again," I said.

"I would be most insulted not to hear how you and your mother are faring," Gostaham replied. "God willing, you shall return and tell us that roses are blooming on her cheeks."

"Thank you," I said. "I remain, now and forever, your servant."

"May God be with you," said Gordiyeh, but her tone was icy. Gostaham frowned at her.

"I mean it," she added quickly.

As Ali-Asghar showed me out, I kept my hand on Gostaham's bag of coins, which felt heavy and solid in my sash. I believe that he regretted his harshness with me and was seeking to make amends. That's why he had finally hushed his wife, if only for a moment.

AS I WALKED toward the Image of the World, I passed the kind beggar with the stump at the top of Four Gardens and stopped to give him a small coin. Then I walked to the meat sellers' section of the bazaar and sought out the fat butcher. By chance, I arrived at the beginning of the last call to prayer; the muezzin's voice traveled clear and pure from the Friday mosque across the square. It made me feel scrubbed clean inside.

"Ah!" said the butcher when he saw me. Then he whispered, "You're one day early for our delights! Let me wipe my hands."

His nails were black with dried blood. "Don't trouble yourself," I whispered back. "Here's your money," I added loudly, counting out the coins so that his assistants could witness me paying. "That should take care of the meat, plus an errand boy's time."

The butcher's face grew red with anger. He had no power over me now that I was paying. Lifting his knife, he began slicing a lamb's heart.

"My mother's health has improved, thanks to your fine meat," I said. "You were very kind to give me the food on credit."

The butcher paused and swept the coins into his bloodstained hands. "How very lucky you are," he hissed.

In a louder voice for show, he added, "Praise God for her health."

"I do," I said. I felt as if I had just escaped the blackest fate of my life. I would be a slave to God, to carpets, or to Gostaham, but I did not want to be a slave to someone else's pleasure ever again.

I returned to Malekeh's house and served the family the meat stew I had made, although Malekeh was not home yet. Everyone looked brighter than they had only a few days before. The boys behaved better, for they were not irritable from hunger. Davood was well enough to move around the room. But the biggest change was in my mother. Her fever had finally abated, and her color was beginning to return to normal. I sent my thanks to blessed Fatemeh for her intercession.

Malekeh arrived very late that evening, with only one carpet on her back and a lightness in her step. "I sold one!" she announced proudly as she walked in the door. A family that had recently moved to Isfahan had bought it to furnish their new home. The wife had recognized that Malekeh's knots were tight and her prices low, and had told her that she would rather help a poor young mother than one of the wealthy merchants in the bazaar.

We all exclaimed joyfully, "Praise be to God!"

Malekeh's boys were excited by the bright silver coins in her hands. That night, after Malekeh had eaten, everyone was so merry we decided to set up a *korsi*. We heated pigeon dung in the stove, put the embers in a large metal vessel, and placed it under a low table. Malekeh threw blankets over it, cautioning the boys not to touch the hot vessel with their feet. Gathering around, we covered ourselves with the blankets and warmed ourselves by the delicious heat of the embers. For the first time in weeks, we drank strong tea and crunched on sugar crystallized with saffron. Malekeh stroked her boys' hair until they fell asleep. Then Davood told jokes, and the rare sound of my mother's laughter filled my ears with the finest music I had ever heard.

DURING THE NEXT two months, my mother convalesced slowly. Since she could not stand without becoming exhausted, from her bedroll she explained which dried herbs to buy in the bazaar and instructed me on how to make her medicines. I steeped them, packed them, and delivered them to Amir, who sold them successfully on his own. The medicine brought in enough money for us to feed ourselves, but we were not able to put much aside for wool. I longed to start another carpet, for it was the only way we could improve our fortunes, and I still dreamed of hiring others to help us.

When I told Malekeh about my hopes, she looked doubtful. "Buy wool and hire women with what money?" she asked.

"How about the silver from your carpet sale?"

Malekeh clicked her tongue against her teeth. "It's too risky," she replied, "but if you gather some money, I will match yours."

In the past, I might have been angry that she would not be persuaded, but now I realized she was right to be cautious. Since I would never earn enough extra money for wool by selling medicines or begging, in the end, there was only one thing I could do. With my mother on her way to recovery, I owed it to Gostaham and Gordiyeh to tell them their charity had made a difference. I dressed in Naheed's old finery—the purple robe with the fur cuffs, and a pink tunic—and went to see them again.

When I arrived, Gordiyeh was absent. Ali-Asghar told me she had gone to see Naheed's mother, which must have meant that the families had been reconciled. He showed me into the workroom, where Gostaham was making sketches.

"Come and sit!" he said, calling out to Shamsi to bring us coffee. "How is your mother?"

"Much better," I replied, "and it is because of you. The coins you gave me bought her fresh meat, which restored her health. Thank you for helping me save her."

"Praise God, Healer of Men," he replied.

I looked at the paper on Gostaham's lap. The design was as beautiful as a park in bloom. "What are you working on?" I asked.

"A cypress tree carpet," he said. The trees were long and thin, with a slight bulge in the middle like a woman's hips. They were surrounded by riotous garlands of flowers. Seeing Gostaham's drawings made me long to be working with him again.

"Amoo," I said, "as you know, I have no protector now, so I must do everything I can to earn honest money."

"True," said Gostaham, "but now it is time you took your own risks, for you will always be one to take them."

He was right. I could not stop myself; it was part of my nature. "Can you help at all?"

"Perhaps, if you can reliably deliver what I demand," he said, with a guarded look. "But can you?"

I knew I had always been a curiosity in his eyes, for I had talent and fire. He had never seen that in his wife or daughters, who had been content with being pampered. But now he had reason to mistrust me, as well. I took a deep breath.

"I promise you, amoo, I have learned," I said. "I almost lost my mother to illness. I have begged in the bazaar and endured the worst insults from strangers. I have made my peace with living humbly. I will not go against your sage advice — at least, not when it comes to carpets."

Gostaham looked off into the distance, and his eyes were full of regret. He cleared his throat a few times before he could speak. "We did wrong by you," he finally said.

"And I by you," I replied. "I am sorry for all the trouble I caused your household, for I have loved nothing more than learning by your side."

Gostaham looked at me as if assessing me anew. I believed he could see the change in me. I was calm, prudent, and strong, not the willful child I had been.

"It is time we made amends," he said. "If you are certain you can do what I require, I have a way to assist you."

"I will do anything you ask."

"What I need is workers," he said. "This cypress tree carpet is a private commission, and my usual assistants are too busy to do it. You know how to read a design now, so you can call out the colors and supervise its creation. I will pay you and two workers a daily wage to make this carpet, and give you the wool."

I was filled with joy. "Thank you, amoo, for your generosity," I said.

"Not so fast," he replied. "The conditions are that I will visit your workshop weekly to make sure everything is proceeding according to my exact plan."

"Of course," I replied. "We will open our home to you. And who is the carpet for?"

"A friend of Fereydoon's," he said.

I was astonished. "So he is no longer angry!"

"He seems to have forgiven all of us," Gostaham said. "And so have Naheed's parents, who restored their carpet commission just a few days ago."

"I'm so glad," I said, for I could feel that Gostaham was more at ease now that his silver was assured.

We sipped our coffee. It felt good to be with Gostaham again. Yet now things were different, for I was no longer his retainer. Although I did not have his protection, neither was I under his and Gordiyeh's sway. He was right, I would always take my chances on things. Perhaps it was better to be unfettered.

"Amoo," I said, "may I show you the design I have been working on?" I had sketched some carpet designs while my mother and Davood slept off their illnesses.

He threw back his head and laughed. "You are most unusual for a girl," he replied. "Before long, you will have seventy-seven people working for you, I am sure."

I showed him the design and asked him to advise me on the colors. It was a simple sunburst carpet with a universe of tiny flowers, a design that I hoped would appeal to young wives who enjoyed shopping for fashionable goods in the bazaar. Gostaham looked at it carefully, but then I watched the lines in his forehead deepen, a reliable sign that something was wrong. He looked up and said, "Don't make this."

I was so surprised, I stared at him.

"If you try to sell this carpet, you'll be competing with rug makers from all over the country who use the same type of design. It's an honorable pattern, but you can do better."

I thought about how long it had taken for Malekeh to sell one of her sunburst carpets, even though it was very fine. I didn't want to have to struggle as hard as she had.

"Then, what should I do?"

"Make another feathers carpet, like the one you gave the Dutchman," Gostaham said.

I winced at the memory of my folly, which had cost me so dearly. It was painful to be reminded of it again.

"That carpet showed you to be a designer whose work cannot be equaled by others," Gostaham said in a softer voice. "That's the only way to make money in this business."

"I'm glad you liked it," I said.

"You still don't understand," he replied. "It is a rare talent to be able to design something fine and dear. You must cultivate that talent, not waste it."

I could feel my blood rushing to my head. After all that had happened, it was hard for me to force the words out. In a low, strained voice, with my eyes on the carpet, I said, "Amoo, will you help me? Because I don't know how to do it alone."

"You're right, you don't know how to do it alone," he said. "I'm glad you finally understand that."

"I do," I said humbly.

"Then, yes, I will help you as much as I can. And gladly."

His enthusiasm emboldened me to ask for an advance on my wages for the cypress tree carpet, especially since Gordiyeh was not there to stop him. He laughed at my boldness and, to my great satisfaction, gave me the silver right away.

I said my farewell and walked to Malekeh's, singing softly to myself. The air was still cool, but the New Year and the beginning of spring were only weeks away. In the distance, the lemon-yellow dome of the Shah's private mosque beamed like a life-giving sun. It made me feel warm from the inside, although my skin was tingling in the chill.

When I arrived home, I told Malekeh and Katayoon the news. They were filled with delight, for we now had several months of paid work ahead of us. Malekeh expressed surprise over the source of the commission. "You went back to your uncle after he dismissed you?" she asked. "How bold you are!"

I smiled with satisfaction. I was bold, but I was no longer rash. I finally understood the difference.

Malekeh promised to match the advance I had received on my wages so that we could buy all the wool for my feathers carpet, which would allow me to start working on it right away.

For the first time in many months, there was so much joy in the household that no one wanted to sleep. We set up the korsi again and warmed ourselves underneath it. It started snowing lightly outside, but we all felt cozy together. I looked around at everyone as we talked and sipped strong tea. Even though we weren't family, Malekeh and Davood behaved as if we were. Although we crowded them terribly, they had never told us we were not welcome. They shared everything they had and praised us for everything we gave. This, I thought, was truly my family, for they loved us and helped us through difficulties without complaint.

"Would anyone like to hear a story?" asked my mother all of a sudden. I sat up, surprised. For months, she had been as silent as a nightingale in winter. Now I was certain she was on the path to good health.

The boys shouted their approval and promised to sit quietly. Malekeh stroked their heads, and even Davood seemed well enough to stay awake through the tale. All of us turned to my mother in anticipation. She looked beautiful again, her cheeks shining from the warmth of the korsi, her eyes sparkling, her thick gray hair pulled away from her face. She began speaking in the honeyed voice that my father had always praised, which lulled me right back to the times we had sat together in our village and listened, held fast in the web of her tales.

First there wasn't and then there was. Before God, no one was.

Once there was a girl named Azadeh who, by nature, was firm and certain in her decisions. From the time she was a child, Azadeh always knew what she preferred: almonds over pistachios, the cooing of doves over the song of the nightingale, her quiet friend Laleh over her talkative friend Qomri. Even when the time came for her to marry, Azadeh did not behave like other girls, who trembled with fear under their veils. She had met her husband once, when he had come to admire her red hair and milky skin, and sip a sour cherry drink with her family. When she saw him and heard him speak with a catch in his throat about his favorite horse, she knew he was a man who un-

derstood tenderness. *Looking toward her mother, she closed her eyes and held them shut for a moment to convey her assent.*

Azadeh and her husband lived together in harmony for two years, at which time he yearned to make the pilgrimage to Mashhad. Admiring her husband's religious feeling, which had deepened during their years together, Azadeh encouraged him to travel, knowing they didn't have enough money to go together. "I will make the pilgrimage another time," she told him kindly, "when my heart is more ready."

Azadeh's husband left on his trip, murmuring thanks to the Lord of the Universe for blessing him with such a jewel of a wife. During his absence, he asked his brother to care for Azadeh like a sister, ensuring that she remain free from want and harm.

Her brother-in-law had always kept his distance, but that changed soon after her husband departed. Early in the morning, when she arose and came out of her room to take her morning meal, her brother-in-law would say, "Voy, Azadeh! Your face is as smooth and white as the moon that is only now slipping into the outer spheres of heaven!" And in the evenings: "Voy, Azadeh! Your hair shimmers like the last streaks of sun giving way to blackest night!" Azadeh would smile politely and suggest that the moon or sun or stars were signaling that the weather would be fine. Privately, she wished her brother-in-law would take a wife.

As the months passed, Azadeh yearned for her husband, and his brother yearned for Azadeh. Whenever he could, he brushed against her clothing or her hair, or stood too near when they spoke, so that she was always inching her body away. She spent long hours alone in her room, and when she emerged for food or other needs, he was always waiting. One day, when she tried to slip out of her room at dusk, she felt a tug at her tunic and saw him crouching near the door in the gloom. Before she could speak, he grabbed her legs, toppling her to the ground. Within moments his body was covering hers, and he was demanding her submission. "Otherwise," he said, his oniony breath hot against her cheek, "I will tell everyone that you pursued a soldier until he could no longer resist you, and the first story your husband hears will be of your adultery."

Azadeh screamed to summon her servant, forcing her brother-in-law to peel himself off her. Then she locked herself in her room in fright. That night, her brother-in-law came to her door, whispering through the lock that he'd give her seven days to yield, which became six and five and four, until all the days were spent.

On the eighth day, a group of men including her brother-in-law broke into her room. While Azadeh sat quietly with her sewing, he announced that she had been declared guilty of adultery. He had brought four witnesses before a judge, each of whom had sworn they had seen her commit the act itself, and she was to be punished that very day.

The men took Azadeh deep into the desert and dug a hole, burying her to the waist. As she stood immured in the sand, she watched them gather stones, which they placed in piles near her. The sun was hot on Azadeh's face and her arms were pinned tightly to her sides, so when the rocks began flying toward her, she couldn't defend herself. Blood streamed into her eyes, and before long she saw circles of light that looked like exploding stars. Her head lolled on her shoulder as if broken. When the men were satisfied that her body held no more breath, they departed, expecting that her bones would soon shine white in the sun.

Early the next morning, a Bedouin traveling through the desert thought that the strange creature he spotted must be a mirage. When he came closer, he noticed that its lips were still moving. The Bedouin unburied Azadeh, slung her body on his camel, and brought her home to his wife, who tended her until her wounds healed.

Although Azadeh's heart was heavy with sorrow, it was only a matter of months before her beauty bloomed again, her hair as red as if it had been fired by henna, her skin as white as milk, her lips like the pinkest corals. Smitten, the Bedouin asked her to be his second wife. When she gently reminded him that she already had a husband, he promised to care for her like a sister, and remained true to his word.

But to most men, Azadeh's beauty pricked like a needle. Such a man was the Bedouin's servant, whose heart stung whenever Azadeh came near. If she passed on her way to fetch water, he murmured passages of soul-stirring po-

etry, but she remained deaf to his pretty words. One night, when he could no longer bear being spurned, he threatened to commit a crime unless she relented. But Azadeh remained firm, refusing him out of respect for her husband. In desperation, his mind clouded by lust, the servant grabbed a stone from the garden and sought out the Bedouin's only child, a baby who slept in her own small bed. He smashed in the child's head, breaking her fragile skull, and hid the bloody rock under Azadeh's pillow.

When the child's death and the rock were discovered, the Bedouin summoned Azadeh, tears streaming from his eyes. "Voy, Azadeh!" he said. "I gave you back your life. Is this how you repay me, with blood and death?"

"Kindest of masters, I beg you to use your reason," she replied. "What motive would I have for killing the child of a man who saved my life? Look around you: Who else might have wanted to commit such an evil deed?"

The Bedouin knew that his servant had always yearned for Azadeh. He struggled to master his feelings, realizing Azadeh was right. She had never done anything to make him distrust her.

"I believe you are innocent," he said slowly. "But if you stay, every time my wife looks at you, she will be consumed by grief. No woman can bear to be reminded of so much sorrow. I am sorry to lose you, but you must go."

The Bedouin gave Azadeh a sack of silver, and she left with only the money and the clothing on her back. Not knowing what to do, she walked to the port and found a ship sailing for Baku, where one of her uncles had gone many years before to make his fortune. She gave the captain all her money, and he promised her safe passage and freedom from harm. But only a few days after they had set sail the captain felt stricken by the sight of Azadeh's flaming hair and her cheeks like blooming roses.

"But I am a married woman!" protested Azadeh, cloaking her hair and body and wishing she had been born as plain as her friend Laleh.

Azadeh fled from the captain's grasping hands and prayed to the Redeemer of Men. To her wonder, the skies began to darken and a fierce wind stirred the water. As the waves became as tall as buildings, even the hardiest seamen began to pray with her. Suddenly, there was a loud, violent crack and the ship split in two, spilling its contents into the sea. In the water, Azadeh felt a piece *of the ship's hull strike her cheek. She rolled her body on top of it, her tunic billowing in the water behind her. For hours, she drifted alone, and though she had reason to believe she would die of hunger or thirst, she was surprised at how calm she felt, for the sky, the sea, and the birds were all unconcerned by her presence.*

After a night and a day, Azadeh spotted a thin strip of land. She paddled herself to shore and threw herself onto the sand, aching with fatigue. Her cheek had swelled like a melon from being hit by the debris that had saved her. She could barely open her right eye.

Not far away, she noticed the body of one of the sailors, who appeared to have drowned. Azadeh crawled over to him, checking his breath to make sure he was dead. Then she discarded her own sopping clothing and donned his, which was stiff with salt. In his pocket she found a knife. She unsheathed it and examined its sharp blade, and an idea came to her about how to separate herself from her misery.

She had always known what she wanted; her decisions came easily. Now, as she approached this one, she hesitated under the burden of doubt. How could she do what her mind was imagining? She sat holding the knife until dawn, when the sounds of fishermen preparing to launch their boats roused her. And suddenly Azadeh, who was too weary to endure anything more, made her decision.

She lifted a hank of her hair and slid it against the sharp blade, cutting as close to the scalp as she could. Then she cut another hank, and another. Clumps of red hair drifted, lifted, and billowed around her, blowing into the sea like some strange creature returning to the deep. When she was finished, Azadeh's scalp felt the night air for the first time, and she shivered with pleasure as if she were being caressed. She placed the sailor's cap on her head, dragged her body away from his, and slept like the dead.

Late that morning, a group of fishermen discovered her as well as some of the bales of silver that had been part of the ship's cargo. Knowing that such a treasure was a matter for the shah, they took Azadeh to his palace to explain what had happened.

To Azadeh, whose body was salt-encrusted and broken, the shah looked as clean as if he had bathed in light. He was dressed in a red silk robe, and his face glowed under a rose-embroidered turban that sparkled with rubies.

"Your name?" demanded the shah.

"I am Amir, son of a sea captain," replied Azadeh in her throatiest voice.

"What a fair youth you must have been before this tragedy!" exclaimed the shah. "Your face has been cracked and bruised, yet God in his mercy has preserved your life."

Azadeh almost smiled, her body tingling with relief at the thought of her own ugliness. Mastering herself, she replied, "All my father's cargo has washed up on your shores, but my father, alas, is lost. I offer you all his goods in exchange for just one thing."

"I give you permission to make your request," replied the shah.

"From now on, I renounce voyaging and moneymaking," she said. "Only build me a stone tower near the sea where none shall visit, and there I shall worship the Leader of the Faithful for the rest of my days."

"It shall be granted," the shah replied, dismissing Amir without a second glance.

Amir walked toward the town square. A few of the townspeople expressed sympathy for his losses and offered poultices for his face. Later, an innkeeper provided him with a bed in a room with other men. They joked with him a little, trying to relieve his sorrow, their eyes sliding across his face with no more interest than if they had been gazing at a mule. As Amir pulled the blankets over his body, he knew he would sleep peacefully for the first time since being left to die in the desert. That night, he dreamed of his stone tower, where he would live free and forgotten, listening no longer to fevered words of love but only to the soothing sound of the sea.

Amir worshipped God in that tower, and his fame as a man of devotion spread across the land. Such was his reputation that when the shah became ill, he called on Amir to become his successor, for he knew of no one more pure. But rather than accept, Amir revealed that he was a woman. Awestruck by this display of humility, the shah called upon Azadeh to select a man among them who would be a fitting ruler.

By then, Azadeh had also become known as a healer. Every day, pilgrims came to the stone tower to beg for blessings and to ask for the gift of health. One of these was Azadeh's brother-in-law. When her husband had returned from his pilgrimage, he had found his brother's limbs paralyzed and offered to take him to the stone tower to seek a cure.

Another supplicant was the Bedouin's servant. He had mysteriously become blind, and the Bedouin promised to accompany him to visit the sage of the tower. The four men met on the road and decided to travel together.

Naturally, Azadeh recognized them as they approached, but in her disguise as a man, they did not know her. When the men asked for help in curing their ills, she demanded that they first confess their crimes. "Reveal all that is hidden within your heart," she told them, "for only then will you be cured. If you leave anything veiled, it is certain that you will remain stricken."

Her husband's brother, shamefaced, revealed how he had lusted after a woman, falsely accused her of infidelity, and brought her to her death. The servant admitted that he, too, had desired a woman and crushed a baby's skull when she would not relent. Once the truth had been uttered, Azadeh offered a prayer to God, who released the men from their afflictions. Now her husband's brother could walk again and the servant could see. Each one begged for forgiveness for his crimes, and Azadeh granted them pardon.

Then she revealed herself to her husband, and all the love that had been denied them for so long gushed forth like a river. Azadeh installed her husband as shah and made the Bedouin her vizier, and justice reigned forevermore in their land.

The boys and Davood had fallen asleep. Malekeh thanked my mother for the story and curled up beside her husband. Only my mother and I remained awake.

"What a tale!" I said. "Azadeh must have had a heart as big as blessed Fatemeh's to forgive those who had wronged her so much."

"It was the right thing to do," said my mother tenderly, holding

341

my gaze. I returned her gaze, and when I saw how full of love it was, I suddenly understood what she meant. She had forgiven me, despite the pain I had caused her. We sat quietly for a moment, and for the first time since we had left Gordiyeh and Gostaham's house, I felt peace in my heart.

My mother and I moved closer together, sitting knee to knee so that we could talk quietly without waking the others. When the korsi went out, we put an oil lamp between us and wrapped blankets around our shoulders. The wind howled outside and the snow turned to freezing rain. When a drop darkened my blue cotton robe, I moved to evade the leak. Despite the chill, we stayed awake and began talking about all we had experienced in recent years: the evil comet, my father's untimely death, Gostaham's peculiar household, and the marvel that was Isfahan. At first, my mother did all the talking, but before long, I began speaking instead. The words flowed out of me, and I felt as if I were in a saint's shrine whispering the truth of my heart into the saint's ear.

My mother listened carefully, just as I had listened to her stories so many times before. Sometimes what I said seemed to surprise her, but her gaze was tender, and I felt as if I were growing into a woman before her eyes. It took until a cock crowed outside, signaling the dawn, before I was finally done.

My mother said, "Daughter of mine, your heart is now as pure as a carnelian, for you have spoken the truth."

She blew out the oil lamp and burrowed under the covers, closing her eyes. Yawning, I took my place beside her, happily tired. As my mother's breathing became quiet and smooth, I thought back to the comet and Hajj Ali's predictions, and how sharply they had afflicted me. Was there any reason I must live forever under an unlucky prophecy, now that the year of the comet had come and gone? It seemed as if Azadeh herself had been under such an evil influence, for her luck had died, but then it returned to burn even brighter than before. Even her suffering had not been in vain, for her heart had grown large enough to forgive those who had wronged her.

I could not guess what fate promised me, but I knew I would strive to make a good life, just as Azadeh had done. I thought of my father, and his love coursed through me like a river. As I began to fall asleep, I could hear him giving me advice. He said, "Put your faith in God, but always fasten your camel's leg."

CHAPTER SEVEN

Winter was almost over at last. The weather had softened, bringing sweet rains and the first warm days of the year. As the New Year approached, we prepared our home and ourselves to welcome it. Malekeh, my mother, and I mopped our tiny room, swept the courtyard, washed the bedding, dusted our few possessions, and scrubbed our tattered clothing and ourselves, so that we could greet the spring with freshness and hope.

We celebrated the first day of the New Year with a bounteous meal of chicken cooked with greens, and took Salman and Shahvali to play near the river. As the boys dipped their feet in the water, they seemed giddy with delight, for it had been long since they could enjoy themselves without cares. After they had finished playing, we sat in a teahouse underneath the Thirty-three Arches Bridge and refreshed ourselves with hot tea and cookies made with soft, sweet dates. The river seemed to dance by our feet, spraying us from time to time with revitalizing drops. It was the first time that all of us, including Davood, were well enough to have an outing together as a family.

The next day, even though all of Isfahan was beginning a fifteen-day holiday, Malekeh, Katayoon, and I began work on the cypress tree carpet for Gostaham. It was difficult to make progress in the courtyard with so many children underfoot and so many neighbors coming and going, especially during the holiday. But we labored through the commotion, for nothing rivaled the importance of creating a rug to dazzle Gostaham.

Shortly after the end of the holiday, Gostaham made his first visit to inspect our work. When he arrived, looking princely in an indigo silk robe over a saffron sheath and a purple turban, I jumped to my feet from behind the loom to greet him. Malekeh and Katayoon showered him with thanks for being our benefactor, while keeping their eyes fixed respectfully on the loom.

Gostaham glanced around the courtyard in disbelief. A dirty child with a runny nose shrank against the door of his home, awestruck by Gostaham's presence, while another in tattered clothes ran for her parents. The weather was already warm, and the courtyard bore the rancid smell of feet, which emanated from shoes left outside the doors. My mother begged Gostaham to sit and accept a vessel of tea, but when the odor reached his nostrils, an expression of barely concealed disgust flickered on his face and he said he could not stay. He did not touch the weak tea that was nonetheless placed near him, with an old but coveted saffron candy that drew a small crowd of flies.

Gostaham examined the rug from both sides to check the tightness of the knots and the accuracy of the pattern against his design, and professed his satisfaction with the few rows we had completed. Then he said he had pressing business elsewhere and turned on his heel. I ran behind him and thanked him for coming.

"God be with you, my child," he said, as if divine help were the only thing that could save me. I watched him mount the horse that awaited him. Before he rode away, he said with something like ad-

346

miration, "Mash'Allah! Neither earthquakes, nor plagues, nor misery will ever stop you from making carpets that delight the eyes."

I returned to the loom with a light step. Malekeh and Katayoon looked at me expectantly, and I showered them with praise and assured them that our patron was pleased with our work. Feeling relieved that we had passed our first test, I sang out the colors like a nightingale until it was time for the midday meal.

After we ate, the others took up household tasks, while I turned my attention to knotting the new feathers carpet. It was much easier this time, for I knew the pattern well and had chosen colors based on Gostaham's criticisms of my first attempt, in an effort to make the design seem even more delicate. I took great pleasure in the work. My fingers seemed to fly over the knots like birds skimming the surface of a river, and the carpet flowed from under my fingers like water.

It was hot in the courtyard, and I had to wipe away the sweat from my brow. From time to time, my mother brought me water mixed with the essence of roses to refresh me. But I was intent on what I was doing and forgot about the children in the courtyard and the sound of braying donkeys bearing their burdens down the street. It was as if I were living within the surface of the carpet myself, surrounded by its soothing colors and its images of eternal tranquillity. Lost in its beauties, I forgot the misery around me. At nightfall, my mother had to pull me away from my work and remind me that I must eat, rest my hands, and stretch my limbs.

My mother recited:

My love is sweet-waisted, like a cypress.
And when the wind blows, my love
Neither breaks nor bends.

It was several months later, and we had just finished the cypress tree carpet for Gostaham. We had laid it out in the courtyard and gathered around in a circle to admire it from above, as it would look to its owner.

"How like the gardens that await us, God willing!" Davood proclaimed. "Its owner will feel soothed when he rests his body upon this treasure."

Salman and Shahvali were so excited that they were running on and off the carpet, until at last they veered into each other and fell into a tangle of arms and legs.

"It's just like being in a park!" Shahvali declared, and indeed with his limbs splayed in every direction on the carpet, he appeared to be entangled in the very heart of a garden.

I began laughing at his boyish disarray, as did the others, and when my eyes met my mother's, Katayoon's, and Malekeh's, my heart soared with joy over the completion of our first project. We had worked well together, with the sense that we were building a future that would benefit everyone. And through it all, like the cypress itself, we did not break, nor bend.

Gostaham sent one of his men to pick up the carpet, and a few days later, I went to see him about it. I wanted to know if we had delivered exactly what he had wanted, and to hear his assessment of our work. I was pleased to learn that the owner liked it so much he had commissioned another of the same size, so that he would have a pair to adorn his Great Room. Gostaham advised him that it would have been cheaper to make them simultaneously, for I could have called out the colors for two groups of knotters. But I was only too happy to accept the commission.

Gostaham asked how my work was proceeding on the feathers carpet, and I told him I worked on it every afternoon.

"Try to complete it soon," he said, "for it's nearly time for the harem's twice-yearly visit to the Great Bazaar."

I stayed silent, but a spring of hope welled in my heart.

"If it is finished, I will grant you permission to display it in my alcove."

At that, I thanked him forty times and nearly ran home to get back to work. I was so eager that I did not heed my mother's warnings but worked on the feathers carpet every day, from the moment it was light until it was too dark to see. When time became short, I hurried my work by knotting by the light of an oil lamp deep into the night.

I completed the fringes just a day before the harem's visit, and when the carpet had been sheared, I saw that Gostaham had been right about the color choices: Just a few delicate variations in the shades had made this carpet superior to the first one. All the elements had fallen into place, like the ingredients in a stew cooked to perfection, and the carpet pleased both the eye and the heart.

Early the next morning, Salman and Shahvali helped me carry the carpet to the Image of the World. They were young enough not to be prohibited, like grown men, from catching a glimpse of the Shah's women. To protect them, though, I sent them home before entering the gates of the square, and carried the rolled-up carpet myself to Gostaham's alcove. His eldest daughter, Mehrbanoo, had been summoned from her family to run the shop. She greeted me with a cool peck on each cheek and said, "It's going to be a long day. I wish I could be doing anything other than this."

She wore a tunic in such a brilliant shade of orange, I was certain it had been dyed with saffron. The tree of life design on her hennaed hands was pristine. From this, I knew how idle she was. I choked back the words that came to my lips.

"Don't worry, I shall devote myself to helping you," I said as gracefully as I could.

Needing no further offer, she sank onto a large, comfortable bolster with a sigh that indicated exhaustion and instructed me to move a bundle of carpets from one end of the alcove to the other.

I bent down and pretended I couldn't move the bundle alone. I tugged and huffed until Mehrbanoo was shamed by her own indolence and arose to help me with it, although she added little strength to the endeavor.

The ladies of Shah Abbas's harem had begun to filter into the bazaar and penetrate the shops. I hung my feathers carpet on one of the most prominent walls in the alcove and waited to see what would happen. Before long, Jamileh, who was as beautiful as I remembered her, walked by without giving our shop a glance.

"There's the Shah's favorite!" I exclaimed.

Mehrbanoo laughed at my ignorance. "Not anymore," she said. "The latest is Maryam. You'll know her by the color of her hair."

When Maryam entered our shop later that morning, I realized it was the same harem woman I had seen years ago, whose hair flamed red like the dawn but who had looked lost and scared. She had an entourage now, spoke Farsi as well as her native Circassian, and appeared to be in charge of her sisters. Her dark eyes and eyebrows made a pleasing refuge from her bright red hair. After greeting us, she began looking at Gostaham's wares and saw my carpet.

"Look at that!" she said, attracted to it as if it were a lodestone. After gazing at it for a long time, she announced wistfully that the feathers reminded her of the birds in her homeland.

I did not reveal that I was the carpet's designer and knotter. I thought if she saw my callused fingers or looked closely at my tired red eyes—if she understood the fearsome work that a carpet demanded—its beauties would be forever tarnished in her eyes. Better for her to imagine it being made by a carefree young girl who skipped across hillsides plucking flowers for dyes before settling down to tie a few relaxing knots in between sips of pomegranate juice.

I knew otherwise: My back ached, my limbs were stiff, and I had not slept enough for a month. I thought about all the labor and suffering that were hidden beneath a carpet, starting with the materials. Vast fields of flowers had to be murdered for their dye, innocent worms boiled alive for their silk — and what about knotters? Must we sacrifice ourselves for the sake of rugs?

I had heard stories about women who became deformed by long hours of sitting at the loom, so that when they tried to deliver a child, their bones formed a prison locking the baby inside. In such cases, mother and child would die after many hours of anguish. Even the youngest knotters suffered aching backs, bent limbs, tired fingers, exhausted eyes. All our labors were in service of beauty, but sometimes it seemed as if every thread in a carpet had been dipped in the blood of flowers.

These were things that Maryam would never know. Instead, I told her coyly that the carpet would distinguish her in everyone's eyes — just like her thick red hair. I argued that any man who appreciated fine carpets, as I knew Shah Abbas did, would take great pleasure and pride in such an unparalleled design.

She replied that she desired a carpet just like it, but twice as long to fit one of her rooms. When she asked the price of a commission, I replied sweetly, but there was iron in my voice. I would not give away my carpet this time. I, better than anyone else, knew the value of every knot.

Maryam didn't wince over the steep price, and after a brief bit of bargaining, we came to a deal. Her eunuch wrote up our agreement, which included a first payment that would allow me to buy the wool. I was so gleeful when they left that I wanted to dance around the shop, for I had finally achieved what I wanted: sold a carpet on my own, of my own design, on my own terms.

The end of the day held an even greater surprise. Right after the guards announced that the bazaar would be closing soon, Jamileh slipped into our shop. She was alone and behaved as if she wanted to conceal her visit. Although she was still beautiful, the faint valleys under her eyes hinted that the first flower of her youth was gone. Rather than the brash confidence she had exhibited when I first served her years before, she showed a touch of weariness and bitterness, for her star had already dimmed in the eyes of the only person who mattered.

Without looking at our wares, she inquired about whether we were offering a carpet with the lightness of feathers. Mehrbanoo and I were both surprised that she knew of it. When I pointed it out, she pretended to examine it and then disparaged it, saying she thought it ought to be cheap, but the lust in her eyes told me she would not leave without it.

"It's a rare treasure: Only one other has been commissioned," I said, and when her face darkened, I surmised that her spies had informed her of Maryam's purchase.

My initial price was very high, but I left enough air in it to be able to give her a discount. Jamileh did not like my price. She pouted, protested, and finally begged, but to no avail. All rug dealers learn to identify naked desire in their buyers and trap those who display it. Jamileh could not hope for a bargain, and she hated herself for having bared her heart.

To console her, I asked Mehrbanoo's permission to give her a free knotted cushion cover. Knowing it would be best for future business to appease her, Mehrbanoo agreed. I think she, too, felt vindicated, for she had heard the story of how Jamileh had talked Gordiyeh into a spectacular discount on the cushion covers, and how Gostaham had had to design and make them at a loss.

Jamileh called in a eunuch to write down our agreement. I was to claim the money later from one of the Shah's accountants, for the women did not carry any silver. She left with the coveted carpet, triumphant despite the price. I knew it would give her great satisfaction to be the first to show her treasure to the Shah, knowing that Maryam's carpet would seem old to him when it was finally delivered.

*   *   *

WHEN I ARRIVED HOME, my mother brought me a vessel of hot tea, and the family gathered around and made me tell them everything that had transpired during the day, including what the women looked like, how they bargained, and how I had managed to get the better of them. To celebrate our success, my mother cooked eggs with dates, and served the meal with fresh bread. As we ate, we began to discuss how we would accomplish all the work that lay ahead of us, for now we had two commissions to fulfill at once.

"It would be best to work on the carpets at the same time, so that we can increase our income," I said.

"True," replied Malekeh, "but the neighbors are already annoyed with us for using so much of the courtyard—more than our share."

"If only we could have our own home!" my mother said, and there was loud agreement.

That began a discussion about how much money we could expect over the next few months. After calculating the amount, Davood declared that it might be possible to afford larger quarters and promised to find out how much they would cost.

It took him only a week to find a house in the neighborhood that most people didn't want, for it had very small rooms. He bargained over the price, receiving a reduction in rent after offering to make all the owner's shoes and to fix any leather goods that needed repair, for he had been a cobbler before his illness. We concluded that our income would still be slim, but agreed that new accommodation was the only way we could get several looms under way at once, and seek to improve our fortunes.

At the end of the month, we moved into our new lodging. It was a humble mud-brick home with two small rooms on either side of a large courtyard, and a tiny, dark room that served as a kitchen. But to me, it was like a palace, for now my mother and I had a room of our own again. The first night, after Davood, Malekeh, and their sons disappeared into their room, I had the courtyard all to myself. I sat there after everyone else had gone to sleep, with a vessel of hot tea, enjoying the snug feeling of being alone yet surrounded by kindhearted companions.

There was ample room in the courtyard for two looms. Davood busied himself with setting them up and stringing them, while Malekeh and I looked for workers. We found five women knotters who needed to earn money and asked them to come for a trial day of work. One of the women was too slow, while another made sloppy, loose knots and would not be corrected, but we were pleased with the other three and retained them.

Before we started, I taught Malekeh how to call out colors for a loom. She supervised Katayoon and one of the workers on the second cypress tree carpet for Gostaham's client, whose design she already knew, while I presided over the other workers on the large feathers carpet for Maryam. In the mornings, the only sound that could be heard from our courtyard was of flowing colors, me calling them out at one end, Malekeh at the other. My mother cooked for us all, and the fragrance of her stews made us work well, in anticipation of the midday meal.

One morning, my mother told me she was making one of my favorite dishes, pomegranate-walnut chicken, and I thought about how Gordiyeh had made me pound the nuts into powder.

"I'm using crunchy nuts," my mother added, as if she could see my thoughts, "because that's the way *we* like it."

She disappeared into the kitchen, and I heard her singing a folk song that I remembered from happy days in our village, which told about a visit from the sweet nightingale of luck.

When the stew was ready, we put aside our work and ate together in the courtyard while I enjoyed the view of the two rugs. I loved watching them transform from scraps of colored wool into gardens of unforgettable beauty.

My mother asked me why I was smiling, and I told her it was because I was enjoying her food. But there was more to it than that. In my village, I had never imagined that a woman like myself— alone, childless, impoverished—could consider herself blessed. Mine was not the happy fate, with the husband and seven beautiful sons, that my mother's tale had foretold. Yet with the aroma of the pomegranate-walnut chicken around me, the sound of laughter from the other knotters in my ears, and the beauty of the rugs on the loom filling my eyes, the joy I felt was as wide as the desert we had traversed to reach our new life in Isfahan.

WE TOILED TOGETHER for many months before we finished the commissions for Gostaham and Maryam. Malekeh worked until her belly became too big for her to sit at the loom, for she had become pregnant with her third child.

Davood delivered the second cypress tree carpet to Gostaham's home, but when he offered to deliver Maryam's, I thought of a better plan. A man would have to wait outside the harem gates while Maryam looked at the carpet and indicated through a servant whether it met with her approval. As a woman, I suffered no such strictures and could present the carpet to her myself.

Davood carried the carpet for me to the Shah's palace at the Image of the World and left me at the entrance. I approached one of the guards and told him I needed to deliver a carpet ordered by one of the ladies. As proof, I showed him the paper written by the eunuch, which confirmed the order.

The guard took me to the side of the palace and delivered me into the care of a tall black eunuch. After unrolling the carpet and checking that nothing prohibited was hidden in it, he escorted me through a group of wooden gates, each manned by a different guard. When I was finally through the last of them, I found myself directly behind the Shah's palace in a forbidden area that contained houses for his women. Maryam lived in one of the best, an octagonal building known as Eight Heavens.

I waited near a fountain on the ground floor, which was open to the air. A high brick wall surrounded the harem buildings, with no doors; the only exit was by way of the gates the eunuchs had ushered me through.

After I had consumed several vessels of tea and eaten half a melon dripping with juice, I was summoned into Maryam's presence. At the top of the stairs that led to her quarters, a servant took my street wraps, and I smoothed my hair and my simple cotton clothes. An old, bald eunuch followed with my carpet on his back. Maryam was lounging in a room decorated with turquoise and silver cushions. She was attended by a woman with large, wise eyes, whom I later learned was a physician revered for her knowledge.

The eunuch unrolled my carpet in front of Maryam, who was wearing a dark blue robe that made her red hair look ablaze. I told her that I hoped the carpet would meet with her satisfaction, though it would always be unworthy of her beauty. She arose, gazed at it, and said, "It is more beautiful than I ever imagined."

"It is my privilege to be your servant," I replied.

Maryam told the eunuch to remove the old rug she had been using and place mine in the position of honor. Its colors blended beautifully with those she had chosen for the rest of the room.

After admiring it, she said, "Why is it that you've delivered this yourself instead of using a man from your shop?"

"I wanted to be sure the carpet met your desires," I said, and then I paused. She knew that was not the only reason and looked at me with curiosity.

"I hope this is not imposing on you," I said, "but I would be honored to know what you think of it, for it is a carpet of my own design."

Maryam looked surprised. "Your own design?"

"I drew the pattern myself," I said.

I could see from her expression that she did not believe me, so I asked if she would call for paper, a reed pen, and a writing stand. After the bald eunuch brought them in, I sat cross-legged next to her, dipped the pen in the ink, and drew one of the feathery shapes, after which I let my pen dance around other common carpet motifs, like roses, cedar trees, onagers, and nightingales.

"Can you teach me?" Maryam asked.

Now it was my turn to be surprised. "Of course," I said, "but as a lady who belongs to the Shah, why would you need to make rugs?"

"I don't need to make them," she replied, "but I should like to learn to draw. I am so often bored."

Her honesty delighted me. Drawing would be a new way to amuse herself inside the harem.

"It would be an honor," I said. "I will come to you whenever you like."

A servant entered bearing coffee in pure silver cups, which were decorated with scenes from legends like the story of Layli and Majnoon. I had never seen such costly vessels, even at Fereydoon's house, and I marveled at their size and weight. The hot drink was followed by fruit heaped on silver trays, sweetmeats, including my favorite chickpea cookies, and cold cherry sharbat in porcelain vessels. The sharbat contained ice, which I had never seen before in a summer drink. Maryam explained that the Shah's servants dug up blocks of ice in winter and stored them underground to keep them cold during the hot months.

After we had enjoyed the refreshments, Maryam asked me to look at another carpet she had bought in the bazaar, and I praised its simple, geometric design, which looked as if it came from the northeast.

"My mother used to make carpets like this one when I was a child in the Caucasus," Maryam said, and then I understood why she wanted to learn to draw patterns.

"If you like, we can study the designs from your native region," I said, and she replied that she would like that best of all. Then I rose and begged her permission to depart.

"I will send for you soon," Maryam said, kissing me warmly on each cheek.

After I said good-bye, the bald eunuch took me to the harem's accountant, who gave me a large bag of silver for the carpet, the largest I had ever held in my hands. It was nearly dark when I was ushered back through the gates to the Image of the World.

As each of the thick wooden gates slammed behind me, I thought about how richly dressed Maryam was, how soft her hands, how glittering her rubies, how perfect her face, how lovely her red hair and tiny red lips. And yet, I did not envy her. Each time a gate closed with a thud, I was reminded that while I was free to come and go, she could not leave without an approved reason and a large entourage. She could not walk across Thirty-three Arches Bridge and admire the view, or get soaked to the skin on a rainy night. She could not make the mistakes I had, and try again. She was doomed to luxuriate in the most immaculate of prisons.

EVERY WEEK, Maryam summoned me to give her lessons in drawing. We became friends, and around the harem quarters, I became something of a curiosity. The other women often invited me to look at their carpets and give my opinion. I had the freedom to mingle with them that no man had, except for the Shah, and they welcomed the diversion of visitors.

Gostaham congratulated me on my work at the harem. He had never been able to develop a loyal clientele among the women, and he encouraged me to use the advantage I had in being able to visit them. He even paid a tailor to make me a fine orange silk robe, with a turquoise sash and turquoise tunic, so that I would look well-dressed and successful when I called on them.

As I got to know the harem ladies, they began to commission me to make carpets and cushion covers, as did their family members and friends who lived outside the harem. Their appetite for beautiful things was insatiable, and we began to have so much business that we had to hire more workers. Before long, Malekeh and my mother had to supervise them, for I was often busy at the harem or at drawing new designs to delight the ladies.

One day, I was surprised to get a commission for a feathers carpet from an acquaintance of Maryam's, who sent one of her servants to our house with a letter. It was written very simply so that I could read it, and before long, I realized that it was from Naheed. Although it did not include anything personal about her life or our friendship, I knew that by this gesture, she was making amends in the best way she knew how. Having recognized the sacrifice I had made by ending the sigheh with her husband (and mine), she had decided to help me in my new life.

I know that most people would never understand why I had traded a life of occasional opulence with Fereydoon for the life of hard work I had now. I couldn't have explained it myself at the time, except that I knew in my heart it was right to leave the sigheh. For I, a maker of carpets, had become an aspirant to the highest things. I couldn't content myself with a secret sigheh, nor pretend to be clean on the outside while I felt dirty on the inside. Gordiyeh would have been surprised to discover that my lessons with Gostaham had spurred this decision, for he had taught me this: Just as when we step into a mosque and its high open dome leads our minds up, up, to greater things, so a great carpet seeks to do the same under the feet. Such a carpet directs us to the magnificence of the infinite, veiled, yet ever near, closer than the pulse of the jugular. The sunburst that explodes at the center of a carpet signals this boundless radiance. Flowers and trees evoke the pleasures of paradise, and there is always a spot at the center of the carpet that brings calm to the heart. A single white lotus flower floats in a turquoise pool, and in this tiniest of details, there it is: a call to the best within, summoning us to the joy of union. In carpets, I now saw not just intricacies of nature and color, not just mastery of space, but a sign of the infinite design. In each pattern lay the work of the Weaver of the World, complete and whole; and in each knot of daily existence lay mine.

I will never inscribe my name in a carpet like the masters in the royal rug workshop who are honored for their great skill. I will never learn to knot a man's eye so precisely it looks real, nor design rugs with layers of patterns so intricate that they could confound the greatest of mathematicians. But I have devised designs of my own, which people will cherish for years to come. When they sit on one of my carpets, their hips touching the earth, their back elongated, and the crown of their head lifted toward the sky, they will be soothed, refreshed, transformed. My heart will touch theirs and we will be as one, even after I am dust, even though they will never know my name.

A FEW MONTHS LATER, Malekeh gave birth to her third child. She and Davood named her Elahay — goddess.

The first time I held her in my arms, I was intoxicated by her sweet baby smell, the dark hair sticking up on her head, her tiny feathery eyebrows, and her feet as smooth as velvet. I lifted her and held her close to my breast, and I thought about how I'd like to teach her everything I knew.

But then a river of feelings coursed through me that I did not expect, and I had to give the baby back to Malekeh so that I could conceal the emotions on my face. I had already entered my nineteenth year, and I was unmarried and childless. I had been too busy making carpets since we had left Gostaham's to think about anything else. But now that I had Elahay to gaze on every waking hour, I began to wonder if there was any hope for me, and whether my future must be to be respected as a knotter but pickled as a woman.

One afternoon on my way home from the harem, I walked by the hammam where I had bathed so many times with Naheed and thought about how much I missed Homa. After my mother and I had left Gostaham's house, we could no longer pay the coin for bathing and had to content ourselves with washing over a bucket while Davood was out of the room. But now I had plenty of silver to pay the entrance fee, and I decided to go in.

It had been more than a year since my last visit. Homa was still working there, as I had hoped, and when she recognized me, she said, "How your place has been empty! How I have thought of you, and wondered about your fate! Come here, my child, and tell me everything."

Her hair was pure white against her dark skin, as radiant as the moon in a dark sky. She took charge of my clothes and led me to one of the private bathing areas, where she sat me down and began pouring buckets of warm water over me.

Homa's dark eyes looked sorrowful. "My child, whenever I thought about you, I feared you had fallen into the worst of all fates — on the street."

"Not quite," I replied, "but times were very hard for us." And I told her about all that we had endured, the words flowing easily as she began kneading my muscles and loosening them.

I recounted how our life had improved after we had begun making rugs with Malekeh's family, and how the commissions had started to stream in from the women in the harem.

"We are planning to buy a home for all of us," I said, "and we can now afford comforts for the children and for ourselves."

I had just bought myself a pair of orange silk shoes, my first new shoes in a long time. The toe was pointed and curved gracefully upward like the spout of a teapot. I loved looking down at them.

Homa's eyes became wide with wonder.

"So your fortunes have changed at last!" she said. "Azizam, you deserve it."

She reached for a kisseh and began scrubbing my legs, and I watched the dead skin sliding away. When Homa turned me face-down to scrub my back, I let my arms and legs flop open, for I felt safe in her care.

"And what of the family you live with?"

I described how well the boys were doing, now that they had enough to eat, and how kind Davood was to my mother, for he believed her herbal potions had cured him. I told her that he and Malekeh had recently welcomed a new child, and when I said her name, I was surprised to find tears flooding my cheeks.

Homa reached for a soft cloth and gently wiped my face. "Akh, akh!" she said sympathetically. "Now you are ready for one of your own."

She turned me on my side, and scrubbed me from my outer ankle to my armpit. "You are not young, but you still have time to bear children," she said.

"But what about my sigheh?"

"There's no reason why you can't contract a regular marriage, now that you have money for a dowry," she replied. "Remember what I told you? The first marriage is for the girl's parents. The second is for herself."

She turned me over and scrubbed my other side.

"But now you must think about what would satisfy you, and avoid making a foolish mistake."

While she scrubbed my palms and callused fingertips, I thought about the marriages I had witnessed among girls my own age.

Maryam had one of the most exalted liaisons I had ever seen, as concubine to the Shah himself, but saw him only when it suited him, and would always have to wonder when she would be supplanted by another favorite.

Naheed had been forced to marry a man she loathed and must content herself with dreams of what might have been with Iskandar, whom she would most likely never possess. Her story was just like that of Golnar and her beloved rosebush.

My village friend Goli was her husband's perfect gift, but in his presence she had been meek; he was much older, and I could see now that she obeyed him like a child.

I was unlike all of them, for I had my carpets and my adopted family to think of. Even if I contracted a marriage, it was my duty and my desire to keep working with Malekeh's family and developing my craft. Each passing month confirmed that my work compared favorably to that of other designers. It also offered the novelty of being the work of a woman, and was popular with the harem ladies. I should never want to give up designing, even if my husband were as rich as the Shah.

Yet my path was not what I had expected when I was a village girl listening to my mother's stories.

"All my life," I said to Homa, "the tales I have been told ended in marriages between a wealthy, generous prince and a beautiful, troubled woman who is rescued and folded into his life."

Homa smiled. "That's the way they go," she replied, pouring warm water over my head, "but not always."

She dug her fingers into my scalp to massage it. "Remember, you are no longer troubled. You have made yourself valuable — even more valuable than you were as a virgin. There's no reason why you can't tell your own tale."

When Homa finished washing my hair, she poured buckets of water over me until my skin glowed. Then she dispatched me to soak in the hottest of the tubs, and I lay there thinking about what she had said. She was right: Now that I was older, unmarried, and had some money, I could make my own choices. I needn't be pick-led, for I had plenty to offer a suitor. But I would never want another man like Fereydoon, even though he was rich, for he saw in me only a mirror of his own pleasure.

I longed for something else, which made me think about my parents. When my mother was so ill that she had almost died, she had told me about the selflessness of my father's devotion. For her, he had sacrificed the deepest desires of his heart not once, but twice. First, he had determined to endure life without a child rather than torment my mother by taking a second wife. Then, after I was born, he had made his peace with never having a son. He was like the humble stone that suffered so much and shed so much heart's blood that it was finally transformed into a ruby. Such was the shining jewel I was now seeking.

After I finished soaking, I went into a private cubicle and lay down on a soft cushion. Homa returned with cool water for me to drink and sweet cucumbers to taste before leaving me to rest. Sleep didn't come, but a rich tale began to weave itself in my mind. I don't know what stuff it came from, for I had never heard it before; per-haps I was making it up myself. Yet I loved it, for it seemed to tell of the lion-man that I now desired, someone as treasured as the length of my life. God willing, our story would one day be written in the brightest of inks, and continue that way until the last page was turned.

"Homa!" I called. "I have something important to tell you!"

Homa came into my cubicle, her eyes shining like stars, her white hair as luminous as the moon. She sat down near me and leaned close to listen, and this is what I said.

First there wasn't and then there was. Before God, no one was.

Once there was a man who was vizier to an aging and cantankerous shah. When the shah demanded the vizier's only daughter in marriage, he refused to give her away. The shah had him executed for disobedience and told the girl that she could win her freedom only if she could knot him a carpet finer than any in his possession.

The girl was locked in a chamber with a tiny window that overlooked the shah's gardens, where his ladies strolled, drank tea, and ate sweetened sesame paste. During the day, she watched them laughing together and amusing themselves while she sat in front of an old loom and a coarse pile of brown wool.

Because she was lonely, the girl left bits of bread every morning for the birds. One day, a bird with a proud crested head and long white feathers entered her cell from a window in the roof. He alighted near the bread, ate a morsel or two, and flew away.

The bird came again the next day and ate a little more. After that, he visited every morning and ate from her fingertips. He was her only companion, and whenever she was especially sad, he would perch on her shoulder and sing to her.

"Ay, Khoda!" she lamented one day, calling on God's mercy. "This wool is so smelly and coarse, it will never make a carpet fit for a shah!"

The bird stopped singing as if he had heard her, and all of a sudden he disappeared. In his place was a fleecy white sheep. She reached out her hand to touch him, for she could not believe her eyes, and discovered that his underbelly had the finest wool imaginable. She sheared it, and it grew right back again. The sheep stood patiently as she cut and cut, and when she had enough wool, he turned back into a bird and flew away.

The girl spun the wool and began using it in her carpet, which became as soft as velvet. The next morning, the bird returned, perched on her shoulder, and sang sweetly while she made her knots. But after a few more days of knotting, the girl became sorrowful again.

"Ay, Khoda!" she sighed. "This rug looks like a shroud, for I have no colorful wool. How shall I make a carpet fit for a shah?"

The bird fell silent and disappeared. In its place, a bowl that had been empty was suddenly filled with bright red flowers. When she smeared one in her palm, it left a streak as bright as blood. She kept one of the flowers alive by putting it into a vase. The others she crushed and boiled into a dye for her *fine white wool. The wool she saturated briefly turned orange, while the deeply saturated wool became scarlet. Then she knotted the orange and scarlet threads into her rug.*

The bird visited the next morning and sang his song, but his beautiful voice sounded faint, and his proud head was bowed.

"My dear bird, did you sacrifice yourself yesterday?" the girl asked. The bird shivered and could sing no more, and since he was too tired to continue, she fed him extra bread and stroked his long, white feathers.

Now the girl's rug was becoming beautiful, like the pleasure gardens she could see from her window. Having finished the borders, she began knotting a pattern of autumn maple trees filled with songbirds. The rich red leaves tinged with orange hues against the brown tree trunks delighted the eyes, and yet she knew the carpet was still not fine enough.

"Ay, Khoda!" the girl sighed. "How can I make a carpet that dazzles the shah? I shall need golden thread to brighten his old eyes!"

The bird was perched on her shoulder, as usual. Suddenly his wings began to flutter, and a small feather drifted to the floor. Then he began trembling so violently, she feared for his life.

"No!" she cried. "For I would rather have you than make a carpet fit for a shah!"

But the room filled with dazzling light as the bird changed from one with a beating heart into one of solid gold, finer than any jewel owned by a shah. The girl marveled at its brightness, for it lit up her cell like the sun.

The next morning, she scattered bread and awaited the bird, but he did not return. Nor did he return the next day, nor the next, nor all through the long winter months. The girl grieved for him every day. To honor his sacrifice, she melted the golden bird, dipped the white wool in his molten blood, and knotted the golden thread into her rug.

When the girl had finished, she asked her captors to allow her to present the carpet to the shah. His retainers spread it before him, and its golden threads seemed to fill the cold hall with sunlight. The shah put his hand to his earlobe and wiggled it in disbelief, for he thought he could hear the carpet's golden songbirds extolling the glories of love.

"What kind of sorcery is this?" he demanded.

The girl told him about the bird that had kept her company for so many days. When the shah commanded her to prove it, she showed him the single white feather that had dropped to the floor. She had attached it to a thread and worn it around her neck ever since.

The shah summoned a wizened old woman known for her magical powers and ordered her to untie any unholy spells from his royal presence. The woman held the feather in her fingers and muttered incantations, ending with, "By the power of God above, you are released from your spell!"

The feather quaked until she lost her hold on it, and then it transformed into a tall man with downy cheeks, lips like tulips, eyes as dark as night, and blue-black tresses like hyacinths.

"Surely there could be nothing stranger than this, not even a carpet that sings!" exclaimed the shah. "Who overmastered you?"

"An evil demon," the youth replied. "He had been chased away by my parents, and he punished them by enchanting me. To torment me further, he gave me the power to transform into anything except myself."

"And what have you to do with this girl?"

The man's voice softened. "When I saw her innocence enslaved, my heart became one with hers," he replied, "for I was in thrall, too."

The shah remained unmoved. To the youth, he said curtly, "You are henceforth my property."

To the girl, he added, "And now you and I shall be married."

The girl jumped to her feet and cried, "By God above, did you not say that you would release me if I should knot a carpet finer than any you possess?"

"I did," the shah admitted.

"And can you swear that there is one finer?"

The shah pointed to the vizier who had replaced her father. "Bring me my finest carpets," he told him.

The vizier rushed to do his bidding, and when the three carpets were laid out to be inspected, the girl examined them each in turn.

"My pattern is finer than the first one," she said. "My carpet has far more knots per radj than the second. And none of these carpets sings to the eye, the ear, or the heart, as mine does!"

The shah did not reply, for he could think of no evidence to contradict her. The girl added quickly, "Nevertheless, I shall agree to give myself to you as your wife, on one condition. Release this man from bondage to you, for he all but relinquished his life for me."

The shah seemed ready to agree, but the wizened woman interrupted. "Great Shah, I beg you to show mercy," she said. "Allow these slaves their liberty, for by sacrificing themselves for each other, they have already become legends."

"It is true that I have never seen two such wonders in a single day," the shah exclaimed, "and yet why should I let them go?"

In a voice of authority, the woman declared, "Because they will be remembered forever—and your munificence will be recognized through the ages."

The shah, who cared deeply about his own reputation, was prepared to improve it. To the girl he said, "I release you, for you have achieved what I commanded. Your carpet is finer than any I possess."

To the youth he said, "I grant her to you, for you let flow your life's blood for her."

The shah gave them a wedding feast that lasted three days and three nights, and they were married on the carpet that had knotted them together. Its golden birds sang to them as the girl gave her consent, for she had found the lion of her heart. Then the two former prisoners served one another with joy and tenderness until the end of their days.

Acknowledgments

This book would not exist in its present form without the unflagging support of my father, Ahmad Amirrezvani, and my stepmother, Firoozeh Firoozfar Amirrezvani. During my three trips to Iran to research this book, they drove me around the country to visit historic sites and museums, indulged me while I made notes and poked around, and answered my endless questions. I owe much to their patience and love.

I would also like to thank my faithful readers, Janis Cooke Newman, Rosie Ruley-Atkins, Bonnie Wach, and Steph Paynes, and my longtime friend, storyteller Ruth Halpern, who shed light on the art of telling tales.

I owe a great debt to novelist Sandra Scofield, whom I met at the Squaw Valley Community of Writers. A born teacher, Sandra offered insights, encouragement, and helpful advice at every juncture.

Bringing a novel to term is demanding not just for the writer, but for everyone close to her. For his unwavering love and support, I would like to thank Ed Grant.

My heartfelt appreciation goes to the hardworking staff at

Little, Brown, especially my editor, Judy Clain, and publisher Michael Pietsch, and their equally dedicated counterparts at Headline Review, in particular my editor there, Marion Donaldson, and deputy managing director Kerr MacRae.

Special thanks also to my agent, Emma Sweeney, for her advocacy and thoughtful suggestions.

Finally, I wish to acknowledge the dedicated scholars who have devoted their lives to understanding Iran. Without their extraordinary work, this book could not have been written.

Author's Note

During the nine years I worked on *The Blood of Flowers,* I felt like Ali Baba in *The Arabian Nights,* who utters the magic words "Open, sesame!" to reveal a cave illuminated by gold and precious gems. In my case, the riches emerged in the form of books about pre-modern Iranian history and culture, which were similarly hidden away on dusty library shelves where few people ventured. I spent hours examining these treasures, and the more I read, the more fascinated I became.

During my explorations I kept returning to the reign of Shah Abbas (1571–1629), a historical period that's hard to rival for great calamities and equally great deeds. When the Shah took power at the age of seventeen, Iran had endured a bloodbath in which members of the Safavi royal court were blinded or murdered in a struggle for power, and many soldiers and large chunks of the country were lost during wars. Shah Abbas was able to chart a course through this chaos. During his forty-one-year reign he proved to be a brilliant administrator, although his approach to justice was harsh by today's standards. For his bravery, ingenuity, and contributions to Iranian cultural life, he is known as Shah Abbas the Great.

I set *The Blood of Flowers* in the 1620s, at which point the Shah had succeeded in defending the borders of Iran, vanquishing his internal political enemies, and creating a climate where the arts could flourish. One of the arts the Shah promoted vigorously was carpet making. Iranian carpets had become coveted in Europe by kings, noblemen, and wealthy merchants and were catching the eye of artists such as Rubens, Velázquez, and Van Dyck. Always alert to a good opportunity, the Shah set up carpet workshops around the country, such as the one described in this book. According to Iran scholar Roger M. Savory, "under his patronage, carpet weaving was elevated to the status of a fine art," so that in addition to being created by individuals working on their own looms, carpets were woven by urban specialists who were trained to make masterpieces for the court. Remarkable examples of sixteenth- and seventeenth-century Iranian court carpets survive in museums and private collections, and a number of rug scholars believe that the carpets of the Safavi period (1501–1722) rank among the finest ever produced.

When the Shah first came to power, his capital was located in Qazvin, a northwestern Iranian city. By 1598, the Shah had moved his capital to Isfahan, a more defensible site in the center of the country, where he undertook one of the most remarkable renovations in urban planning history. Under the guidance of his city planners and architects over the course of about thirty years, the Shah built a city that's still magnificent today. The enormous Image of the World, which earned its honorific because of its size, was bigger than most European city squares of the time. The Shah's palace, his personal mosque, the Great Bazaar, and the huge Friday mosque described in this book are still a wonder to behold, and you can even see the marble goalposts that were used for polo games, which the Shah liked to watch from the upstairs balcony of his palace. Thomas Herbert, a young man who visited Iran from 1627 to 1629 with English ambassador Sir Dodmore Cotton, described the square as "without doubt as spacious, as pleasant and aromatic a market as any in the universe." Like Herbert and many other travelers, I fell under Isfahan's spell when I first visited at the age of fourteen. The city made such an indelible impression on me that decades later it was the only conceivable choice for the setting of my novel.

Although the main characters in *The Blood of Flowers* are fictional, I have tried to stay true to events that would have shaped their lives and ways of thinking. For example, the comet described in the first chapter, and some of the misfortunes associated with it, were recorded with consternation by Eskandar Beg Monshi, Shah Abbas's official historian, who produced a thirteen-hundred-page chronicle about the most significant events of his reign (I used the Persian Heritage Series translation by Roger M. Savory). However, I have taken the liberty of compressing events within the novel even when they occurred outside of its time period.

Every great historical period deserves a great travel writer, and seventeenth-century Iran found one in Sir John Chardin, a French jeweler. Chardin traveled to Iran in the 1670s and wrote ten detailed volumes about his experiences there. Few chroniclers are as thorough in their reports or as entertaining to read. Chardin's observations were an important source for me about the customs and mores of the Safavi period, especially since he was astute enough to record intriguing contradictions such as these: "Wine and intoxicating Liquors are forbid the Mahometans; yet there is scarce anyone that does not drink of some sort of strong Liquor" and "Two opposite Customs are commonly practis'd by the Persians; that of praising God continually, and talking of his Attributes, and that of uttering Curses, and obscene Talk" (from *Travels in Persia: 1673– 1677*).

During his travels, Chardin obtained an almanac from Isfahan and recorded its prophecies, upon which I have modeled the prophecies described in chapter 1. The prediction about the behavior of women is a direct quote from *Voyages du chevalier Chardin en Perse, et autres lieux de l'Orient* (the translation from the French is my own).

374

Many travelers have been fascinated by Persian carpets, and they have been a small but cherished part of my own life ever since I received my first rug from my father when I was a teenager. The carpets described in this novel are generally based on Iranian designs, color choices, dyeing methods, and knotting techniques. Although I consulted dozens of carpet books, two key sources of information were Hans E. Wulff's *The Traditional Crafts of Persia* and Leonard M. Helfgott's *Ties That Bind: A Social History of the Iranian Carpet.* The ideas about the spirituality expressed in Middle Eastern carpets have been discussed in many publications, including the exhibition catalogue *Images of Paradise in Islamic Art,* edited by Sheila S. Blair and Jonathan M. Bloom, and in essays such as Schuyler V. R. Cammann's "Symbolic Meanings in Oriental Rug Patterns." Related ideas about buildings are articulated in *The Sense of Unity: The Sufi Tradition in Persian Architecture,* by Nader Ardalan and Laleh Bakhtiar.

Several readers have expressed curiosity about the prevalence of the temporary marriage contract described in this novel, which is known as a *sigheh.* This form of marriage has been part of Iranian culture for hundreds of years and is still actively used by men and women. My main source of background information was scholar Shahla Haeri's *Law of Desire: Temporary Marriage in Shi'i Iran,* which includes interviews with contemporary practitioners and provides a detailed portrait of this complex and unusual institution.

While researching this book, I also became interested in sharing Iran's extensive oral tradition because of its prevalence in premodern times. Many travelers have remarked that the most illiterate of Iranian peasants could recite long poems; even today, Iranians play a game in which they challenge each other to remember poems and prove their knowledge by reciting them. In addition to poems, the literature that was traditionally shared orally includes a large body of folktales, legends, fables, discourses, and teaching stories about spiritual growth.

The nesting, or layering, of stories was a common practice in the Middle East, one familiar to readers of *The Arabian Nights*. I was much influenced in this regard by the twelfth-century Persian-language poet Nizami, who wrote a book-length narrative in verse about a shah's exploits, called *Haft Paykar (Seven Portraits)*, which includes seven thoughtful tales about love. In my view, Nizami's layering of stories parallels the layering of designs in Iranian carpets, creating a weave of infinite richness and depth.

Of the seven tales interspersed between the chapters of my novel, five are retellings of traditional Iranian or Islamic stories. In cases where I thought it was necessary for the novel, I adapted the original stories freely. The words that begin each tale, *"First there wasn't and then there was. Before God, no one was,"* reflect my rough translation of an Iranian expression that is equivalent to "Once upon a time."

The story at the end of chapter 2 was recorded in Henri Massé's *Persian Beliefs and Customs*. Massé's original source was a book of Iranian tales, *Tchehardeh efsane ez efsaneha-ye roustayi-e Iran,* collected in the Kerman region of Iran and published in 1936 by Kouhi Kermani.

The stories that appear at the end of chapters 3 and 4 were written in verse by the aforementioned poet Nizami. The tale after chapter 3 is based on parts of the tale of Layli and Majnoon, which existed long before Nizami retold it and made it his own. My main source was *The Story of Layla and Majnun,* translated by Dr. Rudolf Gelpke with collaborators E. Mattin and G. Hill, but I used the Iranian name Layli. The story of Fitna the slave girl after chapter 4 appears in Nizami's *Haft Paykar;* my source was the translation by scholar Julie Scott Meisami. Her extensive notes make this wonderful book easy to enjoy and understand.

The tale át the end of chapter 5 is adapted from a traditional Islamic story, while the tale following chapter 6 is modeled on the one that opens the poet Farid al-Din Attar's *Illahi-Nama (Book of God),* in the translation by John Andrew Boyle. Attar, whose long life spanned the twelfth century, may be better known to readers as the author of the famous Sufi parable in verse called *The Conference of the Birds.*

The tales that appear at the end of chapters 1 and 7 are my own. Those tales, as well as the main narrative of this novel, are deeply influenced by the use of language in traditional Iranian tales, as well as by their approach to characters and plot. I was also much inspired for the language of this novel by eminent scholar Annemarie Schimmel's *A Two-Colored Brocade: The Imagery of Persian Poetry.*

The title of the novel is drawn from a poem. Called "Ode to a Garden Carpet," the poem appears in Arthur Upham Pope and Phyllis Ackerman's monumental *Survey of Persian Art,* a forty-three-hundred-page encyclopedia and labor of love published in 1939 by Oxford University Press, which I used as a reference on everything from carpets to coins. The poem is described as "by an unknown Sufi poet, circa 1500," and it portrays the garden carpet as a place of refuge that stimulates visions of the divine.

The narrator of this novel is purposely not named, in tribute to the anonymous artisans of Iran.

About the Author

ANITA AMIRREZVANI was born in Tehran, Iran, and raised in San Francisco. For ten years, she was a staff dance critic at newspapers in the Bay Area. She has received fellowships from the National Arts Journalism Program, the NEA's Arts Journalism Institute for Dance, and Hedgebrook. She worked on *The Blood of Flowers* for nine years, during which time she made three research trips to Iran. She lives in northern California.

970-884-2222